Maggie MASON

Blackpool's Angel

sphere

SPHERE

First published in Great Britain in 2019 by Sphere

1 3 5 7 9 10 8 6 4 2

Copyright © Maggie Mason Ltd 2019

The moral right of the author has been asserted.

All characters and events in this publication, other than those clearly in the public domain,
are fictitious and any resemblance to real persons, living or dead, is purely coincidental.

All rights reserved. No part of this publication may be reproduced, stored in a
retrieval system, or transmitted, in any form or by any means, without the prior
permission in writing of the publisher, nor be otherwise circulated in any form
of binding or cover other than that in which it is published and without a similar
condition including this condition being imposed on the subsequent purchaser.

A CIP catalogue record for this book is available from the British Library.

ISBN 978-0-7515-7783-9

Typeset in Bembo by Hewer Text UK Ltd, Edinburgh
Printed and bound in Great Britain by Clays Ltd, Elcograf S.p.A.

Papers used by Sphere are from well-managed forests
and other responsible sources.

Sphere
An imprint of
Little, Brown Book Group
Carmelite House
50 Victoria Embankment
London
EC4Y 0DZ

An Hachette UK Company
www.hachette.co.uk

www.littlebrown.co.uk

Maggie Mason is a pseudonym of author Mary Wood. Mary began her career by self-publishing on Kindle where many of her sagas reached number one in the genre. She was spotted by Pan Macmillan and to date has written many books for them under her own name, with more to come.

Mary continues to be proud to write for Pan Macmillan, but is now equally proud and thrilled to take up a second career with Sphere under the name of Maggie Mason.

Born the thirteenth child of fifteen children, Mary describes her childhood as poor, but rich in love.

She was educated at St Peter's RC School in Hinckley and at Hinckley College for Further Education, where she was taught shorthand and typing.

Mary retired from working for the National Probation Service in 2009, when she took up full-time writing, something she'd always dreamed of doing. She follows in the footsteps of her great-grandmother, Dora Langlois, who was an acclaimed author, playwright and actress in the late nineteenth–early twentieth century.

It was her work with the Probation Service that gives Mary's writing its grittiness, her need to tell it how it is, which takes her readers on an emotional journey to the heart of issues.

To my children, Christine Martin, Julie Bowling, Rachel Gradwell and James Wood. Your love and support sustain me. Your loving Mum x

PART ONE

A SUDDEN CHANGE

1893–1894

CHAPTER ONE

Tilly stood and rubbed her back. Her hands were torn to bleeding by the thorns of the blackberry vines, but she didn't care. She needed to cut enough of them to finish the baskets she was making to hold the twins' small blackboards and chalks.

Next week, the first week in September, four-year-old Barbara and Elizabeth, or Babs and Beth, as she and Arthur called them, were to start their lessons at the Church of England free school. Tilly was filled with great pride at this – her own young 'uns, learning to read and write! She couldn't believe it. *Eeh, that's sommat I've allus wanted to do. But there wasn't a chance with me Aunt Mildred thinking that learning such skills weren't for the likes of poor folk like us.*

The pain of her Aunt Mildred's passing a year ago ground into Tilly. For all her old-fashioned thinking, her aunt had been a kindly soul and had taken Tilly in when her parents died from typhus in 1868. Tilly had been just a few months old.

'Learn a trade that'll stand you in good stead, lass. It's the only way,' Aunt Mildred had said. And to that end she'd passed on her weaving skills and now Tilly could make anything out of hedgerow pickings and grass – from baskets to hats, cots to plant-pot holders and mats. And all intricately designed using different-coloured materials. But willow was what she most loved working with. Not easy to come by, but sometimes traders had some to sell when they came up to Blackpool from the southern counties, especially Somerset. The finest willow came from there.

Tilly sighed as she thought of how Arthur would never let her put these skills to helping to earn money for the family. Not that they needed it now, but there had been some lean times. He had his sayings did Arthur, aye, and he stuck by them. 'I'm the breadwinner, lass, not you,' he'd say if she broached the subject of selling some of her baskets. 'You're me wife, you keep me house clean, cook me meals, bring up our young 'uns and aye, see to me needs in our bed.'

This last thought gave Tilly a pleasurable twinge. Arthur said she was made for loving, and she always enjoyed it when he took her to him.

Tossing her thick raven-coloured hair away from her face to cool the heat that had risen within her, Tilly knew she had all that men desired in her voluptuous curves. Of medium height, her breasts were larger than most women's. Her tiny waist accentuated this.

'By, lass, God gave it all to you,' her Aunt Mildred would say. 'What with your beauty, and them flashing dark eyes, you'll have trouble knocking at your door. Don't you be bringing it to my door, though, and that's a warning.'

Tilly smiled. Aunt Mildred had a way of scolding you that made you giggle rather than feel chastised.

'Ma, Ma, look.' Babs and Beth's heads were just visible above the tall grass of the field. As she walked towards them, she looked over to where they were pointing and knew the same wonderment that lit their faces at the sight of the tower. A feeling of pride in her Arthur for being one of the workers fitting together the huge iron structure assailed her. Almost finished, the Blackpool Eiffel Tower, as it was known on account of it being modelled on the Eiffel Tower in Paris, now stood at over three hundred feet high.

It was the mayor, John Bickerstaffe, who started it all, or so they say, but all that didn't matter. It was her Arthur getting a job on the building of it that mattered. For that had changed their fortunes. They'd moved from the boarding house in Albert Street that housed a dozen or so families, to their own two up, two down terraced house in Enfield Road, North Shore.

Every thought of Arthur warmed her. Their love for one another knew no bounds. Arthur had been brought up in Enfield Road, just a couple of streets from her. She'd known him all her life, and they'd played together as young 'uns, knowing then that one day they would marry.

Tilly laughed as she looked down at the twins playing with a worm they'd dug up; she never ceased to be amazed at their enjoyment in everyday things.

'Gather yourselves, me lasses, we're to head for home. Your da'll be in by the time we get back, and I've that lovely stew on the hob waiting for us all.'

Tying the vines into a bundle, Tilly slung them over her shoulder and began the mile walk over the fields to her home. In the distance she could see the sea sparkly in the August sun.

Blue and calm today, it could whip up to a churning, angry crashing of waves as quickly as a nod of the head if it had a mind to.

Blackpool had changed a lot over the last few years. Visitors from all over came to 'take the waters', as the posters put it, which meant folk dipping themselves in the mostly freezing Irish Sea, believing it could heal all manner of ailments. Whether it could or not, Tilly didn't know – but she hadn't much faith in it doing so as those who lived in Blackpool ailed just as much as the rest of the country.

But for all that, she knew that the idea brought folk flocking and folk brought money and Blackpool was prospering. Guest houses and hotels were springing up all the time, which bode well for Arthur's continued employment once the tower was completed.

Life was good, and Tilly was grateful; even her sadness at not being able to have any more children didn't mar her feeling of everything being all right with her world. She had her twins and her being damaged inside by their birth wasn't the end of the world. Nothing about her had been impaired otherwise, and she and her Arthur could make love till the cows came home without worry of increasing their family to the extent that they would suffer poverty, as happened with a lot of folk. Look at her best friend, Liz. Five young 'uns under eight and she had her belly up again. The lass was worn out and she never knew where their next meal was coming from.

Tilly and Liz had been friends since childhood. Liz still lived in her mam's house a couple of streets away from Enfield Road. Badly in need of repair, it was a damp, cold place at the best of times.

Thinking of Liz, Tilly determined to call in on her way home and made a detour as she came into Blackpool.

When Liz opened the door to greet her a sea of faces surrounded her, all eager to see who was visiting. Shooing her brood away, and hitching the youngest higher on her hip, Liz, as always, showed how glad she was that Tilly had called round. 'Eeh, lass, it's good to see you. I have the pot on, and some tea that I got this morning – I'll make us a cuppa. Mind, I've naw milk, but it'll be hot and sweet as I've got a bag of sugar an' all.'

'That'll be welcome, Liz, though I ain't got long.'

'Put your bundle down. Eeh, look at the young 'uns, they look worn out. Have you been trundling them over the fields again, Tilly?'

'Aye, we've had a grand day.'

Liz looked tired. The vibrant girl she'd once been had gone. Her fair, always unruly, curly hair looked wiry and lacklustre. Her skin that used to glow was now pale and seemed as though it was pulled tight over her cheekbones. Her once sparkling blue eyes now looked grey and weary and were sunk into dark sockets.

Tilly looked around her as she stepped inside. Despite her poverty, Liz kept her little house clean and tidy. Threadbare rugs were brushed to within an inch of their life, and the floors beneath scrubbed till the flagstones had a sheen on them. Remnants of Liz's mam's furniture – a scrubbed wooden table, and two big armchairs each side of the fire – looked fresh with a crisp white cloth covering the centre of the table and antimacassars of white cotton draping the arms and backs of the brown chairs. 'Sit yourself down, lass. I won't be a mo.'

Glad to take the weight off her feet, Tilly sank into the chair. Beth and Babs had found renewed energy with the prospect of playing with Liz's lot and were soon out in the backyard with them, leaving the little living room a peaceful haven.

'So, what are you thinking of making this time, lass? By, your house is full of beautiful baskets and the like, I've a wonder you can fit any more in.'

Telling Liz of her plans, Tilly was soon full of the twins starting school. 'I can't believe it, we didn't get the chance, did we, Liz? I were working in Dottie's sweet shop by the time I were ten, and that were me lot. I learnt how to count, though, and was good with the money transactions, even though I couldn't read and write. And you fared no better – with your ma taking in washing from the guest houses, you were allus turning that mangle.'

'I have the muscles to prove it an' all, but I ain't ever been interested in learning. And I ain't bothered if me kids do or not. It'll only be more expense for me. More often than not I keep our Alfie at home. He's more use scouting around for what he can make from the tourists. Polishing their shoes, or carrying their bags with their bathing stuff in. He comes home with a good few pennies most days.'

Tilly didn't say anything to this, but she felt the pity of it as, to her mind, an education was a way of opening up the world to the young 'uns and helping them to make more of themselves, though she knew the Alfies of this world would flourish in Blackpool, educated or not.

This thought hadn't died when he came in the door. 'Hello, Aunty Tilly. I've sommat as you'll like. I've been helping in a rock factory today. I walked into that shop on the prom asking for work and they took me in the back and set me on. I helped to roll the rock an' all, and they let me have some bags of the chippings when they cut it. I can sell you a bag of bits for Babs and Beth for a penny.'

Liz gently cuffed the cheeky eight-year-old Alfie around the ear. 'Oy, what're you up to? You didn't steal them bits, did you?'

'Naw, Ma, I were given them, and I did such a good job, helping to keep the floors clean and fetching and carrying the bags of sugar, besides having a turn at the rolling, that I got meself a regular job. Two days a week. Me earnings will be sixpence and pickings of the bits that break off during the cutting.'

'Eeh, lad. Eeh, me little Alfie, come here, and let me give you a hug.'

'Gerroff, Ma. Don't come all sloppy over me.'

'I'll buy a bag off you, Alfie, it'll be a treat for me girls.'

'Ta, Aunt Tilly. Here you go. I've five bags altogether. I'll let me sisters and brothers share one, but the other four I'm going to sell down the prom tomorrow as that's going to be the sideline of me job. I should make a pretty penny or two that way.'

'By, lad,' Liz looked with pride at her eldest son, 'you never cease to amaze me. Now, don't let your da knaw, or he'll be after you to give him some money for his drink.'

'I'll keep it secret from him, Ma, and you've to make sure the young 'uns do an' all. I'll start a stash in that tin I have under me bed, but you can help yourself from it whenever you need to. And I'll cough up me sixpence to you an' all.'

'You're a good lad, Alfie. You're worth twice what your da is, the lazy sod. He's away to his bed at this minute. He came in tipsy again. Lost his job and spent his pay-out on the way home. I'm at me wits' end with him.'

As Alfie went out the back door, Tilly had the feeling that he didn't want to hear about his da as Liz hadn't finished talking before he'd disappeared. 'How do you cope, Liz, love?'

'I don't. I live in fear of being evicted as I'm behind with me rent. And feeding me brood is difficult. Alfie's little offerings help and Larry's coming up to seven now, so he can bring a ha'penny in now and again running errands for them in the street, and he's good with numbers an' all. I don't knaw how, or where he gets that talent from, but he helps at Dottie's sweet shop now. He fills little bags with an ounce of toffees so they're ready for selling rather than old Dottie having to do the job as the customers come in. But she's a mean old cuss and only gives him a farthing now and again.'

'She was allus like that when I worked for her. Look, Liz, I can help you out, lass. I have enough in me purse for your rent – for this week, anyroad.' Tilly dug her purse out from the pocket of her frock and handed some coins to Liz.

'Naw, lass, I – I mean, are you sure?'

'Aye, I am, and I've a big pot of stew on at home. If you give me a pan and send Alfie and Larry with me, I'll fill it for you. They'll manage a handle each to get it back here. If not, I'll put it on the pram and they can wheel it round, how's that, eh?'

'Eeh, Tilly, that'd be a godsend. I've some bread baked off an' all. I can easily fill their bellies with stew and bread.'

'Aye, and if you mix up some dumplings, you can boil the stew up to cook them in.'

'I'll do that. I've got some lard, and plenty of flour. They're things I allus keep in as I can do a multitude of things with them to feed the young 'uns.'

'Don't ever go short, Liz, I'm allus telling you, as I'd give you owt that you need.'

'I knaw, you're a good friend.'

'I mean it. Send one of the young 'uns round to mine if you need owt, and if I've got it, you can have it. Now, I'm to get meself away. I'll have Arthur in afore I knaw it. I'll see you later, lass. Take care.'

Tilly wanted to add that Liz should try to dodge some of the blows that came her way, as she hadn't missed the bruises on Liz's arm. A sigh escaped her. How was it that Eddie had turned out like he had? Though she had to admit, he was always aggressive as a young 'un. She remembered how the four of them, Arthur, Eddie, Liz and herself, would play snobs, a game they played with stones. They'd start with five, four on the ground and one in their hand. They'd toss the one in their hand and try to pick up others before they had to catch the one they had thrown in the air, all having a good time, giggling and teasing, but Eddie would spoil it. Especially if he was losing. He'd kick the stones away, saying it was a daft game. Once Eddie had beaten Arthur up when he'd challenged him to stop being babyish. That had been a changing point in their friendship and had taken a long time to mend. Eddie's family had moved away the next year, somewhere down the Midlands, and Tilly had thought that was that, but he came back looking for Liz a few years later and, against Tilly's advice, Liz fell for him and they married. Eddie was idle. He never kept a job for long, even though there was an abundance of jobs in Blackpool for young men. And what with his temper, his drinking, and aye, his womanising, he led poor Liz a merry dance that she didn't deserve.

As Tilly turned the corner, she was surprised to see a man talking to Mrs Haggerty and Mrs Brown, her neighbours. The three were standing outside Tilly's door. Something about them made her blood run cold.

'Are you all right, Aunt Tilly? You've gone very white.'

Tilly couldn't answer Alfie. She held Babs and Beth's hands tighter as if clinging on to them would ward off the dread in her.

Mrs Brown saw her at that moment. Her head shook from side to side. 'Eeh, me lass, me poor lass.'

Tilly couldn't speak. She stared at the two women. How she'd walked the last ten or so yards towards them she didn't know.

'Mrs Ramsbottom?'

Tilly nodded at the man. He looked official, with his bowler hat and long black coat. 'I'm afraid I—'

'Let her get inside, man.' Mrs Haggerty came forward as she said this and took Tilly's arm. 'You, Alfie, mind the young 'uns for a mo, there's a good lad. Keep them playing, we have sommat to tell your Aunt Tilly. And you, Larry, run and fetch your ma. Tell her Mrs Haggerty told her to come as your Aunt Tilly will need her.'

'What? Why . . . ?' Tilly could hardly voice the words. She had a feeling inside her that her world was coming to an end.

'Come on, lass. Let's get you inside.'

Propelled forward, Tilly went into her house. For some reason she couldn't fathom, nothing about it seemed familiar to her anymore. The usually welcoming living room that led off the street, with its cosy chairs and sofa in beige and brown, and cream rug, covering the polished brown linoleum, looked as though they didn't belong. And she wanted to take her hand and push her shining brass ornaments off the mantle shelf and have them clatter to the floor. Why she should feel like this she didn't know.

'What's happened? Is . . . is it Arthur? Naw, don't let it be. Naaaaw.'

'Sit down, lass. There's been an accident. The gentleman will tell you.'

With this from Mrs Brown, Tilly felt herself being gently steered towards one of the chairs, but she didn't want to sit in that one. That one was Arthur's and he'd be in soon to sit in it himself.

'I'm very sorry to tell you this, missus, but, well, the scaffolding gave way and . . . well, Mr Ramsbottom fell . . .'

Whatever else he said was drowned out by her moaning scream. A sound that assaulted her own ears and revealed the truth to her that there was such a thing as a broken heart. She felt hers split in two when he uttered the words, 'killed instantly.'

TWO

The last three days had passed in a haze of weeping and dealing with folk coming in and out of the house. During that time the inquest had also been opened and adjourned, and she had been granted the right to bury her Arthur.

His body now lay in an open coffin on the table at the back of the living room. The sun streamed through the windows and lit his beautiful face. It didn't matter to Tilly that that face was broken; she knew in her mind the contours of how it always had been – the clear-cut cheekbones and the square chin. The overly big nose, that didn't detract from how handsome Arthur had been . . . *Had been. No, No, I want my Arthur back. I don't want him dead.*

Looking down at him, Tilly wanted to make him all better. To put the crooked, flattened nose back into place, and to heal the slash across his cheek. Touching him, she wasn't repelled by how cold he was, but wanted to get in beside him and warm him up. Cuddle him to her and soothe the pain she knew he must have felt on impact as his bones crumbled and he took his last breath.

Fifty feet he fell. Fifty feet that would have taken seconds to pass and yet, what fear Arthur must have felt in that time.

Stroking his waxen cheek, Tilly whispered her love for him. A cough behind her made her want to scream. She didn't want the lid to be put on the coffin. That would be final. Her Arthur would be gone forever, encased in a wooden box, feet beneath the earth. Never again would she be able to see him, touch him . . .

A hand took her arm. 'Come on, lass, let the men do their job. Say goodbye to Arthur.'

Liz's voice didn't sound like Liz's voice. Her throat sounded sore. Her nose blocked. She too had cried buckets these last days. Holding Tilly, rocking her, trying to give and receive comfort. But there was no comfort, only a black pit that held a future that Tilly didn't want to acknowledge. A cold future with no Arthur. One in which she would never again be held by him, kissed by him. The sound she'd made many times came from her once more. A long drawn-out moan that hurt her lungs and rasped her throat, but she let herself be moved away, let herself be held. Supported by the hateful Eddie, who'd at least shown some decency towards her these last days, she stepped outside.

There, the sun shone and though there was a stillness in the folk that lined the street, the rest of the world carried on unaware of her pain. Birds sang. Horses' hooves resounded on the tarmac of Devonshire Road that ran along the bottom of their street. And then the horses of the dray that would take Arthur to his final resting place in Layton fidgeted. One snorted loudly. All a rude intrusion into her world of grief.

Looking up the street, she saw Babs and Beth wave to her. Mrs Lipton, their teacher-to-be, had offered to collect them and keep them for the day. Tilly waved back and, as she did, she had the feeling that they too would leave her. Panic gripped her. She wanted to run to them and hold them to her and never let them go, but Eddie's arm tightening on her waist stopped her. Repulsion shivered through her. She pulled away from him. No one noticed as at that moment the undertakers stepped out of the house bearing Arthur's coffin.

Everything passed in a daze after that and it seemed like no time had gone by before it was all over – the service, the burial, and the wake held in the church hall. Now Tilly found herself sitting alone, with the ticking of Aunt Mildred's mantle-shelf clock filling the space around her. Her thoughts were of despair. The cost of the funeral had all but taken the money she'd had in the rainy-day pot that stood next to the clock, but when she'd squirrelled away the odd copper here and there, she hadn't had any thoughts that there would be this kind of day to pay for.

Getting up and shaking the pot, the pennies rattled around inside. There'd hardly be enough to pay one week's rent, let alone buy food, though she comforted herself on this last as she had a well-stocked cupboard. But how to get money after that? Even if she could get hold of some wicker and make some baskets, she couldn't make enough to start up as a trader – she'd need at least ten wicker items to even think of going down to the beach to sell. Besides, the season would be over in a few weeks; already those who owned the houses on the promenade were beginning to close them up.

Jobs would be scarce then too, as most traders would close their stalls. And what of the twins? Who would look after them while she worked? Liz had her plate full and she didn't know who else she could ask.

A knock on the door made her jump. She glanced at the clock – ten past ten, no one had ever visited her at this hour!

Opening the door, she had to step back as Eddie lolled towards her, his clothes and his breath stinking of beer and fags. His voice slurred. 'I called on me way shome to shee if yoush all right, darling?'

With her heart pounding a fear around her, Tilly held on to the door trying to prevent him from coming inside, but his weight as he leant on it was too much for her. 'I'm fine, Eddie, ta. Now, take yourself home, it's late and Liz will be looking out for you.'

'That cold fish. I desherve shomeone better. Shomeone warm like you. I could keep you happy like Arthur did. He told me you liked it, he shaid you and him did it every night. Liz only letsh me near her now and again. I go to Prossie Pam a lot. She knowsh how to get a man going. But I could come here, and then you wouldn't mish Arthur sho much.'

Horrified, Tilly stepped further into the room as Eddie leered at her. 'Please go. I don't want you. I wouldn't let you touch me, you filthy animal.' With her temper rising, her fear left her, and she reached for the poker that was kept by the hearth. 'Come near me and you'll get a wallop with this. You're disgusting, Eddie Philpot. Me Arthur's not cold in his grave and you – his supposed friend – makes a pass at his missus. You should be ashamed of yourself. Get out! Go on. Get out!'

Eddie stared at her for a moment, his stance one of a sober man now. 'Well, p'raps itsh too soon, but I knaw you're going to yearn for it, and I'll be ready, me darling. Just give me the nod.'

'That'll be never. You're me friend's man. And I don't want you or any man. Now go, Eddie, just go.'

He went out of the door, leaving Tilly shivering from head to toe. Dropping the poker, she ran to the door and turned the key. The strength went from her body at the sound of the lock clunking into place. She leant her back against the door, but her legs gave way and she slumped to the floor. The same moan she'd hollered so many times these last days came from her as her body gave way to a deluge of tears she couldn't stop. Eddie had just made her troubles threefold as she knew he wouldn't give up. *Oh, Arthur, Arthur. I knaw it would have been lads' talk, but of all the folk to share our intimate details with, you shouldn't have chosen Eddie.* 'Oh, God, help me, help me.'

It was a few days later before Tilly ventured out. She'd had callers, but Liz hadn't been to see her, and this had worried her as to what Eddie might have said about the incident. Had he feared in the light of the next morning that she would tell Liz what had happened, and, not liking the fact that she'd rejected him, chosen to discredit her? Tilly could think of no other reason why Liz wouldn't come around to see how she was and to offer her help. But today, she had to take the twins to their lessons in St Paul's on Edgerton Road and had decided she would go and see Liz before going home.

As she arrived in Fairfield Road, her nerves almost got the better of her and she hesitated before turning down Liz's street. Taking a deep breath, Tilly knew she had to do this. Having no communication with her friend was too much to bear on top of everything else that weighed her down.

Trepidation shivered through her as she opened Liz's door and called out. As Liz stood up from the chair she'd been sitting in, her whole demeanour spoke of her anger.

'Liz, I—Oh, Liz, it weren't my doing, I took the poker to him, I did . . . I'd never, I mean . . . Oh, Liz, please believe me.'

'Take your word over me husband's, you mean, eh? And accept that me husband made a pass at you? Naw, Tilly. I've allus had a jealousy in me where you're concerned. Me Eddie allus fancied you more than he did me when we were young 'uns, and now, the minute you're a free woman, you entice him. I'm proud of how he resisted you and came home to me. He offered you help, Tilly. He called in to see as you were all right, and all you wanted was the comfort of him in your bed, and with you just having buried your poor Arthur. You should be ashamed of yourself.'

'It weren't like that, Liz. It weren't.'

'I think as you'd do best to leave. Me and you have been friends since we were born, and aye, you've been a good friend to me in me time of need, but to do this to me, when you knaw as me Eddie is one to stray and how much that hurts me? Well, I can't forgive you, Tilly, and I never will.'

'It's Eddie you should never forgive. I've done nowt. He called on me with the intention of lying with me. How he could think I'd even fancy him, or anyone for that matter, when me heart's broken from me losing me lovely Arthur, I don't knaw. Eddie's a wrong 'un and allus has been. He don't deserve you, Liz. But . . . but I – I don't knaw how I'm going to manage without you. Help me, Liz. If you never do owt for me again, help me at this time in me life.'

19

For a moment Liz looked unbending. Her arms were folded across her chest. Her body was stiff, making her protruding belly look bigger than usual. But a tear seeped from the corner of her eye, and Tilly realised that to accept the true version of events – that her Eddie had tried to seduce her best friend – would cause such pain to Liz that it wasn't that she didn't believe, she just couldn't allow herself to.

Walking out of the door, Tilly hoped against hope that Liz would call out to her, but she didn't.

To have her heart broken twice in such a short time was unbearable to Tilly. But she lifted her head high in case Liz was watching through the window and walked on unsteady legs towards her home.

Loneliness engulfed her once she closed the door on the world. Making it to Arthur's chair, she snuggled into it, trying to feel his presence and gain comfort, remembering how often he'd sit here and say, 'Come and sit on me lap, lass, and let's have a cuddle.' And how he would start to tickle her until she was crying with laughter – times that always ended in their lovemaking. But instead of giving her solace, the empty feel of the chair and the memories it conjured up caused her to crumble.

Thoughts of ending her life went through her mind, but always the twins held her back. If she did such a thing, then they would end up in an orphanage and the idea of that was too much to bear. They had no one. Arthur's ma was alive still, but she hadn't the time of day for Tilly and hardly took notice of Babs and Beth.

She still lived in Enfield Road, a few doors down from their house, but Mrs Ramsbottom had always thought herself something better than the rest of them and hadn't approved of Arthur mixing with the likes of her, Liz and Eddie, or anyone who lived in Bedford Road, let alone marrying one of them. She'd been brought down a peg or two when her husband, Arthur's dad, had been killed in a cycle accident on his way home from work. She'd needed to take the help of her neighbours then. But still she hadn't relented over her son's marriage.

Sometimes they would pass in the street and all the greeting Tilly would get was a 'humph' followed by some criticism or other, such as the time she'd said, 'Them young 'uns of our Arthur's look like ragamuffins half the time. Haven't you got a hairbrush, girl?'

Tilly had felt her girls snuggle close into her, their shyness overcoming them, and had had to bite her tongue for their sake and say something to placate the sour-faced woman. 'Sorry, Mrs Ramsbottom. It's the wind. I'll plait it for them in future.'

Without speaking to her grandchildren, Mrs Ramsbottom had walked on, muttering, 'Well, see that you do. I'll speak to our Arthur about it. They should have their hair cut short if you ask me.'

When Mrs Ramsbottom would speak to Arthur had mystified Tilly, as for all she knew, they didn't have much contact. Arthur had always said his ma would die a lonely old woman, but it was of her own doing.

Having lived with this situation all her life, Tilly was used to it, and if Mrs Ramsbottom passed her in the street without bothering to speak, it didn't worry her. There was nothing she could do about the woman's outlook, or her rejection of her and her children, and it had never come between her and Arthur for they had rarely mentioned his ma.

Finding herself nodding off, something that happened a lot of late, Tilly was startled by the door opening. Her heart leapt as she imagined it might be Liz, but to her surprise, as if by thinking about her she'd conjured her up, her ma-in-law stood on the threshold. 'Can I come in?'

Straightening herself and rubbing her eyes, Tilly couldn't speak for a moment.

'I'll not keep you. I were wondering how you were faring?'

'Yes, come in, Mrs Ramsbottom.'

Tilly stood and indicated that Mrs Ramsbottom should sit down. 'Would you like a pot of tea?'

'Aye, that'd be welcome, lass.'

The atmosphere was strange as Tilly swung the iron kettle-stand over the fire and she felt glad to escape to her little back kitchen to arrange the tray with cups, saucers, sugar bowl and milk jug, before scooping three spoonfuls of tea leaves into the teapot. This done, she leant her hands on the pot sink under the window and took a deep breath as she looked out into the yard. The last of the pink roses on the bush Arthur had planted against the wall that divided their yard from next door were in bloom. She could hear his voice when he'd planted it: 'There you go, lass, come summer, you'll have a pretty sight to meet you as you work at your sink, rather than that dull old wall.' *Oh, Arthur. Me lovely Arthur.* Tears pricked Tilly's eyes, but she didn't allow them to flow. She swallowed hard and busied herself doing nothing – straightening the tea towel that hung on the rail attached to the back door, tipping some water from the jug into the pot sink to swill it, even though it didn't need it. Then readjusting the curtain that hung around the sink and the draining board, hiding the shelf underneath where she kept items like furniture and shoe polish, soap for washing clothes and the blue bags that she added to the water to make her whites gleaming white.

This done, she listened for the sound of the kettle and could hear it was still sizzling and hadn't come to the boil. Other sounds assailed her then. The ticking of the clock and the faint tweet of a starling who'd landed on the wall. Turning around, she surveyed the kitchen. Counted the shiny copper pans hung above the main stove, which she hadn't yet lit. The thought passed through her mind that it needed blackening, a job Arthur always did on a Sunday morning. He'd stand back when done and say, 'Now, look at that, lass. By, I love seeing it shining and its brass knobs gleaming.' Tilly's eyes travelled downwards to where his slippers still leant against the fender. Her heart dropped like a stone and she gasped for air.

Picking up the tray, she hurried through to the living room and placed it on the table that stood at the back of the room between the back door and the kitchen door. It was as if having Mrs Ramsbottom in the house had brought everything into focus and she felt ashamed of the crumbs and the tea stain that graced the crumpled white cloth covering the table. And as she turned, the sun showed the smears on the windows where the twins had stood on the stools under the sill and watched folk pass by, making patterns by steaming the glass with their breath and drawing with their fingers. The hearth suddenly looked badly in need of brushing as ash and coal dust covered its surface. Embarrassment made her cheeks tingle. But Mrs Ramsbottom didn't seem to notice, she just sat staring ahead.

Crossing over the room and picking up the kettle, Tilly asked, 'Do you take your tea strong, Mrs Ramsbottom?' then thought how sad it was that she didn't know.

'Aye, I does. And with two sugars, ta.'

The sound of the water hitting the bottom of the pot accentuated the silence that clothed the room. And the rattling of the cup on its saucer was almost like thunder as Tilly's hand shook when she passed the cup of tea to Mrs Ramsbottom.

Taking her own tea and sitting back down in Arthur's chair opposite her ma-in-law, Tilly felt even more ill at ease and at a loss as to what to say.

She waited, sipping her tea. After Mrs Ramsbottom took a sip, she blew the steam away. 'By, that's good. Ta, lass.' She cleared her throat. 'I've sommat to tell you. I ain't long for this world. Me stomach's been playing me up for a while, and now I'm spitting blood, and struggling to breathe at times.'

This shocked Tilly. She wanted to say she was sorry, but she could only stare at this little woman who had always intimidated her. Signs of what she'd said became obvious. The weight she'd lost, and the yellow tinge to her skin. How her cheeks had sunken in and there were dark patches under her eyes.

'I've naw kin but you. And I wanted to tell you as I've made all the arrangements. I've paid for me funeral, and that bloke who deals in second-hand stuff will collect all me belongings and empty out me house. If there's owt you want, you can come over and take it.'

'Eeh, Mrs Ramsbottom, I – I don't knaw what to say. I –'

'There's nowt you can say, lass. I want to go. I don't want to stay here now me Arthur's gone.' She rummaged in the pocket of her pinny and pulled out a hanky. 'I look for him every morning to wave as he passes, and then in the evening, when I'd stand on me step and have a word with him.'

This surprised Tilly; she hadn't known of this ritual. It felt strange to hear of something Arthur did on a regular basis that she didn't know of. But then, he never mentioned his ma much and as far as she knew, his only time of visiting her was on a Sunday morning for half an hour. Mrs Ramsbottom's next words spoke of this. 'And when it comes to this Sunday, me first without him visiting, I . . . I, oh, God!'

Her ma-in-law bowed her head and covered her face with her hanky. Tilly jumped up and took Mrs Ramsbottom's cup, placing it on the dresser. Sitting on the arm of the chair, she put her arms around the little woman.

For a few moments they sat like this, both crying, their tears bonding them for the first time ever.

'Eeh, lass, I've not treated you right. And I'm sorry. I – I, well, it were sommat in me as I couldn't surmount. I wanted better for our Arthur than one of the urchins as played in the street. I were wrong. I knaw as you've been a good wife to me son. I could see his happiness, but seeing it only made me more resentful of you. And, well, now I'm turning to you in me hour of need and I'm ashamed of me ways.'

Tilly could only stroke her ma-in-law's soft white hair. Feelings were churning around inside her. Part of her wanted to take this woman and shake her. Tell her of the hurt she'd inflicted with her stuck-up ways and bigoted view of the world, but what would that achieve? There would be no satisfaction in telling someone what they already knew. For

Arthur's sake, it was time to forgive, and for Arthur's sake, Tilly knew she had to take care of his ma.

'I'm getting so weak, lass. I need help, and you're the only one I can ask. Losing me Arthur has finished me, I want to go to him. Him and my Cedric. I knaw as they're waiting for me.'

For some strange reason, this gave Tilly a pang of jealousy, but she quashed it, as she at last found her voice. 'Of course I'll help you, Mrs Ramsbottom, I'll—'

'Call me Ma, lass, as that's what I am, your ma-in-law. Like I said, I ain't been a good 'un to you. I've been a stupid woman.'

Taking a deep breath, Tilly determined to put her earlier thoughts into action. 'Naw. Forget all that. You're here now, when I most need you. And let's hope you have long enough to get to knaw your grandkids. Come on, Ma, we'll get through this together. Me and the kids'll be there for you.'

As she said this, a tiny part of Tilly's grief-filled heart lifted and she knew that she could do this for Arthur, she could care for his ma. And she knew he was smiling down at her and thanking her.

THREE

Tilly shivered as she followed the dray carrying her ma-in-law's coffin. The early November wind had a chill to it that cut through her bones.

The gaping hole in the ground that was ready to receive the coffin was next to the now settled mound of earth covering Arthur. Six weeks had passed. A time when Tilly hadn't allowed herself to be consumed by her loss as she had toiled to keep her ma-in-law comfortable. Neighbours had helped with the washing of the endless soiled sheets, and by giving Tilly a break by sitting with her ma-in-law whilst she tended to her own home and to the twins.

Tilly had come to love Arthur's ma, but felt a deep sadness that she hadn't always been the sweet, pliable woman she'd become as she coped with her terrible pain and faced her death. The disease that ravaged her body didn't have a name but in the end the doctor had put it down to consumption, and he'd shook his head in despair when nothing he did stopped the progress of the illness.

Tilly had cried many a silent tear of anguish as she had tried to make her ma-in-law comfortable and had listened to the moans of agony night and day. But miraculously, during her last two days, her ma-in-law had lain quiet and peaceful, her eyes closed, and her body seeming to work by clockwork until the moment came when a sudden silence descended, and she breathed no more. Then Tilly had wept at all that had befallen her. At how she'd hardly had time to think of missing her Arthur, and at the loss of the woman who'd come to mean so much to her.

Wearily standing between Arthur's grave and his ma's, Tilly didn't feel part of what was going on. The vicar's prayers went over her head. She looked around the small group of neighbours showing their respects and felt the pity of so few being there to mourn, but her ma-in-law hadn't let many folk get close to her. Over the weeks, Tilly had learnt that she'd been brought up in a convent orphanage, and had become wary of everyone in the world, trusting only her Cedric, who'd she met when she was in service and he was the gardener's boy. She'd determined that they should make something of themselves and, to this end, had encouraged Cedric to take a job in the biscuit factory as a delivery man. 'Eeh, he looked lovely in his white coat,' she'd told Tilly. 'He were just as handsome as our Arthur. And I loved him with all me heart. We did well, and we rented this house, but I didn't knaw how to relate to folk so kept meself to meself. I stupidly thought I could make my Arthur achieve even better things than we had, and I wanted him to marry well. But I were daft, as he couldn't have married anyone better than you, Tilly. And I hope you'll forgive me for rejecting you.'

Tilly had told her that of course she did and that she understood.

That moment had unlocked the love she felt for her ma-in-law, and they had become very close. It was painful to say goodbye so soon after finding each other.

Weariness clogged Tilly's bones as she stood looking at the two graves. Both contained her love. *What now? I feel so alone. The world seems a big empty place.* Her thoughts went to Liz. She hadn't seen or heard from her, nor from Eddie, which was strange, as she'd expected more visits from him.

With the wake behind her and it being near time to fetch the twins, Tilly thought for a moment about all that they had gone through. Poor little mites – their hearts were broken over losing their da, and getting to know and being loved by their granny had helped with that, but then as they realised that they were going to lose her too, they'd become very quiet. Tilly had had so little time to give them but had tried to keep their lives as normal as possible, keeping to their routine and encouraging them with their learning. They missed their Aunt Liz and her brood too.

Sighing, Tilly had the urge to do something about the latter and decided to leave early and take a detour along Fairfield Road. She could drop in to see Liz that way and then cut through Claremont Road to the school. She would try once more to convince Liz that what happened hadn't been her fault. Liz would be near to her time and might need help.

As she walked up Fairfield Road and was about to turn into Liz's street, she prayed she'd be received with friendliness. There was a huge void in her life now, and she so needed Liz. Helping Liz with her confinement and with the new babby would fill the long lonely hours that stretched ahead.

'If you're thinking on calling on that mate of yours, lass, you're going to be unlucky.'

The voice of the woman, whose name Tilly didn't know and with whom she'd only ever passed the odd greeting, cut into her thoughts. The woman, who looked in her sixties, and was about the same age as her ma-in-law had been, was leaning on the wall of her house, two doors from the corner of Liz's street. What she'd said had caught Tilly by surprise. 'Why? What's happened?'

'They're long gone. Did a moonlight. I saw them out of me window. Two o'clock in the morning it were. A dray pulled up and all them kids of hers carried stuff out. Not that lazy bugger of a husband she had. He didn't appear until the cart were loaded, and then he sat up front with the driver and left his family to walk behind. There's a new family in the house now.'

'Naw! Eeh, naw. Have you any idea where they've gone?'

'Naw, but didn't he come from the Midlands as I remember that's where his ma and da moved to when he were a nipper? I reckon as that's where they've made for as Liz were having a natter to me about a week afore and she mentioned as there were plenty of work down there. Not that she had a fat chance of Eddie doing any of it. Ha! He were an idle bugger. The only thing active about him was what he had in his trousers. That never lay dormant for long.'

Tilly burst out laughing, something that hadn't happened for a long time, and it felt good. But then she found she couldn't stop. Her body bent forward to take the pain of the laughter that shook her from head to toe. Mingled with the laughter were huge sobs.

'Eeh, lass, naw. Come on in. I knaw as you've been through the mill. Elsie as lives next door to you is a mate of mine and she told me. You've been a very brave lass, looking after your ma-in-law on top of losing your man. Come and have a cuppa with me.'

Tilly sipped the hot liquid and in doing so found some control. 'I'm sorry, I . . . well, I've just come from me ma-in-law's funeral and it was a shock to find out as Liz had gone.'

'It's understandable. I heard as Mrs Ramsbottom had passed on. She were a funny old cus, and she were lucky to have you tend to her. They say as she never gave you the time of day till she needed you.'

'Naw, it weren't like that. Well, it were, but she made it up to me in the last few weeks. I'm going to miss her.'

'Eeh, lass. You've a lot to contend with. Me name's Martha, by the way. I knaw yours, as me mate's allus on about you.'

'Did Liz ever mention me?'

'Naw. Not of late. I were surprised, as I asked her how you were, and she just brushed over answering me. What went wrong atween the pair of you? I knaws there were sommat as you were allus together till you lost your . . . well, anyroad, she's gone now.'

'It were Eddie as caused the problem atween us.'

'Don't tell me. I can guess. He made a pass at you, and afore your Arthur were cold, I shouldn't wonder. I wouldn't put it past him. That dirty bugger, he showed himself to me once. He called me a nosy old cow that could do with a good shagging, and if I weren't so ugly and fat he'd give me a bit of . . . well, then he unbuttoned his flies and lobbed it out. I were shocked. Not only at his action but 'cause I hadn't seen one for a good while and I'd forgotten how ugly they were.'

Once more Tilly found herself laughing, something she'd thought she might never do again. Martha joined in the laughter, a funny cackling laugh that made Tilly double over even more at the sound.

Composing herself at last, Tilly looked at the clock and realised she would be late picking up her young 'uns if she didn't get a move on. 'Well, ta for your company and the cuppa, Martha, both were welcome. But I've to fetch me twins from school now.'

'Aye, well, remember where I live, and don't be afraid to come knocking. I never had any young 'uns of me own, but if I had, I'd like them to have been like you. And I'd love to have had some grandkids running around the place. So, if I can help with your young 'uns, you only have to say. I'd love the chance.'

'Thank you. I might do that, as I do have to find a job. It's that or go cap in hand to the parish relief.'

'Awe, lass, didn't Mrs Ramsbottom leave owt for you?'

'Naw. She had a good pot on her mantle shelf and she kept me going while I cared for her, though I am behind two weeks with me rent, and that's worrying me to death. But the rest of what she had went on paying the doctor's bills and the medicine he prescribed for her. And I can't even sell owt as is left in the house as she'd already arranged for her stuff to be collected by a dealer who'd paid her upfront for it; that were to pay for her funeral. Arthur and me had a bit, but you knaw what it's like. I don't knaw where me next penny's coming from now.'

'Eeh, poor lass. It's not easy being a widow, though I were lucky as me old man were in an office job and paid into a pension fund. With that and owning this house, I get by champion now he's gone.'

This shocked Tilly. She couldn't imagine Martha being the wife of a white-collar worker. Weren't they refined? Well, there was nothing refined about Martha.

'So, what're you going to do now, lass?'

'I don't knaw, I've had naw time to think about it.'

'There's a job going at the greengrocer's on Dickson Road. Joe Simpson as owns it says as he can't manage on his own now that his wife's ailing. She's got a bad cough and I reckon as she'll be the next up the churchyard. Mind, it don't stop her going to her meetings and such at the church, she's allus there or in the vicarage having talks with the vicar about this and that. Allus been a busybody that one. Anyroad, they've never had any young 'uns, so Joe's a bit on a limb now without the help of his missus and he's looking to employ someone. He has a card up in his window. He wants someone for two days a week to mind the shop while he does his deliveries, and he says they have to be able to ride a bike, as they may need to take the orders out now and again on account of his gammy leg that plays him up. You knaw, thinking about it, I'm not sure as you should go for that job.'

'Why? It sounds perfect. I don't knaw about the bike riding, but I could learn.'

'The trouble is, I'd worry over you, as Joe's another who leers at the ladies, and well, love, you're built for the men. They'll all want a piece of you. And them as have an over-active thingy would make your life a misery.'

This time Tilly didn't laugh. She knew what Martha meant. 'I can handle meself, Martha. I took the poker to Eddie, and he soon ran for the door. I'm used to it. I didn't ask to look like I do, and I do try to flatten me chest a bit by wearing a tight liberty bodice, but it's difficult.'

'Aye, you were given a good endowment with them, but you're also a beautiful lass and even without them you'd catch the eye of the fellas.' Martha was quiet for a moment. What she'd said hung heavily on Tilly. She didn't want folk to see her as someone who would catch the eye of men, as that alienated her from the womenfolk. Look how Liz had reacted. Tilly had never thought in a million years that they would fall out. Martha broke into her thoughts.

'I tell you what, call back in with the young 'uns and I'll make some butties for them. I've a loaf baked off and some slices of ham. I cooked a shank this morning and it's nice and cold now on the slab in the pantry. By, I can almost taste it.'

'Ta, I'll take you up on that.'

'Aye, and that job. You give it some thought. And if you think you can handle the odd amorous suggestion, or the occasional tap on your backside, give it a go. If the twins take to me, I'd be willing to walk them to school and fetch them home and give them their tea while you're at work. And I wouldn't want payment neither, as it would be a pleasure.'

Despite all she'd been through that day, and for weeks now, and the sadness at finding Liz gone, Tilly's step was lighter as she left Martha's. At last there seemed a glimmer of hope that she could keep a roof over the twins' heads. After all, she had her basket making too. Earning some money would give her a chance to make a stockpile. She could collect the last of the blackberry vines and make baskets on the days she wasn't at work and every evening until she had enough to start to sell.

Her future suddenly looked brighter, if only she could get this job, and it was all down to Martha, a woman she'd never had much to do with. She knew of her from seeing her occasionally on her way to Liz's and she'd heard bits about Martha's character, and how it was said that she could be crude, and yet stand on her soapbox about anything she didn't agree with. Tilly hadn't seen her as crude – funny, yes, and a bit shocking, but her way of expressing herself was harmless and meant in humour.

Tilly thought again about the job in the greengrocer's shop. She knew Joe Simpson, the owner, who Martha had spoken of, and where his shop was on Dickson Road. She'd shopped there from time to time when she hadn't made it to the market. She'd never noticed him giving her the eye. Maybe he liked older women like Martha. She'd go along there when she had collected the twins, it was only a short walk from the school hall.

Mr Simpson – a good-looking man in his fifties – had thick, dark hair which was greying at the sides and looked slightly unruly, despite an attempt to sleek it back with oil. His hazel eyes twinkled and had a keenness about them more often seen in a much younger man. He sported a waxed handlebar moustache, shaped so that it curled at each end and brushed his cheekbones, giving him a rakish look. About five inches or so taller than Tilly, he gazed down at her through half-closed lids as he eyed her up and down.

Tilly caught a whiff of his hair oil mingled with the scent of tobacco as she breathed in deeply and waited for his answer to her enquiry. Relief filled her that there was no sign in his manner that he was leering at her as Martha had warned that he might.

'Well, you don't look very strong, and I need someone who is. Lugging crates of spuds and suchlike when the farmer delivers them ain't naw light work. Grab that one and let's see how you handle it. Shift it off the floor onto that shelf.'

The weight of the wooden crate of potatoes nearly creased Tilly as she bent down to pick it up. At first, she didn't think she'd manage it, but this job would suit her with its proximity to her home and the twins' school, and especially as it was just two days a week.

Besides this, she'd noted that the vegetables, and especially the fruit, could be better displayed in baskets than in the mishmash of crates and cartons that didn't seem to give them space to breathe. So, maybe Mr Simpson would become her first customer and buy baskets to house his goods. With this thought she made an extreme effort and managed to shift the crate.

'By, you're stronger than you look, lass. You've surprised me.'

Trying not to show the exertion the move had cost her, Tilly took a deep breath. 'So, will you give me a try, then?'

'Can you ride a bike?'

'I can soon learn. There don't seem owt difficult about it.'

'Aye, that's sommat as you can pick up. You can have a go up and down the pavement when the shop's not busy as you can see the comings and goings around the shop from here to the Gynn. But don't venture out on the road for a while as it can get very busy.'

Tilly knew Dickson Road was a busy thoroughfare for horsemen and carriages and was especially so in the season as many of the rich folk who came to Blackpool had houses around the Gynn Square. 'Does that mean as you'll take me on?' Tilly's heart quickened with hope. But then she saw for the first time the glint in Mr Simpson's eye.

'Aye, I'll more than take you on. You're widowed, ain't you?'

Tilly nodded. His words set alarm bells ringing inside her, but she so needed this job.

'And these are your young 'uns? You don't think that you're bringing them with you, do you?'

'Naw. Martha's going to take care of them for me.'

She hadn't told the twins this and both looked up at her with an anguished expression. She put a hand on each of their shoulders and pulled them to her. Their lives had been turned upside down these last weeks and both had become a little withdrawn. Now they looked lost. She smiled down at them. 'You'll knaw Martha, we've spoken to her many a time when we've passed her house.'

'But, Ma—'

'Hush now. Ma's busy.'

When she looked back up at Mr Simpson his gaze was intent and directed at her bosom. Her movement alerted him, and he coughed. 'Well then, I think as you'll suit me very well and that we can become friends. Yes, we'll jog along nicely. And I might have some extra tasks for you that could boost your wages an' all.'

The innuendo was so subtle that Tilly couldn't challenge it, but she hadn't missed his meaning. 'No ta, I've decided this job ain't for me, Mr Simpson, but I might have sommat as might interest you.' She told him about her baskets, but as she did she knew that he'd not take any from her. Her refusal of him had offended him.

'Huh! Well, you're a canny one, I'll give you that. Come in here looking for a job and then try to sell me sommat. Well, I ain't in the market. You can take yourself off now, and we'll say naw more about it, will we, eh?'

She knew what he meant. He knew that she'd sussed his intentions and now he was afraid she'd talk, and his missus would get to hear. With his change of attitude, the last remnant of hope of earning some money left her. What now? With the season having ended there would be so few jobs, if any, available. Suddenly, she knew she had to reverse her decision. She had to find a way of coping if Mr Simpson made advances. She was desperate and that meant she had to take her chances.

'I – I'm sorry. I ain't worked for a long time, and me nerves attacked me. Can I change me mind and ask you to consider me for the job after all? I'll do owt as you have in mind as I need to earn as much money as I can.'

Tilly immediately regretted adding this last. Why had she said that? *Oh, God, he'll expect sommat from me now, and I can't – I can't bear the thought of him touching me.*

She looked down at the twins. Their little faces stared so trustingly back up at her. Two little curly-topped heads. Identical, and yet easily distinguished by Tilly, the twins took after her in looks. Both had her raven-coloured hair and dark eyes.

They were dependent on her. They needed food, and a home. The air was already frosty, heralding the arrival of winter. Her little ones needed warmth – coats and boots and bonnets. She had to provide for them. She had to.

'Well now, on those terms, yes, I'll take you on, and I'd like a sample of the baskets you say you can make an' all. Your idea will smarten up me shop. The wealthy ladies will like that and it might give me a bit more of their business instead of using me as a convenience if they've forgotten to order sommat from the posh shops. Aye, you can make me store into a posh shop. And, I'm thinking, you can do much more than that for me.'

Ignoring this, Tilly smiled. 'Ta, Mr Simpson, I'm grateful. When do I start?'

'The sooner the better for me. Let's say Wednesday. Two days from now. It's half-day closing, so you can do two and a half days this week. Normally, Thursday and Friday will be your regular days, but I need to show you the ropes and can give you some time after shop hours an' all. And if you have a sample of them baskets you're talking about, bring one with you. I like that idea of yours. I like it very much.'

Realising she hadn't even asked about the rate of pay, Tilly broached the subject and was surprised by his answer; it was more than she had expected. 'I'll start you on tuppence an hour, but if you come up to my expectations, I'll give you threepence an hour. And your hours will be from eight forty-five till five fifteen. You'll get an hour off for your dinner when the shop closes between one p.m. and two p.m., but that ain't on pay.'

Trying not to think what his expectations might be, Tilly quickly added up that for the seven and a half hours she worked each day she would initially receive one and three-pence a day. That was half a crown for two days. Only a fraction of what Arthur had been bringing in, but she could manage if she cut everything to the bone. Her rent would take one day's pay, but she'd have plenty left over to feed them, besides having some from her basket making, though she'd need some wicker to do a proper job.

Forgetting any thoughts of what she might have to contend with, the first real, tangible hope filled her since Arthur had passed. 'Oh, ta! Ta, Mr Simpson. And I won't let you down. I'll be here on Wednesday. Quarter to nine on the dot.'

'Righto, and wear sommat a bit brighter, but more practical. I've some bibbed aprons of Mrs Simpson's that you can wear to keep your clothes clean, but I like a lass to look nice.'

Tilly glanced down at her dark grey mourning frock. Its skirt brushed the floor as she walked. Mud from the graveyard clung to the hem. She pulled her shawl around her and patted her black bonnet. 'I've been to me ma-in-law's funeral this morning. I apologise for me appearance.'

'Naw, lass, it's understandable, and you're the type as looks good in owt, but I were just saying how I want you to look when you work. Don't be turning up in blacks and browns. Make an effort to look nice.'

Feeling offended at this and mentally going through her wardrobe wondering what he would think of as suitable, Tilly bade him farewell.

As she turned into Edgerton Road, she gave further thought to what frocks she had that would be fitting for the work and yet were a bright colour. She wasn't short of clothes. If she'd seen a length of material in the market and liked it, she'd had

40

no reluctance to buy it as money hadn't been short. Not that she'd been indulgent, and besides, she hadn't ever had the need for more than a couple of day frocks other than those she wore for doing her housework and a Sunday-best outfit. The grey frock she wore now she'd bought for Arthur's funeral, but she hoped to never wear it again as long as she lived.

Maybe one of her housework frocks would do. One was blue calico, and she had several lace collars and cuffs, so she could press-stud clean ones to it to brighten it and make it look fresh each day. It was a good style too, as the bodice fitted her shape: it had buttons from the high neckline down to the waist before flowing into a gathered skirt. Yes, she thought that very suitable. She'd brush her hair back and pull it tightly into a bun. She looked less attractive like that than her usual style of leaving a few ringlets to bob around her face and neck. *I might even wear a mop cap. Yes, I've a couple that I wear when doing the laundry. They take away any illusion that I'm desirable, even Arthur . . .* She pulled the thought back. It was too painful to think of Arthur teasing her and saying she looked like a skivvy maid in her mop cap and it not being a good image to get him going. *Oh, Arthur, Arthur, why did you have to go? Why?*

Babs stopped this train of thought. 'Ma, when will we get to this Martha's house?'

'You're to call her Aunt Martha, Babs. And it's just around this corner, lass. Look, tell me what you've been doing at school today, eh? I love to hear.'

Beth answered. 'We're to find sommat beginning with our own letter and tell the teacher about it tomorrow.'

This mystified Tilly. She had no idea what their own letter could be. 'Have you thought of sommat, me lasses?'

'Not yet, Ma. I'm to think of sommat beginning with "E" and Babs sommat with "B".'

'Oh, aye, and why are them your letters, then?'

'Eeh, Ma, why d'yer think?'

'Babs! You knaw Ma can't spell, don't be unkind. It's because Babs's real name begins with "B", Ma. "B" for Barbara, and mine is "E" for Elizabeth.'

'So, Babs could have bread, as we'll see some bread at Martha's and you, Bethsy, can have evening, as it will be evening when we head for home.'

Both girls clapped their hands. 'Awe, Ma, you're good at this. We don't have to think about it anymore, do we, Babs.'

'Naw, we have a clever ma. I love you, Ma, you're the best ma in all the world.'

Beth nodded. 'Aye, in all of Blackpool an' all.'

Tilly laughed at this. Blackpool to her girls was all the world they'd seen. She pulled them to her. 'Eeh, me little lasses, I'll allus help you and I'll allus be there for you.'

Their two little faces looked up at her and Tilly's heart ached with love for them, and their love for her shone from them. The moment warmed her.

As they turned the corner, Babs shouted with glee, 'Eeh, it's on Aunt Lizzy's road, can we go and—'

'Naw. Aunt Lizzy don't live there no more, and Aunt Martha's is around the corner, not on the same road. We're here now. Come on. You'll like Aunt Martha, she'll make you giggle. And she's got tea ready for you an' all. I bet you're both hungry, eh?'

With this, Tilly opened the door of Martha's cottage and called out. As she did so, the reality of her new life hit her. She'd be dropping her twins off here and going to face goodness knew what. Though she did have a good idea.

FOUR

Wednesday morning gave Tilly more than an idea as to the way things would be if she continued working for Mr Simpson. But, for the near future, she didn't know what else she could do. At least until the season started next year and she had enough baskets made to sell to the holidaymakers.

It was while she was transferring the apples to the basket that she'd brought with her that her fears were confirmed.

Mr Simpson stood very close to her, which made it difficult for her to bend down without bumping him. His gesture of placing his hand on her bottom could have been a simple measure of keeping her from doing so, but for how his breathing was audible and how he made a sound in his throat told Tilly it was much more.

With her nerves jangling, Tilly's voice shook as she turned towards him. 'This is just an example, Mr Simpson. It's me vegetable basket for home. I made it oval-shaped so I could lay a few different veg side by side instead of on top of each other, but it's only made of blackberry vine. You would need ones made out of wicker, so that they would withstand the wear they'd get in your shop.'

'Hmm, very nice.'

His eyes rested on her bosom.

'A – And I can make them with a design on if you like. The one for apples can have "Apples" written into the weave, and so on.'

'You can do all that? My, you're a clever young miss, aren't you?'

The tone in his voice had set a nerve tingling in Tilly's stomach.

'When can you have them ready for me and what's your price?'

'I'd have to save for the wicker first. There's a trader due to come by soon. I've got to know him, and he usually brings a small amount of wicker up for me, enough to make a basket like this one. Then I have to treat it, and if you want the letters, I have to treat some of the canes in a different way to make them a darker colour so that the letters stand out. The whole process for a wicker basket, from preparing the canes to making it, can take a week.'

'You say he calls at your home? How's he to knaw where you are if it's a day that you're here, then?'

'I'll leave a message with me neighbour, to tell him to call here.'

'Yes. Do that. And I'll order and pay for the wicker we need. Now, what price?'

'For one like this, if you buy the wicker, I'd say two bob.'

'Two bob! Crickey, that's pricey. It's more than I'm paying you for a day's work and I'm going to need at least twenty baskets!'

'Naw. What you could do is to display some products together. In this basket, you could fit carrots and onions, for

45

instance, or apples and pears. Then we fill the baskets from stock behind the counter as and when the produce is sold.'

'Eeh, you've some bright ideas, I must say. So, I'd need ten then? At a cost of one pound. And what about the wicker? Is that costly?'

'Naw. Me trader charges around ha'pence for a bundle depending on the size of the canes and the thickness. They're all graded.'

'Right, it's a deal. I'll pay you each time you complete one.'

The morning went on with him showing her the weighing scales and being pleasantly surprised that she knew how to calculate the weights. Then they had a laugh together as she told him some tales of working in the sweet shop where she learnt how many ounces were in a pound.

'But do you knaw how many pounds in a stone, and stones in a hundredweight?'

'Aye, I does. I didn't have to weigh out such amounts, but I got interested and learnt meself. Me Arthur knew a lot about such things as he went to school, so he helped me an' all.'

'And you didn't?'

'Naw.' She told him about her Aunt Mildred.

With all this and seeing to the customers who came in, the time soon passed by.

'Now, I need to show you sommat out back, Tilly. I've a shed where I keep the stock. It's cool out there and I want you to see how I cover everything with sacking to keep the light off it. Your first job in the morning will be to stock the shop from there. You'll take the crates out there and fill them with what wants topping up in here. When we have your basket system, the job'll be twofold as you'll then display the

46

goods in the baskets and stack the crates behind the counter. Come on.'

Something made Tilly hesitate. She didn't like the sound of the shed out back. 'What if someone comes into the shop? Wouldn't it be best if I went out there and had a look then asked any questions of you if I'm not sure?'

'Naw. I have an ingenious system whereby the shop bell rings in the shed, so I never miss a customer, or let a thieving hound have access to me shop while me back's turned. And I allus take me money bag with me. But it's time to shut up shop anyroad. Come on.'

Tilly waited while he locked the door and pulled down the blind, and then followed him out. The smell of vegetables filled the shed, and the size of it surprised her – it was much bigger than a normal garden shed. Inside there were shelves lining the walls and boxes filled these; all were labelled, and all covered by sacks. The high shelves worried her. But there was a wooden stepladder against the wall. Somehow, she'd have to manage to bring produce down using the ladder.

'Right. So, you see how it's all laid out? Well, when deliveries come, they arrive at that back gate. I let the deliverymen in, and they stack the boxes here. Then the stock has to be rotated, so I put it away once the shop closes, making sure that new stock is placed behind the old, and stock for the shop is allus taken from the front of each box. Got it?'

As he said this Mr Simpson moved towards her. Tilly stepped back. His hand came out and caught hold of hers. His voice gravelled as he said, 'And this is where those extras I talked of will happen. We'll pick our moment. Usually on a Thursday lunchbreak, when Mrs Simpson goes to her meetings at the church. Or if she goes to an extra one. She's allus involved in sommat or other, flower arranging, or church cleaning, I don't knaw.'

His face was so near to hers by the time he'd finished saying this that Tilly could feel his breath wafting across her cheeks. She pulled her hand away. 'I – I'm not for giving owt extra, I'm here to do me job, Mr Simpson.'

His face changed. 'Now that wasn't the arrangement, remember? Oh, we might not have expressed in words what was expected of you, but I made it clear and you agreed.'

With this he pulled her roughly to him. His hand lifted her chin so that she was looking into his eyes. 'You're beautiful, Tilly. You had me heart the moment you walked in me shop.'

Tilly could hardly breathe. She went to protest, but his lips clamped down on hers. Held as if in a vice, she couldn't get away. The feeling wasn't unpleasant – nothing about Mr Simpson repulsed her. He wasn't a bad-looking man, and he was clean and smelt nice . . . *What am I thinking? I don't want this, I don't.*

With an extreme effort, she released herself from him. 'Don't. Don't ever do that again. You're married and twice me age! You should be ashamed of yourself.'

'Naw, it's you as isn't to do that again. I made meself clear what I wanted, and you understood. Agreeing so you could get the job ain't what I expected. Well, you'll find yourself on your arse in the street if you stop me again. Play ball and you can live in clover as there'll be extra for you if you please me. And what does it matter that I'm married? I ain't giving you owt me missus wants. She turned her back to me a long time ago, and I'm sick of using them prossies on Coronation Street. The dirty whores. I want someone decent like you.' He grabbed her arm again. Tilly went to move away but something stopped her.

'You've a lot to offer, Tilly. And I won't make you pregnant or owt like that. This were me solution – to hire a woman as would play ball with me. See to me needs and work hard in me shop. If you don't want the job, you can leave now. I don't reckon as I'll have trouble finding someone who will take me up on me offer.'

Tilly hesitated. Never in her life did she think she'd face such a choice – give herself to another man or lose her home and see her kids starve or, just as horrific, taken from her and put in a home, as would happen if she couldn't provide for them. She knew she couldn't face either of those things happening. The thought came to her that no one would know. She needn't even get involved, just let him do it and get it over with.

'I . . . I'd need sommat upfront. I've not paid me rent and the collector will call this afternoon. I've got to give him sommat, and well, if you say you'll give me extra . . .'

'By, it's like dealing with the prossies.'

'I ain't naw prossie! I've never had anyone touch me but me lovely Arthur, and I don't want to do this, but you've left me naw choice! If I don't go with you, I've no job. No job, no house, and I'll lose me young 'uns . . .' A sob escaped her, and tears tumbled down her face as she thought about what she was agreeing to through her desperation. *Oh Arthur, Arthur.*

Mr Simpson looked shamefaced for a moment, but his conscience was beaten by his need. 'I'll give you owt, Tilly . . . owt. And, I'm not repulsive, am I? The prospect of going with me don't disgust you, does it?'

His voice had an appeal in it. And suddenly Tilly saw him for what he was: a lonely, desperate man. Their needs may be different, but didn't she feel those same emotions? 'Naw, you don't disgust me. But Mrs Simpson, she don't deserve—'

'She won't knaw, and wouldn't care less, I shouldn't wonder. She never wanted it, like I say, and now she's ailing, I've no chance. Come here then, Tilly, there's a good girl. Everything will be all right, I promise.'

Tilly couldn't move willingly, and yet allowed herself to be pulled into his arms. His kisses felt strange. She hadn't really registered the first one, but this time she felt the stiff moustache as if it was a wire fence. Arthur's moustache had been soft and tickly, nothing like this. But despite that something stirred inside her when his hand cupped her breast and gently kneaded it. She was repulsed that it did. She wanted to fight against it but stiffening only seemed to increase his ardour and she found herself led to the back of the shed. His voice a hoarse whisper, Mr Simpson told her that he had some sacking piled up there. 'I'll lay it on the floor for us.'

Again, Tilly's mind screamed that she didn't want this, but the part of her that dreaded the future gave in.

Once on the floor, Mr Simpson was a gentle lover, caressing her, kissing her and removing her undergarments whilst praising the colour and feel of her skin, the shape of her thighs, and the fleshy feel of them. Gradually her doubts left her, and Tilly found that she wasn't unwilling. Not to the point of struggling, though her heart remained as cold as steel. But even that melted a little when his fingers reached the innermost part of her. Feelings boiled up and raced around her blood, leaving her breathless and panting.

'I think you're ready, me lovely, Tilly.' With this he moved to within her open legs and lowered himself into her. The thrill she felt shocked Tilly. She cried out as she took the fullness of him, all her doubts leaving her as she lost herself in the ecstasy of his movements and responded as she had done with her Arthur, in a hungry, animal-like way. Willing the feelings to grow, calling out that she wanted more, moving in the same rhythm that he was, and then it happened. She shook with the intensity of it as wave after wave gripped her body, sending her into a world of extreme pleasure she could hardly bear. A more intense feeling than she'd ever experienced. She couldn't let it go. She clung on to this man who had brought her to this place and sobbed from the joy of it.

As the feeling subsided she became aware of him trying to pull away. 'Let go, for God's sake, let go, I – I can't . . . Oooh, oh, God!'

His moment was on him. Tilly lay and allowed it. When it was over, sobs wracked her. Deep sobs that she couldn't control.

'Eeh, lass, I'm sorry, I'm sorry, I tried to pull out. Happen as no harm's done. But by, I've never experienced owt like that. Let me hold you, me little lass. Let me hold you.'

Tilly went into the soft enclosure of his arms and found comfort. She had a strange feeling of being detached. Not from him, but from the pain that had clogged her since the day that Arthur had died.

She clung on to this man who had done that for her, this man who had done things to her body that had never been done before. He rocked her back and forth. 'There, me lass. Are you all right, now? Everything'll be all right. I'll see to things if we get trouble from this, I promise.'

'Naw, nowt'll come of it. I – I can't have any more babbies.
I – I just feel, well, released. I don't knaw why. I don't even feel
guilty and yet, me lovely Arthur ain't left me long. It's just that
that were nowt like he gave me. Though what we did were
good and we loved doing it. But we never . . . I never, well, I
had a special feeling with you.'

'Oh, Tilly. I'm not Arthur, I'm different. I've learnt a lot of
techniques, especially with the prossies. They knaw it all and as
often as they have it, they like it to be right and to satisfy them.
What you had with Arthur were love. A good love, a love that
you shared exclusive to others. I used to have that with Mrs
Simpson, but we lost it. It were my fault. I've allus wanted more
than she can give, and she found out I'd visited the prossies and
that was that. But you, Tilly. You can give a man everything he
needs. Naw man who had you as theirs would want to stray.'

His words somehow made all they'd done seem right. She
hadn't given anything away that belonged to Arthur. She
didn't love Mr Simpson. And Arthur wasn't here anymore.
She did feel guilty at how soon she'd given herself, but then
she reminded herself that she'd had no choice, and she hadn't
known that Mr Simpson would do what he did to her, not
how he did it. And she'd only consented to save their young
'uns. Arthur would want her to do that.

Something nudged the guilt a bit deeper. Yes, that had been
why she'd consented, but she didn't have to accept it how she
had, or . . .

'Tilly? Are you all right? Are you getting cold? Your body
just shuddered.'

For a moment she wanted to scream that no, she wasn't all
right, but what was the point? She knew that as much as she

hated herself, she would do it again. Something inside her would compel her to.

Once they were dressed, Mr Simpson held her hand and looked into her eyes. She saw him differently as she gazed back. Saw that he was quite handsome, and didn't look his years, though that was helped by the blush that tinged his cheeks. He cleared his throat. 'Well, my dear, I'm thinking differently now. You've pleased me. So tell me, how much is your back-rent?'

This spoiled the moment and made her cringe inside. She truly was a prostitute, no better.

'No. Don't take it like that. I can see what you're thinking. I didn't want to ask, and don't want to pay you, at least not for what we just did. It cheapens it and it was something very special to me, but we must be practical. You have to pay your rent. I'll give you the whole amount plus a little extra to tide you through, then from now on I'll pay you threepence an hour, then what we have together is covered and you needn't feel I'm paying for it.'

This shocked and pleased Tilly. 'Well, me rent's one and threepence a week and I owe three.'

'Christ, Tilly, how many weeks do they let you get behind afore they kick you out?'

'I don't knaw. I've never been behind before. Happen the landlord has heard of me circumstances and is letting me off for a bit. No doubt me neighbours would have told the rent collector.'

'Well, it had better be paid. Here's four bob. That'll give you threepence to get a bit of scrag end for your tea. And you can take some root veg to cook off with it. And, Tilly . . . thanks.

I'll take care of you, I promise. I feel as though I've taken advantage of your situation and that ain't a good feeling, but it helps that you were willing and enjoyed it as much as me.'

They went out of the shed and crossed the yard. Somehow being in the daylight once more brought the enormity of what had happened back to haunt Tilly. Inside she folded and wanted to lie on the ground and scream all the shame out of her, but then she knew that she would have been doing that for certain if she'd refused as she wouldn't have known where to turn.

'I'll see you tomorrow, Tilly. And we'll take our dinner in the shed, eh?'

Despite herself, she smiled up into what she now saw as a kind and loving face. 'All right, Mr Simpson.'

As he pulled the blind up that was covering the front door, he smiled back at her. 'By the way, when we're on our own, it's Joe. Call me Joe.'

With that, he closed the door on her and she heard the blind being pulled down.

What had happened didn't seem as bad as she had thought it would. Joe was a gentle, loving person. Oh, she knew he could be ruthless as he'd showed in the way he'd used her situation to get his own way, but once he had . . . Yes, she could call him loving. And at this moment he was her salvation as well as a solace to her loneliness.

FIVE

Though she cried herself to sleep every night and wailed against the guilt that was her constant companion, and the struggles that beset her, by the time Christmas came, Tilly was used to her new life. She missed Arthur every minute of every hour, but she found great comfort in Joe's arms. She had feelings for Joe. He was good to her, and she needed him as much as he needed her. Her work days were the best of what seemed a long, long week.

Her friendship with Martha helped too. Martha never ceased to make her laugh. Tilly looked forward to when, like now, she had called to pick up the twins. Always there was a hot cuppa waiting for her, and often a bite to eat.

'Eeh, lass, you look tired the neet.'

'Aye, we've been run off our feet. Joe didn't get out to do his deliveries till after we closed. He'll not get in till late tonight. All on account of the Christmas rush.'

'Joe, is it?'

'I . . . well, aye, it is. I've been there almost two months now and all the customers call him Joe, it just seemed natural.'

'I'm only tugging your tail, lass. I'm glad as you're happy there. And you've had naw trouble from him? He's shown you nowt but respect?'

Martha had never spoken of her fear of Joe making a pass since Tilly had taken the position at the greengrocer's, but now she had, Tilly had to look away under the pretence of greeting the twins.

'Tilly? Eeh, lass, he ain't giving you any trouble, is he? I'll be round there with me copper stick if I thought he was.'

'Naw. Don't be daft, Martha.' Thinking it best not to deny it too vehemently, Tilly laughed. 'He chases me around the cabbages now and then, but I hit him with a marrow.'

Martha burst out laughing. 'Ha, they say he has one like a marrow, so you take care.'

Tilly blushed again but covered it with laughing out loud. She'd more than noticed the truth of this.

'Anyroad, I wanted to tell you sommat. I've been planning Christmas dinner. Eeh, I'm that excited to have you and the little ones to sit at me table with me, you don't knaw what you've done for me by accepting me invite. I've spent so many Christmases on me own, I'd begun to dread it.'

Tilly was glad the subject had changed from the goings-on in the greengrocer's. 'Don't forget that I'm bringing the vegetables. Joe's making me a hamper up as a Christmas gift. There'll be all sorts, but sprouts in particular. I love sprouts, oh, and chestnuts an' all. He had a delivery today; what with them and the mistletoe arriving, we've had a funny day. The women were queuing up to be kissed by him.'

'Eeh, I might go down meself. I bet he's a grand kisser, though that moustache'd dig in yer. By, it's years since I were kissed by a man. You miss it, don't you?'

This struck home and a tear seeped out of Tilly's eye. She did miss her Arthur's kisses. Missing him was like a burning ache in her, and she wondered how she'd ever have got through it all without Joe.

'By, I'm sorry, me lass. I shouldn't have said that, and here it is coming up to your first Christmas without your Arthur an' all. But look, lass, I promise you, we'll have a jolly day. We'll make it so for the young 'uns, eh?'

'Will Father Christmas come to me and Beth, Ma?'

'Aye, he will, Babs. He'll bring two stockings so fat with goodies, he'll hardly fit down the chimney.'

Beth clapped her hands. The quieter but stronger one of the two, Beth took everything in her stride. Always there to protect Babs, who went at everything like a bull at a gate and took the tumbles to pay for it.

Bending over, Tilly took Babs in her arms; Beth soon got up from what she was doing and came to snuggle in too. 'I'm making a card for Da. It has a heart on because I love him. Do you reckon as he'll get it, Ma?'

'I do, Beth, love, I do. I'll post it with the address for heaven on it and an angel will come and collect it.'

'I want to make one an' all.'

'I'll help you, Babs. I've plenty of the card that Aunt Martha gave me. Come on, we can do it now, and you can crayon your picture.'

'Eeh, Beth, ta. Would you help me to draw an angel an' all, as that's what Da is now, ain't he, Ma?'

'Aye, he is. He's our angel and he looks after us, just like he's allus done, me lasses.'

'He is, and not all angels are in heaven as your ma's one an' all with how she's took on providing for you both.'

Tilly blushed but said nothing as she watched the girls get down on their knees once more and become engrossed in making their cards. What Martha had said had caused her heart to feel like a lead weight in her chest. Would she ever recover? Had what she'd embarked on made it worse for her? Part of her didn't think so, but part of her was etched with the pain of guilt.

Christmas Eve dawned before Tilly knew it. She'd promised to go to the shop to do an extra two hours to help out. And she and Joe had said they would make time to go into the shed once the shop closed at lunchtime and Mrs Simpson had left to decorate the church. It was to be their first time in almost ten days, as they had been too busy and inundated with orders to fulfil, and their last time for over a week due to the holiday, so both were eager and willing to brave the cold of the shed.

As the snow began to fall mid-morning, and the temperature plummeted, Joe whispered that he would take her to his bedroom. 'I can't have you undressing in this cold, and I can't make love to you with all those petticoats and corsets in the way. I want you next to me.'

His words sent a shiver of anticipation through Tilly, and yet, part of her didn't want this advancement in their status. To make love in the shed was one thing but to go to his room . . . well, that seemed to move things on to a new level. But when the time came, all of those feelings were forgotten as Joe closed the blinds and turned to her. She went willingly into his arms and let her doubts, and any traces of guilt, flow away from her. She needed to be lost in all he could give her.

She couldn't understand why she behaved in this way, or what drove her. She only knew that the solace he offered dulled the pain, even made it disappear, and always she could tell herself that she was doing this for her children.

Tilly was calling out with the abandonment that had taken her when her world was shattered, and she saw Mrs Simpson standing in the bedroom doorway.

'What's going on? Oh my God, Joe! No! No, no, no!'

The words weren't screamed but said in an anguished voice. Joe rolled off Tilly and stared towards his wife, she couldn't move. Not even to close her legs. She lay exposing her most intimate parts as she witnessed Joe's wife, who she knew as Agatha, almost stagger towards a chair that stood in the corner of the room. Her face white with shock.

'Not again . . . I said never again! Why? Why do you do this? I – I try my best. Why do you humiliate me in this way? Aren't I enough for you?' Though she said this, there was no sense that any of what was happening really mattered to Agatha. 'For God's sake, Joe, I even let you have your way last night. I . . . I thought, I . . . I mean, I know you wanted to again this morning, but I was tired, I can't believe that would drive you to this. You're an animal, a filthy animal!'

Her moan was pitiful. Tilly curled herself into a ball trying to ward off the sound. She felt it take root in her and unlock her own agony. An agony she'd warded off and dealt with by taking what belonged to this broken woman.

'Darling, I'm sorry. She enticed me. This is the first time ever, I promise. Ever since I took her on this harlot has tried to get me to be unfaithful to you.' He was kneeling in front of his wife now. 'If only you'd let me this morning. You knaw how my needs nag away at me. I couldn't help it. Oh, darling, please forgive me. She is to blame. She's nowt to me, nowt, but when she offered, I were weak. I love you, my darling baby.'

'Don't! Don't call me that. It's as if you're mocking me. I'm not your baby, and don't ever want to be. I have tried to stick to my vows, but that isn't good enough for you. You repulse me!'

'B – but, I . . . It's not my fault. Agatha, I love you. I'll get rid of her. I'll never set eyes on her again. She's a whore. Her poor husband has only been dead a couple of months, and in all that time she's tried to get this to happen. Showing me that she wanted me with gestures and moving close to me and flashing her eyes. I have sinned, I have been weak, but you knaw I love you, Agatha, don't leave me. Please don't leave me.'

Tilly had never heard a man cry how Joe now broke down and sobbed. And neither could she understand how he could say such things after the way he'd behaved. He'd lied to her about his wife not sleeping with him. Though it didn't sound as though she did it for the love of him, but out of duty to the vows she'd taken.

Agatha sat as if made of stone, looking almost triumphant as Joe's sobs and appeals went on and on. The sound brought home the reality of the situation to Tilly. Something that had lain unattended inside her since the minute she'd been told Arthur was dead erupted and filled her with agony. What had

60

she been doing? Her whole being crashed with the pain of loss. The torturing distress of what she'd warded off hit every part of her. She'd been used. Blackmailed. She'd allowed it all and become trapped by this man who was skilful at lovemaking and had taken her out of herself. Made her forget, made it possible for her to carry on as if . . . as if her Arthur had never existed.

The moan that assaulted her ears came from her this time. From deep within the part of her soul that she'd forced to lie dormant because she couldn't face it.

As this self-analysis seeped into her, so did shame. Shame at the lack of courage she'd shown. She could have found another way. She needn't have jumped at the first solution. Her desperation had caused her to do that.

'Tilly, Tilly! Stop, stop. Oh, Joe, help the girl. Do something.'

'I can't do owt, nor do I want to. She brought this down on herself. Hark at her calling for her dead husband. She ain't given him a thought this day, nor any of the days since the poor bloke was killed. She's nowt, Agatha, nowt.'

A stinging slap burnt Tilly's cheek. The shock of it stopped her cries. She stared at Agatha.

'I'm sorry. I had to do that. You were hysterical. Get your clothes on, come on, let's get you out of here.'

Agatha was taking charge of the situation in a manner that Tilly would not expect of someone who had been so let down. And though only small, she seemed to have grown in height. 'Here, put your pantaloons on.'

Tilly took the garment and started to dress. Everything seemed unreal and her actions were carried out as if by clockwork. Even the sobs that rasped her chest felt as though someone was making them happen.

Turning to her husband, Agatha commanded him to leave the room. 'Go downstairs. Mrs Bilson is waiting for me. She has no doubt heard all that went on, but that is as it maybe. I don't care anymore. I've had enough. Enough! Do you hear me, Joe? You disgust me. First prostitutes, and now this . . . This taking advantage of a young woman in distress. Get out . . . GET OUT!'

If the situation hadn't been so agonising, Tilly would have laughed at the scurrying Joe as he grabbed his pants and almost fell trying to put them on whilst hopping towards the door.

Tilly carried on dressing. Part of her was horrified that someone, especially the gossiping Mrs Bilson, knew what had happened. But the biggest part wouldn't let anything in other than the sheer agony that was akin to her feelings when she'd lost her Arthur.

'Here, let me help you with your corset.'

This was surreal. The thought came to Tilly that this woman's husband had helped her to get the corset off, and now . . . A laugh came from her. A strange laugh that gurgled up and then burst from her. It was like the cackle that Martha made when she laughed. This thought made Tilly laugh even harder. She couldn't stop. Her body hurt with the exertion of it.

'Stop that. Tilly, stop!'

Tilly felt her body being shaken, making the walls of the room seem as though they were coming towards her then going away. 'You're hysterical again, Tilly, STOP IT!'

Once more a sharp stinging slap made her fall silent. Her body folded and slumped forward.

'Come on, Tilly. You have to get dressed and get off home.'

Lifting her head, she looked into Agatha's eyes. 'I – I'm sorry. I don't . . . I don't knaw why it happened. I – I was desperate for money. I – I was losing everything. Joe . . . paid me. I've betrayed my lovely Arthur, and . . . and you. I'm sorry.'

'I know how it is. You're not the first and won't be the last. Joe's insatiable. I have had enough now and will leave him. I cannot stay. I wouldn't be able to stand the scandal. Nothing has ever got out before about him, but now . . . Well, I think we all know what Mrs Bilson is like.'

Taking Tilly's arm, Agatha said, 'Let me help you. You're a victim as much as I am. Joe would have seen your desperation. I did myself but felt happy that Joe was helping you. I knew he paid you over the odds, but I thought that was an act of kindness. I didn't think he'd made you do this.'

Tilly had the thought that she was in the presence of a saint. No other woman would react how Agatha was, but then, by the sound of things, she'd been so badly hurt and perhaps that made her recognise the hurt in others. But how she wasn't condemning Tilly was a mystery to her.

Agatha sat on the edge of the bed as Tilly stepped into her frock and pulled it up to put her arms into it. Though it was a long frock with petticoats attached to the inside of the skirt, Tilly had never known it to be as heavy as it felt now.

As if Agatha had read Tilly's thoughts, she said, 'I forgive you, Tilly. Oh, that don't make me a saint, as I'm far from that, but in forgiveness, I find a path to help me to carry on. It has been the only way with Joe. I keep telling myself that he can't help himself. I know how his feelings are overpowering for him and I try to accommodate him, but no one woman could do that for a man like Joe. He is to be pitied really. I should have taken more care of you, but I've hardly spoken to you, let alone given you my support. How could I have been so blind? He told me that in helping you by paying you more than is the going rate, he felt some recompense for his sins. I believed him and in that, I encouraged him.'

'Naw. You're not to blame.'

'And neither are you.'

Dressed now, Tilly felt like taking this woman into her arms and hugging her. She could recognise the same desolation in her that was inside herself. Every part of her body was shaking with it, her eyes were leaking with it. Desolation that she'd lost her Arthur and had betrayed him, and yes, with the thought of, *What now?*

Huddled in her shawl, Tilly somehow managed to make it to Martha's.

'Eeh, lass, what's to do? Is it the thought of facing Christmas – your first without Arthur? Come in and let's get you warmed up. The young 'uns are having a nap. I allus put them to lie down after they've had their dinner. I've sommat for you an' all. It's a nice shepherd's pie, it's still hot in the oven. Get your cloak off and I'll get it out and ready on the table.'

Cold to the bones of her, Tilly moved towards the fire before removing her cloak and bonnet. The hem of her skirt was wet through from swishing in the snow as she'd walked.

'Reet, lass, sit yourself down and get that inside you. I'll make you a pot of tea.'

'Martha, I've done a terrible thing.'

'Eeh, lass, naw. What're you saying? What's happened?'

Unable to face eating the pie, Tilly shoved it away from her, folded her arms on the table and rested her head on them.

'Tilly? Tilly, lass, tell me what it is?'

How Tilly uttered the words, she didn't know, but somehow, she got the whole sordid story out. Never in a million years would she have predicted Martha's reaction.

'What? I – I, well, I never had you down as like that. And you've duped me an' all. You've took advantage of me good nature and me love of your young 'uns, so as you could carry on like a whore. You've gone down in me estimation, Tilly Ramsbottom. I thought you were doing all you could to keep body and soul together and provide for your young 'uns, not prostituting yourself! I'll thank you to leave and never to come back to me doorstep again.'

'Martha! Naw! I – I'm sorry, I didn't mean—'

'Didn't mean what? To give yourself to the pleasure of another woman's man, eh? To do that under the guise of taking care of your young 'uns, eh? Oh, don't give me that. I warned you what Joe were like, but that suited you, didn't it? You could play on that and get more money out of him. You're a disgrace. You've let me down and you've hurt me all over again!'

'Again? When have I hurt you afore, Martha?'

'Oh, you didn't do it, but a young woman just like you did. She enticed me husband and he . . . he betrayed me. Cut me in two they did. Well, I came out the winner, as the to-do it caused killed him. Caused him to collapse and that was that. Gone. Leaving me with the pain. Well, I ain't for wanting to help someone like her. So, I'd thank you to get out of me house, and never darken me doorstep again.'

Tilly stood. If she thought she'd felt desolation before, it flooded her now. She'd come to love Martha as if she was her own ma, and grandma to the twins. The twins loved her too. This would devastate them. Everything gone . . . All gone, and all because of her own actions.

Not speaking, she went up the stairs to the bedroom and woke the twins. Their reaction nearly undid her as they threw themselves at her and in sleepy voices asked if Santa had been. Cuddling them to her, she couldn't tell them that all they'd been looking forward to was now in tatters. That there would be no Christmas. At least, not the one they'd been expecting, with the paperchains they'd made hanging from the ceiling and the tree lit with a dozen candles stand- ing in the corner. Nor with the presents they were hoping for, though she did have a few of these for them. She'd bought a rag doll each for them, and a yoyo. And had been thinking of getting a spinning top too, but she hadn't been paid before she'd left the shop and so now, she only had enough to call into the butcher to get a scrag end to make a meal for them. They had all been looking forward to Martha cooking the cockerel the twins had helped her to pluck and the chestnut stuffing she'd prepared, and most of all to the Christmas pudding they'd stirred each week since November.

'Why are you crying, Ma?'

'I'm not – well, I am a little. You see, Aunt Martha ain't well and this means that we have to go home and can't spend Christmas with her.'

For a moment they were both quiet. Then Babs got that stubborn look on her face as she said, 'But I want to. We've nowt at home. Aunt Martha and us, we got everything ready.'

'I knaw, little one, but Aunt Martha can't help being poorly.'

'Shouldn't we stay and look after her, Ma?'

This from the caring Beth was typical. 'She doesn't want us to. She can't be putting up with us when she's not feeling well.'

'But she never says she has to put up with us, she loves us. It's not fair!'

'Fair to who, Babs? To you, or to Aunt Martha? Now, come along, we have to leave. You're to say ta to Aunt Martha for all she's done for you, and to give her a hug.'

'We will see her again, won't we, Ma?'

Tilly didn't know how to answer Beth. Her perception was always astounding.

Babs forestalled her. 'I want to see Aunt Martha again, Ma, I want to.'

'We'll see. Now, Babs, don't have a tantrum, you know that upsets Beth and then she has a screaming fit that she can't control. Be a good girl. Aunt Martha needs peace and quiet not two screaming girls bringing the roof down.'

'She's not going to heaven, is she? Ma, Aunt Martha ain't dying, is she?' The sight of Beth's bottom lip quivering brought home to Tilly what her actions had caused. Her beloved twins were going to be heartbroken not to see Martha again, and she'd opened wounds in Martha that had never healed. Not that she'd known they were there, or ever intended to fuel them. But that was it – she'd never intended any of it, and yet, she'd done it. Why? How could she? And as she

67

thought this, she knew it hadn't all been down to the need to make enough money to keep the twins with a roof over their heads and food in their bellies. Some of it was down to the feelings that had been awoken inside her and now rarely gave her peace, and the need to use something to block out the grief she hadn't been able to face.

SIX

Somehow, Tilly got through Christmas. Boxing Day came and went with her hardly participating in anything. Oh, she played with the twins. Hide-and-seek, trying to teach them to manage the yoyo, and though her body laughed at their antics, she didn't – not inside she didn't.

Memories of Arthur assailed her, but not in a comfortable way, in a shameful way. She longed to be able to tell him she was sorry. To face him, and to see the forgiveness in his eyes.

But now, three weeks after Christmas, panic was setting in. Everything she'd saved in the pot on the mantle shelf had gone. The last of it had been given to the rent man yesterday, meaning that she had to do something and fast. And yet, she felt drained of energy. And almost afraid to go out into the street where fingers pointed at her, and curtains twitched each time she took the children to school and returned to pick them up in the afternoon.

She couldn't blame her neighbours; she'd violated their trust in her, and to their eyes, as one put it, she'd thrown everything they'd done for her back in their faces, and almost destroyed Martha.

And now, with not enough oil to light the lamps and her candles almost burnt to the wick, she had no one to turn to. Bitterness entered her as she thought of Joe. His standing hadn't changed. His long-suffering wife still stayed with him despite her saying she wouldn't. No doubt he'd used his manipulative ways to get around her. And his shop still did well, with all that was said about anything was that he was a 'bit of a lad for the women'.

Life wasn't fair! But thinking such things wouldn't right the wrongs. She had to take action today. When she paid the rent up the last time she fell behind, a letter had come to say that if she failed to pay again she would be evicted; it had added that there were plenty of folk waiting to rent the houses. She knew this. Knew Enfield Road was a sought-after location for those who could pay their way because their men were in work.

Plucking up all her courage, Tilly donned her coat. She would have to go to the greengrocer's and ask Joe for the wage she'd earned in her last week in his employ. She was owed at least a shilling as she'd done a lot of overtime. But if he had any decency he would give her more to tide her over.

Tilly stood on the corner of the Gynn for a good ten minutes, watching the shop, waiting for a time when the customers stopped going in and out. She'd chosen a bad time as many mothers did their shopping just before collecting their children from school to save making two journeys in the bitter weather. At last Dickson Road looked empty and Tilly felt she could venture forward.

With her heart banging against her chest she reached the door and, before her courage could abandon her, she opened it. Joe went pale as he looked up at the clanging of the bell. 'What . . . ? Look, Tilly, lass, you'd better not start trouble. You brought it all down on yourself, you knaw you did. You couldn't get enough of me. Or have you come for more? Missing me, eh? In that case, you should go to the back gate and ring that bell, I don't want folk catching you in here. Agatha couldn't stand it and she'd be told. There's allus someone wanting to spread gossip.'

Ignoring this, she spoke at first in a frightened, defensive voice, but then with her head held high. 'I've come for me wages. You owe me. I never got paid for that last week and I did a lot of hours over me time.'

'Ha! You'll be lucky. You'll only get money out of me if you lie on your back for me. You can do that now if you want. Go around the back and I'll let you in. There won't be many folk coming in the shop for the next half an hour, they're all at the school gate and Agatha is out for the afternoon.'

'Naw! I never want you to touch me again. I just want you to do the decent thing by me. I – I'm desperate. I haven't got next week's rent and they'll put me out.'

'Best thing, we'd all be rid of you then.'

'How can you be like this with me, Joe? You lied. You lied to Agatha and to everyone, I shouldn't wonder. You forced me—'

'Forced you, my arse. Look, you knew what you were doing, and you were begging for it. Now, the only thing I will do for you is let you take that wicker out of me way. It arrived just after Christmas. I've decided I don't want the baskets now, it's too much hassle. I reckon as that wicker which I paid for is payment enough for you; you can make

71

baskets and get some money that way. But that's all I'll do for you.'

Tilly wanted to tell him he could stick the wicker where all his talk came from, but she stopped herself as this was a chance for her. She could make some baskets and try her luck door-to-door. She'd thought about that method of selling before, and she still had the huge pram the twins used to use which she thought would be a good carrier for her.

'All right. I don't think you're being fair, but that'll go some way to help. I'll go and fetch me pram and bring it around the back. I've time afore I pick the young 'uns up, as their teacher'll stay with them if I'm a bit late.'

'Aye, you do that, lass.'

The tone of this sent a shiver through Tilly. If only she had someone who could come with her. But no one wanted to know her anymore. At this thought loneliness engulfed her. Taking a deep breath to combat the sadness that had tight-ened her throat, she hurried out of the shop.

She was back in no time, having half run back to her house, and wheeled the pram out of the outhouse and through the back gate into the alley that ran between the houses. This was a shortcut anyway, and one she'd taken a lot lately to avoid her neighbours.

She didn't have to knock on the shop's back gate for long. Light flooded the dusk that had fallen and the gate opened on her second knock. 'I'm coming, no need to knock the gate down.' On opening it, Joe stood there with a grin on his face. 'Eager, aren't you? Come in.'

'Naw, please bring the wicker out here, Joe, and put it in me pram.'

'Oh, and what if I change me mind then, eh? What if I say it's to be paid for by one last shag in the shed?'

'Naw. I wouldn't do that, not ever again. I just want the wicker as payment for me hours that I worked, and nothing more. Please, Joe, do this one decent thing by me.'

'But I want you, Tilly. Look at me.'

He pulled his overall aside and thrust his hips forward. The bulge in his trousers was clear to see, but whereas seeing it like that had always thrilled her and made her eager to follow him out back, now it repulsed her.

'I don't want it, Joe. I'm telling you. I never want you to touch me again. You lied to your wife about me and you lied to me, making me believe I meant sommat to you, and that you'd allus care for me. You blackmailed me. I did it to save me young 'uns and that's all I want to do now. Please just give me the wicker.'

'But I can't do that. Now you've got me in this state, I have to have it, and you're the only one available. I've shut me shop so we can do it. You either let me, or no wicker.'

The feeling of being trapped flooded Tilly once more. She needed that wicker; it would give her a chance of getting out of this mess she was in and save her house. An idea came to her. She peered both ways along the alley through the descending darkness, checking that no one was about. 'All right. I'll do it.'

'Well, show more willing than that, then. You knaw you want it.'

For her plan to work she had to play up to him. 'Aye, I have to admit, I've missed it. And you, Joe.'

'Good lass. There's no need to go without, you knaw. And I'd pay you an' all as you're the best I've ever had, and I've missed having it with you.'

73

Tilly made herself smile. 'Be your prossie, you mean?'

'Aye, why not? I could come around the back of yours sometimes, no one'd see me. Anyroad, let's stop talking, I need it and I need it now. Bring your pram inside. We'll do it first and then load the wicker. It's just inside the yard here.'

This is what Tilly was waiting for. Turning the pram so it was facing the gate, she pushed it inside, keeping her eyes pinned to Joe's and giving him a look of pretended, sexual hunger. Just as he moved to make way for her, she rammed the pram at him with such force he fell to the ground. Pushing the pram to one side, Tilly grabbed the metal rod that kept the gate secured and brought it across Joe's shoulder.

'You bitch! Christ, you've broken me bloody shoulder. You bloody whore, get out! Go on. I'll yell the place down and say you were trying to break in.'

Fearing what this would mean, Tilly took action without thinking and slammed the rod down on Joe once more. The blow caught the arm he'd put up to defend himself, but didn't stop him from yelling out, 'Help, is anyone there? I'm being robbed!'

Fear and hate of this man drove Tilly on. Lifting the rod, she brought it down with all her strength, crashing it across his head. Joe slumped forward before letting out a moan and flopping to the side. He made no more movement. Tilly stood staring down at him, then at the bloodied rod. Dropping it made a clanging sound that reverberated in the silence.

'Get the wicker and go, Tilly.'

Tilly swung around. Agatha stood in the back doorway to the shop. 'Go on. I heard and saw everything. And I could see your intention. I was up at the window. I didn't tell Joe that I'd returned. Hurry. I'll start to scream once you're out of here. I'll give you five minutes, then I'll say I saw Joe answer the door to a man and thought nothing of it. Then I heard Joe call out and looked out of the window again to see Joe lying on the floor. Now go on. And, Tilly, if you've killed him, you've done me a favour. But this is the end of it. Never come near here again. Never!'

Tilly had to force herself to move. She couldn't bring herself to look at Joe again but loaded the huge bundle of wicker onto the pram, manoeuvred it around Joe and out of the gate. On shaking legs, she walked as fast as she could towards the school. Hardly daring to think, hardly daring to breathe.

'Ma, Ma, look what I made you.' Babs came out first and ran towards Tilly. 'It's made out of that scrap paper that we had to bring in to school. It's a butterfly.'

'It's beautiful. Ta, lass. Where's Beth?'

'She's talking to Harry Lynman, he's got a spider in a matchbox and he's her boyfriend ... Ma, you've got blood on your hand, have you cut yourself?'

'Naw ... I mean, aye, I caught it on the pram.'

'Why've you got the pram, Ma? What's that sticking out?'

'I've been collecting stuff from the hedgerows, I'm going to make baskets. Now stop asking so many questions and go and tell Beth to come at once, there's a good lass.'

Though she sounded calm, Tilly felt sick to her stomach. She couldn't take in what Agatha had said. But then the air filled with the sound of a bell ringing

Tilly froze as she knew this was the police.

Beth had joined them and now she jumped up and down. 'I wanna go and see what's happening, Ma. Come on, everyone's going.'

'Naw.'

'Look, Ma, all the others are going.'

'I knaw, Babs, but it'll be gone by the time we get there. Now come along, I need to get all of this bramble home.'

'Naw, Ma, the horses have stopped. It's just around the corner. Please, Ma.'

Someone shouted, 'It's at the greengrocery shop. I can see Agatha, it must be Joe.'

Babs pulled away and ran to the corner. 'It's at the shop, Ma, where you used to work!'

'Aye, well, there's nowt you can do, nosy parker. We're going home.' With this Tilly turned the pram and marched away from them, hoping they would obey her and follow her. Her stomach was churning. Her nerves were fraught. She had to get away.

As soon as she opened her back gate, Tilly pushed the pram inside and ran in to the lav. As she heaved over the bowl, this brought the tears and weakened her body. When the bout passed, she leant against the wall and sobbed.

SEVEN

Despite the cold, Tilly donned her cloak later that evening and opened her front door. Stepping outside, her breath vaporised in the cold air, and her cheeks tingled. But she'd hardly been able to breathe inside and had felt panicky since the twins had gone to bed leaving her alone. The image of Joe lying in a pool of blood wouldn't leave her mind, and still she couldn't believe what Agatha had done in letting her disappear out of the gate. Would she keep to that? Would she really tell no one what had truly happened? *Oh God, I'll hang if Joe is dead and it's discovered that I killed him!*

'Evening, Tilly. What're you doing outside at this time? You'll freeze your lugs, and besides, there's a dangerous man on the run.'

Tilly jumped round to see Fred Wimpole, the local street bobby. 'Oh! I – I were just needing some air. H – Have you come to see me about sommat?'

'Naw, why should I? We're patrolling all night on the lookout. Have you heard what happened to Joe Simpson?'

'Naw . . . I – I heard the police when I fetched the young 'uns home.'

'Aye, well, he's dead . . . Hey, are you all right, Tilly?'

Tilly had involuntarily gasped in fright. In her heart she'd known Joe was dead, but to hear it confirmed terrified her. 'Aye, it were a shock, that's all.'

'Oh . . .' Fred coughed. 'Sorry. I forgot about . . . well, you knaw. You and him . . .'

Tilly cringed. 'It weren't my doing, I – I mean, he took advantage of me. I – I needed the money.'

'You don't mean you prostituted yourself, do you, Tilly, as that's an offence?'

'Naw. I mean, he blackmailed me. I needed the job, but well . . .'

'Say no more about it. I've known you since we were young 'uns and I don't believe all that is said. I knaw as you'd need a good reason to go with him. Being destitute makes the best of us into wrongdoers.'

'I did do wrong, Fred. I knaws that. But it were as if it were the saving of me. I couldn't deal with Arthur's passing, and that sort of blocked it out. I'm ashamed of meself and can never undo it now. I've tainted Arthur's memory.'

'As I see it, after what you've just said, you were still in shock and took whatever course you could to save your young 'uns from the poorhouse. He's to blame, that Joe. He were an animal to make you do that, and that's speaking ill of the dead.'

'Ta, Fred. Naw one's believed me or asked for me side of the story.' This wasn't strictly true, as Agatha had believed her, but she couldn't go into all of that with Fred.

'Well, he's gone now. And Agatha said she saw a strange man talking to Joe at the back gate, and then the next thing,

78

Joe were on the floor. We think he tried to fight the bloke off when he realised that he was there to rob them. But this bloke's still at large, so you be careful.'

'I will, Fred. If owt moves in the street, I'll go straight back inside and lock me door.'

'You do that. And look, don't worry, the gossips'll move on to someone else afore long. Well, I'm to get on my way. Goodnight, Tilly.'

Tilly felt a weight lift off her shoulders. Whatever the reason for Agatha letting her off, she couldn't fathom, but she'd stuck to it and now Tilly knew she was in the clear.

She felt no remorse at Joe's passing. It was a rare truth, but he deserved what he got. She was to get on with things as best she could. Tomorrow she would begin to prepare the wicker for making a basket. Tonight, she would draw some designs and work out how to weave them. Then with a fair wind, she could have a couple to sell afore rent day.

As she turned to go in, she saw someone coming along the street towards her. It didn't frighten her as she knew there wasn't a dangerous man about. The gas lamps were lit in the street, and as the figure came into the light of them, Tilly could see it was Agatha. She held her breath. Then turned to go back inside, not wanting to face the woman.

'Tilly? Tilly, wait, I'm on me way to see you.'

Tilly didn't answer. Her heart was thumping. Had Agatha changed her mind?

'Can we go inside, Tilly? I don't want to be seen.'

Tilly stepped aside, then followed Agatha and closed the door.

'Eeh, Agatha. I'm sorry, I'm so sorry, but ... but, please don't change your story. I can't go to prison, I'll hang!'

'Aye, you would, as folk don't see our side of things. Well, that ain't going to happen. I'll not change me story. I'll play the bereaved widow, but inside I'll be glad. Joe Simpson broke my heart and wore me out.'

With this, Agatha started to cough.

'Come near the fire. Such as it is, you'll get some warmth in your bones from it. You shouldn't have ventured out.'

'I had to. I had to know that you were staying strong. I saw and heard everything and realised that you were playing Joe along and had a plan. I knew you weren't intending to go in the shed with him. I could have stopped you, but I didn't, I willed you on. I wanted to see someone punish him, and yes, even kill him. I – I know that is a terrible thing to say, but I would never have got free while he was alive. My life has been hell.'

'I'm sorry, Agatha. Eeh, but coming here at this time of night … And it's a wonder you didn't bump into Fred Wimpole – he passed by a short while afore you came along.'

'I know, I saw him talking to you. I dodged into the alley and hoped he'd not walk down there. He didn't. But if he had seen me, he'd have been curious as to why I was on your street, and maybe worried that I wanted revenge or something. That would have foiled my chances of speaking to you.'

'Aye, it would have looked suspicious to him. Can I make you a hot drink to warm you up? That cough sounds terrible.'

'It's not as bad as it sounds. But yes, I would like a tea, thank you. I don't take milk. And don't worry about my cough. It affects me when I go into different atmospheres, or get upset, but I made out I was more ill than I am as I couldn't bear working in that shop any longer and not doing so gave me freedom.'

Pouring the tea, Tilly handed Agatha a cup. 'I'm still not for understanding why you saved me, Agatha. I mean, I caused you so much pain and you could have got rid of me an' all by turning me in.'

'I know, but Joe destroyed enough lives. I didn't want him to destroy another. There have been those before you whose marriages have broken up because of them falling for Joe's tricks and being forced to be unfaithful to their husbands. One ended up in the poorhouse. I couldn't bear for that to happen to you. You've been through enough.'

Tilly still felt sick and afraid of all that had happened and, yes, of what she was capable of. *I killed a man. Me! Oh God!* But there was comfort in what Agatha was saying.

'Look, Tilly, I know it is a terrible deed, to have killed a man, but part of me coming here is to try to make you see that this wasn't your fault – none of it. Not succumbing to Joe, or killing him, which was self-defence, as I see it – fighting off a would-be rapist. Because that was what Joe was. He didn't rape by force, but by blackmail and any other means he could. Then, being as skilful as he was, the women couldn't stop letting him do to them what he did. It's a very sordid tale.'

'What about you, Agatha? What will you do? I'm grateful for your concern and forgiveness of me, but what's your life going to be like now? You can't run the shop as you're not fit enough, the work's hard. It'll be impossible for you on your own. I could and would be willing to run it for you but that wouldn't sit right with folk around here.'

'I'll let you in to a secret, but it must stay as that. I am in love with the vicar, and he with me. My visits to the church weren't all they seemed. Not that we've done anything wrong – far from it, as our love holds respect and the desire not to taint it by sinning. But now, we can be together in the future. I am going to sell and then move away. Malcolm will then apply for a position near to me and after enough time has elapsed we will marry.'

'Eeh, I'm so happy for you, lass, and I'll not breathe a word, I promise. Somehow, that's lifted me guilt.' *Aye, and I can now see the real reason Agatha is on me side. In my eyes, she's as guilty as me of Joe's killing.*

'But what about you, Tilly? How are you going to manage?'

'I have the cane that Joe bought for me to make baskets for the shop.' Tilly told of her plans and then tried to explain why it was that she'd come to the shop earlier.

'So, you never got your pay? Well, I'll put that right. And I'm so sorry for how Joe treated you.'

'I'd say naw, but I'm desperate and I did earn it. I worked hard and sacrificed time with me young 'uns to help out as the shop were so busy. But I – I, well, I feel bad.'

'Don't. Here, I have two shillings in my purse, will that cover it?'

'Aye, it will. Eeh, you don't knaw what you've done for me, Agatha. I'm still in a state over it all, but you've helped. I can only say ta, and I'll never forget you, and I hope with all me heart as things work out for you.'

'And I wish the same for you, Tilly. Well, I'd better get back. I don't like the dark, and neither do I want to spend time on my own in my home at the moment. But I'll probably call in on Malcolm and find comfort with him for a while. Even if I stay the night at the vicarage it won't seem bad to anyone; after all, it is natural to turn to a man of the cloth at such times.'

'You do that. And think on. If you go to his bed, you'll not be sinning as much. You're a widow now, not a married woman committing adultery. And if it worries you to lie with him afore you're wed, then get him to marry you afore you do!'

This tickled them both more than was warranted and they laughed out loud. To Tilly, it was a healing laughter in many ways, and though she knew she'd never forget, and it would take her a while to get over what had happened, she knew Agatha was right. She'd never meant to kill Joe. She was defending herself from him raping her in his own subtle way. This, she knew, was the best way she could look on it, and she knew too that by doing so she would find a way to cope.

PART TWO

1894

A GYPSY ENCOUNTER

EIGHT

Though she trundled the streets no one bought a basket from Tilly. And so, with rent day looming she decided to try her luck the following week and walk all the way to St Anne's where the posher folk lived.

By this time, she had four baskets made: two small ones suitable for pegs or for holding bits and bobs, one shopping basket and a much bigger basket which she'd shaped to hold walking sticks and umbrellas.

She was greeted by a maid at the first house and refused permission to see the lady of the house, being told that, 'M'lady would never deal with hawkers,' and to 'use the back door in future.' But the young woman had added that if she came back with suitable items for Cook or for herself, then they might be interested – suitable items being a basket to collect the vegetables from the garden for the day's meals, and something for the maid to carry her cleaning materials around the house. Then they could get the money from the housekeeper, if she agreed the baskets would help them in their work.

As she'd walked out of the gate, Tilly didn't feel rejected but more that she'd learnt a valuable lesson. And the girl had been nice in her manner.

At the next house, she was overjoyed to sell the two small baskets for sixpence. The staff had been looking for something unusual to buy for their mistress for her birthday and loved the idea of the baskets for her embroidery silks and needles.

With a feeling of joy at the first sale of her very own creations and thinking that everything was going to be all right, Tilly allowed herself to sit a moment on a bench facing the beach. Here, she took out a slice of the cake she'd baked the night before and which she had wrapped and stored in the bottom of the pram. As she watched the seagulls diving for fish, squawking as they did so, and the sea churning before crashing onto the beach, she enjoyed every crumb. Oh, but what she'd give for a drink! However, she dared not spend any of her money on one.

'Buy some lucky heather, lady.'

The voice startled her. She looked up into the weathered face of a gypsy woman. And then at the beautiful dark-skinned girl who was with her. The woman had a kerchief of many colours holding her hair out of view, but the girl's lustrous locks flowed down her back, leaving long ringlets over her shoulders and around her face.

'Heather it is that will bring you luck, pretty lady.'

'No, ta. Not that I couldn't do with the luck but if it has to be bought, then I can't afford it. Sorry.'

'What's that you have in your pram?' The woman leant over and pulled out the shopping basket. 'My, but that's a fine bit of weaving. Where did you get it?'

'I made it. Me old aunt taught me the skill and I've found

many ways of weaving in designs. I'm like you, trying to sell me wares to make enough for a crust.'

'How much? This would look good with me heather and pegs in and I wouldn't keep dropping them like I do from this rag sling.'

'Sixpence.'

'Threepence and some lucky heather.'

'Aye, it's a deal.'

'Why don't you be coming to visit us and bring more of your wares? I'm thinking that some of the women would be wanting such useful items. They're for weaving out of hedgerow vines, but nothing to match these.'

'I might do that. I saw an encampment as I crossed the fields to get here from Blackpool, is that where you are?'

'It is so. And it is welcome you'll be made. Now, let me see your palm, I've a powerful feeling about you.'

Tilly held out her hand. She knew these gypsies had a way of seeing into the future, and she'd like to know if everything was going to turn out for her.

'Hmm, it isn't all good. You've a terrible secret weighing on your heart, and you've a lot to go through afore you find happiness. I've a mind you once had that, but sommat was for snatching it from you and you've lost your way. But it will come to you again, though you must beware of false friendships. Women will always be seeing you as a rival for their man's affections, and that will be your downfall, so be careful how you are around the married men as they will lust after you.'

Tilly felt unnerved and blurted out, 'I have to go. Me young 'uns'll be coming out from school afore I'm home at this rate. Ta for buying me basket.'

'Afore you go, mind what I said about bringing your wares to us gypsy women, we might be able to help with the selling of them.'

Shaken by the encounter, Tilly hurried away, deciding that she wouldn't take the shortcut across the fields. It had only been the fact of the ground being frozen that had given her the idea of taking her pram that way. But she was afraid to now as the gypsy woman and her all-seeing eyes had unnerved her.

Walking along the path towards Blackpool, the rain began to fall, and the ice-cold wind whipped her skirts. It was as she came in sight of The Foxhall Inn that she lifted her head to see a gang of ruffians barring her way. One of them asked if she had a penny to spare. 'I've a thirst on me for a beer, so I have. Now, a pretty lady like you won't be refusing me help, will you?'

Tilly knew at once they were gypsy lads. They were dressed in dirty, ragged clothes, and each had an earring in one ear. 'I've not got naw money, I'm sorry.'

'Ahh, but we know that to be a lie.'

'I'm telling the truth.'

'Didn't we hear that you'd sold some wares today?'

'How do you knaw that?' *God! The gypsy woman! She's sent them to rob me!* Tilly knew it was a possibility. Gypsies lived by their wits, and took what they needed to survive. They were rumoured to have stolen children, and it was said they could see into the future. Their whole way of life was one of chance. She should have been more careful. Selling to a gypsy was bound to have its risks. The girl the woman had with her could have been back at the camp in less time than it took for

90

Tilly to walk half of the journey she'd trodden. And these lads could have come across the fields and easily got here before her.

'Just hand over the money, pretty lady, or are we to take you around the back alley and be having our way with you instead?'

'Let's be doing that, Phileas. She's a tasty bit. I'd like to give her a shagging.'

'Ha, Jonas, you wouldn't be up to it, this is a real woman you're looking at. Besides, Janey will give you hell if she's for finding out.'

'Naw, don't. Here, you can have a penny.' Tilly's panic made her clumsy as she fumbled in her pocket for her purse. As she pulled it out, it was snatched from her hand. 'Naw, naw, please. Please don't take it all, I have young 'uns to feed and me rent to pay.'

Her pleas went unheard as the lads ran off, their laughter and jeers filling the air around her and taking all her newfound hope with them.

Two days later, Tilly stood on the threshold of the money lender's house and knew that no fresh hope was to be given to her. She'd already shamed herself in going around to see Agatha, but hadn't found her in. A call at the rectory had only given her the information that Agatha had gone to stay with her sister until the funeral. The vicar had instructed his house-keeper to give some provisions to Tilly and these were handed over with a begrudging 'humph', and a snide, 'You reap what you sow, lass.' But even though the words had stung her with the truth that was in them, Tilly had felt grateful for the warm loaf, homemade jam and slab of lard. She still had flour and sugar and could make cake and flat bread.

'And what do you want, then?'

Tilly looked up into the rough-skinned, pock-marked face of Mr Pimpkin, the money lender. His waistcoat hardly buttoned over his portly stomach, his sideburns curled, almost meeting beneath his chin and brushing against his huge moustache. It was as if all his hair had fallen downwards as his head was shiningly bald.

'I need a loan, sir.'

'Oh, aye, and how do you propose to pay it back, eh?'

'I'm hoping to sell me baskets. I have sold some but ...' Tilly explained what had happened to the money she'd made.

'Ha, what I knaw of you, you probably had banter with them, hoping to get money for sommat else, and it backfired. Well, I'm a God-fearing man, and I don't lend to the likes of you. Folk'll say as I'm being paid in kind, as you did with poor Joe Simpson. Be away with you.'

Tilly turned away, humiliated and dejected. *Oh, God, what now? Only one basket left, I've no others ready to sell. I'll lose me house for sure.*

With no one to turn to for help, her heart wept with the thought of being homeless, unless she took herself to the workhouse. But what of the gypsies? Didn't that old woman tell her to come to her? But then, hadn't they caused all of this?

Her mind tried to think of another way those lads could have known she'd sold some baskets other than being sent deliberately. Maybe they'd seen her earlier with more baskets in her pram?

Somehow, Tilly had felt there was an honesty in the older woman. Maybe the girl had set her up unbeknown to her companion?

Deciding that she had to act, to try to save her home and her girls from being taken from her, Tilly determined to finish the basket she'd started and to sit up all night if it took that long to finish another one. The one she'd begun was for the cook of the house she'd first called at and was boat-shaped and suitable for gathering vegetables. She could make one to carry the maid's cleaning tools and then go back to that house, calling on the gypsies on the way. It was a risk, but hopefully she'd find the woman and would be given the help promised.

With this plan formed, a little of the hope Tilly had lost seeped back into her. The rent man was due the following afternoon. If she had a part-payment for him and promised the rest and a week's rent the next time he called, she might just save the day.

Cross at herself now for wasting time begging instead of doing something about her situation in a practical way, Tilly hurried home.

With an aching back, Tilly finally inserted the handle of the vegetable basket just as the clock struck three a.m. Pushing the bodkin, the pointed metal tool with a wooden handle which she used for this and for inserting the stakes to begin the basket, caused her great pain and made her eyes blur with tears, but she wiped them away, and made one more determined effort. At last, she could look with pride on the finished article.

She sank back in Arthur's chair and allowed her tears to flow.

Beth woke her. 'Ma, Ma, we've to get ready or we'll be late for school.'

Disorientated, Tilly took a moment to realise that she must have fallen asleep in the chair. She moved herself stiffly.

'Ma, I'm hungry.'

'I knaw, Babs. I'll just go to the lav, then I'll get you some of that bread and jam that the vicar gave me. How will that be, eh?'

For answer, Babs clung to her legs as she stood. 'Wish Da was sitting in his chair.'

This shocked Tilly as neither of the girls mentioned their da often. 'Aye, lass, so do I. I tell you what, if it's not too cold on Saturday, we'll pick some of them bluebells from the wood and take them to Da's grave, eh?'

'I like visiting Da's grave but I want to see him.' Beth joined in with this and it cut Tilly's heart.

'Oh, Beth. We can't, but he can see us. He watches over us. How about you say good morning to him while I go out back?'

Shivering with the cold, Tilly nipped to the lav. There, she felt a desolation descend on her. 'Oh, Arthur, Arthur.' For a moment, she could have given in to her weeping again, but she pulled herself up. Babs and Beth needed her, she was to be strong for them. No matter what was going on in her life, they mustn't suffer.

Getting back into her warm kitchen, she scurried about preparing the bread and jam and a hot cocoa for each, leaving it to cool while she bustled them upstairs to dress.

'Last one ready'll be the fool of the house.' With this there were squeals of delight as they tugged at their clothes, and let her brush their tangled hair, vying to be the first.

'Babs's last,' Beth declared. 'Babs is the foo-ool.'

Tilly quickly allayed the tantrum this would cause. 'Naw, she's not, I am, look at me, I'm all tussled from sleeping in the chair all night.'

They both chorused, 'Ma is the foo-ool.' Picking up a pillow, Tilly pretended to go for them both, then collapsed in a heap of laughter with them, holding them to her – her two precious bundles of joy. 'Right, off you go downstairs, and eat your butties and drink your cocoa while I get meself tidied up.'

Both did as she bid, and as she watched them go, she realised that fun had been missing from their lives, and she must be the one to put it back. Arthur had always played rough-and-tumble games with them while she'd sat and watched and egged them all on. Well, now it was down to her to be Ma and Da, and she was determined she would be. *Aye, I'll bring the laughter back into this house. I have to. Me little lasses deserve no less as none of me troubles are their doing.*

When she reached the encampment, Tilly's courage nearly deserted her. She'd been close to changing her mind after dropping the children off, but she'd made herself do this. She looked around her and saw a hive of activity going on by the covered wagons. Women huddled around a flaming brazier, shaving pieces of wood, which she presumed would end up as pegs. Men hammered away at scrap metal, warmed by a second, bigger brazier, and dirty-looking children laughed and squealed as only children can as they played with a mangy-looking barking dog, and all to the background of mouth organ music that lifted Tilly's heart. Looking in the direction of where the music was coming from further upset her nerves as she saw it was Phileas who was playing the instrument.

He stopped when he caught sight of her and stood up with a grin on his face. Tilly tugged her shawl around her body as his leering voice called over to her, 'If it isn't the pretty basket maker. Or are me eyes playing tricks on me?'

A young woman stood up from where she'd been sitting with the group of peg-makers. Holding the edge of her gaily coloured skirt, she flipped it back in a gesture that challenged.

'Awe, Betina, it is that you have nothing to worry over, you are the most beautiful girl and aren't I going to make you me wife one of these days?'

Betina flounced away but was called back to work by the woman who had bought the basket from Tilly. 'Get on with your work, Betina, there's no need for jealousy. For sure, we'll be keeping Phileas in check. Now, basket lady, what is it we can do for you? Have you thought on me offer?'

'Aye, I have, and I have a pressing need, as you probably are for knowing. Phileas and another called Jonas robbed me of me money that day after I left you.'

'No! And I wasn't for knowing.' Turning, she looked into the face of the girl who'd been with her that day. 'So, that was the urgent thing you needed to return to camp for quicker than me, Lucy? Well, it's a good gypsy girl you'll make, but we never take from them as I need sommat from. You heard me say as this woman was welcome amongst us. Me saying that makes her one of mine. I am not for being pleased with you.'

Lucy kept her head down and it was obvious to Tilly that this woman was an important person amongst them as they all seemed to look up to her and respect her word.

'Well, missy, it is sorry that I am, but I can't be giving you back what you lost. No doubt it has been spent. But we can help in other ways. What's your name?'

'Tilly, short for Matilda.'

'Well now, that's a lovely name. Mine is Lilly Lee. I see you have baskets there. Come, and let us see what you have.'

'Aye, but I think I have customers for them, I was just going to deliver them. I – I have me rent to pay tomorrow or I'll be evicted from me home, and I haven't a penny towards it now.'

'That's a sorry tale. Well, I'm telling my lot now, they're not to touch you or thieve from you. And I told you afore, we womenfolk would be glad to learn the skill that you have and will help you sell your wares. Call back this way when you've done your deal, but afore you are going, show my women the wonderful weaving you do.'

The women crowded around, all making noises that said they were in wonderment of her work.

'There now, didn't I tell you we'd be interested? Now, don't forget to call back this way.'

Tilly nodded, then looked over to where Phileas had sat. But he'd gone. Glad of this, she took hold of her baskets and left. What had happened had given her a little hope but had also left her feeling unsure. Could she really trust Lilly Lee? Should she return? Would the gypsies be of help to her, or would they steal what, if anything, she got for her baskets? She wished that everything wasn't so unsure in her life. Oh, how she wished she could turn the clocks back. But there was no going back, and she knew she had to deal with her life as it was and take any help that may be offered.

NINE

As Tilly walked away from the encampment, she could feel the glare of dozens of eyes boring into her and she guessed it would be those of the women. She hadn't gone far when a movement in the hedgerow beside her made her jump. She peered into the bushes but couldn't see anything, then laughed at her own nervousness as she imagined it was only an animal.

It was when she climbed over the stile to get onto the road that led into St Anne's that Phileas jumped out in front of her. 'So, pretty lady, was it me you dropped in to see?'

'Naw, you thieving tyke. I need help and Lilly Lee had promised me that, and I'd hoped to get some of me money back. You've put me into dire straits – me young 'uns may not have a roof over their heads tomorrow.'

'Here, I have a penny left of it. And it is sorry I am, I didn't know you were a friend of Lilly Lee. It is that we have to live by our wits and take our chances where we see them. I'm for getting my own wagon soon, and then I can take a bride. If you would be that bride, I'd be a mighty happy man.'

'What! Don't be daft, I've only just met you and I don't like you, you're a thief. Besides, I just heard you propose to Betina.'

'Och, she's nothing to me. She's hardly matured into a woman and I haven't the fancy for her. It's just what me family are wanting of me, to join the Lees and the Gaskins, as me and Jonas are, but the moment I clamped me eyes on you, I was for wanting you. I'd take care of you and your young 'uns. I can put meself to earning a pretty penny and me wagon will be the finest there is.'

'Me answer's naw. I'm not long widowed and not looking for a husband.' To her shame, she couldn't add that she couldn't give herself to another yet. Shaking this thought away as it would tear at her heart to remember her own despicable actions, she turned away from Phileas.

With every step she took, she feared he would follow and try to stop her, but he surprised her by letting her go on her way. Her mind stayed with him, though, as she walked the last half mile. There was something magnetic about him. He had dark skin and deep blue piercing eyes with thick, dark lashes that framed them. His strong, handsome features and his tanned and honed body all made for a man that any woman would find attractive. But his ways and his lifestyle were so alien to her that she couldn't imagine life as his wife, nor did she want to.

At last she came to the house, and made her way around to the kitchen door, praying as she went that she would sell her baskets.

The door opened to her knocking and the same maid answered. 'Oh, it's you again. You're soon back. Well, let's see what you have.'

'Who is it, Florrie?'

'It's that woman I told you of, Cook, the one with the lovely baskets.'

The door opened wider and a much larger woman peered at Tilly. She had a kindly face and twinkly brown eyes. Her cheeks dimpled when she smiled and, as she brushed the stray hair that had escaped her bonnet away from her eyes, she left a trail of flour on her forehead.

'Well, now, let's have a look at what you've got, lass.' Cook wiped her hands on her stark white pinafore. 'Eeh, that big one looks just what I need. How much?'

Tilly drew in her breath, and quickly said her price as she exhaled. 'Ninepence.'

'Eeh, lass, away with thee. I'll not get that much out of the housekeeper here, she's a mean old cuss. Can you not give me a more reasonable price?'

'I could go to sixpence, but that has to be me final price.'

'And what about the other one for Florrie? That would do you nicely, wouldn't it, Florrie?'

'Aye, it would an' all. By, you've a talent for the basket making, lass. But your prices are too high. You'll not get sixpence each for them; I'd say as housekeeper'd only pay that for the two. After all, in her eyes, we're managing with how we are now so she won't see them as essential.'

'Aye, Florrie's right, but if that's all she does offer, I'll add a penny. What about you, Florrie? You could add a ha'penny surely, and I'll tell you what, miss, I can make you up a few goodies an' all. You look half-starved.'

'Ta. Ta ever so much. If you can get that deal with your housekeeper, I'll take it with what you can add.'

'Right, come on in, lass. Florrie, pour the lass a cuppa out of that pot. I'll go and tackle Housekeeper.'

The tea was lovely, hot and sweet. Tilly relaxed in the

warmth of the kitchen, which was heated by the huge cooking range, and she savoured the smell of baking bread. The long wooden table that looked as if it had been scrubbed within an inch of its life held the remnants of a baking session, with flour sprinkled on it and a mound of pastry waiting to be rolled standing next to a mixing bowl holding a wooden spoon. There were flour and lard next to this. The rest of the kitchen had an air of cleanliness about it and yet also a welcoming feel, with its huge pot sink and pretty gingham curtains. Shelves housed gleaming pans and strings of onions, and an array of spoons and kitchen implements hung from hooks beneath them. A large dresser held practical china and standing on top of a row of cupboards was a bowl of eggs and another of fruit. Tilly sighed. How nice it must be to work in a kitchen like this.

'And what is a hawker doing in the kitchen and drinking tea? What are you thinking of, Cook? This young woman could have fleas for all you knaw.'

'Naw. She ain't one who trudges the roads from one town to the next. Look at her, she's as clean as you and me, aye, and nicely dressed an' all. Down on her luck, I'd say, and trying to make an honest penny. She told Florrie on her last visit that she makes these baskets herself. You just take a look at them, Miss Atkins, they're quality. She has a real talent.'

The thin poker-faced woman who'd entered the kitchen with Cook came over to where Tilly sat at the table. Picking up a basket, she examined it. 'Well, you're not wrong there, Cook, this is fine work. But are you sure you can't manage without it? It isn't as if the garden's a mile away, it's only over there.'

Tilly looked through the open kitchen door. Outside a path wound its way to a gate which she imagined led through to the walled kitchen garden. For a moment she thought she might lose the sale as it did seem that the basket wasn't necessary, but Cook and then Florrie chimed in.

'I knaw, but the basket I have is worn out. I'm forever losing carrots and whatnot through the holes and having to retrace me steps to collect them. I need a new one and this one the lass is offering will last a lifetime by the looks of it.'

'And I need sommat that will hold all me bits and bobs, so I don't have to keep going backwards and forwards to the cleaning cupboard.'

'Oh, all right. Sixpence for the two, you say?'

'Aye, ma'am. I'd like more but that's what I've agreed.'

'I'm not addressed as ma'am. Miss will do. Here. Take this and be on your way. And there's no more where that came from so don't be making return visits.'

Tilly waited. 'Well? Is there something else?'

Tilly looked from the cook to Florrie, but neither seemed to remember their promise of giving her extra. She rose from the table and went out of the door. *How can people be so deceitful? Aye, and cruel.* Both of the women knew she was relying on the penny and ha'penny they'd said they'd chip in, and she would have been grateful for the supplies Cook had promised too.

But her faith was restored when she heard a voice call, 'Hey, you, basket maker, hang on.' Turning, she saw the maid looking flustered as she hurried towards her.

'By, you move quick. Here, this is what we promised, only we couldn't give it to you whilst the housekeeper was there, she'd have gone mad at us. Cook's put a few things in this bag for you, and here's the money. Good luck with your trade, lass, you deserve it, and ta for our baskets. You've done us a service.'

'Oh, Florrie, ta. That's good of you.'

'Aye, well, I wished I could get to knaw you, you seem like a nice person, but I don't get much time off, and when I do, I go back home to me ma in Blackburn. So, I'll say me goodbyes.'

Tilly felt sorry that she couldn't get to know Florrie better. She so needed a friend. She'd been lonely since Martha had fallen out with her, and despite how they'd parted, she really missed Liz and often wondered how she was, and if her baby was born yet and how her brood were. They were nice kids. Sighing, she turned towards Blackpool. As she did, she caught sight of the tower and her heart lurched. It was to have its opening ceremony soon, an event that Arthur had looked forward to. 'We'll all go,' he'd said. 'Aye, and we'll have a smashing time. It's going to be grand, Tilly, just grand, and I'm that proud to have had a hand in building it.' But then, neither had known what the tower would be responsible for. Now it loomed like a painful reminder of her life before Arthur fell from it.

Looking away, she turned into the gateway and climbed the stile. Not an easy thing to do with her long skirt and petticoats catching on the posts, but eventually she dropped down the other side. Shivering now as hitching her clothes had let the cold late February air have access to her body, she tugged her woollen shawl tighter around her and folded her arms into it, although she found this difficult with holding the bag that Florrie had given her. Her cheeks tingled with the wind that whipped across the open fields, but her bonnet kept it from freezing her ears. With her head down, she picked her way across the ruts of the rough ground and thought of her plight in only having eightpence ha'penny to give to the rent man. But she didn't let that get her down. She lifted her head and made up her mind to face what life had in store for her with courage. Her girls deserved that of her.

'So, you're coming back to us, then?'

Once more, Phileas made her jump. 'Aye, I am. Needs must. I believe Lilly Lee when she says she can help me. And I knaw I can help the women in the camp learn me skill. Me coming back has nowt to do with you, or your daft proposal.'

'Is it daft that it is? Well, what if I was to make you?'

His tone frightened Tilly. The threat it contained was tempered by the lust that thickened his voice. She looked around her; there was no one in sight. Fear clutched her, but she held her head high and glared at him in defiance. 'I don't think you would get away with that. Your own clan would stop you. Lilly Lee said she would keep you in check. And I wouldn't cross her if I was you.'

'But you're a burning desire that I have and have had since I met you in Blackpool. Aye, I know I took your money, and I'm sorry, but I didn't know then that I would ever see you again, though I wanted to.'

This eased Tilly as she heard less of a threat and more of a plea, so she softened her approach to him. 'Look, I ain't saying I don't find you attractive, but I ain't looking for no man. Stick with Betina. She knaws your ways and your lifestyle is hers too.'

Phileas grabbed her arm. His face came close to hers. 'I mean to make you mine one day. And that's a promise.' His eyes burnt into hers.

'Let go. I'll scream if you don't and that will bring the wrath of Lilly Lee on you.'

'It is that you are a feisty woman, and it is that I can see a passion in you.'

'Please let go, Phileas, you're hurting me.'

But far from letting her go, he pulled her further into his arms. Though she tried, she found it impossible to get away from him. Her arm was now twisted up her back, causing her pain. His face was close to hers, so close she could feel the warmth of his breath brushing her cheek. His whispered words, 'You're mine,' shuddered through her, not with fear, or with repulsion, but with a deep answering feeling that allowed him to kiss her lips.

The kiss was gentle, loving, and drew her in further to the magnetism of him. But then as suddenly as she'd given into him, she came to her senses and pulled her head away. 'Don't. I don't want to.' The plea was as much to reassure herself as to reject Phileas. As he let her go relief flooded her.

Phileas turned and walked away, leaving Tilly shaking uncontrollably. *What is it that has been unleashed inside me? Am I some kind of demon? How can I behave like I do? No one will ever come near to my Arthur. I love and miss him so much. But then, why am I seeking comfort in such a way? Forgive me, Arthur, forgive me.*

Her body sank to the ground. Her heart wept. She was lost. A lost soul taking anything offered to her to assuage her grief. *I have to stop this. They'll allus be plenty offering. I must be strong. I must.*

Rising, Tilly brushed down her skirts, now wet and clinging to her legs as her underskirt had come into contact with the wet grass. She stood, undecided as to what to do. Should she go back to the road and return home? Give up the chance of the help Lilly Lee had offered? Looking up at the weak winter sun, masked by a haze of cloud that she feared may hold more snow, Tilly made her mind up. Turning, she walked towards the gate. By the position of the sun, noon had passed and the rent man usually came around two. She'd go home and face him and see what her fate was to be.

'You were warned the last time, Mrs Ramsbottom, that if you fell behind again, we would be repossessing the house. I'll take what you have, but you're to make it up and give me a full rent next week, or that is what will happen. You'll be out on your arse.'

Closing the door and leaning on it, Tilly bit on her lip. Her fingers went to her pocket and curled around the ha'penny she'd decided to hang on to. It wouldn't have made any difference to her situation to have given it to him.

Tears stung her eyes, but she swallowed hard. She'd done enough weeping. A week was a long time. She could make a few baskets in the first half of it if she sat up all night, then she could trudge the second half and pray that she sold them. What Cook had given her – a loaf, and a pot of dripping, a pie wrapped in muslin that just needed popping in the oven, and a jar of preserved plums – would feed them all for a couple of days, along with what she had left of what the vicar's housekeeper had given her. Some of the dripping she would spread on bread for the twins' tea. And with the rest, she would make dumplings. The ha'penny would buy her some root veg which she would cook, together with the dumplings, and that would feed them for the rest of the week. Sighing, she tried to convince herself that things weren't so bad. She still had a mound of coal in the coal house to keep them warm, and to boil pots of water so she could steam some of the cane to blacken it. This would weave in well with the different shades of brown she'd created by soaking the willow for varying lengths of time. Soaking the cane was also how she made it pliable so she could use it to make her patterns. There was still plenty of posh houses in St Anne's, and she might get as far as Lytham where there were even more wealthy folk.

TEN

A few days later, Tilly was struggling to push her pram through the four inches of snow that had fallen and was quickly melting, as it always did, since the salty Blackpool air refused to let it settle for long.

Although she was hardly able to put one foot in front of the other, she was glad of her thick leather boots. Arthur had them made for her last winter, and she'd found them out, and donned a pair of his socks to stop them chafing her ankles. Her limbs ached through lack of sleep, but she had six baskets made and only two days to sell them in.

As the ladies she was hoping to sell to didn't do their own shopping, she had only made one shopping basket. Three of the other baskets were of the kind that she had sold on her first day, that could hold the materials the ladies used for their embroidery, and two were vegetable baskets of the same kind Cook had bought as she was hoping to get a sale from another maid for that.

It was this one that had taken the longest – not because it was patterned, as it was made in plain, dark brown cane, but because she'd had to trudge the alleyways looking for discarded

109

wood to make a base. This had taken a whole morning after dropping the twins at school. She'd made a wonderful find, though – an old chest of drawers which hadn't been put out long as it was still dry. She'd taken just the drawers as the bottoms of these were of a thin wood, which she had easily sawn into shape, leaving her plenty for future baskets. Usually she went along to the woodyard on Grasmere Road, and Mr Jacques, the owner, would cut her a few shapes from the offcuts, but she hadn't the money to pay him. She'd been proud of her efforts in cutting the oval herself and cheered that she'd found this way of getting free wood.

Boring the holes with her bodkin had given her blisters, and her fingers were sore from cutting the cane with the large cutters; sometimes it took both hands to get enough leverage to cut through the thicker bits of cane. She still had plenty of cane left after making these items and hadn't forgotten the idea for the greengrocery shop. As soon as she saw it open again, she would tackle the new owner and hope that he would be interested in buying baskets from her.

Thinking this had raised her hopes and kept her working long into the night until she could do no more and had had to take a few hours' rest.

Keeping to the road, as going over the fields wasn't an option in the snow, she passed the house where Florrie worked, and looked hopefully towards it. A joy filled her as she saw Florrie coming out of the door carrying a shopping basket.

'Florrie!'

'Eeh, hello, basket lady! Are you off selling your wares again?'

'Aye, and me name's Matilda, only I'm known as Tilly. Where are you off to, then?'

'I've to go to Mandy's Stores, as they didn't put any sugar in our order, and Cook's going mad. She was doing a batch of baking and ran out. What about you?'

'Oh, just trying me luck. I've to start about four doors down as I didn't get further than that the first day when I called here.'

'Awe, and you'll find a lot of the houses closed up for winter, as some folk go to their London houses and come back for the summer season. Eeh, lass, you look worn out, and you've lost weight you can't afford to lose. That coat's hanging off your back.'

'I knaw, I'm having a hard time of it.' As they walked, Tilly told Florrie that she'd had a job but had lost it. She didn't tell her everything, just that her boss had made a pass at her and her refusing him had led to his sacking her.

'What? Eeh, that's a sorry tale. And you say as the neighbours believe that you were to blame and so they shun you? They sound a bigoted lot. But, lass, you knaw as you're to be careful around menfolk, you're a good eyeful for their lust. I have naw such worries, looking like the back end of a horse, with me fat face.' Florrie burst out laughing at her own description.

Tilly smiled. 'You don't, you daft apeth. You've a lovely homely, welcoming face, and your eyes, well, they're a colour I've never seen afore – sometimes they look blue and sometimes they look grey. You should make more of yourself, your hair doesn't do you justice pulled back like that.'

'I have to wear it like this or Housekeeper goes mad. She's allus pulling Cook up for the stray bits that escape her cap.

Anyroad, I ain't looking for no man so it don't matter. I'll be twenty-eight next birthday. How old are you, Tilly?'

Florrie linked her arm through Tilly's as she said this. It felt good, not just because Tilly had had no close contact with another for so long, but because she felt a surge of love in her for Florrie. 'I'm twenty-five. I had me twins by the time I were twenty.'

'I had a young man at that age an' all and we planned on marrying, but when I went home on me leave days, he'd met someone else and got her in the family way. I were broken-hearted.'

They'd reached the end of the road and were entering the square that housed many shops. 'By, we've walked by a lot of houses and you've not called in on any of them. I'll leave you here, lass, and hope to see you again.'

Tilly didn't want Florrie to go and could sense the reluctance in Florrie too. 'Aye, and I hope to see you again an' all. I'm sorry about your young man, but you knaw what they say: there's plenty of fish in the sea. Don't give up, Florrie.'

'No one would want me now. Anyroad, ta-ra for now.'

'I might bump into you as you come back, as I'm going to turn around and call at the houses on me way towards Blackpool.'

As she watched Florrie walk away, Tilly felt almost bereft. She'd been so lonely, and it had been lovely talking to someone of a similar age to herself and having that feeling of being close to another. She liked Florrie. Liked her a lot and hoped that friendship would grow between them, though she didn't see how with the commitment Florrie had to her ma as far away as Blackburn.

At the first house she called at she sold one of her baskets for tuppence ha'penny. It was a small basket that hadn't taken much material or time to make. The maid had bought it saying it would do nicely for her to put her darning wools in. At the next three houses she was turned away, but surprisingly the door to the fourth house was opened by a gentleman.

'Well, what have we here?'

'Sorry, sir, I was hoping to talk to the maid.'

'Oh, I don't bother with maids. I only come to this house occasionally, and I come for peace. I like looking after myself. One can get fed up with having dozens of people scurrying around the house and getting under one's feet. How can I help you?'

His intense stare made Tilly nervous. Fair-haired, he had bushy blond eyebrows and a moustache; his body was very thin – puny, she'd call him. And he wore glasses perched on the end of his nose.

Tilly told him why she was there.

'Well, now. I have no need of baskets for the house, but I like the look of that oval one. I am a botanist and that would be handy when I go out collecting my specimens. How about I give you ninepence for it?'

'Oh, ta, ta very much, sir.'

Tilly skipped down the path, glad to get away from the strange man who gave her the creeps, but so happy with her sale. She almost bumped into the gatepost with her pram she was that excited. Four more baskets to sell, and she could have her rent money and the extra she had to pay to catch up the payments. Happiness filled her.

'Well, lass, you look like you did well there. It's nice to see a smile on your face.'

Tilly was even happier to see Florrie coming back from the store and told her the good news. 'Eeh, Florrie, I'm a good way towards getting me rent this week now.'

'But what do you do for food? By, Tilly, I'm reet sorry for you, lass. And I wish I could help. Look, I've an idea. You carry on doing your calling, and I'll see if Cook's got owt she can give you. I'll sneak out and hide it just under the bush by our gate. If there's nowt there, then I ain't been able to get owt, or I couldn't get by the housekeeper's eagle eye. But I'll do me best for you. Ta-ra, Tilly, I'll look out for you another day.'

Tilly had no luck at any of the next three houses she called at and began to feel despondent. She was ninepence ha'penny short of her needs, and fear began to trickle through her. By the time she reached the bush where she hoped against hope Florrie had been able to leave her something, she'd been refused twice more and found two empty houses.

But she cheered when she saw the chequered cloth tied in a bundle. Finding it quite heavy to lift, she wanted to shout her thanks to Florrie, but knew she wouldn't hear. Just then she became aware of how bitterly cold it had become, and she realised that snowflakes were beginning to fall again.

Around her was a wonderland of beauty. Trees with their boughs laden with snow, rooftops still patched with the white of the previous snowfall and red tiles where it had melted, and bushes and shrubs with their tips dotted with white, all looked like a fairyland, but as the snow began to drive into her face, Tilly realised that she would have to give up trying to sell any more baskets and get home.

Having to take the long route along the road added at least a mile and a half to her journey, so with her head down she pushed the pram with all she was worth to try to hurry along, only looking up into the snow occasionally to keep herself on track.

Everywhere seemed deserted and silent as she passed by the last house of St Anne's and there were only sand dunes on her left and fields on her right, but then behind her, and into the silence, came the sound of a horse's slow trotting and the wooden wheels of a cart. She prayed the driver would see her and avoid her. But suddenly the air was filled by a loud, screeching whinny of a horse in distress. As she turned, she saw the belly of a huge carthorse, his legs scrambling the air before an almighty crash took over the space around her. Bending as far forward as she could, the horse's hoof clipped her shoulder, jarring her until she nearly fell over, but as she steadied herself Tilly could see the cart was on its side. A familiar voice shouted, 'Steady there, Rhona girl, whoa up!'

The horse calmed and its driver, who she was certain was Phileas, climbed on all fours from under the side of the cart. 'Who is it that walks the highway in such conditions? Can you not see what damage you've caused?'

'I was tucked into the verge but couldn't walk on it as I have a pram.'

'Tilly, is that you? Are you hurt?'

Not realising before that she was, or how much, a pain suddenly streaked down Tilly's arm and her shoulder smarted. 'Yes, I can't move my arm.'

He was by her side in an instant, still holding on to the horse's rein which he'd grabbed. 'Let me see.'

'Naw, don't take me coat off, it hurts, and I'll freeze.'

'Well then, I'll right me cart, and if its axle hasn't twisted, I'll get you and your pram onto it and get you home.'

Tilly didn't want this but knew she had no choice. The weather was worsening. Snow was blinding her to everything around her, and she was shivering with cold. Her arm hurt so much she wanted to cry out, but her lips seemed perished and numb.

Before long they were trundling along at a snail's pace. Tilly clung on desperately to her pram with her one good hand, afraid it would slide off the back, and pressed her feet as hard as she could against the other side of the cart to try to stabilise herself and prevent herself from sliding off. Pain consumed her.

'Phileas, this is hopeless, I can't hang on much longer. I'll have to walk.'

Her voice was taken on the wind and didn't penetrate the huddled figure of Phileas sitting on the driver's bench behind the horse. Exhaustion took Tilly and she felt herself letting go of the pram. 'PHILEAS!' This time he heard her and pulled the horse to a stop.

When he came around to her she told him of her plight. 'Well, it is that you'll have to come and sit up next to me, me darling. I've some rope, I'll secure the pram.'

Tilly didn't want to sit next to him, she didn't want to be in such close proximity, but she had no choice.

With his scarf over his mouth it was difficult to get the gist of what Phileas was saying, but she knew he was getting worried as it was becoming increasingly difficult to keep the horse going. At last they came into Blackpool, and though the snow was falling just as thickly it didn't stay so long as the roads were busier, and householders were brushing the pavements clear.

When they reached The Foxhall Inn, Tilly leant towards Phileas. 'I can take myself home from here, thank you. Will you lift me pram down for me?'

'No, it is that I need to tend to that shoulder and see what the injury is. I'm taking you to your home.'

'I don't want you to. Phileas, please let me down now.'

The horse came to a halt at Phileas's bidding. 'It is a powerful stubborn woman that you are. If you get down, I'll not let your pram off, but take it to the camp. We can share your wares, and whatever it is you have in that bundle.'

Despairing and with pain throbbing through her arm, Tilly gave in. The last thing she wanted was to let Phileas know where she lived, and yet she couldn't allow him to take her pram. Her money was tucked under the remaining baskets and she so needed the food in the bundle.

Reluctantly, she directed him. 'But I have to call at the school. That clock just chimed three, and me twins will be waiting for me to collect them.'

'Aye, I remember you saying it was children you had, and that you'd lost your man, how is it that you're managing? Sure it is you need a man to take care of you.'

'I don't, I'm doing okay with me baskets.' They were trotting quite fast now and soon the church came into sight. 'There, that's where my twins are.'

Phileas reined in Rhona.

With great difficulty and the use of just one arm, Tilly managed to get down. The snow had now stopped, and she saw several of her neighbours standing by the church wall. One called out, 'So, it's gypsies that take your fancy now, then? Eeh, Arthur'll be turning in his grave.'

'Shut up! I'm not a gypsy's lass. His horse reared at me and hurt me shoulder, he is just giving me a lift home.'

'Ha! A likely story.'

The twins came out at that moment and Tilly was able to cover up her humiliation by greeting them and taking them to the cart. 'Don't want to get up there, Ma. I don't like it, it smells.'

'Oh, Babs. It's only to take us around the corner.'

'No, Ma. Everyone's looking.'

Pain almost overtook Tilly, leaving her no energy to argue. 'Very well. Eeh, you're a one, Babs. Phileas, I'm going to walk with me young 'uns. Can you get me pram down, please? I only live around the corner from here.'

Phileas looked taken aback. He could hardly voice his threats in front of everyone and didn't have a reason to refuse. Jumping from the cart, he told her under his breath that she wouldn't beat him.

With her pram down in front of her, and Phileas trotting away, a relief entered her. 'Hold on to the pram, girls, I can't hold your hands as I only have one hand to push the pram with.'

When she reached home, Tilly tentatively took off her coat, all the while calling out in pain. Babs and Beth stared up at her. 'Ma, Ma, have you hurt yourself?'

'Aye, I have and badly. Help me with me coat.'

Once her arm was out of the sleeve, Tilly was shocked to see the blood seeping through her blouse. A huge patch of red spread from her elbow to her shoulder. The pain was agonising, and she couldn't lift her arm. 'I need you to get a knife, Babs, and carefully cut the sleeve of me blouse. Beth, go and get a towel, and the rest of that sheeting I've been ripping up for rags. It's in the basket at the bottom of my bed.'

With this done, Tilly instructed them to fetch the liniment from the shelf under the sink. Soon, between them they had stemmed the blood, dressed the gaping wound and, with a great effort from Tilly not to scream as she feared frightening them, had her arm in a sling. A very loose sling, that didn't really do the job. Still in agony, Tilly did something she'd never done before. She sent the twins out in the dark together, to go along the street and ask Mrs Gilly to come back with them. 'Tell her I have money to pay her, good girls, and don't let go of each other's hands.'

Mrs Gilly came in a few minutes later. 'And what do you want, Tilly? If I'm seen coming in here, me name'll be mud.'

When Tilly explained, and Mrs Gilly took a look at her injury, her attitude changed. 'By, Tilly, I think your shoulder is out of its socket. The cut is bad, as is the bruise, but it's the dislocation that's the worst. It has to be put back. Eeh, this is going to hurt, lass, but I have to do it.'

Mrs Gilly was known for her ability to cure all. In her youth she'd been a nurse and had many tales of nursing soldiers returning from the war that had taken place back in '56 between South Africa and the British. Now in her late sixties, she was still a strong woman and supplemented her income by tending to folk and charging a penny or two.

'Now, girls, you're not to be frightened. Your ma will scream, but what I do will be for the best for her. Do you want to go to your room until it's done?'

119

'Naw, I'll stay and hold Ma's other hand.' Babs sounded brave as she said this, but Tilly could see the fear in her eyes.

Mrs Gilly didn't accept this, 'I'd be happier, Babs, if you'd care for Beth, lass. Look, your sister is crying. Take her upstairs, there's a good 'un.'

With the twins out of the way, Mrs Gilly took hold of Tilly and led her over to the chair. 'Now, I'm going to tug and twist. It'll be quick, but very painful. I've known grown men to pass out with the pain. So, sit yourself down, and I'll take hold of your hand and lower arm. That's right. Now, I'll put me foot on the chair to help me with leverage.'

Tilly trembled with fear, but wanted to be out of the pain she was in. Closing her eyes, she waited. When the tug came the pain consumed her. But though she begged her to, Mrs Gilly didn't stop tugging and twisting. At last there was a click and the pain eased. 'There. It's gone in. Well done, Tilly, you did better than a lot I've done that to.'

Tilly opened her eyes, and as droplets of sweat dripped into them from her forehead, she blinked them away. Mrs Gilly's face was red and drenched in sweat. Tilly's voice shook as she thanked her. 'Eeh, I've never been through owt like that afore. I'd rather have a dozen young 'uns.'

'Aye, and that could happen the way you're carrying on, Tilly. What's to do with you? When your Arthur were alive, you were a respectable wife and mother, and we all loved and looked up to you. You've let Arthur down as well as us and yourself, not to mention them young 'uns upstairs.'

Tilly didn't bother to tell Mrs Gilly that she couldn't have any more babbies, as that would have given her another stick to beat her with. 'I – I don't knaw. He ... Mr Simpson, he blackmailed me. I were desperate for money.'

'Aye, well, so a lot of us have been, but we didn't resort to sleeping with another woman's husband to get it.'

Tilly couldn't say anything to this.

'Now, let me clean that wound. I see you have liniment and a clean bit of sheeting. I'll bind it up for you, but your shoulder should be all right now; keep it moving is the trick. Gently, but don't hold it stiffly as they have been known to stay like that.'

When all was done, Mrs Gilly asked for tuppence for her services. Tilly went to her pram that stood at the back of the room and lifted the baskets out with her good arm. She stared down to where her money had been in a leather pouch. Nothing. Frantic, she moved the bundle Cook had left for her. Still nothing. 'Oh, naw, naw.'

'What is it?'

'Me money's gone. Oh God, Phileas must have rummaged and found it.'

'Who's Phileas?'

When Tilly explained, Mrs Gilly folded her arms and tutted. 'Been up to your tricks again, Tilly, eh?'

'Naw. Naw.' In despair, Tilly sank down on to the nearest chair, unable to control the sobs that wracked her body.

'Now, now, no need to take on like that. We reap what we sow, lass. Well, I take it you can't pay me? Well, I rather like that shopping basket and that must be worth a couple of pence. I'll take that as payment.'

Tilly nodded. *A couple of pence? I'd get at least a sixpence for it.*

Leaning back, she knew it was the end of the road. With her arm incapacitated, she couldn't make baskets for a while as it took a lot of strength and agility to do so. Nor did she have the strength to walk the streets to sell the two that she had left. She was beaten.

As the door closed behind Mrs Gilly, Tilly realised that she had no choice but to take herself and her girls to the poorhouse.

ELEVEN

Tilly held on to the pram. Her girls had a hand on each side of it, their knuckles white as they clung on.

Four days had passed and, as she knew he would, the rent man had told her to be out by Saturday. She'd managed to take the base of her pram out and had packed the space under it with as many of the twins' clothes as she could. Amidst these she'd tucked her tools that had belonged to her Aunt Mildred – her bodkin, her scissors, her sharp knife with the bone handle, her round-nosed pliers and her loppers for cutting willow, and her large cutters for the thicker cane. On top of that she'd put blankets as the journey to Manchester would take her days, even if she did get help from the gypsies, as she intended on going to the encampment and begging one of them to take her. They owed her that much as Phileas had got her into this position by twice taking the money she'd earned.

The blankets would cover the twins at night time, and for herself she'd put Arthur's big thick coat in the pram. The thought of wearing it over her own at night gave her a warm feeling; she'd think of it as him cuddling her.

Food had not been a problem these last days as in the bundle from Cook and Florrie she'd found a cooked ham shank, and she still had some of this on the bone. There'd been some pickles too, and some tatties and a cabbage, and she'd made a dish of ham and cabbage that had lasted two days. With the rest of the ham, pickles and a full loaf she'd baked off, she knew she could feed them as they travelled.

The snow had cleared now, leaving a few wedges of it in the hedgerows, but with a further drop in the temperature, frost whitened the world and icicles hung from rooftops and the branches of trees.

'I'm cold, Ma.'

'I knaw, Beth, but we'll soon warm up if we walk quickly, lass.'

'Are we never going back home, Ma?'

'Naw, Babs. I did me best, but with me injury, I couldn't make me baskets and had no other way of making the rent money. I'm sorry, me lasses. I tried.'

'It's not your fault, Ma. God's to blame for taking our da. Everyone needs a da, and we loved ours.'

Babs was filled with wisdom and a perception deeper than others of her age. 'We did, lass, and we miss him, but you knaw, he'd want us to allus be brave.'

'I can be brave, Ma. But Beth isn't strong like us.'

'Well, we have to be her strength then. Can you do that for her, Babs?'

'Aye, I can, and I'll allus look out for her. Come on, Beth, come this side and I'll hold your hand.'

Tilly stopped a moment to let Beth change her position. When she came around to Babs, Babs cuddled her.

The sight of them brought a lump to Tilly's throat. She'd known she'd made mistakes since Arthur had died, but now she felt sick to the stomach at her actions and what they had brought down on her and her little ones.

Still not able to cross the fields because of the weather, she took the roadway towards St Anne's, thinking that once she got to the stile she and the girls would climb over and she would leave the pram in the hedgerow. They could cover it with whatever they could collect to hide it, and then make their way to the encampment. If the gypsies would take her in a cart to the poorhouse, then she would ask them to pick the pram up on the way. They should help her, they stood need to but, in her heart, she had doubts. They didn't see helping themselves to other's belongings as wrong, just a survival tactic.

By the time they reached the stile, Tilly was exhausted. The girls had tired long before they'd left Blackpool and she'd ended up sitting them on top of the pram with the blankets wrapped around them and pushing the weight of the pram had drained her of energy.

'Come on, me lasses, help Ma with covering the pram. The gypsy encampment is just through this field.'

'I don't want to go there, Ma, they frighten me.'

'Naw, Babs, don't start. You'll frighten Beth and you promised to look out for her. We've naw choice, lass. Come on, now. Grab some of that brush and let's get the bonnet of the pram covered, I can push the bottom half under the hedge. We don't want anyone stealing our stuff while we're gone, do we?'

*　　*　　*

When she came within sight of the camp she was met by the familiar smells of burning bonfires, smouldering iron and another scent that was strong and seemed to be of alcohol. There weren't many folk milling around; some men were working over an anvil, which was where the hot metal smell came from. Another was nearby shaving a horse's hoof. A group of children with ragged clothes and snotty noses were chasing a mangy dog, just as they were last time she visited, and she wondered that they hadn't anything better to do. And then a young girl, obviously heavily pregnant, stood up from where she had been sitting, her arms folded across her chest. She called something over to the men. Tilly couldn't understand what it was.

The rest of the women, or Jonas and Phileas, were nowhere to be seen.

One of the men shouted back using the same language the girl had. At whatever he said, the girl shrugged, then in a challenging way asked of Tilly, 'What is it yer wanting? What brings such as you here?'

Tilly held herself upright, ignoring the 'such as you' part, and kept her voice steady. 'I've come for help. Phileas has made me homeless by stealing me earnings for the second time, and I reckon as you lot need to do sommat about it. Me and me young 'uns have nowhere to sleep the night, or any night, and I need to get to the poorhouse. I think there's one on the way to Manchester.'

The girl spat on the floor. 'Me brothers are not for being 'ere.'

'I'll wait then. Where's Lilly Lee? She won't turn me away.'

'It is that they're all out, selling stuff. Phileas and Jonas are for getting supplies. They'll be back in an hour.'

Most likely buying stuff with my money! At this thought Tilly felt her temper rising. 'Well, I'll wait till they come back, like I said. Only me young 'uns are cold and hungry. I had to leave me pram at the stile. I've got food and blankets in there for them, but me shoulder is badly hurt and I can't get it over to here.'

'I'll be fetching it for yee.'

Tilly swung around and saw that the young man who'd been preparing the horses hoof was the one who had said this. He looked similar to Phileas, sun-browned, weathered skin, muscly body, dark hair and eyes, but his face was softer looking, as if he had a kinder heart. He wore a red band around his forehead and his hair curled over it.

'Ta. I'd be grateful to you.'

'You be getting yourselves around that fire and get some warmth into your bones. Cilla, move yourself, and make our guest at home.'

The children had stopped playing and stood around staring. One little girl of around the twins' age came up to them. 'Is it that you have a name?'

'Aye, I'm Babs and this is Beth.'

'How is a body to tell you apart?'

'I don't knaw; me ma's the only one as can. Me teacher gets it right most of the time as she says I'm the chatterbox one.'

'How is it you have a teacher, then?'

'We goes to school.'

The little girl looked puzzled at this.

'What's your name, then?' As usual Babs did the talking and Beth just looked interested. Tilly didn't interfere. She wanted to get the girls close to the fire, but they seemed quite happy.

'I'm for being called Pearl. Come away and play with me. I've some hoops, and it is some poles I have in the ground. We have to be trying to get the hoops over the poles. Only Raggarty – that's the dog – is for running away with the hoops and we have to be chasing him to get them back.'

'Can we, Ma?'

Tilly let them go off with Pearl. She didn't see any harm in the game. The dog seemed good-humoured and was enjoying the game as much as the young 'uns.

'It is as you can come and sit with me if you want to. The fire is throwing out a fair heat and the wagon is keeping the draught from me back.' At this from Cilla, Tilly looked back towards her and saw that she was now sitting and patting the empty seat on the bench next to where she sat.

'Aye, I don't mind if I do. I'm freezing.'

When she sat down the smell of alcohol was even stronger from where they were; she looked around and saw that it was coming from a shed to her left. Cilla must have guessed what she was curious over. 'That'll be the gin. I'm distilling it for the shenanigans tonight. It's almost ready, and it is that it is Phileas's birthday, and so there'll be a party when the sun goes down. No one will want to miss it, so I'm for doubting you'll be taken on your way this night.'

'Oh, but we've nowhere to stay.'

'Sure you can stay here. There's a wagon empty over there. It belonged to Flannigan, the eldest of our clan. But he was taken on his final rest this last summer. It's to be mine and me husband's, but it is lazy that he is and taking his time in getting it ready. He is for having the bed made bigger, and that is it. There's a lot of fixing to be done to make it me home, so we're still in the one his mammy and pappy had. That one over there. It's a much smaller wagon. I'm for wanting more room when me babby comes along.'

'Is your husband out an' all?'

'Aye, it is that he has to bring home firewood. We get through a powerful lot of it as each family lights their own cooking fire in the evening. But this big fire never goes out. It is the hub of the clan, where we meet and dance around, and for we womenfolk to do our work by.'

Tilly was thawing out, as the fire gave out intense heat. The wagon behind them, Cilla told her, acted as their main store and was never moved. Sacks had been nailed to the bottom of it, forming a skirt that stopped the wind from hitting their backs. Lots of squeals and giggles could be heard, and when Tilly looked towards where they were coming from she saw that the twins were having a good time and joining in with everything. Beth had her head back laughing louder than she'd heard her do in a long time.

A peace settled in Tilly, and she relaxed, only to stiffen at Cilla's next words.

'Mind, it is that the women won't be best pleased to see you here. I didn't like it meself when you appeared. They have a rumour going from one to the other that Phileas is hankering after you, and it is that Betina is upset.'

Tilly shivered. 'But it's not of my doing. I hate him. Look what he's done to us. I've worked hard trying to keep a roof over our heads, and he comes along and takes what I earn.' With saying this everything tumbled out of Tilly. How she lost Arthur, the greengrocer job she had, and her lie about what happened there, how Lilly Lee had helped her, only for

Phileas and Jonas to rob her. Everything up until the horse had hurt her. By the time she'd finished the tears were rolling down her cheeks.

'I'm powerful sorry for you. Phileas is a bad 'un. Though it is that he has his gentlemanly side too. Lilly Lee sees to that, for she has had guardianship of him since his pa, the last of the Gaskins in our clan, passed on. His ma had died giving birth to Jonas. Oh, there's a mighty clan of Gaskins he could go to up in Yorkshire, and we meet up with them from time to time, but he wants to stay with Lilly Lee. Lilly Lee is wanting to marry her clan to the Gaskins and sees Phileas as the way to do it. It is plain to all that he is not for loving Betina. The beauty that she is has not caught his eye, but he has sworn and so he must. Though rebel that he is, if it is you he is wanting, then he would throw all Lilly Lee has done for him back in her face and up and take you for his bride.'

'Well, he needn't think that is going to happen. Aye, I see him as attractive, but how he carries on is dreadful, and his life is different to mine.'

'Is it for being better or worse than the poorhouse, then? I'm for thinking not worse by a long way. We gypsies are free. As free as the wind. We are for having a hard life, but a good one. We have food in our bellies, gin in our blood, and the love of the clan members to take care of us. We are never for going hungry or cold, as it is nature that takes care of us, and we have the talent to earn our bread. Sure, there's nothing wrong with the gypsy life. God-fearing we are. Oh, I know we take from those who have, but didn't the Good Lord say that a man is to be helping himself?'

Tilly smiled at this. 'I don't think He put it quite like that and if He did, He didn't mean it the way you've taken it. But there is one thing I knaw: He wouldn't sanction you taking from the likes of me and making us homeless.'

'It is that most of us wouldn't. But, like I am telling you, Phileas doesn't always follow our ways. Here comes Jeremiah with your pram. Now he is different to Phileas, and to most of the clan. It is that he likes to preach the word, and to keep us from burning in Hell. He is for being a Godly man and hasn't yet looked on any of the girls with an eye to marriage. Young Lucy, the girl who alerted Phileas to you having money the last time he stole from you, is for having a fancy for Jeremiah, but he doesn't look at her. Lilly Lee says that Jeremiah isn't of this world and will be going to his maker soon too.'

Tilly again shuddered. And a deep sadness entered her at this as she looked to where Jeremiah was walking towards her pushing her pram. She had the strange feeling that she wanted to reach out to him and to save him from whatever fate had in store.

As he came closer he held her gaze. His face changed, and his look turned from one of inquisitiveness to one she couldn't discern. For a moment her world rocked as Arthur seemed to be looking at her, not Jeremiah, and it was as if he could see deep into her soul, where her recent sinning was laid bare before him.

When Jeremiah spoke, his words sent a feeling through her that she was in the presence of a being who wasn't from this earth. 'It is that you have many cares, lady. Not all of them are for being brought down on you by Phileas, but by your own impetuousness. And it is that which will be your downfall. Unless it is that you change your ways and how you hope to gain what you want.'

'I – I don't knaw what you're talking about.'

'I think that you do. You are for gaining what you want through sinning, and this is not how you should be leading your life.'

'Oh, Jeremiah, it is that you are a holier-than-thou busy-body. It isn't for you to go around telling folk they're sinners.'

'Oh, but it is, Cilla. I am the one who is set to save many souls. I must do my Lord's bidding.'

'Am I to take it that you will not be giving your soul a night off then? Is it that you won't be attending the music and dancing this night, nor having a drop of me gin?'

As Jeremiah walked away, Cilla let out a cackle of laughter. 'It is that he'll be as drunk as the next one come midnight, you mark me words.'

Though Tilly smiled, she had the strangest feeling spread through her body. There was something unworldly about Jeremiah. Something that she couldn't put her finger on. But somehow she knew that it would be an action of his that would change her life. What it would be, she couldn't imagine, but she couldn't shake the feeling.

TWELVE

When the women returned, Phileas and Jonas were with them. Tilly could see them walking towards the camp; all had bundles in their arms. When they came closer she saw that the men's bundles were bigger than what the women carried, and that some of the women just had their sling bags, which she knew they carried their pegs in, whilst others had a second sling bag she guessed held more supplies. Lilly Lee was lagging at the back of the crowd and held the basket she'd bought from Tilly. This brought to Tilly's mind the day she had met Lilly Lee. The memory gave Tilly renewed confidence that Lilly would help her.

As the gypsies, led by Betina and Phileas, came into camp, Betina stopped her progress and stared at Tilly. Without speaking, she turned and flounced off, entering a wagon to the left of the camp.

'What is it that you are doing here then, pretty lady?'

'Don't come the innocent with me. You stole me money again, Phileas. You've made me and me girls homeless. I've come to ask for that to be put right.'

'What is all this, Phileas? Why have you been up to your tricks again? Didn't I tell you that Tilly is one of mine?'

'She never comes near to you, unless she needs something, Lilly.'

'I've been busy, trying to earn me way. Only for you to snatch it from me.'

Lilly sighed. 'It's getting dark and me bones are for giving me trouble. Let me sit while you tell me your tale, Tilly.'

Phileas turned away and went towards the wagon that Betina had gone to. Tilly wanted to run after him and claw him to pieces, she was that angry. But she sat with Lilly Lee. Babs and Beth, who had been happy playing for the last hour, came and sidled into her. She put her arms around them.

'Are these your wee ones? My, they are pretty little things. I take them as mine, from this moment.'

Tilly's heart stopped at this from Lilly Lee. 'Naw, no one's having them. They're staying with me.'

'Och, it's a figure of speech. It means they come under me protection.'

But Tilly wasn't so sure. She didn't like how Lilly Lee was smiling her toothless smile at the girls and she pulled them both closer to her body.

The feeling took her that she'd like to get up and run away from here right now, but she desperately needed the help of the gypsies. She didn't know who else to ask. Having told Lilly Lee about her plight, Tilly waited. But Lilly Lee didn't speak; she sat staring, chewing on her bottom lip.

The girl called Lucy stepped forward and gave Lilly Lee a smoking clay pipe. 'I thank you, Lucy, it is that I am in need of me pipe while I think.'

Nothing else happened for a few moments. All those who had returned stood around waiting. Lilly Lee at last spoke, and as she did puffs of smoke came from her mouth and down her nose.

'It is that you should all go about your business. We have shenanigans to get ready for. You girls need to be cooking in preparation and, Cilla, is it that the gin will be ready?'

'Aye, it will, but I have to filter it into the jugs and put it to cool.'

'Well, you should be doing that and leaving me with Tilly.'

The camp became a hive of activity. Even Phileas and Betina reappeared and set about doing chores. Phileas's task was to dig behind the wagon – why, Tilly couldn't imagine – and Betina joined in with some of the other women who were sorting the potatoes. Tilly imagined from what they were doing that they were picking out the ones most suitable for roasting in the fire. A couple of other women were tending to a huge pot, roughly chopping vegetables and throwing them into it, and another two lads of around fourteen years old were skinning the rabbits they'd carried into camp over their shoulders.

'Now then, Tilly. It isn't good to be thinking of taking these little ones into the poorhouse. There it is that children perish. I will speak to the men over there, but it is that I am thinking you should stay with us.'

Tilly gasped. 'But you knaw the trouble I have with Phileas.'

'Aye, it is that rumours are rife as to his feelings towards you, but he is betrothed and if you are for being here under me watchful eye, you can come to no harm. I'll be arranging his wedding sooner than it is set for, as his wagon is nearly completed now. It's a grand wagon. See, it stands over there, and Betina is for making her furnishings and embroidering her linen for it. Betina's pappy has worked hard on perfecting it. We have one over there that you can take as your own.'

'But Cilla has told me that's for her and her husband and child. Eeh, Lilly, she'd be sore at me if I took that from her. I could see when she told me that she is longing for it to be ready.'

'This is the truth, but she will have to wait. I will get another built for her. She is deserving of a new one. But I'll not leave it to her husband to do the work. He is a waster if ever I saw one. He came to me clan from a travelling circus. And he has seen the side his bread is buttered and never gone back to earn his living, or to take his bride with him. It is that I am to see to him being sorted out. I will get Jeremiah on to building her a lovely wagon. He is the best wheelwright and black-smith for miles – he can make anything out of iron – and we womenfolk will stitch the canvas, while the wooden body will be fashioned by Derry, who is the finest carpenter.'

Tilly didn't know what to say. To her the prospect of living with the gypsies was terrifying, and yet, not more so than living in the poorhouse, where she may be separated from her children and hardly see them. And of where she'd heard, as Lily Lee said, tales of children dying from disease because of the filth of the places. And she'd heard too of the low food rations given, for long hours of hard labour.

'Ma. Ma.' Babs tugged at her sleeve. 'Naw, Ma. I don't want us to stay here.'

'Little one, you will be safe. Didn't I see you playing with Pearl and having a wonderful time? That can happen every day. Your mammy will work with us. She'll be teaching us the basket work, and she will stay around camp and be with you as she makes her baskets for us to sell. Sure, you will be happy and well fed.'

The idea began to appeal to Tilly much more than the poorhouse did. But what about Phileas?

'Lilly, it is that I have something to say.'

Jeremiah had come over to them. Once more his eyes never left Tilly and she began to feel uncomfortable in her own skin.

'It is a good thing what you are doing offering to take in Tilly and her children. I think it is God who is for sending her here as she is in need of saving from herself. In the poorhouse she will need to use what she has to better things for herself, and she will, which will lead her further down the sinful path she has been on. Here we can protect her. I will make her wagon weatherproof and fit it with the up-to-date facilities. Together, we will help her not to be casting her eyes towards Phileas and taking what he is offering. Joining us is a good solution for her plight. Me and the men are for it, as I spoke to them before I came over.'

Tilly looked up and gave Jeremiah a look that said how she felt about his summing up of her, but at the same time she wondered how he knew what secrets she held in her heart. He was a strange man, and yet, he had something about him that she was drawn to.

'Well, Jeremiah, what it is you think Tilly has sinned over, I can only guess, but you are judgemental, and for me, I would say that if there is any sinning that has been done, it will have been against her, not by her. Now get back with the men and let me get on with me arranging of everything.'

Jeremiah immediately obeyed.

137

'Now then, Tilly, you are not to be taking any notice of Jeremiah, he is troubled by what he sees. I have been at trying to get him to channel it away from his religious aspirations and to use it to tell fortunes, as there is no doubt he sees things. But he is harmless and is the same as us all when he relaxes. He likes a good time. He works hard, and will make a fine husband for some girl, if only he could stop condemning all who fancy him as sinners. He does himself no good.'

Tilly didn't answer this; her mind was in a quandary. *What shall I do? What Lilly is offering is pulling me to accept.* 'I'm willing to give it a try, Lilly. But if I'm not happy, you must promise to let me go. And if I make me money, I have to be able to keep some of it so that I can make sommat of me life for me and me young 'uns. I'm not of your folk, and your way of life is not mine. Eeh, I can't imagine living like you do, even as I'm accepting your offer.'

'It's a done deal. Spit on your hand and take mine.'

The thought of this was repulsive to Tilly as she saw Lilly spit into her palm. But something compelled her to do it. The feel of the wetness as she clasped hands with Lilly Lee sent disgust through her, but she tried not to let Lilly Lee see this. The old woman had shown her nothing but kindness.

'This is the first joining of us. When I am ready, we will become blood sisters.'

How this was to be done, Tilly couldn't think, but she decided not to delve into it. 'I have to feed me young 'uns now, Lilly Lee, and to get me things in the wagon. Ta ever so much. You've saved me from a fate I wasn't looking forward to.'

'And I need a pee, Ma. Where are the lavs?'

This from Beth brought Tilly's own need of wanting to relieve herself into focus.

'We have no lavs, me darling, it is that you go where nature intended. Behind your wagon. See how Phileas is digging over there? He is filling the hole he used and is making a new one. It is the cleanest way and puts back into the earth that which we take out. And if it is you need to wipe yourself clean afterwards, you pick a dock leaf for the purpose. Och, you'll soon get used to it.'

Tilly didn't think she ever would. She stood up and went towards her pram. The girls followed her. As she pushed it over to her wagon, she wondered at what she'd consented to, but then, what choice did she have?

Beth began to cry, and the sound made Tilly realise that she had to be strong for her girls. She was to make the best of their situation, so that they did too. 'Come on, you two, naw tears. We're starting a new adventure. Naw more school for you, just endless hours of play.'

'But I want to go to school, Ma, I'm learning me letters. And I were going to show you how to do them an' all.'

'I knaw, Babs. Well, p'raps I can make enough money to buy you some learning books, eh? You're bright, you'll take what you knaw now and learn more to add to it.'

Pearl had joined them. 'Aye, and Jeremiah can read. It is that he tries to teach us, but Lilly says there's no point. He taught himself, and he'll teach you if you're wanting to learn. I'd join you.'

'There, you see. Eeh, lass, this is going to be different for us, but we can make of it what we want. And I knaw it will be better than the poorhouse.'

'I'll be for taking you to have a pee. I'll show you how it is that we straddle the hole and wipe ourselves on the doc leaves.'

Tilly couldn't believe a little girl like Pearl could speak with such wisdom and without any inhibitions. Everything seemed a natural function to these gypsies. After all, didn't Cilla say she and her husband stayed in her ma's wagon? From what Tilly could see there were no separate rooms in the wagons, so when they made love, as surely her husband would want to, they must have to do it in front of her ma. The idea of it had Tilly blushing. As did thoughts of how they would be living. There was no screen around the hole at the back of the wagon, and the canvas covering the wagons wouldn't shut out noise, so everyone on the camp could hear everything that went on inside.

Even though her home hadn't been a palace, it was a million miles away from all she had to contend with in the camp, Tilly discovered as she asked questions of Pearl. Water had to be fetched in buckets from the well in the farmyard of the owner of the land, who allowed them to camp there in exchange for the lads helping on the farm. There was a water wagon, which was driven to the farmyard every couple of days. A huge pan was heated on the main fire and everyone helped themselves from this and took water back to their wagons to wash. Food was mostly poached, stolen or fetched from the market, with the women doing the cooking in their own wagons, or using the main fire. To this end, Tilly discovered that she had a wood stove in the wagon.

Altogether she was pleasantly surprised to find how spacious the wagon was and the storage it gave, as under the bed at the back of the wagon were drawers and a cupboard which provided adequate space for hers and the twins' clothes, not that she had brought much for herself, just a change of underclothes and another day frock. To one side there was another cupboard that housed some crockery and another one which was empty. Next to the bed there stood a rocking chair and then another cupboard that had a grid in the back of it, making it very cool; this she assumed would be for milk, eggs, butter and meat, though where she would get these she had to ask Pearl again. 'We are for having a store cupboard; everyone has to pay a little for supplies and then it is topped up with the money. Lilly Lee will be for sorting you out.'

Tilly didn't know where she was to get money from in the beginning, as she had no cane; she'd left it all in the backyard of her home. Now she wished that she'd found a way of bringing it with her. But she did have some food and this she brought in, looking around as to where to prepare it.

'Here, see, you are for having a table; it folds down. When you want to use it, you pull it up like this and then pull down the leg. And then it is that you get your stools; they are here.' From the space that the table had been folded into, Pearl showed her that there were four stools that collapsed to a very small size.

'Ta, Pearl, you've been a big help to me, but it's freezing in here. Can you tell me how to light the stove?'

'I'll be fetching someone to do that for you.' With this Pearl disappeared.

Tilly looked around her. Everything fitted in this small space as if by magic and she wondered what else she would discover. 'Well, little ones, climb up on the stools and I'll soon have you filling your belly with that ham I have. Keep your coats on for now, though.'

'It'll feel strange eating our tea in our coats, Ma.'

Tilly looked at them both. Their cheeks were rosy, but there was no sign of sadness in them, which gladdened her. The thought came to her that there would be many much stranger things to learn about this new life. Part of her didn't want to. She wanted to be as she was, a Blackpool lass living as all Blackpool lasses do in their two up, two downs, with water coming from the tap and a lav in the yard. Sighing, she turned her attention to unwrapping the food she had. *Eeh, I can't see a time as I'll ever live like that again.*

THIRTEEN

'So, pretty lady, you are in need of help. Here it is that I have some kindling and logs, I'll soon have you cosy.'

Tilly froze as Phileas came up the steps.

'Now, it isn't that you should be afraid, I'll not bring any harm to your door.'

'You already have! How can you look me in the eye when you have brought me to this?'

'To what? Isn't it that you will be happier here than in your brick house that you couldn't heat or pay the rent for? Here, everyone will see that you have all you need.'

'You stole me money. Every penny I earned. You don't knaw how I sat up night after night making those baskets to sell to keep a roof over me young 'uns heads. You're despicable.'

'No, it isn't that I am, as me motive was to make you come to me and that has now happened. For sure, I'm going to talk to Lilly Lee and have her allow me to break me promise to marry Betina, as it is you that I want. Now, here,' his hand dug into his pocket, 'I am for having your money here and you can have it back, pretty lady. You can buy all you'll need from our stores.'

'Eeh, I wouldn't marry you if you were the last man alive.' Snatching her money up from where he'd put it on the table, Tilly shouted, 'Now, get out! Get out of here. I'll light me own fire, thank you!'

'What is it that is going on?' The curtain was pulled back and Jeremiah stood there peering in.

'I don't want Phileas in here and told him to leave.'

'Why is it you're here, Phileas?'

For a moment Tilly thought he would voice his intentions, but he didn't; he turned and, pushing by Jeremiah, stormed out of the wagon.

'Is there anything you are needing, Tilly?'

'Aye, I need me stove lighting, and I don't knaw how it's done.'

Without another word Jeremiah set about the task. Tilly watched how he scrunched up the paper as she did in her own home, then lay twigs in a heap. After this he lay sticks and then small pieces of wood before striking a match to the paper. 'Now, you close the door and pull out this damper, and it is that you can have the top of the stove open or leave the plate in place for cooking. Always be sure there's enough draught to send the smoke up the chimney, then when it is that you have a good glow, you can push the damper in and it will burn slowly. Never be letting it go out. There's a pile of wood by the store wagon, and you help yourself from that. But be remembering to close the fire down at night. Push the damper in and the grate plate in place.'

Already Tilly could feel the heat filling the wagon. With the warmth her mind settled, as she'd not been able to imagine keeping the wagon warm or ever feeling cosy again. That

144

feeling was visiting her now, and though the space was small in comparison to what she was used to, she felt that it was homely and determined she would do her best to find it in herself to live in this way and to make a happy home for her girls.

'And so, they tell me that you are a basket maker and will bring those skills to our clan. Where is it you get your materials, as the basket you were selling to Lilly Lee is quality? Not like the efforts of the women here who work from the hedgerows.'

Once he heard where her materials were, he said, 'You be leaving this to me, and they'll be with you by morning.'

Tilly didn't protest. She knew he would have to arrange a break-in at her old home to get through to the backyard, but she didn't care – the cane was hers, so there was no stealing involved. Asking him to get other things that she'd left behind and needed didn't pose him a problem. He said she would have all she wanted from her home as long as the landlord hadn't cleared it out. Something Tilly knew wouldn't have happened yet as she'd been given till midnight to get out. Now she wished she'd have kept her keys, but she'd posted them back through the letterbox thinking that she would have no use of them and had to turn her back on all her possessions.

By the time the party was in full swing later that evening, Jeremiah and the lad he'd taken with him were back with a fully laden cart. He'd told her he'd sheeted it down, so she had no need to worry about it until the morning. 'Even if the heavens open, your things will be keeping dry.'

At this moment Tilly felt as if her life was settled and she had to admit that she didn't feel sad about the move, nor afraid. Here she was amongst friendly folk, who, except for Lucy and Betina who were jealous of her, treated her well and welcomed her and her girls. Babs and Beth looked the happiest she'd ever seen them as they danced around with Pearl and the other little ones, trying to flounce their skirts in the same way that they did and lifting their arms in a heart shape above their heads.

'Will you mind if I take your little ones and dress them as we dress? I'm for thinking they will enjoy their dancing all the more.'

'Eeh, ta, that'd be lovely. I don't knaw your name, as I haven't heard it spoken.'

'I'm Jasmine. That is me wagon over there. I'm the dressmaker and I have many a pretty frock that will fit Babs and Beth.'

'Oh? Are any of the little girls yours?'

A shadow passed over Jasmine's face. 'It is that the Good Lord has not seen fit to bless me with children of me own. It is shame that I bring to me husband.'

'Naw. It isn't your fault. But I knaw how you feel as I'm not able to have any more. Having the two of them damaged me.'

'Oh?'

The feeling that Tilly got from all the young gypsy women visited her now; it was as if they saw her as a threat. Maybe even more so with this admission as they may have thought the prospect of having a child would have deterred her from having relations with their men. But if only they knew that

146

she didn't need a deterrent, as she didn't want to go with any of them. Yes, Phileas had aroused her feelings in the beginning, but not now; now she loathed him. And she was appalled at what she'd done with Joe just after Arthur died. *Never, never again. I'm to try to repair the sin I committed.* But a voice in her head told her that the feelings she got when a man showed his need of her could well let her down.

'Have you tried me gin yet, Tilly?' Cilla's voice broke into her thoughts.

'Eeh, Cilla, lass, I were thinking you would be cross with me for taking the wagon you wanted.'

'Ha, that isn't the way of me. I'm glad as now I get to have a new one made for me, when I was only considered worthy of having that old one. So, don't worry, and come and have a sip of me gin.'

'Naw, I haven't ever been a drinker. A little at Christmas, and that's me lot.'

'It is that it'll warm you through. I'm for hoping it will bring me babby into the world, for I'm fed up with lugging it around in me belly.'

'By the sound of you, you've had a few already.'

'Aye, I'm ... hic ... feeling very happy.'

Tilly took the mug Cilla held out to her. Sipping tentatively, the liquid burnt her tongue; swallowing it had her throat on fire.

'Ha ha, will you look at our pretty lady! It's soft that she is.' Everyone burst out laughing at this from Phileas.

Embarrassed, but not wanting to show it, Tilly controlled her cough and wiped the tears from her eyes. 'Eeh, that's like firewater, but I'll have me mug filled again.'

The laughter was of a different kind this time as the men threw back their heads. But Tilly could see that their wives weren't as amused.

Betina cast an angry glare at Tilly. 'Play some music, Raymond! This is supposed to be a party, but it is that it is turning into a sideshow.'

'Och, Betina, away with your jealousy.'

Phileas's words sent Betina running for her wagon. Tilly hoped that Phileas would have the decency to run after her, but no. He came over to Tilly and stood with his head cocked at an angle that showed he was full of himself. 'Will you dance with me, pretty lady?'

If she'd thought him handsome before, he was devastatingly so tonight. His hair was sleeked back, revealing the gold ring in his ear, and his baggy white shirt showed how tanned he was. His trousers clung to the contours of his legs, and his red and white spotted neckerchief gave him a rakish air.

'Naw, I don't knaw how to dance, and besides, it wouldn't be right. You should go after Betina and bring her out to dance with you.'

Leaning forward, he whispered, 'She is nothing to me. It is that I desire to hold you in my arms and kiss you as I did in the field.'

Tilly turned away. As she did so, she saw all the younger women glaring at her. She didn't want to alienate them. She had thoughts of settling down and becoming one of them, not for them to see her as a rival for their chosen man's affections.

Jeremiah saved her.

'Phileas, go and see to Betina.' As he said this, he reached for Tilly's hand. 'I will lead you to dance as it is customary that when a guest attends they begin the dancing.'

'Oh? I am still a guest then?'

'Aye, until the clan get used to you. But I am thinking that you are going to have to take care as there is nothing as vicious as a woman scorned and, as I see it, you could be the cause of that happening.'

'I don't mean to. I don't want any man.'

'That is not for what a man reads in you. You give off an air of needing the passion of the night.'

Tilly snatched her hand away. 'Eeh, you've got a side to you. How dare you speak to me like that? I'm not a harlot. I'm—'

'Is it that you protest too loudly? Or am I for being the wrong man? If you refuse me, you will render an insult on me, as I am for being looked up to and the only one entitled to lead you into the dance.'

Tilly looked around. She caught Lilly Lee's eye. Lilly had her arms folded and her lips clamped tightly together. She nodded towards the patch of grass that had cleared of folk. The gesture was a command, and Tilly knew that she must obey it.

Taking Jeremiah's hand, she allowed him to lead her to the clearing. The silence around her made her more nervous than she was. 'I can't dance. I don't knaw how, I've never been taught.'

Jeremiah leant towards her. 'Take my lead and let the music light up your soul.'

The strains of the music from the guitar were haunting. Slowly, Jeremiah took her hand and stepped away from her;

his steps were light and his body, clad in a white shirt, small bolero-type waistcoat and tight black trousers, looked graceful as he leant back. Still unsure what to do, Tilly remained still, then suddenly she felt her body jerk and she was twirling under the arm of Jeremiah. The movement excited her as at the same time the pace of the music quickened and became louder. With another twirl, the gin she'd drunk began to heat her stomach and make her head feel light.

Now she could feel the music as if it was caressing her and she began to sway, twisting her body, twirling, and arching her back. The pin holding her hair came loose and she felt her thick, raven tresses swirl around her neck and shoulders. Lifting her hand, she unclasped the last pin and brought her hair over her face, swishing it back so that it cascaded down her back.

Jeremiah was twirling her again. The music was strumming through her and was at one with her soul. Her brow dampened with sweat and she could feel her neck perspiring too, wetting her hair and trickling down her body, but still she twirled and swayed in time to the music, until Jeremiah caught hold of her bruised arm and tugged her. Then she stood a moment, pain searing through her, and yet, feeling exquisite. The moan that came from her seemed to disappear as, oblivious to all sound and everything around her, she sank to the ground.

Coming out of the faint, she could hear the children crying out to her. She opened her eyes, went to reassure them, but the pain in her arm made her holler out her agony.

'What is it? Tilly, what is hurting you?'

She wanted to respond to Jeremiah but couldn't.

'It will be her arm. She was injured by my horse when I came across her in that blinding snow. Rhona reared and hit her with her hoof.'

Jeremiah lifted her, causing her more pain, and she knew her shoulder had come out of joint again. 'M – my shoulder. It – it's dislocated.'

'Ma, Ma . . .' Tilly turned her head towards her girls; they looked like visions in the frocks that Jasmine had dressed them in. One, a bright purple colour, hung in layers edged with black lace and the other was in the same style but in a bright red.

'M – Ma's all right. Me – me arm, that's all, me bonny girls. You look so pretty. Ma l – loves you.'

'Come, little ones, come with me.' Jasmine took the girls to her and held them close. A feeling took Tilly that she wanted to snatch them away and hold on to them, but she couldn't. Jasmine steered them away.

'Well, it is that we have to put your shoulder back, Tilly. Cilla, bring a cup of your gin.'

The pain took reality from Tilly, consuming her. 'Please, please, just pull it back into its socket. Pl – e-ease.'

'You're to sup this first as it is a powerful pain when we pull it back in.'

'Aye, I knaw, I've had it done. Just hurry.'

'Drink this.'

Gulping down the gin, Tilly began to swirl into a dizzy place that wanted to draw her deeper in. The pain eased, but then suddenly became excruciating again as Jeremiah tugged and twisted it. A crack signalled it had gone back into place, and the pain eased once more. She lay back, her mind playing tricks on her as she imagined it was Arthur who'd made the world right for her. 'Oh, my love, my love.'

'It is that you will be all right now, Tilly.' Jeremiah's voice confused her.

'Where's Arthur?'

'Who is this Arthur?'

'He was her man. She was widowed a few months back.' Phileas's voice.

'No, no . . . I don't want me Arthur to be dead.'

A gentle arm lifted her head, then her whole body off the ground. 'I'll be taking her to her wagon, and I'll stay with her till she is resting.'

'I can do that.'

'Phileas, go to Betina. She it is that you are betrothed to. You have insulted her enough this night.'

'But—'

'I know that Tilly has been for upsetting your world, Phileas, but you have to fight the feeling. It will pass. For sure a man feels the need to sow a few wild oats before it is that he settles down.'

'You're not all-knowing, Jeremiah. A man cannot give his love on command. Lilly Lee arranged the marriage with Betina, but I have no feeling for her.'

'Whish, now. The women will hear you.'

Lilly Lee came into view. 'What is it that is holding you up, Jeremiah? Get Tilly to her wagon, she is shivering, she could be getting the pneumonia – I heard a wheeze on her chest.'

With this, Phileas turned and walked away.

When they reached her wagon, Tilly was once more reminded of Arthur as Jeremiah's gentle way with her was just

152

how Arthur had been. She tried to sort out her thoughts that swirled around, making her imagine she could see Arthur. It was him carrying her. His arms that held her gently, lovingly. She snuggled into his body.

Darkness surrounded her. The arms that held her lowered her, but she didn't want to leave their comfort – their love. Her body was lowered onto the soft mattress. But the arms didn't let her go. She didn't want them to. She pressed herself against the firm chest and clung on with her good arm.

'It is that you are safe now, Tilly. Let go and lie back. I will send one of the women to help you get into bed.'

'Naw. Don't go. Don't leave me again, Arthur.'

'Arthur is with you, I am sure of that. Dream of him and he will come and be by your side as he is always for being.'

'But ... I want ...'

'There, there.' She felt her arm being removed from around his neck. She tried not to let that happen, but he was too strong for her. The blanket came over her, but she wasn't cold. She was warm. Warm in a beautiful way. Warm in the arms of her Arthur.

'Don't go.'

'Och, you'll be all right. It is the drink that we gave you. Go to sleep. You're not alone, you only have to call out and we will come running. Sleep now.'

This was whispered in her ear. It had a hypnotising effect on her and she let herself drift off.

A movement woke her. She didn't know how long had passed, but all was quiet outside. Tilly shifted her body as she felt someone getting into her bed. *Arthur?*

His hand lifted her skirts and found her thigh. 'Oh, Arthur.'

'Shush.'

She tried to snuggle into him but all he seemed to want to do was to take off her pantaloons. She felt her suspender give with a snap. She could hardly breathe, she so wanted him. Her hand explored and she found he was naked. He was kneeling over her now. She caressed him, lowering her hand till she held the hardness of him. He felt different. But then, it had been such a long time.

In answer to his whisper to her to help him with her pantaloons, she arched her back. Opening her eyes, everything was pitch black, but she could see his form. 'Oh, Arthur, Arthur . . .'

'Shush.'

Arching towards him, she accepted him entering her. A moan came from her as she filled with the pleasure of him giving himself to her. But then Arthur did something he'd never done before. He clamped his hand over her mouth. His movements became rough, deep and hard. She couldn't breathe. Struggling, she tried to free herself. Awareness hit her as if someone had thrown a bucket of water over her. And she knew. This was not her Arthur.

When at last she heard the deep-throated sigh and felt him pulsating inside her, Tilly took advantage of the moment she knew would weaken him and twisted her body from under him. Gasping in a deep breath, she went to scream, but he moved quickly and clamped her mouth again.

But though it didn't come from her a scream did fill the air. Whoever her assailant was let go of her. A light lit the wagon, blinding Tilly. Finding herself unable to move, Tilly could only listen to the sound of a woman wailing out her distress. It was then that she felt an excruciating pressure on her neck. The world spun around her. She was sinking into a deep black hole. As it encased her, she welcomed the peace it promised.

FOURTEEN

Tilly didn't know how many hours later it was when she woke. Her head ached, her arm throbbed with pain, and it felt to her that a thick fog had descended. Memory seeped into her, catapulting her into a sitting position. Nothing around her was familiar to her. She was in a bed, but not the one in the gypsy wagon. A nurse stood by her looking down on her. 'You're awake then?'

'Where am I?'

'You're in Blackpool Victoria Hospital, love. One of our first patients.'

'What? How ...?'

'Rest back. Don't try to move around, you've had a nasty fall. Luckily, the gypsies found you and were able to put your shoulder back in place. They brought you here and an elderly woman with them paid your fees, more than enough for us to get you better.'

'But ...' Tilly couldn't make sense of this. She remembered nothing more than someone raping her. She lay back, trying to sort out her thoughts. Her mind gave her Arthur visiting her and ... No. It hadn't been Arthur, but who then? Phileas? Jeremiah? No, she was certain it wouldn't be Jeremiah.

Her confused, uncertain thoughts increased the ache in her head till it was a blinding pain that she cried out against.

The nurse brushed her hand over Tilly's brow. 'You're burning up. Rest now, I'll be back in a moment.'

Tilly found she could do nothing other than rest; her body seemed as though it was a great weight and she found it difficult to breathe. She was being crushed! She could no longer stay awake, and sleep dragged her into a deep black hole.

As if from a great distance voices – anxious voices – spoke words Tilly couldn't grasp. She had the strangest feeling that she was floating, leaving her body behind. Glancing down, she saw herself lying still, unblinking, staring up at the ceiling. Panic gripped her. Reaching towards her body, she shouted, 'No, I don't want to die!'

'You're not dying. Not now, love. Eeh, you've been through the mill this last week, though. You've had pneumonia. By, we thought we'd lost you a few times, but the crisis has passed. You're going to be all right now, lass.'

'I'm so hot. Where am I?'

'You're in the isolation ward. You feel hot because we've had steam concentrated on you. We had to keep a humid atmosphere to help you to breathe. We're disconnecting it all now, though, and I'll open a window. Then I'll bath you and change your bed. You can't go back to the main ward yet, but thank the Lord, you're on the mend. By, you gave us a few scares, lass.'

By the time the nurse had washed her down, Tilly's mind had begun to clear. 'Has anyone been to see me, or asked after me?'

'Naw, love. We don't even knaw who you are yet. The gypsy man and woman who brought you in said you were a stranger to them.'

'But I – I don't understand, they did knaw me. They took me in when I lost me home … Oh, God! Me young 'uns. Nurse, they have me young 'uns. I have to get out of here.'

'Oh naw, you're not going anywhere. And that's a strange tale you're telling. You mean, they've got your children? Why would they say they didn't knaw you?'

'I don't knaw. Oh, Nurse, help me, please help me … I want me babbies.'

'Look, calm down or you'll have a relapse. Let's sort this out. You might be having confused thoughts, which isn't surprising given how unwell you've been. As I say, we nearly lost you a couple of times. Your body had no resistance to the infection as there was nowt of you. You were suffering starvation and that made you too weak to fight. Besides, the injury to your shoulder was very severe and had to be operated on. For most of the three weeks you've been with us, you haven't known what day it is as we have kept you asleep.'

'Three weeks! Naw! I don't understand.'

'Oh, aye, you've been with us for three weeks, love. Gypsies brought you in and paid enough money for your treatment; they said they'd found you.'

'But they didn't. I …' As her head cleared completely and all came back to her, Tilly explained to the nurse what had happened. 'Then, that night they had a party and …' Although it embarrassed her to tell of how she had been raped, she let it all out.

'Well, I've never heard the like. And they have your twin girls, you say?'

'Aye, they do. Oh, Nurse, what am I to do? I have to get out of here and go to them and find out why they denied knowing me and to get me girls back.'

'You're not strong enough to. And I reckon as this is sommat as the police should deal with. I'll ask me matron what I should do. In the meantime, your best bet is to concentrate on getting better, lass. You're still very poorly, and no good to your daughters as you're not yet able to care for them, and by the sounds of it, have nowhere to house them either.'

The talking Tilly had done and her anxiety for Babs and Beth had exhausted her. Closing her eyes, she tried to tell herself that everything would be all right. That Lilly Lee had just done the best she could and was probably afraid to say that she knew Tilly. *Yes, that's it! Lilly couldn't say she knew me, and that she had me Babs and Beth, as she'd be afraid they'd be taken from her care. She's just waiting for me to come back, that's all.*

With this thought, Tilly drifted back into a deep sleep.

She didn't know how long it was before she was woken, but a gentle hand on her good shoulder and the voice of the nurse calling her name brought her out of her slumber. Opening her eyes, Tilly looked into the face of a policeman. He had a grave expression and was shaking his head. Tilly glanced over at the nurse and saw that she too looked grim. 'What? What's happened? My girls . . . Oh, God!'

'I'm sorry, lass.' The policeman, a rounded man whose buckled belt seemed to make him a man of two halves, the top half bulging, the bottom half slim, continued to shake his head. 'The gypsies have long gone. Their encampment is bare.'

159

'Naw! It can't be. What about Babs and Beth? Naw, naw ...'

'Is that the name of your children?'

'Yes. I mean ... well, their real names are Barbara and Elizabeth, but ... Oh, God! Please tell me the gypsies haven't stolen them.'

'Well, we will have to make enquiries. Can you prove that you did have daughters? And how did you come to be with the gypsies in the first place? This is all a bit of a tale, to be truthful with you.'

Tilly, though distraught, realised that she would have to tell the whole story to the policeman. *He must believe me! He must!*

When she had finished the policeman shook his head again. 'Well, that's sad, lass. And aye, I remember the poor bloke who fell from the tower. I attended the incident. I'm very sorry for your loss. And it seems it were a bad day the day you met the gypsy woman. Your troubles increased with getting into their clutches. You did well to try to provide for yourself, and they took all you gained. They're a bad lot. Well, some of them are; most are hard-working and don't cause any trouble. But the two you've named, Phileas and Jonas Gaskin, are notorious and have been in front of the magistrate a few times.'

'Can you find them? Please, go after them and bring me girls back to me, please.'

'That's not simple. According to the farmer who let them have the land, they've been gone these three weeks or more. He heard nowt of them going. He just looked out of his window one morning and saw that they were gone. But he's used to that. He says they come and go as if by magic. But then when he went to feed his pigs that day, two of them were gone as well and a load of his animal feed from his barn, besides a churn of milk that was to be collected that morning. Yet he never heard owt of them in his yard. They're like ghosts when they want to be. They have a way of killing animals without the animal making a sound. They're canny. And that is why so many folk are afraid of them.'

'But they may not have got far.'

'Oh, the farmer says they will have. He says they could have gone by midnight that day and made it to Liverpool by midday the next day; they'd be long over the water to Ireland by now, as he reckons as that's where they go when they leave his. He was surprised, as it's not usually until a bit later in the year. But he reckons as they won't come back. They've never stolen from him afore, and have allus been an asset, with the help they give him, and their way of being able to cure sick animals, and them shoeing his horses for nowt. But now they've stolen from him, that'll be it. They'd never do that if they intended on returning.'

Tilly had a sinking feeling that the policeman was going to do nothing. *Babs and Beth, me babbies gone! Naw, I can't bear it.* A sound filled the room. Her pain cut into her, taking all knowledge from her except the loss of her young 'uns. 'Why, Why?' Her mouth gaped open, spittle ran down her chin. Her eyes leaked tears she didn't know she was shedding. 'Why?'

'Eeh, lass, its naw good taking on. I wish it were different but gypsies are known for taking young 'uns. We get many a message from other police forces asking us to check any gypsies that come into the area. It's a mystery to us as to why, as they seem to have a large brood themselves. It must be a money-making thing: they must take them abroad and sell them to childless couples. But it's unusual for them to take

161

any as old as yours are as they can speak up for themselves and ask questions. I'm at a loss to tell the truth.'

Tilly gasped as she thought of Jasmine and her childless state and how much fuss she'd made of the girls. She had been almost possessive of them during the party, and hadn't she dressed them up to look beautiful, and in gypsy clothing too? *Oh, God, make this all go away. Make it so that it never happened.*

By the time Tilly left the hospital, three weeks later, she was a shadow of her former self. Most of the time she'd lived in a silent world not communicating with the nurses or the other patients. Her mind had blocked out the horror of losing all her family as it was impossible for her to comprehend, as was the idea that she had been such a different, happy person almost seven months ago. That all she had should have been taken from her – her lovely husband, her children, her best friend, Liz, and her new friend, Martha.

The nurse who'd cared for her the whole time she was in the hospital had tried to help her, but Tilly couldn't let her. If she did, it would mean facing it all and making it real. Then this morning she'd come and told Tilly that though she wasn't as well as she should be, they were discharging her as the money left for her care had all gone.

In a daze, Tilly had dressed in the day frock she'd had on when she'd been brought in. It had been washed, as had her underwear, but all hung on her thin body as if they belonged to a much bigger woman. Donning her shawl, she'd found that she'd needed it as although the springtime sun had shone through the hospital windows, its weak rays hadn't really taken the chill off this April morning.

And now as she stood inside the warm kitchen of the big house where Florrie had worked, Tilly was facing having lost Florrie as well.

'Eeh, lass, look at you. Me and Florrie wondered what had happened to you. Florrie's ma took ill suddenly, and she had to go home to care for her. She went to your street to find you, to tell you before she left, but you'd moved out and no one knew where you'd gone. What happened to you?'

Wearily, Tilly told Cook all that had transpired.

'By, lass, that's terrible. Here, dry your eyes. I've never heard the like. What're you going to do?'

'I don't knaw. I came here to see if you and Florrie could help as I've naw one to turn to.'

'If only you'd come a week back, we were struggling to fill Florrie's position, but we have now. It would have been ideal for you, a roof over your head, and a chance to save some money. But, lass, all I can do for you now is to give you some provisions and a bit of money. I wish I could do more. Where're you going to live?'

'I don't knaw. I've nowhere and no one. Not even ... Anyroad, I'll sort sommat.'

As Tilly left the kindly Cook, she could hardly carry the bag of provisions and the huge coat Cook had laden her with. Her legs ached from her walk to the house, and pain wracked her body. After she'd gone a little way, she felt too weary to continue without a rest, so crossed the dunes and sat on the edge of them where they met the beach. By the sun's position above the sea she knew it was late afternoon. The days were drawing out now as spring would soon give way to summer, so it wouldn't get dark for a couple of hours yet. Feeling chilled, she lay back and covered herself with the coat, thinking that she'd rest a while.

When she woke, darkness had fallen. The swish of the waves breaking on the sand sounded very near, alerting her as to the tide coming in. Shivering, she stood. She so needed to relieve herself. Looking around, she saw that the beach was deserted and though hardly strong enough to hold the weight of her skirts, she squatted where she was.

No fear entered Tilly at being alone. She seemed unable to feel anything about anything anymore. Even the pain of not knowing where her children were had dulled at this moment. *It's as if I've been cut adrift by the world and everyone I knew in it. Tomorrow, I'll have to go to the poorhouse and hope they take me in.*

FIFTEEN

Gathering her things, Tilly clambered back over the dunes. Blackpool was ahead of her. Lights from all the houses and guest houses twinkled in the darkness, making it a sight of wonderment. Judging by how many she could see, she knew it couldn't be late. She'd walk there and hope to find a boarding house for the night. Cook had given her enough for that. Then, when she was in her room she would eat the sandwiches Cook had made for her.

She hadn't reached Blackpool before the clip-clop of horse's hooves and a familiar voice calling, 'Whoa, boy!' froze her to the spot.

'Tilly, will you jump up on me cart now?'

'Jeremiah!' Relief flooded her as she had thought that it was Phileas. Almost as she registered who it was, he was by her side. 'Awe, me Tilly. I've been waiting for you this good while.'

'What? How? And where's me young 'uns?'

Jeremiah's height blocked out the lights of Blackpool, making her world dark once more. A shudder rippled through her.

'Is it that you're cold, me Tilly?'

'I'm not your Tilly. What have you done with me girls? Where did you all go?'

'Get up into me trap, Tilly. Let me take you to me wagon, it is parked in Thornton. There you will be safe; I can get you warm and feed you. I'll tell you everything when we arrive.'

'But they said you'd all gone. That'd you'd taken me babbies with you.' Tilly's voice shook with her tears. Jeremiah gently soothed her. ''Tis that is what happened, but me conscience wouldn't let me go along with it. I could not do anything about your little girls, but I left the clan and made me way back here to find you and protect you.'

'But how did you find me? How did you knaw I would be walking along here?'

'I've been watching the hospital. Isn't it that I've walked the length of Whitegate Drive, passing the doors of the hospital, waiting for the moment you walked out of there? Then when you did, I was for knowing that I couldn't approach you in the daylight in case you screamed the place down, so I kept me distance. I saw your struggle to get to the house in St Anne's but daren't fetch my horse from where I'd tethered him, as I feared I would be for losing sight of you. Then I watched you rest . . .'

Tilly gasped at this, thinking of her action in relieving herself, but what he said next made it seem unlikely that he was there at that time.

'I saw you fall asleep and took that chance to fetch me horse. I passed you not many minutes ago, but went by, as I was to turn around. It is that I mean you no harm, Tilly, I only want to help you. I cannot get you out of my mind and have prayed to the Good Lord night and day for you to get well.'

Tilly trusted Jeremiah. He would help her, she was sure of it. She took the hand he'd extended to her.

'Oh, Tilly, you've gladdened me heart. I'll be for making everything right, I promise.'

'You'll get me young 'uns back for me, won't you, Jeremiah?'

'As God is me witness, it is that I cannot promise you that but I will do what I can while I have breath in me body.'

What Lilly Lee had said about Jeremiah not having long in this world visited Tilly as he said this. Strangely it awoke her, for the first time, to how he struggled when doing a task, as if exertion tired him. 'Are you unwell, Jeremiah?'

There was no answer forthcoming to this as he helped her to sit in the trap and tucked a blanket around her.

'Hold on to the side. I'll get Stormy up to the best pace I can as we've a fair way to travel.'

Clutching her bag between her legs and with the coat slung over her shoulders, Tilly held on for dear life as the trap swayed from side to side.

Blackpool promenade was alive, even at this time of night, as couples walked hand in hand and carriages carried groups to their destinations. Boarding houses glittered as every window was lit with gas mantles, and the electric lighting along the street gave a hazy glow to all around her. Tilly still found this a magical sight and couldn't comprehend how electricity could be used to light the streets.

On the other side of the promenade, the sea had whipped up a frenzy now the tide was in and she could hear the waves crashing onto the beach.

The noise of street vendors could be heard above the sound as they extolled the virtues of what they had to sell. 'Hot spuds'll warm your bellies.' 'Toffee apple for the lady, sir? None finer.' 'Fried fish at Ma Fielding's, across the road, madam. The best in the country, caught fresh this morning.' And on and on it went, bringing back to Tilly all she loved about Blackpool. That is until they reached North Shore, then the joy that had begun to seep into her left her as she looked at the tower, now finished, and awaiting its opening day next month. Part of her longed to see what the finished building looked like inside, but the biggest part of her knew she would always hate it. It would forever be a painful reminder of how her life had changed.

By the time they reached Bispham all around them had quietened down. Tilly called out to Jeremiah, 'Stop, please stop. I can't go on.' Her arms ached from clinging on and her body was cold to the bones of her.

Once Jeremiah had pulled up, opposite Red Bank Road, the hub of Bispham village, with its shops and cafés, he tethered Stormy to the rail, where the horse started to chomp on the grass.

'It is sorry I am, Tilly, for causing you distress, but it is that I'm trying to get you to the warmth of me wagon.'

'I knaw, but I can't go on, not at that pace I can't.'

Here the lighting was still by gas and only a small area was dimly lit. Jeremiah's shadow crossed her as he climbed aboard the trap. 'Let me take hold of you and help you down. That's fine now.' As she climbed down, his arms enclosed her and the memory came to her of when that had happened before, and how like Arthur's his hug had been. The same sensation took her now as she leant into his body. 'I'm after trying to warm you, Tilly. Please don't be for mistaking me actions as I'm an honourable man, not like that cowardly, take all he can get Phileas.'

'I – I didn't want him to do what he did, Jeremiah. I didn't knaw it was him. Not at first, I was in a stupor. I thought it was me Arthur come to me.'

'I am for knowing that. I tried to convince Lilly Lee that it was Phileas who had sinned, and it was a surprise to me that she'd not have any of it, as she was the one who'd told me you were sinned against, not a sinner. It is that I am for knowing that now. But you have a powerful way of drawing a man's passion without trying. Even from me.'

Tilly drew back from him. 'I trust you, Jeremiah. I shouldn't have cuddled into you, but I'm in need of some comfort.'

'And you will find it in me arms, Tilly. I can control that which you do to me emotions, even though it is a powerful fire burning in me. But I won't lust after you. I will love you and be taking care of you. If later you consent to being me wife, then I will show you me true feelings.'

'Oh, Jeremiah. Ta. Ta ever so much. I've not felt safe around any man since me Arthur died. Even me best friend's man tried it on with me and lost me that friendship. Why? Why do men want to do just one thing with me?'

'It is something you were born with, a passion that shines from you, and your body is shaped for loving and exciting men. You are naive to it all, and so, wrong is done to you, but I will shield you.'

With this she found herself in the circle of his arms once more. Never since Arthur had held her had she known a feeling like she felt at being so close to Jeremiah. The strength of his body matched that of Arthur's, as did his height, so her head rested naturally on his chest. His heart beat the same rhythm Arthur's had, and the smell of his clean body and fresh clothes were similar to Arthur's. Tilly didn't ever want to leave this place she'd found – this solace, this help.

'We will have to make our way, Tilly. We still have all of two miles to go. I'll lay those sacks that I have at the back of the trap over the floor, and you can be lying yourself on them. Then I will cover you over. I'll be travelling very gently so you can sleep.'

When Tilly next woke it was to hear birds in the dawn chorus. Her body was warm and cosy and she didn't want to move. Memories came back to her, some seared her heart, but with the realisation that she was safe, a little peace settled in her.

Jeremiah must have lifted her from the trap and lain her on his bed, without waking her as she had no memory of getting into the bed herself. With this thought came the knowledge that he must have taken her frock off as she was only wearing her undergarments. How she could have slept on through that she did not know, but she had been exhausted.

The sound of coughing caused Tilly to sit up. Rasping, hacking coughs tore at her heart as she realised that it was Jeremiah suffering the bout. Once again she asked herself if he was ill and what it was that ailed him. But these weren't her only thoughts as she felt a deep concern for him, deeper than what would be warranted in the circumstances of hers and Jeremiah's short acquaintance.

Calling out to him made the coughing stop. A spitting sound gave her knowledge that the cough hadn't been a throaty one, but a clearing of Jeremiah's lungs. A fear trickled through her and she knew, she didn't want to lose him. Didn't want him to be ill.

His voice came to her. 'It's sorry I am to have woken you, Tilly.'

'Where are you, Jeremiah? I cannot see much.'

'I'm on the floor. I've no shelter outside so stayed in here with you. Wait a moment while I lift myself. I'll stoke the fire up, and get some hot water on the go. You'll be needing a wash and a hot drink.'

'Knaw. I'll do that. You climb up onto this bed and get comfortable. I can't think of you lying on the hard floor. And that cough . . . Oh, Jeremiah, it doesn't sound good.'

'Don't be worrying. It is the legacy of a fire. We travelled the road past a farm one day, only to see it was alight. I went in to help the farmer and his wife and inhaled a lot of smoke. It has coated me lungs. Sure, it's only the early hours of the morning that it affects me.'

Tilly knew this wasn't so, as she'd noticed how short of breath Jeremiah had become earlier. Her worry deepened.

'The main thing is for being that I got the farmer and his wife and family out of the burning house. The Good Lord was for guiding me to them. And but for this cough, I'm fine so I am.'

Tilly was out of bed and feeling for her frock. 'You're not, and you knaw it an' all. Now, do as I say, only light the lamp first as I'm afraid of tripping over you.'

Once the light flooded the wagon, and Jeremiah was sat on the bed, Tilly could see the space she was in wasn't dissimilar to the wagon Lilly Lee had given to her, only this interior was much more lavish with the cupboards and drawers being elaborately carved and inlaid with patterns; the floor was covered by a ruby-red carpet that softened her tread and the walls and ceiling were lined with pleated, cream-coloured silk. The effect was stunning, and so unexpected for the home of a man.

'I can see that it is surprised that you are, Tilly. Sure, the look of me home surprises everyone, but it wasn't of my making. I was left it by an old aunt who was a gypsy princess, and I kept it as it was in memory of her. It is royal blood that I am from – the Romany gypsies. But I am the last of me clan and was given to the Irish when I was a youngster. They are not of the same thinking as me.'

Tilly had witnessed how they held Jeremiah's insights with a certain disdain. As she busied herself putting a log from the bucket onto the stove, closing the lid and pulling out the damper, she asked, 'Is it true that you can see things, Jeremiah, things that have happened when you weren't there, and things that might happen in the future?'

'It is. And not all that I see pleases me, or is comfortable to live with.'

'When you first met me, what did you see that led you to say I was a sinner? By, you gave me the creeps.'

'I saw that you had gone against the vows of marriage . . .'

'I didn't. By, I'd have never hurt me Arthur, nor did I feel the need to. He was everything to me.'

'It may not have been your own marriage vows, but you tainted others'.'

'Aye, well, as it turned out, I didn't do that either. What I did helped the wife to live a much happier life in the end, and I were in a desperate situation, but I'll tell you about it another time. What do you see for me now? Am I to get me lasses back?'

Jeremiah was silent. Tilly knew the answer wasn't going to be to her liking. Into the silence came the shrill whistle of the kettle. The sound made Tilly's blood run cold.

'The nettle leaves are dried out and in the tin above your head, Tilly. Drop six of them into the kettle and let them steep a while.'

'Nettles?'

'Aye, they are for making the finest tea.'

Tilly did as he said, curious to taste this new idea of a pot of tea. A brew to her was made of the black tea leaves bought from the corner shop in a small oblong box with 'India Tea' written on it, not nettle leaves. But she said no more about it, not wanting to offend Jeremiah.

'You didn't answer me question. Eeh, you're a dark horse, Jeremiah. You see sommat, don't you? You knaw what's going to be the outcome. I want to knaw. The not knawing is driving me mad.'

'I'll be for telling you once we have our brew, but you prepare yourself, Tilly, as what I have to say won't be what you want to hear.'

She was sitting next to him when he next spoke. Her hands shook as she clasped the enamel mug.

'It isn't that I see an outcome, Tilly. I am for knowing where the clan have gone.'

'Then take me there. Please, Jeremiah.'

'Jasmine and her husband left the clan that night. Lilly Lee thought it to be a just punishment on you that Jasmine should take your children.'

173

'But I didn't do owt!'

'It is what it is. And I'm for not knowing where Jasmine would go. She too is a Romany. I can only be assuring you that she will love your girls and give to them what you cannot. Try to be happy that they are being well cared for and cherished. Where would they be with you? In the poorhouse? Oh, Tilly, Tilly, don't cry.'

His arms came around her once more, and Tilly went willingly into them, wanting the love she sensed he had for her – the only love shown to her from anyone other than her children for a long time.

The tears came in a deluge, but they marked a change in Tilly. She would never give up on having her children with her again, but she knew that finding them at this moment was an impossible task. She could only hope that they remembered her, and that they would seek her out once they grew up and were able to make their own decisions. She would hang on to that hope.

'There, it is that you are calmer now. Acceptance is for being the only way, my Tilly. I feel that it is that you are being punished for something you did, but I also see that one day everything will be good for you and you will find happiness in the future.'

'Eeh, it's easy for you to be so vague and make it sound as though you have the all-seeing eye. I'll never be happy until I have me babbies with me.'

'You will. I promise you. Time will heal and send you someone to protect you.'

Not wanting to go into this further, Tilly asked about her immediate future. 'What's to happen to me? I've to sort sommat out. Without me little ones to care for, I can get a job, but I need a home until I can save enough to get meself housed.'

'Sure, you have a home with me, and there'll be no thinking of getting a job. It is that you can make your baskets. Didn't I make sure I had all of your materials aboard me wagon? And then you can sell them. I will bring in money too. I'll shoe horses as we travel and mend broken farm machinery. There's all manner of ways to keep ourselves, but first, I need to ask you, Tilly. Will you become me wife?'

'Oh, Jeremiah. It isn't a year since I was widowed. I have love in me for you. But the way of life you describe isn't what I'm used to. I don't knaw if I can be happy travelling. Besides, if I leave Blackpool, how will me babbies ever find me?'

'Let us try living together for a while. It's a promise that I won't ask anything of you until we're wed, and if that never happens, then I'll be an unhappy man, but will know it is that I have done right by you.'

'You mean you will stay here until I can sort sommat and let me live here with you?'

'Aye. I will do that.'

At this reply, Tilly knew the love Jeremiah had for her was a true love. A love that was willing to give her freedom and a love that she so badly needed – wanted. 'Well, we can only give it a try. Ta, Jeremiah.' With this, Tilly stifled a yawn.

'It is that you are exhausted. Sure, you only came out of the hospital yesterday. Lie down, my Tilly. Rest awhile. I will lie beside you, but you have nothing to worry over.'

It felt good to snuggle into Jeremiah and to know that nothing was demanded of her. Sleep came within a few minutes, as did her swirling, disturbing dreams, taking her to places she didn't want to go – the backyard of the shop and seeing Joe's body sprawled out in front of her, and a noose swinging above it.

Waking up in a sweat, Tilly blinked at the light of day shining through the wagon door. The curtains were tied back, letting in the cold as well as the light. The sound of Jeremiah whistling a jolly tune lightened her frightened heart and settled her thoughts. *Dreams will always haunt me, but I am safe . . . safe.*

The feeling was alien to her, but felt good. Jumping off the bed, Tilly went to the door and looked out.

'So, it is that my sleeping beauty is awake. And here I am preparing supper.'

'Supper! Eeh, how long have I been sleeping?'

'All day. But your body must have been in need of it, so don't distress yourself.'

'I'll get my coat on and come and sit by the fire. By, it's enough to chill your lugs off.'

'What? Oh, Tilly, it is that you have some funny sayings.'

The companionship she found as she sat with Jeremiah was different to any Tilly had ever known. Even Arthur hadn't always given her his attention when they had sat together in the evening, her mending the twins' clothes and him smoking his pipe and nodding off at the same time.

Though the memory gave Tilly pain, she was soon coping again as she listened to Jeremiah's tales of his travels. Listening gave her a kind of peace concerning Babs and Beth, as what he described sounded an idyllic life. One of hard work, but also of camaraderie and protection, and in her heart she had liked Jasmine, and knew that she would love the girls. Sighing with the weight of her loss, Tilly tried hard to come to terms with how life was going to be without her lovely babbies. Tears flowed from her, as she knew they always would, but hopelessness was a sorry state that couldn't be sustained, and she was to get on with life as best she could.

As she took the plate Jeremiah handed her and inhaled the delicious aromas of spit-roasted rabbit and hot, blackened baked potato, she told him, 'Tomorrow, Jeremiah, I'll begin to make some baskets so that I can help to bring in some money, then when I'm stronger, I'll walk the streets selling them, but look for a job at the same time.'

'We'll see. For sure there is no rush.'

Tilly was inclined to agree with him. Here with Jeremiah, she had no worries about tomorrow. Not for her own welfare; he, she knew, would always take care of her. A peaceful feeling nudged the knot of hurt. If only she could have her babbies with her . . . *Naw, I have to stop thinking of the impossible, or I'll go mad.*

'Jeremiah, have you any of that gin you gave to me. I like how it stops me thinking sad thoughts.'

'Aye, I have so, and I like a drop meself. I'll have to teach you to make it, if you stay with me, for it is a powerful medicine if used in moderation. It can be the helping of you, or the ruination, so take care how you think of it.'

As she gulped down a half-mug, Tilly knew gin was to be her salvation and learning to make it would be her mission. She loved how it lightened her mood and made everything in her world come right.

★   ★   ★

With her head pounding, Tilly rose early the next morning and made for the pail that hung from the side of the wagon. Dunking the scoop, she brought it dripping with water to her mouth and drank thirstily.

'So, you're feeling the wrath of overindulging then, Tilly? Isn't it that I cautioned you to take it easy on the gin?'

'I'm sorry, Jeremiah.' Looking up at him standing in the doorway of the wagon, with the winter sun lighting his silhouette, Tilly felt a pang of guilt as memory assailed her. She'd sought more than he wanted to give her, and had embarrassed herself, crying to him to make love to her.

Shame filled her and made her cheeks tingle.

As he climbed down the steps she felt a little wary as she knew he wanted to confront her.

'Tilly, what you wanted, I couldn't give. I love you. I'm not an animal to feast on.'

'Forgive me, Jeremiah. I – I, well, it was the gin.'

'And that is your downfall, Tilly. You always have someone, or something, to blame for your sins. You never take responsibility. You drank the gin, knowing the effect it has on you.'

'You're right. I'll not touch a drop again.' But even as she said this, Tilly felt an urge to drink the fiery liquid this very minute. To seek the solace it offered – the blotting out of all the pain.

'Come here.'

Snuggled up to him, Tilly found forgiveness. Some of her shame left her, but the urge for more gin didn't.

PART THREE

HOPE DIES BUT
IS REBORN

1894–1895

SIXTEEN

The three months they'd been together had passed in companionship, and their feelings for each other had deepened. They'd worked hard – Jeremiah having laboured for the farmer whose land they were on, and Tilly making and selling her baskets for an ever-increasing market as word got around about the quality of her wares and how she delivered on time.

Every hour Tilly was haunted by her last images of Babs and Beth dancing with Pearl, laughing and giggling, swirling around to the music, their lovely gypsy frocks floating around them, and this increased the pain and sadness in her, but she fought it, throwing herself into her work and into looking after Jeremiah.

'Will we cook outside tonight?' Jeremiah broke into her thoughts. 'I've been making a brazier from an old oil drum Farmer Smith has given me. I'll bring it back with me and get it lit early.'

'Eeh, that'd be grand, not to have the wagon filled with the smell of rabbit stew. I'll pick sommat up at the butcher's for a treat. I'll see what he's got going.' Tilly smiled to herself as she continued washing her face and began to brush out her hair. How was it she'd lived with a man at such close quarters and found it possible to love him enough to respect his wishes of not being intimate? Every night she'd wanted him to take her to him as he'd rolled out the straw mattress he'd made from hessian sacks and lain on the floor next to the bed.

Jeremiah, she'd long discovered, was like no other man she'd ever met. His ways were determined by his deep faith in God, and his need not to sin. His kindness shone from him, as did his love for her. A major part of that love was respect for her, something she'd never experienced, not even from Arthur.

Not ever thinking that she would compare Arthur unfavourably to another living soul, Tilly had to admit to herself that Arthur had always taken what he wanted from her, whenever he wanted to. Oh, she'd been willing, but now she could see clearly that whether she was feeling up to making love or not, his demands would have had to be seen to. Always, he satisfied her, but now, with him gone this last twenty-one months, and having the experience of the ways of Jeremiah, Tilly knew that her life had been like any other woman's – used as a skivvy, taken at the whim of her man, and having her own needs crushed to provide for his. For hadn't Arthur stopped her from pursuing her basket making as no more than a hobby, often deriding her work even? He would say that she did make some useful items, and he was glad it kept her happy, but as for her thinking of selling any of her work, no. 'Besides,' he'd say, 'no lass of mine is going to go out to work. I'd be laughed at. I'm the breadwinner and you should be satisfied with what I put on the table.' Oh, she had been, but that hadn't stopped her wanting to add to it to make their lives even better – nor had it quelled the longing in her to show off her talents.

Now she didn't come up against any such objections. Jeremiah praised her work, was in awe of it even, and often helped her to cut the thick cane into lengths she could work with. And he welcomed what she brought in from her labours. But then, that was the way of the gypsies. All the women were expected to work and to help to provide for the family. It was one of their customs that Tilly fully agreed with.

Shaking herself out of these thoughts and feeling disloyal, Tilly brought the brush through her hair, not taking heed of the knots that had formed as she'd slept her usual, restless sleep. The pain of ripping through the tangles was a welcome distraction to the churning of her mind.

'Here, let me, it is that I like to do that for you.' Taking the lovely mother-of-pearl hairbrush from her hands, Jeremiah looked deep into her eyes. The sun blazing through the open curtain that was their doorway shone onto him, lighting the goodness that showed in his face.

His actions were soothing as he stroked the brush through her long tresses, taking the strain off by holding firm when he came to a knot so that she didn't feel anything other than a slight tug.

'You have beautiful hair, me Tilly. See how it now reaches your waist. Sure, it is as a woman should never cut her locks, it isn't natural to do so.'

'I've never worn mine this long afore, and I don't knaw as I can keep it so if the weather keeps getting warmer, it makes me sweat.'

'You should braid it and pin it on the top of your head, then tie a scarf around from the front. The gypsy women are always for wearing a scarf to keep the sun from burning them and to protect their beautiful hair from drying out.'

Tilly sighed. She knew Jeremiah wanted her to be like his people, but she couldn't be. She was a Northern lass, brought up in ordinary ways which were alien to his ways. She knew too that he yearned to get on the road and to travel from place to place; he talked often of wanting to be in the south for the fruit picking by the autumn, and on the way to attend the many fairs the gypsies held; some he said were where they traded their horses and held events of skill and bravery. But Tilly didn't want to leave Blackpool. Even being in Thornton was too far out for her.

Turning her towards him, Jeremiah once more looked into her eyes. 'That sigh was full of sadness, my Tilly. How can I make you happy?'

'You do. You're a wonderful friend to me.'

'But you know that it is that I want to be more than a friend. I want you, my Tilly.'

He surprised her then by lifting her chin and after a moment bringing his lips to hers. Though she tried not to, Tilly found that everything she was responded to his kiss, causing him to pull away. 'Oh, Tilly, it is that we are made for one another and will find the completion of us in coming together, but I have to know that you will be happy living my life with me. I cannot change. I cannot live the life of the Englishman, in a box made of bricks – I would be stifled. My heart is on the road. In me mind I'm travelling along with the wind in my face, humming to the rhythm of the clip-clopping of Stormy's hooves, with excitement building in me heart at the prospect of the next adventure.'

Tilly knew that Jeremiah was different from every other man she'd ever known, that he'd made concessions for her and sacrifices that no other would make, and it came to her that now it was time for her to make some too. 'Eeh, me lad, I want you. I want to be your wife. And as such, I'll follow you wherever you go.'

Jeremiah stared at her. His face, showing his shock, gradually changed to show that his dream had been realised. Tilly was rewarded with a beautiful smile. Jeremiah's eyes filled with tears. 'Me Tilly, me lovely Tilly.'

Once more their lips joined, unleashing the suppressed passion they had for one another. Tilly went willingly with Jeremiah as he gently led her to the bed. 'Sit there a moment, my Tilly, for I have to perform the gypsy ritual of making you mine.' His voice was thick with his need as he turned and opened the drawer.

Trepidation entered Tilly as she saw the glint of the knife he'd removed and how he reached for the gin bottle. Pouring some of the alcohol over the blade, he came towards her. From a cupboard under the bed he took a pristine white cloth embroidered with his initials. Laying this over her arm, he clenched his teeth, then sliced a surface cut into his wrist. Tilly watched the blood seep through the cut. 'Close your eyes, my Tilly.'

For a moment Tilly wanted to snatch her hand away but she didn't. She waited, felt the slice of her own wrist and winced against it, but then felt Jeremiah's arm touch hers and him lift the cloth over them both.

'Open your eyes, my darling. For now it is that you are mine.'

Looking at their joined wrists and the blood seeping through the cloth, two different shades, one very dark and the other a bright red, Tilly felt a surge of joy zing through her veins. 'Tilly, I take you as me wife. Before God I swear to love, protect and care for you, and always be by your side. I vow that I will never take another to me, or look in the direction of another woman with lust in my heart. All that I am is yours.'

Tilly swallowed hard. Jeremiah was staring intently into her eyes. She knew it was her turn to make her vows. 'I – I'll allus love you and honour you. I'll allus be faithful and look after you. All that I am is yours.'

Jeremiah removed the cloth; both cuts had stopped bleeding now. 'Tilly, you are now my wife according to the old Romany tradition. Once we get with more clans, we will have a proper gypsy wedding. The priest will come and there will be much merriment. I love you, Tilly, and know you will bear me fine sons.'

Tilly's heart skipped a beat. She had thought he knew about her not being able to bear more children. *But then, I only told Jasmine and she wouldn't have had time to tell everyone with the shenanigans going on and then the confusion around putting my shoulder back in place. Oh, God!*

'What is it? Why the look of dismay, my darling?'

Tilly knew instinctively that she was to keep this a secret from Jeremiah. That his pride would take a massive blow, and he'd be angry that she hadn't been truthful with him on the many occasions they'd talked of marriage.

'Nowt. Just me thoughts. I'm fine.'

'Come into me arms, my beautiful bride. I cannot take away all of your sadness at the loss of your family, but I can make you happy despite it all.' His eyes veiled over. 'And it is right now that I am wanting to make a start.'

With this, he pulled her closer to him and lowered his lips to hers. Never before had he kissed her with such abandonment, such passion. When his tongue explored her mouth and his hands caressed her breasts, a moan of sheer ecstasy came from her throat.

Frantically, they helped each other out of their clothing, and fell onto the bed. Her cry now was a desperate plea to her husband to take her, to make her his own. When he did, her world exploded time and again as Jeremiah loved her – touched her, kissed her, stroked the heart of her, and brought her to a place where she almost couldn't bear the exquisite sensations she was experiencing. When at last he stiffened and hollered out his own release, he bore down on her, holding her, calling her beautiful. 'My wife, my wife, my own.'

As they lay in each other's arms, they spoke words of love to one another as they rejoiced in the feeling that their souls had been joined, and in the inner peace they'd found with the release of the deep, pent-up emotions and sexual tension that had been between them for so long.

When Jeremiah kissed her the passion rose in them once more. But this time was a gentle giving of love and a discovery as they explored each other's bodies.

As they lay in the peace of the aftermath, Jeremiah traced his finger along the silver marks to the side of her body that had been a legacy of carrying her twins. 'These are your medals, my darling, for it is that your body held your girls and nourished them, and they will always be joined to you. You will see them again, I know.'

Tilly wasn't able to answer him but listened instead as he went on to tell her of his dreams of one day going back to his native Romania, to see if he could find any other Petulengros that he may be related to.

'By, it's good to have a dream. I've had many in the past. I allus wanted me own place to sell me crafts from. There's naw end to what can be made out of cane and wicker, and I'd love to tackle making things like chairs and, well, all manner of things.'

'Aye, with your talent that's what should happen, but as me wife, we won't be in one place long enough.'

'What if we find somewhere that we love, couldn't we stay?'

'It is as you don't know the way of things for the gypsies, Tilly. In a clan we are safe, but on our own many things that happen around us can be put at our door. Only yesterday the farmer hinted that a delivery was light. It is that those you think trust you don't. Rather than think his supplier left him short, he'd be thinking that I had helped myself. It won't be long before that is being turned into hatred of me and he hounds us off his field.'

'Eeh, but that's unfair.'

'I know, but it is a perception that we are all alike and not to be trusted, something that isn't helped by the likes of those of us who do go too far, such as Phileas and Jonas who would rather live their lives preying off others than working hard. But let's not dwell on the whys and wherefores, I don't want you to worry your pretty head. I have a mind that we should both take the day off from our labours. We can ride Stormy to the seaside and take a dip in the water. And have ice cream, then finish the day with a hot tattie, or some fried fish. Let's make it a proper wedding day.'

Tilly laughed. 'I think as you've done that already, me lad.'

'Ha! That's just for being the start, me lovely Tilly, I'm going to be at you day and night, I promise.'

Tilly blushed. She'd welcome him no matter how often he wanted to make love to her. Happiness soared through her. Part of her life was sorted. She had Jeremiah to love and care for her, if only . . . Pulling herself up, she vowed not to spoil the day he had planned with 'if onlys', but to be strong and hang on to the fact that Jeremiah had said that she would get her babbies back one day.

This was easier said than done as they sat on the beach watching families playing on the sand and in the sea on this lovely afternoon that, although only early May, had the warmth of mid-summer. The pain of missing them ground into Tilly.

'Right, me Tilly, it is that I'm going to race you to the water.' Jeremiah stripped off his shirt and trousers as he said this, leaving him standing there in just his long underpants, acceptable bathing gear for men.

Tilly looked down at herself clothed in her long grey skirt and long-sleeved white blouse. 'But I have no bathing suit!'

'Here.' Rummaging in his sack-type bag, Jeremiah brought out some coins. 'There's a stall at the back of the beach that's for selling them; go and buy one and I'll sit down on the sand until you return. Oh, and you could do with buying some

189

cloth for making up some more clothes for yourself; the two outfits you are having already are for seeing better days.'

Feeling like it was Christmas, Tilly ran across the soft sand in her bare feet towards the stalls. This was a place she loved. Tucked up against the sea wall were dozens of stalls selling everything from doughnuts fried on a brazier to fine silks from India. How often she'd longed to have one of these stalls for herself and stock it with her baskets. As she walked from one to the other, she noted that there wasn't one selling basketware. Sighing, she turned her attention to the shouts of the stallholders, whose calls whipped up an excitement in her that took away her disappointment at knowing that her dream may never coming true.

'Ribbons for a pretty lady's hair?'

'The finest wool blankets made from Shetland sheep wool.'

'Silks from exotic lands. Look, lady, t'would make you a fine shawl.'

Tilly giggled at the thought of her wearing a silk shawl. She'd only ever worn a knitted one, and that would do her, but she had to admit the silks in wonderful colours conjured up a picture that excited her: of a land baked by the sun, and beautiful ladies wrapped in these colourful silks, just like the pictures she'd seen as a child.

'Discreet bathing suits for the ladies.'

'How much for one to fit me, sir?'

'Sixpence, please. I have black and navy. Which do you prefer, madam?'

Choosing the black one, Tilly walked on. She smiled at her changed fortunes and how it was that gypsy folk could find the money for anything they needed.

Not sure now about the cloth she would require, she was looking through at what was on offer when a voice calling her name startled her. 'Tilly, Tilly, it is you, ain't it? By, I thought you'd long gone and wouldn't show your face in Blackpool again.'

'Hello, Martha.'

'So, where have you landed then? Not the poorhouse, as they'd not let you roam around, and by the look of you, not on your feet either.'

For the first time, Tilly realised just how shabby she appeared in her worn clothes. She pulled her shawl closer around her. Shame prickled her as she didn't want to tell Martha that she was living with a gypsy, but a defiance helped her. 'I'm surprised you're interested in owt to do with me, Martha.'

'Eeh, lass, that's not the way of it. Disappointed in you I might be, but I've not stopped thinking of you and your girls. Where are they, then?'

Tilly turned her head towards the sea, hoping her bonnet would cover the devastation which must show on her face.

'Well?'

'They're being taken care of by a friend.'

Martha had a sceptical look on her face. 'There were rumours that you were hooked up with them gypsies as camped near St Anne's. You ain't sold them to them, have you?'

Tilly gasped. That this woman who'd been a close friend should think that of her showed how low her name had become amongst her neighbours. 'Th – they stole them!' This came out on a gasp as a sob wrenched her chest.

'What? Good God. Eeh, I've never heard the like. My poor Tilly, I could just give you a hug.'

191

This shook Tilly; she'd expected only the wrath of Martha.

'So, what is taking you so long, Tilly? It is that this is one of your friends, then?'

Tilly swivelled around. Jeremiah stood looking at them both. The concern on his face at her tears turned to anger. 'Not a friend, I take it. What business have you, lady, in making my wife cry?'

'Your wife! Eeh, and here I was ready to take you in, Tilly, on the strength of the lie you just told me. Married to a gypsy, are you? Ha, I didn't think that even you could stoop so low. And you, scum, don't you know the rules of the beach? No undressing when there are ladies present. There's a time for your bathing and a time for the ladies. You're disgusting. Good day.'

The encounter stung Tilly. She watched the stiff back of Martha disappear and lamented losing her as a friend once again. She'd come to love her, but seeing the loathing on Martha's face had stung her deeply.

'Come on, me Tilly. Don't be letting what she said worry you. Sure, it is what I told you of – the treatment of us gypsies by folk who are not always fit to wipe our boots.'

Tilly turned away and walked back with Jeremiah to where they had left their bags, conscious now of the looks of disdain and the tutting coming from folk they passed, and all within hours of becoming a gypsy wife.

Those around them looking at her with derision had been her own folk such a short time ago, but she had crossed the divide, and now had to take their wrath and admit to herself that she was a gypsy. The thought didn't sit easy with her.

Taking her hand, Jeremiah seemed to sense her thoughts. 'You've to stop thinking of my people in the way you were brought up to think of them, Tilly, but hold your head up with pride at being a gypsy yourself now.'

'Oh, Jeremiah, I didn't knaw it would be like this.'

'And is it that you can take it, Tilly?'

Tilly looked up at him, saw his beautiful dark eyes full of concern, and love. She remembered the despair she had felt at being used by one of her own and the rejection by her own people when she had most needed them and she nodded. 'Of course I can and I will be proud to be your wife, but I will never forgive the rest of the clan who stole my babbies, and don't want to be thought of as being of the same as them.'

'I hope one day you will understand. They saw you as a harlot not being fit to look after your girls. They had to abandon you because of the harm caused to one of their own. But they couldn't abandon your children, nor, in their eyes, leave them to be brought up by you ... I know it is a bitter pill to swallow, but that was the judgement. And if you are for looking at it from their eyes, you will see that they didn't do wrong.'

This astonished Tilly. Her anger rose. Giving Jeremiah a look of utter disbelief, she stormed off. *How dare he agree with those who have done such wickedness by me?*

'Come back, Tilly. Tilly.'

Tilly turned and almost burst out laughing to see Jeremiah holding their belongings and hopping towards her with one foot in his trousers and the other leg of the garment flapping in the wind behind him. But then the inevitable happened and he fell flat on his face to a round of gleeful applause from onlookers.

Tilly's anger switched from Jeremiah to the crowd gathering. 'There's nowt for you to stare at, it's not a sideshow!'

Running back towards Jeremiah, she sat down beside him. 'Eeh, I'm sorry, me lad. I shouldn't have run from you.'

'Tilly, Tilly, you had every reason to do so. Wasn't I defending me people in the vile act they carried out? It's me that's sorry. Let's get out of here and go to a quiet beach where we should have gone in the first place. It was daft of me to bring you here.'

Within half an hour they were lying on a small beach at Skiphole Creek, much nearer to where their wagon was on the farm at Thornton. It was as if they were the only people in the world, even though just ahead of them a fisherman sat in his boat which was bobbing up and down on the ripples of the water. Other boats were moored near to them but were unoccupied. Moorhens ducked and dived in and out of the water and a mother swan swam past leading her brood.

The smoke from the fire Jeremiah had lit formed a straight line heavenward.

'This is wonderful, Jeremiah.'

'It is that, and a much better way of spending our wedding day than amongst braying crowds. And we will take that dip. But first it is that I will wade quietly into the water to catch us a fish, while you go behind that bush and get your bathing suit on.'

When she appeared in the knitted garment, with its leggings down to her ankles and sleeves down to her wrists, Tilly felt a little foolish. She'd never imagined wearing such a garment, but at the same time she loved the liberation of it, the freedom from her corsets and many underskirts, and skipped with joy to the water's edge.

Jeremiah raised his finger to his lips. She'd never seen him so still. He looked like a statue of a god. Suddenly, he dived, then rose from the water in magnificent triumph as he held a large pike aloft. The grin on his face Tilly could liken to that of a boy who'd been given a treat. The fish squirmed in his hand, but he managed to land it on the bank.

Drawing his knife, he gutted the fish, turning Tilly's stomach as she watched the life go from the beautiful creature. A moment of violence that brought into stark focus the life she now led.

'Is it squeamish you are?' Jeremiah laughed out loud. 'Sure, all the fish I bring to you, and you buy off the counter, have been through this process. Seeing it is harsh, but we have to live as the Lord himself lived – from the sea, the land and the birds we can pluck from the air.'

Tilly smiled. The feeling had passed, and she knew Jeremiah was right.

'Now, I'll put this to cook, and we'll have our swim.'

'Eeh, Jeremiah, I've never been taught to swim. I thought we would just paddle.'

Turning from the fire where he'd pierced the fish with a stick and had balanced it high above on two prongs, Jeremiah laughed once more. Tilly loved his laugh and how it creased his face and made his eyes twinkle. But her amusement and admiration of him turned to terror as he ran towards her and scooped her up, taking her towards the water's edge. Her screams echoed around the quiet creek, causing the fisherman to up his rod and paddle his boat away.

'Now we're truly alone, my Tilly.'

Once in the water, he dunked her under it. Shivering from the shock of the icy cold water, Tilly gasped for breath once she surfaced. 'Naw, naw, Jeremiah, don't.' But her body went under for a second time to the sound of his laughter.

The next time she surfaced he held her to him. 'There, me sweet Tilly, is it that it's not so cold on the second dunking of you?'

Even though she hit out at him for giving her such a horrible experience, she had to admit to herself that the water had seemed to warm by a few degrees.

Jeremiah laughed as he avoided her blows. 'It is sorry I am, me Tilly, and I won't do it again, I promise. Instead, now it is that you're used to the water, I will help you to float, and then you will learn to swim.'

Floating whilst he supported her felt wonderful to Tilly, and even more so when Jeremiah began to caress her with his free hand, taking hold of her gently between the legs and applying pressure with his thumb so that it dug in through the woollen garment. She found herself catching her breath with the pleasure of the sensations his action caused.

Lifting her without speaking, he lowered his lips to hers. Tilly sank into his kiss, arching her body towards him.

The water slowed their progress as Jeremiah carried her to the grassy edge.

There he made love to her in his own unique, gentle and exquisite way. Then together they relaxed into a love that Tilly had never experienced, not even with Arthur. Because Jeremiah's love was complete, unselfish and totally hers, leaving nothing for himself.

After a few moments, they dried themselves on the rough hessian Jeremiah had tucked into his bag, giggling while they did so. Still flushed from their lovemaking, they sat and juggled the hot fish in the palms of their hands and ate the delicious white flesh.

Tilly thought she had never been happier. She'd learnt lessons today – of the bigotry folk could display, of the happiness to be attained despite pain, and of the deep love a wonderful man could give her. *Oh, my girls, be happy. Ma will come for you one day, but until I do, live your lives in a good way and never forget me.* With this a peace that held a raw pain descended on Tilly.

SEVENTEEN

The journey to Coventry that they set out on a week later had taken them many days. Sometimes they'd camped on a verge, and at others in a field, but each time they had only stayed a few hours for Jeremiah to rest. He was eager to get to the Coventry fair.

'It is where we will meet up with many of my brothers, and you can sell the wares you have already made, and those you can make on the journey,' he'd told her.

The travelling had been tiring, but exciting too. Tilly had loved seeing the different landscapes as the hills around her gave way to flatter land, allowing her to see for miles. She loved, too, delving into the hedgerows for vines, while Jeremiah hunted for a rabbit or a wood pigeon for their dinner.

Sometimes the clattering of their pans hung from the sides of the wagon grated on her nerves as the wheels hit rut after rut in the road, but mostly she liked the gentle tinkling of them when the wagon had a softer sway to it.

'I'm after buying a new horse at the fair, Tilly,' Jeremiah told her. 'Stormy is needing a companion, and a helper. We will be able to tether one to the back of the wagon when travelling, and then be for swapping the animals over when the one pulling us gets tired.'

This seemed much kinder to Tilly as sometimes Stormy looked all in when they finally halted his progress.

When they reached the fair a week after leaving Thornton, Tilly forgot her tiredness as she was caught up in the atmosphere, and the noise. It seemed that music came from every corner of the world as she alighted. Exciting music that prompted the gypsies to dance. Tilly watched fascinated as beautiful dark-skinned girls twisted and twirled to the clapping of the men.

'That is the marriage ritual dance, Tilly. Sure, the young bucks are after seeking a bride and will grab the one that takes their fancy. If they manage to give her a kiss, then she is betrothed to him.'

Tilly frowned, thinking this unconventional, and a bit demeaning of the girls, almost as if they were cattle in a market, and when the music stopped, and the grab began, she was horrified to see some girls desperately trying to avoid the suitor who wanted them, and them being thumped into submission by the boys.

'It is a barbaric practice at times, I am for admitting, but tradition is tradition.'

'Did you not ever join in, Jeremiah?'

'Aye, and I found myself a willing bride, a beautiful lass.'

Tilly wanted to ask more about this, but Jeremiah had marched off and it took all her effort to keep up with him as the crowd jostled her.

A man caught hold of her arm. Tilly gasped as for a moment she'd thought it was Phileas. 'Are you taken, me pretty girl?'

'I am. Let go of me.' Frantically she screamed for Jeremiah. But he was nowhere to be seen and the man had no intention of letting her go.

'I think I have grabbed you, now stand still and let me kiss you.'

'Naw, naw, let me go!'

A slap stung Tilly's face. Stunned, she felt the man's arms tighten around her waist, drawing her into him. Gasping for breath, Tilly tried to struggle, but his huge, solid, muscly frame was too strong for her – she couldn't move. His lips came down on hers and she smelt his stale breath and body odour, making her retch.

The man took no heed of her convulsions but opened his mouth full of black and yellowed teeth and bit down on her lip. Lifting his head, she saw him bite his own lip until it bled, then come towards her again. 'Naw, naw.' Writhing her head had no impact; he simply grabbed her hair and held her as if in an iron clamp.

Suddenly, his body was wrenched from her. Falling backwards, Tilly landed heavily on her back. She stared at Jeremiah. His face was contorted in anger; his body, stripped to the waist, seemed pumped up to twice its size. His fist landed smack into the man's face. The man hardly toppled; it was as if a fly had brushed by him in its flight. Fear filled Tilly's heart, but that quickly turned to terror as she saw this giant of a man pull himself to full height. Others around began to make noises of anxiety.

Staring at Jeremiah, the man looked grotesque as he lifted his fists in the air and flexed his muscles. His chest almost burst out of his shirt; blood dripped from his lip. Helpless,

Tilly lay where she was and watched as the man's fist went towards Jeremiah, as if in slow motion. A sickening crack brought a gasp from the gathered crowd. Jeremiah crashed to the ground. Tilly opened her mouth to scream, but nothing came out as she stared in horror at Jeremiah's still body.

Words she didn't want to hear filtered through to Tilly. 'Och, Tibias, it is that you've broken his neck? There's not a breath of life in him.'

'Naw! Naw, Jeremiah! Jeremiah.' Tilly crawled towards where Jeremiah lay. Her own blood left a trail down her chin – tears blurred her vision, and the shock she felt left her oblivious to everything around her; she just wanted to get to Jeremiah.

Cradling his head in her lap, Tilly's holler filled the space around her. When it passed, and she looked around, the man who had grabbed her had vanished and those milling about had the look of not wanting to be involved.

'What clan is the gentleman from, miss?'

The voice from behind her sounded caring. Tilly turned her head. A man whose persona carried authority stood looking down at her. 'We'll see to things, so we will, but his clan should know of his passing.'

'That man murdered my Jeremiah!'

'No. As it was witnessed by many, me included, it was the deceased who threw the first fist. No one does that to Granville the Giant and lives to tell the tale.'

'But ... He ... Granville was molesting me! Me husband did nowt other than defend me honour.'

'I see. Well then, he died a hero and will receive a send-off that is befitting.' Turning, he called out, 'Petra, will you womenfolk come and see to the deceased wife?'

'It is that she's not one of us, Ramon, she's not a gypsy, and the fate of her man is down to her.'

'Naw, I did nowt. Granville attacked me, he bit my lip, I couldn't get him off me.'

'Why was it you were roaming without your man? Any woman at the fair is deemed to be up for grabs if she is on her own.'

Tilly looked down at Jeremiah. He must have known that and yet he'd walked away from her. Why, why?

The answer came from Petra.

'She's a harlot. The Lees had to rid themselves of her when it was that she tried to take Phileas from Betina. Then she used her wiles on Jeremiah, so much so that he left the Lees who'd sheltered him since birth and took this woman into his wagon. Lilly Lee it was who told me that Jeremiah, who we thought would grab our daughter this year, had abandoned his folk for a whore.'

Tilly couldn't believe what she was hearing. Had Jeremiah gone from her to find this girl? But then, if he had, she knew it would have been to make his peace with her and her family. Why hadn't he thought of her safety, though? Why had he even brought her here?

Remembering the look on his face as he'd walked away from her, Tilly knew he'd shown the determination of someone who had a task to do. An honourable man, he had chosen to do it and then come back to his wife, she was certain of that. He must have thought that she was keeping up with him and looked back to check, and it would have been then that he saw her plight. *Oh, Jeremiah, my love.*

With this scenario helping her to cope, she realised that Petra had mentioned Lilly Lee. 'What Lilly Lee told you is not the truth. Her and her clan stole my babbies. Where is she? Is she here?'

Petra walked away.

'From what I am hearing, you caused this to happen. Away with you, get out of the sight of us. I cannot be guaranteeing your safety when the tale Petra has to tell circulates amongst the clans.'

The terror that had given way to grief clutched Tilly once again as she looked into the now angry face of the man and saw a hatred in him that shuddered through her. Around her a few men had begun to circle the scene; all looked mean and full of hate for her as their eyes bore into her. The man put up his hand. 'She is leaving, give her the chance to do that, then see that our brother's body is given the send-off he deserves. It isn't for being his fault that he fell into her clutches.' Bending towards her, he put his arm under Tilly's and lifted her up. 'This way. Do not be for protesting. This is your last chance to leave here alive.'

Why he was helping her Tilly didn't know. She could only imagine that he was of a similar character to Jeremiah, who she knew would have done the same if he saw anyone in need of help.

'Where is your wagon?'

Tilly looked around her, saw the perimeter fence with many wagons side by side, and horses grazing on the verge. 'There. And that is Stormy, our horse.'

'I will fix your wagon to him, then you must leave. Take the road you travelled and never cross a gypsy's path again.'

Something in the way he said this left Tilly no room to protest. Her fear drove her on. It wasn't until she was a long way down the road that she'd travelled with Jeremiah that she halted Stormy. They were by the last gateway that Jeremiah had pulled them in to. Here they had spent last night. Him eager to tell her of the fair, her snuggled into him, catching his excitement. Then Jeremiah loving her till she'd cried out from the joy filling her. But not one mention of this girl he'd been betrothed to, and was, she was sure, on his way to make peace with. *Oh, Jeremiah, Jeremiah, why? Why?*

Seeing to Stormy, unhooking him from the wagon and giving him his nosebag to feed from, Tilly led him to the same stream Jeremiah had the night before. When the horse had drunk his fill, she took him back to the wagon and tethered him to the fence. A powerful horse, who Jeremiah had found difficult to handle at times, Stormy was pliable and seemed lost. Tilly was certain that he knew his master was gone, and it was as if he also knew he needed to be gentle with his mistress.

With Stormy settled to grazing on the grass verge, Tilly sat on the bed inside the wagon. Her thoughts were a confusion of what had happened. Where had the man they called Granville disappeared to? But then, one thing she had learnt about the gypsies was that they looked after their own. Someone would have persuaded him to make himself scarce. Maybe the man who helped her, who seemed to have an authority over them all.

She couldn't sort her thoughts out to accept that Jeremiah was gone. To do so caused her so much pain.

Searching for the gin consumed her as she longed to lose herself in the oblivion it offered. When she found a bottle in the drawer under the bed, she almost tore the cork from it, though it gave easily as they had already started this flagon and had recorked it. Holding the neck of the bottle to her lips, Tilly gulped the gin down.

By the time night fell, she was oblivious to everything. Her mind swam in and out of consciousness and she was exhausted from crying, her grief for Jeremiah and her babbies released by the effect of the gin.

Days later, having been brought home by Stormy, even though Tilly hadn't been aware enough to properly see to his needs, a very tired horse turned in to the gate of the field in Thornton.

Sobered a little, Tilly did then rouse herself to unhook Stormy and to give him a nosebag. The horse ate hungrily, and Tilly felt her guilt at her mistreatment of him. Leading him to a trough filled with water, she patted his neck while he drank his fill. When he had, he shook his head and then muzzled into her as if looking for comfort. Tilly clung on to him and sobbed. Gently Stormy nudged her, telling her that he knew what was in her heart.

Leading him back to tether him near to the wagon, she watched him graze, and thought how lost he looked. Almost as much as she was. But though her head pounded, and her body didn't want to work, Tilly knew she must conquer her despair, and clean herself up and go to see the farmer. She needed him to agree to let her stay a while until she could sort out what to do. She still had her baskets hanging on the wagon – those she had hoped to sell at the fair. And she knew there was a tin full of money under the bed. Money that Jeremiah had intended to buy a new horse with, and enough to keep them for a while as they'd had plans to travel further south after the fair had ended. She would offer to pay the farmer a rent.

Two weeks later, waking up from the stupor that the last of the flagons of gin had put her into, Tilly tried to gather her thoughts as her stomach attacked her, demanding to be fed. She couldn't remember the last time she'd eaten, though she had kept the stove going and had brewed umpteen cups of nettle tea between drowning everything out with the gin.

In the larder hatch, she found some eggs, and she remembered somehow getting to the farm to buy some fresh milk the evening before even though she'd run the gauntlet of the disdain of the farmer's wife.

It wasn't long before she sat hungrily wolfing down a plate of scrambled eggs and a cup of hot milk. Feeling better after this feast, Tilly knew that she must get herself to town. Her thoughts were to enquire after a stall on the beach. How she could sort all of this out, she did not know. It was as if she was in a bubble that was protecting her and telling her what she had to do.

But it was at night that the bubble fell apart, leaving her vulnerable and seeking solace in the gin. Part of her desire to go to town was to replenish her supply of it.

Getting there wasn't going to be easy. The trap was still tied to the fence where the farmer had allowed them to leave it, pending their return, or if they never returned, they'd told him to take it as his own. Although she'd watched and admired Jeremiah's skill at driving it, she didn't know if she could manage that or not. *Eeh, I'll not knaw until I try.*

One thing she knew, Stormy loved her. He seemed to have found comfort in snuggling his neck into her and was gentle in his dealings with her. When she'd walked to the farm, he'd followed her and waited for her. It was as if he was trying to protect her. She felt safe with him by her side. And confident, too, that he wouldn't fight her attempt to harness him to the trap and would do all he could to help her manoeuvre him.

After what to Tilly seemed an easy journey, she tethered Stormy to the rail of the promenade as the usual hustle and bustle went on all around her. The hot July sun meant that families had spilled onto the beach – now a kaleidoscope of colour as deckchairs occupied almost every space and sunshades fluttered in the gentle breeze. The women wore clothes of many colours, all light and gay, and the children ran around in their bathing suits. The donkeys sported gaily coloured blankets and the calm sea provided a deep blue, almost lake-like backdrop to it all.

Tilly had passed the Tower, and noted the crowds mulling around it. Her heart had skipped a beat as her imagination had given her Arthur's broken body on the ground, but she'd taken a deep breath. Something in her had changed. Yes, she still grieved for Arthur, but now her heart bled for Jeremiah and that pain took precedence over her feelings at Arthur's loss.

As she looked over the prom, the excitement emanating from the stalls beneath her made her catch her breath. Voices calling out their wares drifted up to her. She could do that. She could call out, 'Finest baskets for sale! Orders taken for any design you need!' She had been rehearsing doing so for days now.

Patting Stormy, she told him she wouldn't be long, then she walked towards the slope that would take her down to the stalls. Her feet dug into the sand as she made her way towards the first one. 'Excuse me, sir, can you tell me how I arrange to have a stall?'

'Eeh, lass, you don't arrange owt, you just come down and set up. Mind, you have to be early to get a good pitch, and then you might be bullied off it as some old hand might think they have exclusive right to where you've pitched. Why are you asking? What's it a young lass like you got to sell?'

Tilly didn't miss the implication as his eyes travelled over her body and she felt herself judged once more. Holding her head up in defiance of his assumption, she told him of her baskets.

'Well, they sound like a money earner for you, lass. There's nowt of that nature being sold here as I knaw to.'

'Ta, mister. I'll be here tomorrow. I might see you.'

'Aye. Bring a blanket to lay out and you can pitch next to me. I'll save you a spot, then you'll catch them as come down the slope and them going back up it. Me name's Dan, by the way. Me folk have been selling knick-knacks down here for a few years, ever since holidaymakers started to come in their droves.'

Tilly looked at his wares – jars containing sweets, boxes of silks for embroidery, dried-flower arrangements and trinkets of many colours, as well as pipes and smokers' boxes. All looked beautifully displayed and attractive.

'I'm Tilly. It's right good to meet you, Dan.' A man of around forty, Dan never took his pipe out of his mouth while he spoke, though no smoke came from it. He was balding

– what hair he did have left was fair in colour and curled around the bottom half of his head – and portly, though not unattractive, as his smile lit his face and made his blue eyes twinkle.

Despite his earlier insinuation about what he thought she was selling, Tilly liked him. She smiled at him as she waved, telling him she had to leave but would be back.

With that sorted, Tilly thought to go to the farmer where the Lee clan had camped and ask him if she could bring her wagon and camp there for the season. It would be much nearer for her to get to the beach. Once the season ended, she hoped to find a more conventional way of living and have enough to rent a home for herself.

She had a sadness in her as she approached Stormy. The horse showed his eagerness at her return, fidgeting, shaking and nodding his head the moment he caught sight of her. If she was to live a normal life in a little house of her own, she would have to sell him, and the thought didn't sit easy with her, for he had been so loved by Jeremiah and had also been her salvation these last weeks.

Sighing, she put these thoughts to one side. They were for the future and who knew what could happen before then.

Steering Stormy towards St Anne's, Tilly began to worry as she thought over the plans she'd made. Yes, she had enough stock for a couple of days, or maybe a week if trade was slow, but what after that? How was she going to get the wicker she needed? How was she going to find time to make the baskets? She still had some cane left; perhaps she could soak it and then take it to the beach with her and make baskets as she waited for customers. But what about the bases she would need?

These worries crowded her, giving her the feeling that it was hopeless. But then she remembered, she wasn't penniless, and she could delay the start of her venture and go back to the woodyard along Grasmere Road. Henry, the owner, would cut her a few shapes from the offcuts as he always used to. She would go now and order some. Turning the cart, Tilly headed back along the promenade, feeling happier at the thought that she had covered all avenues. Everything would turn out all right, she told herself, she just had to think through any problems and come up with a solution. She smiled as this thought gave her a feeling of being empowered. *I can cope, I have to. Naw one is going to take care of me. It's all down to meself to do that. And I knaws as I can.*

EIGHTEEN

It was as she passed The Foxhall Inn that she changed her plan. She was nearly out of gin. *Maybe I should buy a bottle, and sit a while on the promenade? It won't hurt to wait until tomorrow to get my bases, and I can go back to Thornton for one more night.*

No argument to this presented itself. With the thought of the gin, Tilly had let the pain of her loss back in and justified her actions as only wanting to deaden that pain. She needed to seek comfort, just for an hour. Enjoy relaxing, looking out to sea and letting her thoughts drift.

'Whoa, Stormy, lad.' Dismounting, Tilly led Stormy towards the layby on the other side of the tram track. Tethering him, she ran across the road.

As she opened the door to the inn, smoke from pipes and rolled cigarettes swirled around her and alcohol fumes assailed her, increasing her urge for the gin. A man popped his head through the hatch of the carry-out counter just inside the door. He looked taken aback for a moment – probably unused to seeing a woman customer. 'What d'yer want, love?'

'How much for a bottle of gin, please, sir?'

'More than you've got by the looks of you. It'll cost you all of five pennies.'

'I have that and more. I'll take two of your finest, ta.'

Outside, Tilly had a moment when she regretted what she'd done. She might need that money in the future to help to keep herself going, but she calmed her conscience with the thought that there was plenty left. Tying the bag of coins to her belt, she clutched the gin, and crossed back over the road. *Maybe I should go to the woodyard and get back to Thornton, and then enjoy a drink? I can light the brazier and sit in its glow whilst baking a spud for me supper.*

But the pull of the gin was too much for her. She'd just have a drink on the bench and enjoy the afternoon sun for a while.

The first sip burnt her mouth. This gin wasn't as good as the gypsy brew, but she'd get used to it. Taking a much bigger swallow, Tilly felt its warmth begin to creep through her. Her head felt light. Behind her, Stormy snorted, but she ignored him. Just a couple more sips and they would get on their way.

The sea looked beautiful. Calm and glittering, reflecting the sun's rays. Folk on the beach were beginning to pack up their picnic baskets and gather their children to them. All looked as though they were behind a net curtain. Tilly took another swig and then another. Liking the devil-may-care feeling, she put her head back and glugged the gin down her throat. Her eyes began to feel heavy. Stormy whinnied, but she took no notice and let her eyes close.

When she opened them again, it was dark. Her head spun. She turned, clutched the bench and tried to rise. Through her hazy vision she registered that Stormy had gone, but she couldn't think where he could have gone to. Her mind drifted. Maybe she'd dreamt that she had a horse?

Her stomach churned. Retching, Tilly leant forward. Once the bout of sickness passed, she reached for her gin and, lifting it to her lips, she tried to take a swig, but it yielded nothing. Throwing it on the floor in disgust, she fumbled for the second bottle. Finding it, she rummaged for the corkscrew. She must have had one. Then she remembered that the bottle she'd thrown down had made a sound as if it had hit something metal. Bending over, she felt around. Her fingers found the blessed tool. Her heart lifted. Wiping away the tears that for some reason were tumbling down her cheeks, Tilly expertly opened the second bottle.

The next thing she knew she was bathed in light once more and the sun's rays were warming her. Everything around her swam and she struggled to focus. The smell of the salty sea churned her stomach.

With this second bout of vomiting, Tilly's head cleared a little. A woman and a child walked by.

'Mummy, is that lady ill?'

'Don't look, Simon. Come along, hurry by.'

Tilly wanted to call out to them to help her, but her lips wouldn't work. Her mouth tasted vile and her throat rasped as if she was trying to swallow a piece of wire netting. She shifted to ease the discomfort of feeling as though she was sitting on cold, wet grass. The movement gave her the strong smell of urine. Shame prickled her. Then memory shocked her into turning around. It was then that her worst fear was confirmed. Stormy had gone! But where to, and who would take him and her cart?

Panic gripped Tilly. Instinctively her hand went to her belt, but her purse had gone too. *No! Oh God. What am I going to do?*

The pain in her head increased. The sea breeze chilled her to the bone. She allowed her tears to run down her face as she rocked backwards and forwards, begging God to help her.

A couple walked by and she cried out to them. They didn't look at her. They hurried on. Turning her head to look left and then right, Tilly saw that the promenade was quite busy – folk taking a stroll, others hurrying as if on a mission.

Her stomach cramped. Bending over to ease it, two empty gin bottles came into view. Puzzled, she tried to remember how long she'd been here.

Behind her the road thronged with horse-drawn vehicles – some with open carriages, some covered. A little way down the road a wagon-type cart pulled by two horses was coming towards her. It slowed and stopped behind her. Two men jumped down from the driver's bench.

'There she is.' They strode towards her. Tilly's heartbeat quickened.

'Come along, slut, you're coming with us.'

The man who'd said this was big and bulky. His waistcoat strained against the buttons holding it around his paunch. His cravat looked grubby and a brown mark ringed the collar of his shirt. His hair and face seemed to be the same colour as ginger curls met ginger freckles. He grabbed her arm, digging his fingers into her flesh. 'By, you stink, you dirty tyke.'

'Leave me, let me go.' Fear gripped Tilly. Her voice gravelled as her words choked her dry throat. Coughing weakened her.

She had no strength to resist the tug of the men as they pulled her towards the wagon. Nor could she ask who they were or where they were taking her, though the man's next words told her this and a sense of dread engulfed her.

'You're for the nuthouse. Come on.'

Tilly wanted to protest. For a moment, she couldn't think what the nuthouse was, but then it came to her. 'Naw, I'm not mad. I ... Oh, God ... help me, someone help me. HELP ME!'

The scream choked her once more and with this bout of coughing she retched again, spewing vile-tasting bile onto the ground.

'You filthy, stinking tyke! Grab her, Cyril. Let's get her in, there's decent folk having to be subjected to this.'

Tilly's body hit the wooden floor of the wagon. Her breath left her lungs, her stomach cramped, she couldn't move. A foot kicked her. 'Gerrup. You'll do naw good on the floor. Get onto this bench beside me.'

Tilly looked up into the face of an old woman. She took the arm the woman extended and somehow managed to get up as the wagon swayed from side to side. When she sat next to the woman on the hard wooden bench the woman shuffled her body away from her. 'No offence, but you pong like you've wet yourself and let it dry and wet yourself again, and your breath stinks of stale alcohol.'

Shame once more tingled through Tilly. Her fuzzy mind wouldn't give her why this was happening. They'd said they were taking her to the madhouse – the asylum – but this woman didn't look mad, just old and very poor. Her long black frock was torn and the pinafore covering it had very few signs that it was once white. What hair protruded from her mob cap clung to her head in greasy, lank strands. But then, as if to deny what Tilly had been thinking, the woman started to laugh, a cackling laugh that showed her one blackened tooth hanging from the top of her mouth. The sound and the look in the woman's pale blue piercing eyes left Tilly in no doubt that there was a madness in her.

Cringing away from the woman, Tilly felt a kind of fear different from any she'd ever known tighten her stomach muscles. 'Naw, naw! Let me out of here! I'm not mad. Help me!' But though she'd wanted to shout, the words came out as a hoarse whisper, which set Tilly off coughing and gasping for breath.

A piercing scream filled the wagon, increasing Tilly's dread. The old woman had gone from laughing to screaming without taking a breath. Tilly watched as she stood and began to claw at the canvas between them and the two men. The wagon came to a halt. After a moment the flap was undone, and the angry face of the ginger-looking man appeared. Behind him was the quieter, thin, weedy man, whose strength she knew belied his appearance. 'Shut up, Irene. Sit down or we'll tie you up, d'yer hear?'

Irene carried on screaming.

Within seconds the men were climbing into the back of the wagon. 'Right, shift yerself, you stinking whore, let us get to her.' With this Tilly felt a vicious kick on her shin. She cried out, but this earnt her a blow across her head. 'Sherrup. Don't you start an' all.'

Tilly put her hand up to ward off a further blow but wasn't quick enough. Her body shot back under the force of the punch. Her head hit the wooden bench. Everything swirled around her; the green canvas roof seemed to descend over her, covering her in darkness. She struggled against the suffocating feel of it, but a painful crack to her forehead had her surrendering to the blessed peace it now offered.

When next she woke, Tilly thought she was back in the hospital again, and a sense of relief flooded her. Someone came to her bed. Disappointment filled her to see that it wasn't her usual nurse. She went to turn her body to sit up, but found she couldn't move; something was holding her to the bed. Struggling made no difference. The nurse didn't answer her pleas of 'What's happening to me? Why can't I move?' Instead she just put her free hand under Tilly's head and lifted her, placing the spoon she was holding in her other hand to Tilly's mouth. 'Open your mouth, you dirty piece of nothing.'

Shock held Tilly rigid. Why should the nurse insult her like that?

'Open, I said.'

Tilly did as she was bid. The liquid the nurse poured into her tasted vile and she spluttered. Her head thudded back down onto the pillow as the nurse let go of her and clamped her nose with her fingers. Her nails dug into Tilly's skin. As she jerked backwards, the liquid trickled to the back of her throat. 'Swallow. NOW!'

Tilly had no option but to gulp, but then went into a fit of coughing and heaving as her body tried to reject the stinging nasty-tasting liquid. She couldn't breathe. At last the nurse let go of her nose. 'You're getting up today, missy. I'm not changing any more of your stinking wet beds.' With this the blankets were pulled off her, leaving Tilly shivering with fright and cold. 'You've bloody wet the bed again, you filthy tyke. Ugh, you stink.' A slap stung Tilly's arm. Feeling as though she really was nothing, Tilly turned her head away.

The straps that bound her had dug into her flesh. As they were released, they peeled bits of her skin off. But though it smarted, Tilly was too terrified to complain.

'Sit up and swing your legs over the side of the bed.'

Tilly tried to do this but couldn't. Her body felt weak, battered and bruised.

'I said, GET UP!'

A ripping sensation seared Tilly's scalp as the nurse yanked her by her hair to a sitting position. The strength of the woman astounded Tilly. Her thick arms were covered in hair, giving the impression that she was really a man. But though lifted to a standing position, Tilly's legs wouldn't hold her, and she crumpled to the floor. A vicious kick winded her. Between gasps she begged, 'Please, please, naw more. Naw more. I – I can't take it.'

'Ha, I'm only just beginning. You mental cases need keeping in check, and yer'll not get the better of me, oh naw.'

'I – I'm not mad. I drank too much. I'm sorry . . .'

'Naw sane person sits on a bench for two days, drinking two full bottles of gin and wetting herself. Calling out obscenities you were, and to decent folk who go to Blackpool for a rest and medicinal purposes. You're nowt but a drunk.'

Tilly couldn't get her mind around this. Yes, she'd seen the two empty bottles of gin on the ground, but why couldn't she remember shouting at folk? Why would she? She'd never been aggressive in her life. But at the mention of the gin a craving swept through her. 'I need a drink.'

'There's water by your bed. Get up and get it.'

'I can't. Help me.'

'Naw. Can't you smell yourself, eh? Can't you feel your sodden nightdress clinging to you? I'm not touching you. And I'm warning you: if you don't get up and get yourself to the sluice where I can scrub you down, you'll knaw to it.'

Tilly didn't know where the sluice was but could see a door leading from this ward so thought she would have to make for that. She could see that there were six beds in the room, and none of the others were occupied. Making an extreme effort, she pulled herself up by holding on to the bed and swaggered towards the door. Misery wept from her every pore.

Reaching the door, she clung on to it, all energy drained from her.

'Go on. That door on the left, get in there.'

Somehow, Tilly found herself in a room with walls tiled in green. Looking around, she saw a lav. The stench coming from it churned her stomach. Plonking herself down, she wondered how the lav was emptied, but then saw a trapdoor to her left.

The sound of running water had her lifting her heavy head. A pain shot down her neck as she did so. And yet, she felt a haze coming over her. To her right was a huge sink and the nurse was engaged in filling a bucket from a pump on the draining board.

Suddenly, yanked off the toilet to a standing position, Tilly gasped as the cold water hit her, and then cringed at the sight of the carbolic soap and scrubbing brush the nurse picked up once she put the bucket down.

Pain seared Tilly. Hot burning, sore pain as the nurse viciously scrubbed her, then doused her in another bucket of cold water. 'Right, sit on that chair.'

Looking behind her, she saw a basket chair with many of its strands loose. The thought crossed her mind that she could mend it easily, but then a mad laughter built up inside her at such a notion. The laughter came from her lips without her bidding it to.

'Shut up, mad woman!'

The slap hardly stung Tilly. Her body was so racked with pain that she couldn't register the extra hurt of the blow. But she did register the scissors the nurse had taken off a table in the corner of the sluice room. Desolation swamped her at the feel of her head being pulled this way and that, and the sight of her raven locks falling to the ground. Her mind gave her Arthur, and how he'd loved her hair. Running his fingers through it and letting it fall onto her face. But suddenly, it wasn't Arthur, but gentle Jeremiah, brushing her hair and telling her never to cut it. His dark eyes shining as he looked down into hers, his hand tenderly stroking the tresses he'd smoothed, telling her that she was beautiful. A sob jolted her throat. She had known the love of two wonderful men, but both had left her. As her head was tugged backwards to enable the nurse to get to the front, a picture of two little girls danced before her eyes. For a moment confusion wouldn't reveal to Tilly who they were. When her mind cleared, and she looked into the eyes of Babs and then Beth, her spirits slumped into a deep dark hole.

Tilly didn't know how many days had passed before she once more began to register what was happening around her. A scream had catapulted her from the dream world she'd descended into. But though she'd lived many days and nights through this dream world, she had come to realise that the moment the nurse thought she was coming out of the stupor, the nasty-tasting white liquid was again poured down her throat to put her back into the dark hole.

Sitting as if slumped, Tilly tried to think through what she should do. Pretending to be zombie-like seemed the best strategy. If she stayed calm and pliable, then they wouldn't give her any more of the liquid. She had to act as if she truly was mentally ill.

Putting her head back, Tilly picked at her clothes as she had seen the other patients doing and looked around her as if she was staring into space. But really, she was taking in her surroundings and who was in the room with her.

A long room with cream-painted brick walls and light coming in from high, barred windows, it was scantily furnished. A table stood in the centre, which seemed to Tilly to be almost as long as the room. Around it were many chairs with what could have been dead bodies sitting on them, so still were the occupants. Some asleep on their folded arms, leaning on the table, some sitting bolt upright staring into a space in front of them.

As Tilly scanned the occupants, her eyes fell on a woman sitting at the other end of the table. It had been this woman who had let out the scream. But now, she sat quietly looking up at the ceiling. Tilly tried to focus on her as something about her jingled a memory that Tilly couldn't grasp hold of. The woman's face held no expression. Tilly tried to clear her mind of the fog that clouded it. She knew the woman, she was certain of it, and yet nothing about the hollow cheeks and lank greasy hair that had a few kinks as if it was once curly could help her bring to mind who this was. *Curls – who did I once know with dark curls? . . . Oh my Lord! Liz! Naw, it can't be!*

Tilly squinted her eyes and stared at the woman. The woman shifted her head from looking upwards and stared back at Tilly. 'Liz? Liz, is that you, lass?' There was no response.

Tilly looked around. The nurse had left the room. Getting up, Tilly shuffled as she'd seen the others do. When she neared the woman, she knew for certain it was Liz. 'Eeh, Liz, what're you doing in here, lass?'

Liz looked at her with a blank stare. No sign of recognition registered on her face. 'Liz. Oh, Liz, what's wrong with you? It's me, Tilly. Eeh, lass, what's brought you to this? Where's Eddie and the young 'uns?'

A terrible noise came from Liz. Tilly shot round. Her eyes watched the door; if the nurse heard and came in, she'd be in trouble. Shuffling away, Tilly kept her head down. A hand grabbed her. The old woman with the one tooth grinned at her. 'She's mad that one. Aye, her name's Liz, but she ain't got no man now, and naw young 'uns either. All burnt in a fire that took a building of the poorhouse. They were asleep in that building. Now one knaws where Liz were, but it weren't in her own man's bed.' The woman's cackle of a laugh rang out. Tilly shrank from the horror of what she'd heard, and in fear of the woman whose eyes seemed to be lit with the very fire she spoke of.

Gasping, Tilly made it back to her own chair. Her body slumped under the weight of the shock of this news. *Oh God, it can't be true, not them lovely young 'uns . . .* A picture of Alfie,

Larry and the three little girls, May, Freda and Lettie, came to her. Happy children, despite the poverty they lived in. And what of the babby Liz was expecting? Her heart bled with grief for the little family and for poor Liz. Though she wouldn't spare an ounce of emotion for Eddie, as to her, he'd got his just desserts.

Despite the horror of it all, a small hope flickered inside of Tilly. *Maybe me and Liz can become friends again, and I can help her – please God let it be so. It would make this place more bearable having Liz by me side.*

NINETEEN

A few weeks later, opening her eyes to the warmth of the sun streaming through the windows, Tilly yawned and stretched herself. All was quiet around her as others slept, but from outside came the dawn chorus of birds as they practised their notes and vied with each other to sound the best. For a moment the beauty of the sound gave Tilly the hope of a new day, but as the reality of her situation hit her, she sat up. Not that she felt altogether down about her circumstances as her memory gave her Liz being brought into the same dormitory the evening before.

Tilly hadn't seen Liz since that first day when she'd been manhandled out of the room and she hadn't been able to find out from anyone where Liz had been taken to. The dread of what might have happened to her had given Tilly a heavy heart.

But despite this worry hanging over her, Tilly hadn't rested on her laurels, but had formed a plan for herself and had carried it through. She'd determined to show small signs of recovery. Not much notice had been taken of her during the time she was quiet and pliable, and so now, she had progressed to making herself useful – soothing others when they were distressed, helping them to feed when all energy had sapped from them, and tidying up their belongings when they had thrown them about in frustration.

All of this had resulted in her being put to work helping the cleaning lady, Bertha, a kindly, matronly person who liked to chat. Tilly already knew all about her aches and pains, her hard life, and her good-for-nothing husband, as Bertha called him. But she hadn't opened up about her own life to Bertha.

To do so would not only be painful, but she wasn't ready to trust anyone yet. She did ask questions, though, just the odd one now and again. Her aim was to find out all she could in the hope of something occurring to her that would help her to get out of here.

Making herself useful was having an effect, as she was being treated a lot better than she had been in the beginning. It also helped to pass the long hours.

It was while Tilly had been helping Bertha to clean the dining hall that she had formed an idea that might finally convince the doctor who came to see them all a couple of times a week that she wasn't mentally ill and that it had been misfortune that had brought her to this point.

Seeing the state of the chairs had triggered the idea. The seats were made of woven wicker and the frames of cane. Most needed repairing and some were dangerous and ready to give at any moment.

Tilly knew she could mend them and make them like new at a fraction of the cost of them being replaced, and finding out from Bertha that this institution was run by a charitable organisation had fuelled the idea further.

Charities were always short of money. *Maybe, when the master of this place does his rounds, I could offer to mend the chairs?*

Tilly felt excited at the prospect and began to think that it could really happen, to the point that she often worked through in her mind how she would tackle the job. She knew the frames were rickety due to the seats and legs needing rebinding. She'd require tools, and some pliable wicker, but that could be ordered in for her. She knew the cost of these and how much could be saved as opposed to replacing the chairs.

With this hope that Tilly had held in her for days now, her thoughts of the future had seemed much brighter, and with Liz back in her life too she would make it happen for them both.

Creeping out of bed, Tilly went along the row of beds, all placed just a foot apart. When she came to the one Liz was in, she saw her lying on top of her covers, curled up in a ball. Going to her side, Tilly looked down on her once best friend and the pain of what had happened to Liz assailed her afresh. The feeling came to her that she wanted to take Liz in her arms and make everything right for her, but she knew she could never do that. Putting out a hand, she stroked Liz's wiry, tangled hair.

Liz moaned in her sleep. 'Liz, Liz, it's me, Tilly.' Though whispered, her words seemed to bounce off the walls in the hush of the dormitory. Tilly looked around her, afraid of the mayhem that could be caused if she woke the others, but no one stirred.

'Eeh, Liz, lass. Let me help you.'

Liz's eyes opened. Against the darkness of her sockets, they looked bluer than Tilly remembered them. 'Liz, it's me, Tilly.'

226

Another moan and Liz's eyes filled with tears.

'By, lass, how did we get to this? Do you remember me, Liz? Tilly, your friend, Tilly.'

'Tilly?'

'Aye, it's me. I'm here, lass.'

'Oh, Tilly ... me young 'uns, they're ...' A gasp that held deep pain came from Liz. It sliced into Tilly's heart.

'I knaw, lass. I knaw. Let me help you, Liz.'

Liz uncurled. Her hand came out and Tilly took it in her own.

'Naw one can help me, Tilly. I just want to die. I – I should've been with them, but ... Oh, Tilly, hold me. Please hold me.'

Tilly climbed onto the bed and held Liz to her. 'Can you talk about it, Liz? It might ease your load a bit. I longed for someone to talk to when me Arthur died.'

'I weren't a good friend to you, Tilly. I'm sorry, lass, but me Eddie, he told me you'd tried to entice him in to see to you as you were missing what Arthur gave you, and I believed him.'

'I knaw. Don't worry about it. It never happened like that, but then, I don't have to tell you what Eddie were like.'

'I – I loved him, Tilly. For all his faults, I loved him.'

'Aye. There's naw accounting for love at times; it's a powerful feeling that allows more than it should.'

'An – and me young 'uns ...' Another painful gasp. 'They're gone ...' The words were a hoarse cry of anguish.

'Tell me, Liz. Tell me what happened.'

Slowly, and peppered with tears and pain, the terrible story unfolded. Liz held nothing back, admitting that she was in the bed of the master of the poorhouse when it happened. 'He – he promised me so much, Tilly. He said he'd get me and me family out of there and into one of the alms houses.' These, Tilly knew, were houses built by a charitable organisation to accommodate the poor, but she'd thought they were mainly for the old and widowed, not families as huge as Liz's was. She didn't say this but let Liz carry on with her story.

'He fed us extra food. Other young 'uns in there were dying of hunger and disease, it were the only way I could protect mine. Oh, but I didn't ... I ... Oh, Tilly, they died, they all died.'

Tilly held Liz to her, trying to give her strength but feeling the utter hopelessness of doing so. 'We all do things, Liz. Things as we wouldn't dream of doing normally. But it's all to help us, and them as we love, to survive. It's a ma's instinct. No matter what it takes, we do it.'

Liz's sobs wracked through Tilly, nudging her own pain and bringing her to breaking point. Her own tears spilled over. 'We're in same boat, Liz. I feel your pain, lass. I lost me young 'uns an' all.'

'What? Babs and Beth ... dead? How? Oh, God, Tilly!'

'Naw, not dead – stolen. Taken by the gypsies, but awe, Liz, me heart's breaking.'

Once she had told Liz what had happened, they fell quiet. Tilly had left nothing out, feeling that what she'd done would help Liz to see that she wasn't the only one to have fallen off the right path.

'You mean, Joe and you ... You, Tilly? I can't believe it, you were never that type.'

'Naw, and neither were you, but it were needs must. I wanted to stop me young 'uns from starving and to keep a roof over their heads. We're naw different to each other, Liz.'

'Naw, but God, we've been punished.'

With this, Tilly found a small hope seeping into her. Liz's voice had become stronger as they'd talked, and there were no signs of the madness Tilly had observed in her the last time she'd seen her. 'We can help each other, Liz. We're all we've got now.'

Liz eased herself into a sitting position. 'Can we heal, Tilly? I don't think I can, not ever.'

'Naw, me neither. But we can find a way of living with it all. Of making things better for ourselves.'

'How?'

'I've an idea, I'll tell you of it ...'

'Eeh, lass, do you think it will work?'

'I don't knaw. But until I find out, there is a way of helping yourself, Liz. If you're pliable and cause naw trouble, then it's better for you. Naw screaming out and venting your pain. If you manage that, then you might get to be treated better. I have, and sommat may occur for us.'

'What? What can occur? We'll never get out of here, never.'

For a moment the truth of this and the hopelessness of it wrapped Tilly in misery, but then the thought came to her that never was a long time. 'Look, this place is for them as are mad, and we're not mad. We have to prove that to them, and then apply to be released, even if it is to the workhouse. Awe, lass, I knaw as me plan's a long shot, but if I get lucky and they let me try to repair them chairs, then I can say I need help and that you used to help me back home.'

Liz was quiet.

'We can do it, Liz. We can.'

'Oh, Tilly, I haven't the strength.'

'I knaw, lass. But believe me, you will find it. I did. I had to. Like I told you, I even fell in love again after me young 'uns were took.' The pain of Jeremiah's loss dug deeply into her, but as before, she wouldn't let it in. She couldn't. On top of everything else that cut her into pieces, it was too much. She had to stay strong. Not only for herself, but for Liz.

'Eeh, Tilly, why? We were just two lasses from a back street in Blackpool. We didn't do no harm to anyone, why? Why . . . WHY?'

'Shush, Liz . . . Please. That's what I'm talking about. Outbursts like that. You've got to control them. I knaw as you want to scream and scream. I do meself, but it won't do nowt to help our cause.'

'I'm . . . sorry . . . Oh, Tilly, hold me again, lass. I feel safe in your arms. Help me. Help me.'

Tilly held Liz tightly, feeling the sobs wrack her body, knowing the pity of it all, and trying not to allow it to release the huge lump knotting her own heart.

When Liz came to a calm place she looked up at Tilly. 'Ta, lass. I can feel your strength and it helps me. Eeh, I used to be the strong one and you the cossetted one with how your Arthur looked after you. But I never envied you, as I thought as you deserved it. You were allus kind and allus there for me. I should never have believed Eddie.'

'Let's put that behind us. We have each other now, Liz. We can get through this and make sommat of ourselves. Come on, let's get to the bathroom afore this lot wake. Oh, and, Liz, try not to take that white stuff they give us. It fugs up your brain. Hold it in your mouth then when they turn away, spit it out. We need to have our wits about us.'

'Won't they knaw?'

'They might guess, but I reckon it's how you behave that determines if they bother about it or not. Look at me: doing a job that keeps me busy, and working with Bertha is a source of information for me. I found out from her more than who runs this place; I also knaw that we're in the country somewhere between Preston and Southport. Aye, I knaw as it seems a useless bit of information, but you never knaw what might come in handy. I learnt that from the gypsies, who live on their wits on a daily basis.'

'Eeh, I can't imagine the Tilly I knew living the life of a gypsy.'

'It weren't a bad existence, and some of it I enjoyed. Anyroad, let's get sorted as I knaw sommat else from Bertha. The bloke who manages the charity is paying a visit today. He's coming early, that's why there's so much hustle and bustle and why I wanted to get up and make meself respectable nice and early. I'm hoping he stops to chat to me this time. Last time he spoke to a few as he walked around. He got nowt but abuse, but with us looking clean and tidy and alert, he might choose us this time.'

When the manager of the charity arrived, they all stood as he was introduced. Mr Jenson, a huge man with a stomach that vied with his waistcoat for release, had dark curly hair and a pleasant, chubby face, with skin that any woman would be glad to have – smooth, dewy and with a pink glow. There were other feminine traits to this man too. His hair was longer than most men wore it these days and it wasn't greased to keep it controlled and close to his head but flowed to below his ears and bounced when he walked. His lips were plump and formed an almost perfect heart shape. Tilly had the impression that he didn't like women. A man in his position would usually take advantage of the females he ruled over, but he showed no interest in any of the nurses, or patients. Instead, he gave an air of them all being very distasteful to him.

This Tilly saw as a disadvantage to her quest. It would be easy to use seductive tactics on a man to get what she wanted. *Dear God, what have I come to that such an idea should occur to me?*

This thought was splintered by a crashing sound. Jumping out of her wits, Tilly looked over to where the noise had come from and saw that a chair had collapsed under a large lady and she was now on the floor screaming blue murder. Tilly's immediate thought was to look heavenward and thank God, but then she felt guilty as the poor lady cried out in pain.

Mr Jenson, flanked by the master and the matron, hurried over to the woman. Around them other women sobbed; one began to fit and fell on the floor, her body trembling and froth protruding from her mouth.

With the chaos that had broken out now taking the attention of the master and the matron, Tilly gathered all her courage and seized the moment by going to the assistance of the poor woman who'd been unceremoniously dumped on the floor. Taking one arm, she gestured to Mr Jenson to take the other. 'It's Gertrude, sir. She's not violent, poor lass; she's upset and afraid, that's all.' Tilly had had many dealings with Gertrude, calming her and sitting with her to reassure her.

As they lifted her a tirade of abuse came from her. Spit sprayed from her mouth.

'It's all right, Gertrude, lass. Here, there's an empty chair for you over there, a stronger one.'

Mr Jenson kept hold of Gertrude's other arm and together they steered her towards the chair Tilly had pointed to. As they did so, Tilly took a deep breath and dared to broach the subject that held all her hopes. 'There's a few chairs that are in a bad state, sir. I – I . . .'

'Don't speak to Mr Jenson until you are spoken to, girl. And what's this? You dare to get him to help with a patient! Oh, Mr Jenson, I do apologise. This girl knows what she's up to. We have to watch her – she's wily, that one.'

'Don't fret, Matron. I volunteered to help. Besides, she has a point: there is so much that is in need of attention. I'll try to apply for more funds, but I don't hold out much hope.'

At the risk of bringing Matron's wrath down on her head once more, Tilly blurted out, 'I could save the trust money, sir. I'm a basket maker and work with all sorts of materials. I could mend them chairs for a lot less than it would cost to replace them.'

'How dare you!'

'No, Matron. Let's hear her out. What's your name, girl?'

'Tilly, sir. I mean, Matilda.'

'Well, Matilda, tell me about how you can mend the chairs.'

Gaining courage from his interest, Tilly explained how she would go about mending the chairs, using the language of her trade to impress him as she described the tools she would need. 'These can be bought locally at an ironmonger's but the cane I'd need ordering from Somerset where they grow the finest. I'd need a barrel an' all to soak the cane in to make it pliable and to get the colour of it just right. I could make them chairs like new, sir.'

'It's preposterous!'

'No, Matron, on the contrary, it's very interesting. Tell me, girl, have you an idea of what the repairs would cost?'

'Aye, for the one as just collapsed, I'd say no more than four and sixpence, and for them as are just showing signs of wear, about one and tuppence. Whereas new chairs would cost you all of ten bob each, sir. And for all me tools, which would be the biggest expense, I think you'd be looking at around eleven shillings.'

'Good gracious, I would say that we have to take this offer up, Matron. I wouldn't even have to apply for more money from the central fund.'

'If you say so, sir, but if you ask me, this one is spinning you a yarn. She's cunning, like I say.'

'I can prove me skills to you, sir. I'd need to be able to use two chairs – this one on the floor, and one not so badly damaged. I'll salvage the willow that was used to weave the seat from this one and repair the other one with it and then you can judge for yourself.'

'How long will that take, Matilda?'

'I could have it done by the morning, sir. That's if Matron will let me off me duties and can find me a pair of strong scissors.'

'I think we should do it, Matron. I'll come back tomorrow to see her work. And I want her to be given a fair chance. Find her somewhere quiet and let her get on with it.'

'Very well, sir, but I do think you will regret this. You don't know these patients like I do.'

'To be honest, Matron, I can't see a resemblance between Matilda and how she conducts herself and these other poor souls. What does the doctor say about her?'

'I'd have to look at my notes, sir.'

Seeing another chance for her, Tilly spoke up. 'I'm not mad, sir, I had a rough time. I lost me husband and me children and were made homeless. I drowned me sorrows in the gin bottle one night and found meself in here the next day.'

Matron looked as though she would explode. Mr Jenson looked astonished. 'Can that sort of thing happen, Matron? Surely the poorhouse is a better option than us having to house those who fall on hard times.'

'She ain't telling the truth of it, sir.'

'I am, that's how it happened. I'm not sick in me mind, I had a setback, that's all.'

'Well, we won't discuss this now; the other patients are getting more and more upset.'

At this from Matron, Tilly noticed for the first time how the noise in the room had increased in volume as distressed patients called out for their mothers, or to God to let them die.

'We will look into your case, Matilda, but in the meantime, let's see what sort of job you do on mending one of the chairs. Go and pick one that you can repair and let me see it in the state it is in today and compare it tomorrow. Now, Matron, I know all of this doesn't meet with your approval, but I am asking you to just give the girl a chance.'

'Yes, sir, of course, sir.'

Tilly's heart soared. She hurried to where she'd been sitting, winking at Liz before picking up the chair and carrying it to

Mr Jenson. 'This one only needs a little repair work doing to it. These strands here need replacing. I could do a proper job if I had a hammer and some small tacks, sir, as I could take the repair from the edge and I could rebind it around the frame, and that would make it really strong. But if you're just wanting to see me weaving skills, I can do a job that will demonstrate them to you.'

'No, let's have a proper job. Matron, the handyman will have what Tilly requires. After breakfast take her to him and let her explain what tools she needs to borrow. I'm looking forward to seeing the results. Now, let us leave and let the staff get everyone quietened down.'

As he walked away, Tilly thought what a nice man he was, not at all like the impression she'd had of him. Hope soared in her as she made her way back to Liz. Liz squeezed her hand. 'Eeh, lass, you did it! By, you could be on your way.'

'If I do manage to get out of here, I'll not go without you, Liz, I promise. I'll get going on the work on them chairs, then I'll ask if you can help me. You mind what I said, though – you have to show you're better. Work hard at it, as nowt they do in here will help you. Turn to me if owt gets too bad for you to cope with, and I'll get you through it.'

Liz didn't answer this, but gave a lovely, watery smile that warmed Tilly's heart. Life was tough, but having Liz by her side would ease her, and helping Liz, Tilly knew, would also help herself to heal. *That's if it's ever possible that I can.*

TWENTY

Matron was surprisingly good over all that Tilly needed, even if she did provide it with an air of someone who was certain that the venture would fail.

For Tilly, the task wasn't an easy one. The old cane was brittle, and she had to soak it to make it pliable. It really needed a lot longer than she could give it, but as soon as some strands of it could be moulded, she used these to rebind the back of the chair frame to the seat.

It was when she moved on to the weaving of the seat, having cut out all the old cane, that she felt the familiar joy of her work enter her. The feeling helped her to overcome the pain of the blisters that formed on her hands as she hacked away with the too-blunt scissors to get the cane to the correct lengths.

At one o'clock, when the dinner bell rang, Tilly wasn't sure that she could finish the task, but kept hopeful even as she washed her stinging, bleeding hands under the cold running water in the closet room.

'How's it going, Tilly?'

Liz looked bright-eyed as she asked this, her eagerness for good news oozing from her.

'Better now, though I've had a struggle. I knaw as a work-man shouldn't blame his tools, but the lack of the correct ones is hindering me.'

'Eeh, look at your hands, Tilly. I've never seen them like that afore.'

'Naw, it's the combination of the wrong tools, and them as I do have being blunt, as well as the cane not really being fit for the job. But I'm mastering it now.'

'By, you're an inspiration, Tilly. I've allus admired your skill with wickerwork, but now you're showing you have the mettle to take on the world. It's helping me to see as it can be done.'

'Good. Keep hold of that, Liz. We're going to win through, lass, we're going to win through, I promise you that.'

Not feeling as sure as she sounded, Tilly tucked into the bowl of slop that had been put in front of her.

Gertrude was still distressed from her experience that morning and she wasn't responding to being shouted at to eat up her soup. Tilly longed to go to her to help her, but thought she'd better not; she was afraid of causing trouble for herself. Not that that would bother her normally, but there was so much at stake for her and Liz.

It was when the nurse's temper flared, and she emptied the soup over Gertrude's head, that Tilly forgot her resolve and stood up. 'Naw. You can't do that, leave her alone! She's just upset, that's all.'

'Ha! Upset, is she? Well, let's see how she likes this then. Maybe this'll cool her down.' As the room went quiet, the slap the nurse landed on Gertrude's face resounded around them. Gertrude fell backwards with the force of the blow and her chair toppled.

Tilly's chair scraped the floor as she stood and made to go over to help Gertrude. But she found herself held in a strong grip. 'Naw, naw, don't, Tilly. They're hoping you'll do sommat like this. They've used poor Gertrude to goad you. Don't take their bait.'

Tilly hesitated. Looking over at the nurse, she saw a fleeting smile of satisfaction cross her face. Realising that Liz was right, she sat down, mentally apologising to Gertrude for letting her down. Not that she could have done anything really, but just to show the woman some support might have given her hope. Sighing, Tilly looked down at the piece of meat floating in the greasy liquid in front of her and allowed a tear to seep out of the corner of her eye. She'd long ago learnt that life wasn't fair – at least, not to women like those sat in this dining hall, and those who misfortune visited.

'Well done, lass. You'd have made no difference, only made things bad for yourself. Gertrude will have forgotten all about it by now. Look at her, she's tucking in like a good 'un.'

Tilly knew this to be true. None of the women in here, except herself and Liz, knew what time of day it was, and all took knocks but carried on, not remembering anything about what had happened five minutes earlier.

'Poor sods, but then, Liz, maybe they're better off than us as I've wished a thousand times to be in that state of oblivion. I even tried to make it happen by making a friend of the gin bottle.'

'I knaw, lass. I've hit it meself a few times, but it's not the answer. What you're doing – working your way to a better life, is what'll win out in the long run.'

'You're perky – full of pearls of wisdom. Did you do as I said and not swallow the white stuff?'

'I did, and I feel near back to me old self. I spat it out into me skirt. I bent over when they weren't looking, then I covered it with me wraparound pinny.'

'That's good, Liz. The only way seems to be to face everything. And we can, together, we can. Right, I'm to get back to me work on that chair. You nod off in an armchair somewhere, so as it looks like you're drugged.'

'That won't be hard to do. I've felt weary ever since . . . well, anyroad, I'll not let all that into me mind.'

'Naw. Best not to. Get a rest, love. And Liz, you're still the best friend I ever had.'

Liz's eyes filled with tears. One spilled over, and Tilly pulled her sleeve over her hand and wiped the tear away with it. 'Work at getting strong, lass.'

With this, Tilly rose and went towards the corridor. The nurse called after her, but she ignored her, and kept her back straight.

Once back in the room they had allocated to her, a small anteroom off the handyman's workshop, Tilly let out a sigh.

'Oh, it is that you came back, then?' The connecting door to the workshop had opened and the handyman stood there, smirking. 'Only Nurse Fazely was after telling me that she could spoil your attempt to ingratiate yourself with the trustees. We had a bet on, so we did.'

'Aye, well, she nearly succeeded an' all, but I didn't let her.'

He stood, one arm above his head, holding the door jam; his eyes roamed her body. 'You're a pretty thing, or could be if you were dressed right and a comb was put through your hair. I like the curves of you. I could be after making things better here for you, aye, and making you feel good, too.'

Tilly's insides lurched.

'Is it that I don't hear you objecting? Well, I'm for having a key to the door . . .'

'Naw. Don't touch me.'

'Look, it's sorry that I am. I thought . . . Well, it is that I was told you're one who takes a payment for your favours.'

'Shut up! I'm not. I'm not a whore. I'm a person, not someone for men to leer over.'

'Aye, well, it's my mistake. I'll be getting back to me work, but first, will you promise me as you'll not be saying anything about this?'

Tilly looked into his eyes. They were what she would term Irish eyes – a lovely blue and watery. Honest eyes. His hair was brown, and his features strong – handsome, compelling. Something told her that he'd acted out of character, probably set up to seduce her as another weapon that could be used against her. 'Naw, I'll not say owt.' As she said this, she noted the stockiness of him – muscle, not fat – and knew he would have great strength and could easily overpower her. That he didn't said a lot for him.

'Is it that you like what you see, eh?' He was grinning now.

Tilly swallowed. The sound of his soft Irish lilt, so similar to Jeremiah's, was having an effect on her. Feelings were awakening. Thinking them long dead, she was surprised how quickly they had jumped into life.

'I'm for knowing that your name's Tilly. Well, I'm Tommy. I'll just be a knock on this door away if you're wanting any help. I hope as you'll forget me first dealings with you, Tilly, and we can be friends.'

Tilly blushed. She went to ask him to stay a while, but a noise in the corridor saved her from such a foolish step which would surely have made Tommy think she was changing her mind.

A voice drifted to her. 'I think I'll call in here and see how that girl is getting on. No doubt struggling to fulfil the lies she told Mr Jenson. I'll catch up with you later, Nurse.'

Tommy's whisper surprised her and confirmed her earlier thought. 'They think they can catch us at it. Look busy, Tilly.'

Tilly felt herself shaking as the door to the corridor opened.

'And what's wrong with you? Having a turn, are you?' Her eyes looked from Tilly to Tommy.

'I dropped in to tell Tilly that I am at her service, Matron, but it is that she doesn't need me to help her in any way.'

The matron's eyes shot up. 'Huh! Maybe not, but I still think she's bitten off more than she can chew. How you duped Mr Jenson I will never know. However, he will realise the truth tomorrow as I see you're nowhere near finishing that chair.'

'Naw, I'm getting on just fine, ta, Matron.' Tilly bent down and picked up the frame of the chair. 'I've rebound the joint here, and I've begun to weave the seat now. Look, I have the anchors in place. That part were easy as the holes are already bored into the frame of the seat. Then I threaded the cane through and twisted and plaited it into place on the outside. Now I have to do the same on the other side and then weave the other cane through the framework. It's taking me a mite longer than it usually would as I'm working with old brittle cane and need to soak it.'

'Oh? Well, I – I didn't think . . . I apologise, Tilly. I thought you saying you could do this was all a bluff. I see now that you are remarkably skilled at this work. Get about your own work, Tommy, and let the girl get on.'

This last came out as if it held a warning. Tilly was convinced now that Tommy had been set up and the Matron turning up was all part of a plan to discredit her. However, she had to give Matron her due. She was willing to eat humble pie. This proved itself in her next words.

'Well, carry on. I think Mr Jenson is going to be very pleased. And, well, maybe you have been diagnosed wrongly. Let's see how you go on from here.'

Tilly's heart rose from where it had sat in the bottom of her stomach since this encounter had begun.

Looking towards the connecting door, part of her wanted it to open again and for Tommy to come in and chat to her. But was it just a chat she wanted as she couldn't deny the feelings that being alone with Tommy had given her? *What's wrong with me? How can I feel this way after all I have been through and with the grief I feel cloying at me?*

The truth hit her as if a bolt of lightning had struck her and given her the root to her problems. *I've sought comfort with men. I've taken solace in the pleasure they can give me. And my instincts are telling me to again! Well, I mustn't. I must fight the urge as in doing so, I'll be a stronger person, I'm sure of it.*

And as if to make this a truth, Tilly felt the strength coming into her. Picking up the seat, she renewed the effort she'd given to get this far with the repair and let her mind work through how she would manage men from now on. *I'll not use them for me own needs. Aye, I knaw as they lust over me, but I must make them see me for who I am. And in doing that, maybe I'll come across differently to them.*

The more these thoughts began to develop, the stronger Tilly felt.

Within a couple of hours, Tilly had achieved the repair work. Now she needed to bind the seat into place. This didn't take long. Standing back and admiring her work, she wiped the sweat from her brow and set about tidying up the bits of cane and putting the tools she'd used into a neat line on the bench under the window.

Tired but uplifted, she picked up the chair. She would ask Tommy to look after it overnight; she didn't trust leaving it here for anyone to tamper with.

As she knocked on the door, and Tommy greeted her with no trace of the lust he had first shown, Tilly had a powerful feeling of freedom enter her, filling her with confidence. She was her own woman.

Tommy readily agreed to take the chair and lock it in his workshop. 'You've done a good job, so you have. It looks like new, Tilly . . . Tilly, I—'

'Naw, don't say owt. It weren't your doing, I realise that. I hope that we can be friends, Tommy. And thanks for helping me out by conveying to Matron that she was wrong. I'll see you soon. Night.'

'Night, Tilly. You be sleeping tight tonight, for I'm thinking the work you've done on this chair's going to change things for you.'

Tilly smiled as she turned away. It felt to her that she was entering a new phase. *Aye, I were a decent living woman when me Arthur were alive, but I lost me way with him going. I'm back on the right path now, though. Me future looks much better, and I'm going to do all I can to make it so.*

Almost skipping back to the day room, Tilly looked around for Liz, but couldn't see her. There was no one to ask, so she made her way to the dormitory, intending to wash and rest for an hour before supper.

She found Liz lying on her bed, curled into a ball, just as she had been that morning when she had first arrived in Tilly's dormitory. Worry dug her painfully in the chest. 'Liz? Liz, are you all right, lass?'

A sob deepened Tilly's worry. 'Liz, oh, Liz.'

'I can't do this, Tilly. Not taking me medication makes me face it all. I need it blocking out. I want my babbies, Tilly, I want them back.'

'Oh, Liz, don't, please don't, lass.' Tilly couldn't continue. The knot inside her that had been serving to keep her together broke and she slumped down on the bed next to Liz and sobbed her heart out. The strong woman she'd been a few minutes ago was forgotten, replaced by a lost one whose heart was breaking for the loss of her lovely little Babs and Beth, and Arthur and Jeremiah. All this came to the surface as she gave way to the terrible pain that consumed her.

The supper bell woke them both. Bleary-eyed, Tilly stretched, then felt Liz do the same next to her. They looked at each other, each with swollen eyes. 'We'll be all right, Liz, lass.'

'Aye, we will.'

'Come on then. We mustn't be late.'

'Eeh, Tilly, I have to pee. You go on, don't wait. I don't want owt to stop you from being in the good books, lass.'

'Naw, we're in this together. Hurry up. You knaw how long it takes some of them to respond to the bell; the nurses'll be too busy rounding up the known offenders to notice that we're late.'

When Liz came out of the bathroom, Tilly's heart sank at the sight of her. From looking quite perky, she looked gaunt once more, the hollowness of her cheeks exasperated by her bulging eyes. 'Eeh, you look a sight, lass.'

'Ha! Hark at the kettle calling the pot black! Have you looked in the mirror lately?'

Tilly giggled. Liz joined her, letting out a silly sound that was somewhere between a laugh and a hiccup. This tickled Tilly further and she laughed out loud. It did her heart good to hear Liz do the same.

Linked in arms, they made their way to the dining hall, their laughter filling the space around them. It was a laughter so near to tears, but what did it matter? It lifted their spirits and that's all that mattered to Tilly.

The next day, Tilly took her handiwork to Matron's office where she and Mr Jenson were waiting. Mr Jenson smiled as he looked at the chair. Something like triumph crossed his face, and he gave Tilly a grateful look. Tilly knew he'd been willing her to succeed to justify the faith he'd shown in her.

Matron gasped as she looked at Tilly's handiwork. 'Well, I never. It's like new. Well done, Tilly.' Cocking her head in a knowing way, she looked straight into Tilly's eyes. 'I have a feeling about you, Tilly. I don't know what it is, but I am beginning to see a very strong and determined woman where I saw only a cunning, mental wreck of a human being before.

I think you are going to earn your ticket out of here, though where you will land up is another matter. Wherever it is, don't let it be on the end of a bottle neck drinking yourself into a state again. Not that I blame you. I've been reading the doctor's notes and what you have told him about yourself. He says you are delicate and can be tipped over the edge at any time and are therefore safer in here receiving essential treatment. However, I think that treatment has long found itself elsewhere other than inside you. Well, well done, you. I like a fighter.'

This speech so shocked Tilly that she didn't know what to say. But joy filled her and spilt over in a little giggle that she hoped wouldn't be misinterpreted by this woman, who Tilly now thought could be a valuable ally to her.

'I entirely agree, Matron. Matilda doesn't seem as though she should be here in the first place. But as she is, we'll make use of her time.'

Tilly felt she could have jumped a mile into the air to release her joy. But she thanked them both and did as Matron bid her and went to find Bertha to give her a hand.

A week later the cane arrived, as did the barrel and the tools Tilly had asked for. Mr Jenson came to see her too.

'I want to know about the baskets you make, Matilda. You have amazed me with your craftsmanship.'

After telling him what other things she made out of wicker, cane and hedgerow pickings, he stunned her by saying he had a wife. Tilly had never dreamt. But she was glad because she found him to be a very nice man and to think of him as loved and a family man warmed her heart.

247

'I think I'll order some more of that cane and get you to make a basket for me, Tilly. A basket to collect vegetables and flowers in. One that will make a nice present for my wife.'

'You're better off buying willow, sir. It's more pliable, and I can change the colour of it to make the basket two-tone.'

'Really? And where do I buy that from?'

'From the same supplier. All the best materials come from Somerset. I used to have a trader bring me some up every few weeks. I was planning on opening a stall on Blackpool Beach when I fell into the despondency that had me hitting the gin.'

'Hmm, that's a shame, as your plan sounds as though it would be a very good thing for you. My wife and I often go to Blackpool and walk along the stalls; she loves a bargain and can be tempted into buying anything that takes her fancy.'

'Just the sort of customer they like along there.'

'Well, now, you get started on your work, and I'll check your progress on my next visit. Are you sure you have everything you need?'

'Well, sir, I could do with a helper; there's a lot of work to do. There's a woman in here who lived on my street back home.' Tilly mentally crossed herself against the lie she was about to tell. 'She used to help me to make baskets then and has a grasp of the basics. She could help speed up the process for me.'

'Who is it, Tilly?' Matron, who'd stood quietly by listening to the conversation, now chimed in. Her tone was suspicious.

'Liz. We grew up together and our recent circumstances are similar in what we have lost. We'd be good company for each other while we worked and help each other along.'

'Have you any objections, Matron?'

'No, no. As you said before, those who show willing to better themselves and a possibility of getting well deserve a chance and that's what we'll give them. Neither has been any trouble, but mind, Tilly, if ever you prove to be, all this will stop, and you will be back on your medication and following the regime the doctor originally laid down for you.'

Tilly didn't miss the threat in this. Matron was hard to fathom. One minute, Tilly thought she would be a good ally; the next she felt afraid of her and the power she had.

Thinking more about Matron's character as she walked the corridor to the workshop, Tilly let her original assessment of Matron find its place in her. She had two sides to her. The one allowed the cruelty that went on in this institution and the other could be very wise and all-knowing and show friendship. Something told Tilly to be on her guard in her dealings with the woman.

The smell of the cane when she opened the door to the room where she'd mended the first chair lifted Tilly. Yes, she would encounter problems along the way, but she was set now on a path to her freedom from the confines of this building, and she mustn't let anything interfere with that. She had to achieve that freedom for her and Liz. Or die trying. *Aye, lass, set your sights on them gates opening up and that'll get you through them.* A smile lit her face. *You're on your way, lass, you're on your way.*

TWENTY-ONE

Three weeks later, and with the view outside showing autumn had taken possession of the world, Tilly stood at the window of the workshop looking out. 'We've not had a breath of fresh air in all the time we've been here, Liz. I'm longing to just go outside and run along that grass. I'd lie down and roll down that slope, hearing the crisp golden leaves crunching under me.'

'Aye, I knaws what you mean. Like we did when we were kids in Blackpool and me ma took us to the park.'

'They were carefree days, Liz. Allus your ma would find a farthing to buy us an ice cream from the bloke who had a cart. I can see it now. His cart had the words "Stop me and buy one" on the side and your ma would stop him and the three of us would share a big ice cream between us. Eeh, thinking about it, I can almost taste it.'

'Aye, and she'd walk us down the prom an' all and let us go for a paddle in the sea.'

'And me Aunt Mildred used to get cross when I went home with the stains of the ice cream down me front and sand all over me skirt. But she never stopped me going the next week.'

'Naw, and she used to give the farthing to me ma now and again so it were her treating us.'

'By, I never knew that. She were a good old soul. She taught me the skill of basket making.'

'And now you're teaching me, though I haven't the knack for it, nor the talent as you have, Tilly. I'm enjoying it, though.'

'You're a big help an' all. You've learnt how to bend and twist the threaded canes to keep them secure – that saves me a lot of time.'

'Do you really think this will lead to our freedom, Tilly? Not that I feel like a prisoner. I feel like I were brought to the right place as I needed help. But you. You should never have been brought here. I'm glad you were, though.'

'Me too. Oh, I knaw as that's a funny thing to say, but I'd never have found you again, Liz, if I hadn't. And God knaws what would have happened to you. You knaw, I often think that God abandoned me, but I reckon me landing here was all part of his plan.'

'Now don't go getting all religious on me. It were a coin-cidence and that was that.'

'Aye, maybe.'

The connecting door opened, and Tommy walked in. 'It strikes me as there's not much work going on in here. It is that I've put the kettle on in me workshop; are you wanting to join me in having a cup of tea?'

Tilly marvelled at how Tommy treated her. He had apolo-gised for his behaviour, saying that he'd never behaved like that before and would never again. 'It is ashamed as I am and me mammy would turn in her grave at me antics, but I think it is that you know that I was told a different tale about you than you are, Tilly.'

That had been a week after the incident and neither had mentioned it since. Now, Tommy treated her with respect and had become a good friend. Although Tilly couldn't deny that she found him very attractive, the new her had kept to her resolve.

'By, that'd be welcome, ta, Tommy. You're right about the work, but we're well ahead and were just reminiscing and saying how we'd love to go outside, even if just for a few moments.'

'To be sure, I can make that happen. I've a door as leads to outside. The one next to me stove. It's not for being over-looked. It goes to me yard where I keep all me gardening tools.'

Tilly looked at Liz with an excited, devil-may-care look on her face. 'Let's do it, Liz. Naw one'll knaw.'

Liz jumped up. 'I'm game. Eeh, I can't remember the last time I had the open sky above me head.'

'Come on, then. It is that I feel sorry for you both. Neither of you should be in a place like this.'

'We're hoping not to be once we've completed this work. It's how we hope to convince them that we're not mad.'

'So, how was it you came to be here?'

Tilly told him briefly, while they waited for his kettle to come to the boil. Once it began whistling, they waited, watching him brew the tea. As he stirred the pot, he looked intently at Tilly. 'So, it's wee ones that you have? Your heart must be breaking. That you both should come to this . . . And is it that the longing for the gin is still in you, Tilly?'

'Naw, I never think of it now. Me dreams are all of getting out of here.'

'And what is it that you will do if that happens?'

Tilly took the steaming enamel mug from him as he handed it to her. 'I have me trade. I just need a start and then me and Liz can set up a stall on Blackpool Beach.'

Tommy was quiet for a moment. 'Well, let's get outside now it is that we have our tea.'

Once outside, Tilly took a deep breath and heard Liz do the same. She looked over to her and they both giggled. 'Eeh, it's grand, Liz. It makes me want me freedom even more.' Tilly looked around her. The yard wasn't big. The wall surrounding it was too high to see over and she looked longingly at the gate, wondering if it led to the fields she could see from the windows of the dormitory.

'Don't even be asking. I could be hanged for letting you out here, so it is that I can't let you go outside of the yard.'

Tilly smiled. Not for the first time Tommy had guessed her thoughts. She gazed at him as he took a sip of his tea. A lock of his hair had flopped forward. She knew nothing about him and was curious. 'So, Tommy, how did an Irishman like you come to be over here and doing this job?'

'It is a long story. My love of gardening brought me to this place, once I landed in England. My family are farmers and it is that I love to work the land. Not that mowing and hewing and planting are for coming anywhere near what we do on our farm back home. But, when me pappy died, our Patrick inherited. He is ten years me senior, and always one for bossing me about. His ways became insufferable to me when he took over. For sure it was a skivvy he took me for, so I upped and came over the water. I've heard nothing from him since, although me family's solicitor is knowing where I am. He's a bachelor is Patrick. And though I wish him no ill, I am the next in line. I wanted to be sure someone knew where it is that I am.'

'So, you're waiting for him to die?'

This from Liz angered Tommy. 'Why would you be saying such a thing? Come on, the both of you, and get inside. I've to get back to me work and the risk I'm taking for you is not worth it, so it isn't.'

Once the connecting door had closed between them, Liz said, 'Eeh, I think I touched a raw nerve there.'

'Well, it was a bit cutting, Liz.'

'I knaw, but it did sound like he was; I just didn't think. I'll apologise to him when we next see him.'

'Aye, well, let's get on. By, that were good standing outside like that. And it's done you good an' all. Your cheeks are pink. Makes you look much better.'

'And yours are an' all, Tilly. By, you look lovely. And I reckon as Tommy's got an eye for you, you knaw. No doubt you'll be living in a big farm in Ireland one of these days.'

'Ha, that'll be the day. Naw, I'd be happy just to get back to our Blackpool; there's naw place like it, Liz.'

Liz let out a big sigh. 'Don't you ever think how painful it'll be to go back? It frightens me.'

'Naw, it's where me heart is, and me memories, and I feel closer to me young 'uns there. I can go to the places we went together and imagine them dancing around me . . . Anyroad, don't let's talk of them, it grinds a pain into me that's hard to cope with.'

'Me an' all. But we're doing all right, ain't we, Tilly? Things are a lot better since we started this work.'

'Aye, we are, lass.'

They both fell silent, their work occupying them for the next hour until they heard the bell for supper.

'Right, let's make our way to the slop hall.'

Tilly laughed at Liz, but knew what she said was correct – what they served up was slop. 'Eeh, I wish they'd give us sommat decent to eat. I get hungry working like we are.'

'I knaw, Tilly. I feel awful 'cause I nicked that Mabel's bread last night. Well, she never eats it and me stomach were gnawing away.'

'I've done that afore now. There's a few that make me wonder how they survive, poor souls. They leave what they are given but who can blame them, the food is often disgusting. One of these days I'm going to talk to Mr Jenson about it.'

'He must knaw. He visits at breakfast time.'

'Aye, but they never serve till he goes. I don't think he knaws the half of it.'

Tilly got her chance the next day. Mr Jenson arrived as usual just before breakfast, but then went out of the room with the matron. Tilly thought that was that, but later, when she and Liz were engrossed in their work, he entered their room. 'Don't get up, girls. I came to see you working. I find it all fascinating. And to tell you what a good job you are doing. The board is thrilled with what you have achieved.'

'Thank you, sir … Sir, is it all right if I speak to you on sommat as is worrying us both?'

Mr Jenson was quiet for a moment, and Tilly almost lost her nerve. 'Well, I expect you want to ask for your release, but I can't help you there. I agree you should be discharged, but that is the doctor's domain, not mine.'

'It's not altogether that, though that's on our mind and we're working towards that day, but there's a lot that worries us about the other patients.'

Mr Jenson drew in a deep breath, almost as if to ward off anything unpleasant. But he didn't stop Tilly; rather, he nodded his head for her to continue.

Tilly blurted it all out. The cruelty they witnessed and the lack of good food. 'Or any food at all, sir. Sometimes there's nowt offered to some of them as needs help with their feeding.'

'What? Good Lord! Is this true?'

'Aye, it is. But, sir, please don't say who told you. See for yourself by varying your routine. Life will be hell for me and Liz if Matron gets to find out it were us.'

Mr Jenson held his chin in his hand and glanced towards the window before looking back at Tilly. 'Look, I can't take this in. There's adequate budget for food et cetera and it all gets used. But then, I ask myself, why would you say these things and invite me to find out for myself if they aren't true? Leave it with me. But not a word to anyone. I will bide my time and will take steps to discover what is really going on. In the meantime, keep up the good work and I'm sure everything will come right for you both.'

With this, he left the room. Tilly was shaking from head to foot. She looked at Liz but got no comfort there as Liz was trembling too. Her face was deathly white. After a minute she said, 'Eeh, Tilly, I never thought as you'd say owt. You've got some clout, lass, I'll say that for you.'

'Aye, well, let's pray as it's never found out as it were me. I can't think on the consequences if it were.'

Nothing happened for days, making Tilly very jittery, but then a commotion erupted a week later when Gertrude, who'd been subdued for a long time, suddenly started to wail during dinner. The sound made the hair stand up on Tilly's arms. It was akin to a wolf howling. Gertrude had no food in front of her, as was normal for her. Half-starved, she was skin and bone. After a couple of days of helping her to feed, the nurses had given up and just not served her for two days, leaving her slumped over the table after being dragged there as if she was a sack of potatoes. Tilly had tried to help her but had been bawled out for doing so and, always afraid of upsetting the thin line she trod, had given up and prayed that Mr Jenson would soon act on his word.

Her prayers were answered, as the door opened just as a nurse swiped Gertrude across the head, sending her clattering to the floor. The nurse then lifted her foot and kicked Gertrude in her side.

Not aware she was being watched, the vicious nurse turned on Aggie, who, distressed at what was happening, began to scream hysterically. Lifting the bowl of slop in front of Aggie, the nurse emptied it over her head.

'Good God! What do you think you are doing?'

The nurse shot round. An expression of sheer horror crossed her face. She looked from Mr Jenson to Matron, who stood next to him and for a moment appeared as though she was going to faint. Recovering, she shouted in her most commanding voice, 'Nurse, what is the meaning of this?'

The nurse, a huge woman with pockmarked skin and fleshy jowls, stared as if struck dumb.

'You're dismissed. Please leave the building immediately!'

The room went quiet. Not even poor Gertrude curled up in a ball on the floor uttered a sound. The nurse broke the silence. 'Oh no. If I go, you go. All of this is your doing, Matron.' The title was said with utter disrespect. 'It's you that keeps the rations low and orders that the patients are kept drugged. And it's in your pockets the money that's meant to be spent here goes. And it's you that advocates the treatment we dish out to these mad bastards. It's you who is to blame for all that goes on in this place – this so-called asylum. Ha, there's nothing of an asylum about it, it's more like hell on earth.'

'Shut up! Shut up this instant! You're a liar, a liar!'

A sound began to fill the air, a moan that became a wail, but it wasn't coming from just one patient, but all of them. Liz's hand found Tilly's and, in that moment, Tilly realised just how delicate Liz was as her hand was shaking. Clutching it tightly, Tilly looked into Liz's face. 'Don't worry, love, it'll be all right. Mr Jenson'll sort it.'

Liz had a look of terror on her face. 'Liz, Liz, lass, I'm here. Nowt's going to happen to you. Hold yourself together. Keep strong. We're nearly there, I promise you.'

A tear seeped out of Liz's eye, followed quickly by more, and yet she wasn't making a sound. 'Liz, Liz, love. I'm here.' But Tilly's words were drowned out by the noise that had started up as patients banged their bowls on the table. Tilly stood up. She looked into the eyes of Mr Jenson. His face held shock and it was as if he was rooted to the spot. Tilly guessed the poor man hadn't really believed her and hadn't expected to find himself in a room full of raging women. He just didn't know what to do.

Seeing the nurse storm out and the matron follow her, Tilly turned to Liz. 'Liz, help me. We must be strong for the others. They need us. Come on. Wipe your eyes and help me to calm them.'

With this, Tilly started to go from one to the other of the women, speaking to them gently, stroking their hair, giving each a hug, until gradually they became calm. She looked over and saw that Liz was doing the same.

'Help me with Gertrude now, Liz. Let's get her off the floor.'

As they went to try to lift her, Mr Jenson seemed to come to his senses and crossed the room to give them a hand.

With Gertrude sat on her chair, Tilly released a sigh of relief. All were quiet now.

'Thank you, Matilda. Will you and your friend stay with them and keep up this good work? I have to call a medical doctor in. These women need help. I am seeing them all properly as if for the first time. They all look half-starved and uncared for. How did it come to this? How?'

Tilly felt sorry for him. He had been duped by the cunning, cruel matron. 'Is there any staff I can call on to help you? Surely there should be more nurses on duty.'

'Naw, there's never much staff about. They'll be some in the kitchen, but usually one nurse and the matron are the only ones in attendance.'

'Oh, Lord.'

Tilly looked around at the now quiet women as Mr Jenson hurried out of the room. Some were almost asleep as they had put their heads on their arms which they'd rested on the table.

'What can we do, Tilly? I don't knaw where to start.'

'There's not much we can do, other than help them to a more comfortable place. We'll walk them one by one to the rest room and get them into the chairs; most will nod off and won't remember what's happened. Take Ruby and Elsie – they can shuffle along if they have hold of your hand. I'll take Jean and Hettie – they can manage to walk as long as they can hold on. And I'll encourage Patsy to follow – she's sprightly on her legs. Let's hope getting them out of here helps them as they all look scared out of their wits.'

Getting Gertrude to an armchair proved the most difficult. She was obviously in extreme pain, but they managed it and Liz found a rug to put over her knee. Gertrude managed a smile. It lit her face and for a moment, Tilly saw a deep love in her eyes. Bending over and hugging Gertrude, she kissed her cheek. 'You're going to be grand now, Gertrude, everything's going to get better, I promise.' Gertrude's arm came around her neck. Tilly let her hold her like that for a moment. To her these women were starved of love.

'Shall I get the tea trolley, Tilly?'

'Aye, that'd be a good idea, lass, I could do with a cuppa meself.' Tilly and Liz had often been called upon to take the tea round in the afternoon, before they'd been allowed to get back to their work. Usually the huge pots were ready for them and the trolley laid with cups of milk and sugar. Whether it would be now or not, she didn't know but suspected it soon would be as the kitchen staff would be well aware of what was going on and eager to show willing. Looking around the women, Tilly saw a sea of faces staring towards her, their expressions a mixture of hope and bewilderment. An idea came to her.

'Why don't we have a sing-song, eh, ladies?' An Irish ballad came to Tilly's mind: 'The Wind Beneath the Barley'. She'd heard Jeremiah sing it on many occasions when they'd sat around the blazing brazier on a dark night. The only songs she knew were Irish ballads as most other music she'd heard had been from the organ on the prom, which she thought was magical as she'd watched the cardboard punched with holes being wound through a machine. A wonderful sound. Taking a deep breath, Tilly began to sing.

> 'I sat within the valley green
> I sat there with my true love . . .'

A beautiful voice joined in with her. Tilly looked over at Maria, a quiet soul who shuffled around all day lost in her own world. But now, as she took up the song in a lovely Irish lilt, she came to life. Her voice filled the room. Tilly had never heard anything so beautiful. She stopped singing along; this moment belonged to Maria. Everyone else was silent, but not in a lost way; their faces showed their enjoyment of the wonderful sound.

As the last note died, they all cheered. Tilly looked around at each one; all were smiling. Encouraged, Maria went into a foot-tapping ballad and the room became animated as some clapped along to the lively tune and others tapped their feet.

Again, there was applause when Maria's song came to an end. Then, as Liz came through the door pushing the trolley,

Mabel, a woman who had never spoken but often moaned in a disturbing way while she rocked backwards and forwards, got up and walked to the piano in the corner of the room. Lifting the lid, and then seating herself with a flourish, she began to play. Tilly didn't know what the music was called, but it was beautiful – haunting – and watching Mabel was fascinating as she lifted her hands high between bars of the music, and swayed her body, giving the impression that she was a professional musician.

Tilly looked at Liz. Her face showed the astonishment that Tilly felt.

When the music ended, they all clapped once more and were joined by a male voice calling, 'Bravo, bravo!' Mr Jenson had slipped unnoticed into the room.

Mabel stood and bowed dramatically before walking back to her seat in the way Tilly imagined a ballerina would.

'Well, well, that was wonderful. What's that lady's name? She has obviously been a concert pianist.'

'I don't knaw her full name, only that she's called Mabel. We're just about to serve a pot of tea, sir, would you like a cup?'

'I very much would, Matilda, but I have a lot to sort out. I have sent one of the kitchen staff on an errand, so more staff should arrive soon. But don't worry, their ways will change, or they'll all be taking the same road Matron and that other nurse have already taken. Still, I won't burden you with the troubles of this place. If you can keep everyone happy for an hour or so, I should have everything in place. There are going to be some changes around here. These poor women are going to be looked after according to the trust's vision.'

Tilly couldn't imagine what vision could have resulted in the misery she had suffered here, and these poor souls had continued to suffer, but she hoped it included them being fed well and cared for with love, as well as something she knew they must long for as she did herself – to be able to walk around in the beautiful gardens that Tommy had fashioned. She hoped with all her heart that was what the vision was.

TWENTY-TWO

Christmas came and went. It was a time of change, as all that
the board had decided upon was gradually put into place. To
Tilly's surprise, the attitude of the remaining staff improved
greatly. It took a while for them to gain the trust of the
patients, but as they did, the atmosphere lightened. Good,
decent wholesome food was served at each meal, and plenty
of it, and there was always enough staff to coax and feed those
who were refusing to eat.

Tilly could already see a change in many of the women.
Some were putting on weight; some were now strong enough
to walk, when they had only managed a slow shuffle before.

The musical afternoons continued, with Mabel playing a
few beautiful numbers for them to listen to, followed by a staff
member playing music-hall songs that most of the women
knew and sung along to.

The level of transformation in such a short time amazed
Tilly. A proper routine was in place and the women responded
to it, knowing when it was time for their baths – something
they'd rarely had – or to get themselves to the dining hall
when it was mealtimes, instead of having to be almost dragged

in there. Happiness was the main feeling everywhere, though of course there were a few upsets when someone would ask for their mother, or their nanny. These times distressed everyone, and tears abounded.

'You should be proud of yourself, Tilly, lass. This were your doing.'

'Naw, but I'm glad as I found the courage to speak up. I wonder what the new matron will be like; the staff are saying that she'll arrive today. I hope she's nice.'

'Aye, and I hope with her in place we can see the time when we can be discharged. It needs someone at the helm who can sort sommat out for us. I sometimes think we'll rot here, Tilly.'

'Naw, that won't happen. But I can't see us getting out with nawhere to go. At least, not to total freedom. To the poorhouse, maybe.'

Liz shuddered. Tilly didn't know how to comfort her; her own heart was heavy at the prospect of maybe swapping one institution for another. But what it must be like for Liz to think of going back to the place where she lost everything she had in the world, she couldn't imagine.

It was a week later that they were called in to the new matron's office. A small woman with tiny features that made her sometimes appear childlike, her appearance belied the commanding air she had that brooked no nonsense, and yet made you think that she understood your problems and could deal with anything in a kindly way. The staff loved her and didn't baulk against any changes she wanted putting in place.

'Ahh, Tilly and Liz. Now, I won't go around the houses. I've been looking at your notes and taking in the work you have been doing and your general welfare. And I find myself bemused as to why you are in here, especially you, Tilly. Once we had sobered you up the mistake of you ever being brought here should have been rectified and a more suitable place-ment found for you. You, Liz, I can see did need the support we offer for a time, but you have become much stronger and I think would cope better away from the confines of this place.'

An excitement bubbled up in Tilly, and by the way Liz had grabbed her hand, she knew she was feeling it too.

'But, where to send you, that is the thing. With a good start, I believe the skill you have could set you up, Tilly, and that would also sustain Liz as I know you work well together. I am in awe of the work you have done. That, however, is coming to an end as I see there are only a few minor repairs needed on the chairs you have yet to work on.'

Matron leant forward. 'Sit down, both of you. I'm craning my neck looking up at you.'

As Tilly sat down in one of the two chairs that faced the matron across her desk, her heart was thumping. Partly with fear, and partly with hope, till she didn't know which one would win. Her future was so uncertain.

'I have spoken to Mr Jenson on this matter, as, although the medical aspect of your case is nothing to do with him and therefore he cannot discharge you, your welfare is the respon-sibility of the board of trustees. I have also spoken to the doctor and he has felt for a long time that you both should leave here, but there was never anything in place for him to discharge you to. He did advise the previous matron, but, well, that's by the by now.'

Tilly held her breath. She couldn't imagine what decision had been taken; she could only hope against hope that it was one that would give her and Liz a chance.

'And so, Mr Jenson had an idea that he should approach the board about ongoing help for you. It appears there has never been a case of anyone ready to leave here until they died and so, what to do about such a situation when there was no family support in place is something that has to be discussed. Obviously, there is the poorhouse . . .'

Liz's gasp caused Matron to pause. She looked at Liz with kindly, understanding eyes. 'Please don't worry, Liz, I will do all I can to stop that happening. Now, in the meantime, I want you to finish the work you are doing and start to prepare yourselves for leaving here. Oh, I am aware that with not knowing where you are going to it won't be easy to get excited about it, but rest assured, all that can be done is being done and we do have your welfare at heart.'

'Ta, Matron. It's a relief to us, isn't it, Liz?'

'Aye,' was all Liz could manage. Tilly could see she was fighting an inner battle.

'Well, off you go. As soon as I know any more, I will let you know.'

Tilly thanked Matron once more and took Liz's arm. Once outside the office, they looked at each other. The moment they'd longed for was on them, and now they didn't know how to react. All Tilly could think to do was to open her arms. Liz came into them and they hugged. Clinging on to each other in an exchange of love, and comfort.

'We'll be all right, won't we, Tilly, lass?'

'Aye, we will. We'll help each other. We'll get through whatever is thrown at us.' Tilly tried to sound brave, and to not let her dread of where they may end up consume her. She wanted to savour the feeling of knowing she was at last getting out of this place and try to look on the future with hope. It wasn't easy as neither of them had anything in all the world except each other. But then her heart nudged her, and she had to let in that she did have more. Somewhere, she had her lovely little Babs and Beth.

With this thought a huge sob took her and she buried her head in Liz's shoulder, who seemed to know what had set her off.

'We'll find them, Tilly. We'll never give up till we do. We'll ask the gypsies, 'cause they'll be back – they make a good living in Blackpool and they'll not give that up. Even if it ain't the same clan as took your young 'uns, someone must knaw sommat.'

The deep breath Tilly took didn't soothe the pain in her, but helped her to steady herself. She knew she had to conquer the feeling that had taken her. All the crying and longing in the world wouldn't alter things. She had to make a life for herself and Liz. And that life had to be in Blackpool, so that if ever her young 'uns tried to find her, she'd be where she was when they had left her.

Getting back to their work room, Tilly found that she was coping with the feelings that had overcome her and the excitement she'd initially felt had seeped back into her. Knocking on the adjoining door, she couldn't wait for Tommy to answer. 'Tommy, Tommy, are you there?'

The door opened. 'What is it that you're so happy about? I can hear in your voice that something has changed.'

'We're leaving, Tommy. At last, we're leaving.'

Tommy was taken aback for a moment. His look was of disappointment not joy. He changed it quickly and smiled. 'That's grand, so it is. And you are both deserving of it. But though I'm happy for you, I'm sad too. It is that I will miss you.'

'Aye, and we'll miss you, Tommy.'

Tommy looked at Liz as she said this. But his glance was only fleeting as his eyes went back to Tilly's and his gaze deepened. 'Can I have a wee while alone with you, Tilly?'

Tilly felt uncertain for a moment. She'd seen more and more that Tommy had feelings for her, but she didn't need the complication of having a man in her life. She just needed her freedom. 'I – I don't knaw, Tommy, I—'

'I am just wanting a word. I have something I need to say.'

'I need to go to the lav.' Liz was already at the door that led into the hall as she said this. 'Just give Tommy a mo, Tilly, he's been a good mate to us.'

Tilly wanted to stop Liz leaving the room, but it would seem petty. It wasn't that she was afraid to be alone with Tommy, as she trusted him now and had long accepted that he'd acted out of character when he'd first met her. It was just that she wasn't sure she could face what she thought he would say.

As the door closed on Liz, Tommy moved towards Tilly. She jumped back. His look was one of shock. 'Sure, you're not afraid of me are you, Tilly?'

'Naw. I'm just a bit unsure. Tell me what you want to say, Tommy.'

'Well, it is that I love you, Tilly. I know as I set off on the wrong foot. I wasn't for knowing you, and well, I thought . . . Well, I mean . . . No, there's no excuse for how I behaved. Is it that you will ever forgive me, Tilly?'

'I have. I'm just afraid of what you want from me now. I don't knaw if I can give owt. I'm like an empty shell, Tommy. There was a time a long time ago that I were a happy lass. I had the man I loved, and me little twins . . . but all that changed, and I lost me way. I can't explain it, but I need to find meself again. I have to get meself back to sommat of the woman I used to be. Going from one relationship to another ain't helping, as each time the pain piles higher. I'm afraid if you ask, I'll give in and I'm not ready.'

'Then I won't be asking anything of you, Tilly. But know that I am here for you. I love the bones of you and it is that I want you for me wife. But I'm willing to wait, if it is that you can give me some hope.'

Tilly was quiet for a moment as she tried to untangle the mixture of emotions coursing through her and to control the feeling that was urging her to go into Tommy's arms and seek the comfort she knew she would find there.

'I can see it is a battle you're having with yourself, Tilly, me wee darling, and I'm for wishing it would be won in my favour, but it is patient that I can be, so don't feel you have to be giving me an answer now.' Tommy opened his arms, and Tilly swayed towards him. Held close to his body, a feeling took her that this was where she was meant to be now. And that she never wanted to leave the warmth, the protection and the love Tommy was giving her. But then a warning trickle of doubt entered her, and she pulled away. Tommy sighed a deep sigh.

'What you found in me arms is always there for you, me Tilly.'

'Ta, Tommy. And ta for allowing me time to make me decision. I do have feelings for you, I'm just not ready.'

'Well, it is that I can live with that. So, it is back to Blackpool you intend on going?'

Relieved to be on safer ground, Tilly nodded. 'I don't knaw how, but I'm hoping to set up the stall I've talked to you about. I'm going to ask Mr Jenson if I can take the tools with me, but it all depends where they send us to live.'

'I don't doubt you are after being able to make a living, Tilly, your work is superb. That basket you made for Mr Jenson was beautiful, and similar ones would be well sought after, so they would. But how is it you will afford to buy the material you are needing?'

Glad to be on safe ground, Tilly told Tommy how she can gather material from the hedgerows to fashion baskets from.

'Well, I'm for finding that remarkable, so I am. But, Tilly, it is that I can be helping you. I have a good amount put by, and I receive an amount each quarter from me family estate, depending on the profits of the farm and the holdings me father left in trust for me. Let me make you a loan to help you to get established.'

'Oh, Tommy, would you? Oh, you don't knaw what a difference that would make to me life. If I could just rent somewhere for me and Liz to live, I can make a go of things and pay you back, I knaw I can.'

'Well then, it is done. I'll be for making the arrangements to have the money ready for you. It will take me a couple of weeks. I can be lending you ten pounds; will that be enough to get you set up, now?'

'Oh, Tommy, that's a fortune! Oh, ta, Tommy. That's enough for us to stay in a boarding house while we look for a cottage to rent, and we can pay the rent for a few weeks and so have time to stockpile some baskets to sell once the season gets started. Then I can pay you back in a couple of seasons, I knaw I can. Trade is brisk in Blackpool. The streets throng with those coming to take the waters and they're all monied folk who spend as if there's naw tomorrow.'

'Well, it is that it's a done deal. I only wish as I could find something to do that will keep me near to you, but I'm not a sea and sand man; I need me green fields and the caring of the land to keep me happy. And, Tilly, I'll be praying every day that you'll come back to me to be me wife. But in the meantime, I'll come and visit you. And I hope it is that you will come to see me. I have a nice cottage on the edge of these grounds.'

Tilly felt a twinge of longing to do just that. To be going to Tommy and his little cottage. To make a life as his wife and to be safe and cared for. 'One day, Tommy. Maybe, one day. I just need me freedom for a while. A time when I'm beholden to naw one and can run me own life and be responsible for me own destiny. Of course, I have Liz to care for an' all, but that will be good for me and keep me from being lonely. Loneliness is a powerful thing and can lead you to take decisions you never should take.'

'It is that I know all about loneliness, Tilly. But mine will ease, knowing you feel something for me and there is hope for me future. Never forget that I love you, Tilly.'

Something in Tilly wanted to tell Tommy that she loved him too, but she couldn't sort out her feelings towards him. Yes, he meant a great deal to her, but was it love? Surely, if she had to question it, then it couldn't be. Sighing, she was relieved when the door opened. Liz didn't appear straight away but called out to see if she was welcome.

'Come on in, Liz. I've some news that will ease our worries, lass.'

Liz looked pale as she came slowly into the room. She had an air of a scared rabbit caught in the light of the poacher's lamp.

'We're going to be fine, lass. Tommy here is going to make us a loan that'll see us right.'

'Eeh, but that's grand.' This was said with relief and saw Liz rushing at Tilly and hugging her.

'We're on our way, lass, it's really going to happen.'

The joy Liz showed lifted any lingering doubts Tilly had.

Tommy interrupted them, 'Before it is that you get too excited, I have to tell you there's a price to pay, ladies. And it is that I'm to be made welcome whenever it takes me fancy to pop up to Blackpool. And I'm going to do something I've put off for a long time: I'm going to buy meself a horse – that's if I can find stabling for it roundabouts. Then I can ride into Blackpool at me whim, so I can.'

'You'll allus be welcome, Tommy.' With this, Tilly impetuously kissed him on the cheek. Tommy caught hold of her arm, but as she jumped away, he let go. She smiled shyly at him. 'Eeh, Tommy, you'll never knaw how much what you're doing for us means to us, will he, Liz?'

'Naw, but we'll do our best to show you, lad. We'll give you good old Blackpool hospitality when you come.'

'I'll want more than that, so I will. I'll want you to be showing me the sights, especially the famous Blackpool Tower. I never thought such a feat could be achieved. Is it that it is as high as folk say or are they at exaggerating?'

Tilly laughed, and then felt surprised that she could do so. Always before, on hearing the tower talked of she'd felt a pang of pain, but now, she too wanted to see it again, and aye, go inside and see what her Arthur had lost his life for. She'd look on it as a tribute to him to do so.

Liz was looking at her with a worried expression.

Tommy cottoned on to Liz's concern. 'Is it an eejit that I am? I was for forgetting what you told me about your husband. I'm powerful sorry, Tilly.'

'Naw, it's all right. I'm proud of his part in building such a magnificent building and am longing to go inside meself. We'll do that. Me and Liz won't visit till you come, Tommy. Oh, and there's so much else to show you an' all. The Grand Theatre, the North and South Piers, and the Winter Gardens . . . Oh, so much.'

'It is that I am excited already. Is it that these Winter Gardens are somewhere I could work and do me gardening?'

Tilly and Liz laughed out loud at this. 'Eeh, Tommy, naw. It's a grand building, housing a skating rink, and places where you can sit out of the cold in beautiful surroundings. And when I left there was more building going on to add a ballroom that it was said would rival owt they had in Buckingham Palace and, best of all, a big wheel was being constructed just outside. Eeh, I can't wait to see it, it'll be grand.'

'By, lass, you never mentioned owt about all of that. Eeh, Tilly, I can't wait to get home.'

And in that, Tilly knew Blackpool was home to her and Liz and there'd never be anywhere that came up to it. She could almost smell the sea, and the roasting tatties, and taste the doughnuts the vendors offered, and she could feel the hustle and bustle of the beach stalls. She longed to be there. To have her own stall. Could it really happen?

Trying to settle down to work was difficult, but their chatter helped them. Waiting to hear when they could be released proved almost too much for them, but at last a few days later, Matron sent for them.

The doctor was present when they were ushered into Matron's office. He stood with his hands behind his back, a tall gangly man with a monocle held in one eye which lifted his brow and gave him a look as if he was permanently enquiring. He constantly tweaked his waxed moustache and shifted nervously. Clearing his throat, he spoke. He had a squeaky voice, that Tilly knew would grate on her if she had to listen to him for long.

'Sit down, please. Now, I am here to formally sign your discharge papers. I'm very pleased with the progress you both have made. It is rare; in fact, I can't remember it happening before – for someone to be discharged from here. So I am looking on you both as a triumph for my methods in treating those whose minds have become unbalanced.'

Tilly wanted to tell him not to, as nothing he'd done had helped them; they had helped themselves, and one way of doing that was by not accepting his potions. But her joy was such that she couldn't be bothered, she just wanted that piece of paper that said they were free.

Matron brought her attention to her. 'Now, you're not to get too excited. We are not sure what we can fix up for you yet and will be leaving the date off the release papers until we can come up with a suitable solution. Unfortunately, Mr Jenson isn't having much luck with the board. They're reluctant to sanction making funds available to help discharged patients to go forward and feel we should keep you until you can make arrangements for yourselves or approach the poorhouse to take you. A false economy, if you ask me.'

'Matron, we do have plans now, and a means of funding them an' all.'

'What? How?'

Tilly explained what Tommy was willing to do for them.

'Oh? Can he really afford that much? You shock me. Well, Mr Jenson will have to investigate this thoroughly before we can agree. What do you think, Doctor?'

'I don't know Tommy very well, but I can't see how he can afford to loan such a sum. I'm wondering if this is some kind of scheme these two have dreamt up. I would be reluctant to sign their release on these grounds; after all, there are all manner of ways they may intend to earn their living.'

Matron looked shocked, and Tilly wanted to fly at him as she hadn't missed his assumption, but she kept her head down; she didn't want to appear rude, or to upset what now seemed an unsure proposal to set them free.

'There, you see. That one looks guilty already. No, Matron, my pen won't be touching that discharge paper for a while yet, at least until you are sure of where they can go. And please be certain that it is a place of security where they will have to continue to follow Christian values. I'll bid you good day.'

With this, the doctor left the room. Tilly stood there feeling shocked and afraid. She hadn't known the doctor was a religious man, nor that he was so judgemental. Why should it be considered that two young women on their own would only be able to make their way in life by unchristian means?

A silence followed the doctor's departure. Liz broke it. 'What did he mean, Tilly?'

'He thinks as we're going to get up to no good to fund our way. But that's not true, Matron. We intend to work hard. We'll rent a cottage and we'll collect vines from the hedgerows and make baskets and all sorts, and then when the season comes, we'll take a stall on the beach and sell our wares. We'll pay Tommy back in instalments. It can work, it can. Please, please let us try.'

'Go back to your work. I believe in you and so does Mr Jenson. We will do all we can. I promise.'

Feeling a little better, Tilly stood. 'Ta, Matron, we'll not let you down.'

Tommy reassured them that all would be well, and this proved to be so just a few days later, when, armed with a letter from Tommy's solicitor and a ten-pound note, Mr Jenson and Matron gave them the news that all was in place for them.

'Now, there is no need for you to go into a boarding house, either. I have a friend who owns some terraced houses on Bonny Estate. He has one vacant one. Let me see ...' Mr Jenson consulted the paper he had in front of him. 'Yes, Back Brunswick Street. Do you know it?'

'Aye, we does, sir. They're nice houses and just the right size for us.' Tilly felt Liz shift uncomfortably beside her and hoped she wouldn't pipe in about the houses being small terraced houses, all crammed together with narrow roads between them and most overcrowded with families squashed into them, as they were never going to get a chance like this again.

'Yes, and we have something else for you. I managed to get an extra two pounds for you from the board. How they gave in, I do not know, but I pointed out to them how you had saved them twenty times that by mending the chairs, and to add to that, I have the sixpence three farthings I owe for the beautiful basket you made for my wife. She loves and wants more of your handy work. I will have your address, so will let you get settled and then will call on you. I think this extra money will be more than enough to furnish your home. Your rent will be one shilling a week, so if you can sell two baskets a week, that will cover that. Although with what Tommy has loaned you, you have enough for at least a year, leaving you plenty for food, and for setting up your business. I want to wish you both the very best of luck. Be our first success story, ladies.'

Tilly liked being called a lady – she wasn't used to the title – and rewarded Mr Jenson with a huge smile.

'Well, that's happiness for you, Matron.'

'It is, sir. And good to see. Tilly and Liz, your time here hasn't been wasted, and I hope you will look back and remember the best of your stay. For one, Mr Jenson has told me that it was your appeal to him to make things better that resulted in the well-run home we have now. You can be proud of yourselves. Now, I will hold on to this money for you and make the final arrangements. I think you can look towards the weekend as your release date, I just need to get the papers signed by the doctor. Do you think you can finish our chairs by then?'

Matron had a cheeky smile on her face and gave them a wink. Tilly giggled. 'We'll work our fingers to the bone. Naw, I'm only funning. Aye, we've nearly finished; they should all be done by tonight.'

Tilly couldn't believe it as they sat on the train. Her eyes took in every bit of the journey from Preston, and she couldn't wait to alight at Central Station. They were booked for three nights into the Talbot Hotel opposite the station – the time they thought they would need to sort out their home. Liz placed her hand in Tilly's. And her old saying came out, making Tilly smile. 'We're on our way, lass.'

Tilly returned to looking out of the window. *Aye, we are on our way. On our way to a new beginning. There's a lot we have to face now we're on our own, and the road won't allus be an easy one to travel, but we'll travel it together, Liz and me, and we'll make the best of it an' all.*

PART FOUR

A NEW BEGINNING

1895–1896

TWENTY-THREE

As the train pulled into Central Station, Tilly gripped her hands in front of her chest, for the excitement that took her was almost too much and she felt the need to contain it, to stop herself from yelling out at the top of her voice, 'I'm home!'

As was typical of Blackpool in late March, the wind whipped around them when they stepped onto the platform. Holding on to her bonnet and doing her best with her skirt, whilst clutching her suitcase, she giggled at Liz. Liz only managed a small smile, and that, Tilly could see, was almost swamped by the tears filling her eyes.

'Come on, lass, we're home.'

'Aye, and though I'm happy, Tilly, lass, I feel me loss more here than anywhere.'

Tilly risked letting go of her bonnet to hug Liz to her, but the move wasn't a good one as the bonnet took on a life of its own and whipped off her head. Dropping her case and running after it as it danced along the platform had her laughing into the wind. But best of all was the sound of Liz joining her in that laughter.

At last she caught up with the bonnet and stepped onto its brim to stop its antics. Out of breath, she bent down to pick it up. Going back to where Liz had stayed with their cases, she bent in a fit of giggles. 'A forgotten lesson, Liz: allus have ribbons on your bonnet when in Blackpool.'

Just saying the name of her home town made Tilly feel the excitement of it, as did the hustle and bustle of the crowds around her arriving from all corners of England, as they alighted different trains on different platforms; Central Station in Blackpool was the largest station in the country and brought visitors to the very heart of the town. The folk around her, calling for porters, or hurrying towards the exit carrying their own baggage, would all have come for an early season break and were nothing like the numbers that would arrive for the Easter bank holiday in a couple of weeks. The thought of that event put an urgency into Tilly. *I have to get some stock made for then; I can't miss the busiest time of the early part of the year.*

'By, we've a lot of work to do, Liz. I reckon we should spend just two days getting what we need for the house – the big items of furniture – and then, if you're in agreement, you can spend your time making the house into a home, and I will get on with making baskets. I want enough to set up a stall for the Easter holidays.'

'Eeh, Tilly, you're pushing it, lass. It's a lot to ask of ourselves in just two weeks!'

'It is, but if we miss this opportunity, then we might not earn much for the next couple of months until the season starts to get busier. Though I could do what I used to do and take me baskets from door to door, but it's a thankless task most of the time.'

Saying this brought Cook, and Florrie, of the house in St Anne's, to her mind, and she determined that she would visit and find out from Cook if Florrie was all right. Part of her hoped that Florrie would be back at the house in her rightful position, but that would mean that she would have lost her ma, and Tilly wouldn't wish for that. *I doubt they've thought any more about me. Oh aye, they were kind, but after all, I were just a lass who'd come begging at the door of their master's house. But for all that, I felt a deep feeling for Florrie. There was just sommat that drew us together and I knaw as Florrie felt it an' all.*

'Aye, I remember you saying when you told me of the gypsies. Eeh, Tilly lass, we've been through the mill, haven't we?'

'We have. And, like you, I'm feeling the pain of it all now I can smell the sea air. It brings it all back. But we've to stay strong, you and me, Liz. If we don't, we'll go under. We've been there once, and it wasn't a good experience. We must stop ourselves going there again. We've to push ourselves to the limit.'

Brave words, but they were said over a lump that had formed in Tilly's throat as familiar sights and smells assailed her – the fishy aroma from Robert's Oyster Bar, the tang of the salty air, and the delicious smells of the potatoes cooking on the coals of a brazier, across the road on the seafront. Then there were the unique sounds of Blackpool – the rumbling of the trams, the calls of the tradesmen and stallholders to attract custom, and the tinkling of bells around the necks of the beach donkeys, all mixed in with the excited buzz of holiday-makers' chatter. All this brought back memories that were difficult to visit.

'Right, best foot forward. We'll drop our bags at the Talbot Hotel where Mr Jenson has arranged a room for us, then we'll have a hot tattie, or fish and chips, before we go to the flea market to see what we can pick up for our cottage.'

'I reckon we should go and look at the cottage first, Tilly, and get an idea of what we need. We don't even knaw the size or layout yet.'

'Aye, I think that's a better idea. I wasn't thinking straight. Here's the hotel, now. Eeh, I never thought the likes of us would stay at a place like this, Liz.'

Tilly looked up at the hotel, a white, two-storey building with its woodwork painted in black. One sign to the side boasted that there was a bowling green to the rear.

The receptionist looked them up and down, making Tilly feel conscious, for the first time, of how their clothes showed their humble status in life. Not the usual guests to stay in this hotel, and she wished now that Mr Jenson had gone along with their suggestion that they stay in one of the back-street boarding houses.

Her grey skirt, though clean, looked crumpled, and her long purple jacket was worn at the cuffs and lapels. She'd been wearing it when she'd been picked up by the van and whisked off to the asylum, and though it had been cleaned, it was shabby. Liz looked even worse, in a brown frock that had long since faded and showed signs of wear as the lace that adorned the collar was tatty, and a couple of the buttons that formed a straight line down the centre of the bodice had lost their covering. On top of this she wore a grey three-quarter coat that looked fit for the rag bin. Both had removed their bonnets, and Tilly knew her hair was an unkempt mess as it had been since the scissors were wielded by the horror nurse who first took charge of her.

Taking a deep breath and mustering all the dignity she could, Tilly checked them in and then asked for a porter to take their bags to their room. 'We'll be back later. We won't want dinner, ta.' With this she almost pushed Liz towards the exit. 'Eeh, lass, we're not of the class that madam's used to.'

'Naw, we're not, Tilly, but our money's as good as the next person's, and don't you forget that. We could be two rich, eccentric old maids for all she knaws and she should have more respect.'

Tilly laughed at this, and felt lifted, not least because it showed that Liz still held a spark of her old self inside her.

The house they would be renting from Mr Jenson's friend was in good order. A two up, two down, with the lav out the back, it backed onto an alley, and looked out at another house identical to it and seeming to only be an arm-stretch away from it. This was the pattern for all the streets on the Bonny Estate. One end of them came out onto Bonny Street and then the promenade, and the other onto Central Drive.

But though crammed together, the houses were respectable and well looked after. The children playing outside were neatly dressed and looked cared for and all the steps were scrubbed and the windows shining.

'Eeh, Tilly, lass, we've fallen on our feet here.'

'Aye, we have. And it won't take much furnishing. For a start we'll need a bed each. There's that good-sized cupboard in each bedroom so that's plenty of room to store our clothes. Then down here we need a sofa and a rug and a small table.

Perhaps a cupboard for the kitchen and a table and a couple of chairs. What do you reckon, Liz?'

'Aye, we can make it cosy later when we've got some money saved, 'cause we've to get pots and pans, and crockery and bedding, and that lot what you've mentioned would take a good slice of what we have.'

'Aye, you're right. So, let's get down to the market and see what we can do.'

By the time they moved in, on the third day of being back in Blackpool, they were both very pleased with what they'd managed to get, if sad as to why they came to have so much, as their luck was a neighbour's sorrow. Molly Watson, as she'd introduced herself, had collared them as they'd left the house intent on going to the market. 'Excuse me, I hope you don't mind me asking, but are you moving in?' she'd said.

Thinking her the nosy one of the street, Liz had answered her. 'Who wants to knaw?'

'Eeh, I ain't minding your business or owt. I'm just in a bit of a predicament and I thought I could help you.' She'd gone on to explain how her ma had passed away and how she had been given the task of clearing the house and only a week to do it as the landlord wanted his key by then. 'I wondered if you might be interested in any of me ma's stuff. It's good quality and has been looked after.'

'By, I'm sorry for your loss, lass,' Tilly had told her. 'But aye, we might be interested. We can look at it anyroad.'

Everything in the house, which was only a few streets away, was just as Molly had said – very clean and in good order. Molly had shocked them then by saying, 'I only want three quid for the lot. All the furniture, bedding, crockery, everything. I've taken what I want to remember me ma by, so you can take the rest.'

They'd jumped at it and now it was all in situ and looked lovely, from the oak dresser that stood at the back of the living room, to the ruby three-piece suite, and the huge rug that stretched from the fire to the back wall, which, though faded, still showed the rose pattern on the beige background.

'Eeh, Molly, were your ma rich, lass? This stuff's much better than any we thought to get hold of.'

'Naw, she worked for the Clefton family and they gave her bits when they didn't want them. She got some nice pieces, and though she had them for years, she loved them and looked after them. They're not my taste, but I'm glad as you're both happy with them.'

'More than happy, ta, love.'

They both liked Molly. A little bit older than them and in her early thirties, she hadn't asked them any questions about their background, but had taken them on face value, and been a great help to them, mucking in and helping them with the move. A small woman, Molly had bright red hair that she found difficult to tame, and a perky face that always looked interested and ready to smile. When she did smile a dimple appeared on each of her cheeks, and her hazel eyes twinkled. She was a mum of two boys: Gerry, eleven, and Brian, twelve. Nice, quiet lads. Molly seemed to be the one in the street that solved everyone's problems as, more than once, other women had joined them and asked her how to make something, or if she could sit with their ma, or look out for one of their young 'uns. All had accepted Tilly and Liz and made them feel welcome and as if they belonged.

When they sat having a cuppa after they'd made the beds and unpacked the towels and other linen, Tilly, feeling she ought to tell Molly a little about themselves, asked, 'I suppose you're wondering about us two, Molly?'

'Aye, I'm curious. You both have wedding rings on, but don't seem to have your men or any young 'uns.'

There was a silence for moment, then Tilly took a deep breath. What she told was that they had grown up together and had both been widowed, and about what had happened to their children. Tilly didn't tell of anything that happened after that, only to say that they'd both needed a home so had decided to set up one together.

'By, me lasses, that's a sorry tale. I feel for you both. But I see you don't want to talk about it all, not in depth, so just to say that if ever you do, you can drop in to mine, and I'll give you a ready ear. So how are you going to keep yourselves?'

This bit was easy to tell of, and Tilly had to be shut up in the end. 'All right, Tilly, we knaw as you're excited, but there's naw need to bore Molly with all the details of how you make your baskets, love.'

They all laughed at this. 'Sorry, Molly. Liz's right, I'm that excited, and eager to get going.'

'And you get your materials from the hedgerows? That's amazing, lass. Why don't you take me lads with you and show them what you need and how to cut it? They can do some gathering for you whenever you want them to.'

'That'd be grand, and I'm hoping to catch the trader an' all. He allus comes up from the south and has everything on his cart. He used to bring me some cane to order.'

'Do you mean the fellow who goes around the streets with a horse and cart and sells from the back of it?'

'Aye, I do.'

'Well, he's due round soon. He came about a month or so ago and I ordered an Indian rug and two cushions. Lovely they were; I love owt from far-off countries. My Will says as I'm daft putting such stuff in a house like ours, but if you like nice things, it don't matter where you live if you can get them. Why shouldn't you have them, eh? Anyroad, I'll make sure he calls on you, or if you write down what you need, I'll order it for you.'

'I – I can't write, Molly. I never went to school.'

'I'll do it for you, love. Just tell me what you want.'

Embarrassed, Tilly explained what she needed. 'If it's the same bloke, he'll knaw what I mean.'

With this, Molly left, and Tilly and Liz slumped back into the comfort of two chairs either side of the fire.

'Tilly, lass, I'd love to learn to read; as you knaw, I'm in the same boat. Me ma didn't think learning was for the likes of me and our lot and, well . . . I were the same with my young 'uns. I never made them go to school.'

Tilly didn't take Liz up on this. It was good to hear her talk of her children without breaking her heart. So, she just kept the conversation going.

'Me too. I've allus wanted to learn. Imagine sitting here of an evening with the fire roaring and us quietly reading a magazine, or a book even. Eeh, it'd be grand. Still, once I get me materials, there won't be much time to dwell on it. I'll go to the field tomorrow.'

★   ★   ★

Tilly was surprised to find so many vines from the blackberry bushes, and some, though winter had played havoc with the undergrowth, were in excellent condition. As she hadn't a cart, or a pram, she tied what she had in a bundle and strapped this across her back. The willow pieces from branches that had fallen, or that she could hack off, were the longest and heaviest to haul, so these she put in a sack and dragged them behind her.

On reaching home she was exhausted and had taken a few funny looks from folk.

'You did well then, lass. I should have come with you and helped you, but anyroad, I've not been idle. I've emptied the last of those sacks and found a place for all the linen. By, we've plenty of everything, Tilly. Drop that lot outside. I've a big pot of water bubbling away and I've dragged the tin bath in. You have a sup of tea – it's all made – and I'll fill the tub for you. You'll feel better after a soak.'

'Eeh, ta, Liz. I'll be glad to teach Gerry and Brian how to get me material for me. It'd be worth paying them to do this job, I don't seem to have the strength I used to have.'

'We'll get sorted.'

The sound of the tea filling her mug cheered Tilly. She sat on a kitchen chair at the plain wooden table they'd bought – its surface had been scrubbed to within an inch of its life, and yet it was still strong and sturdy – and relaxed as she let the tea revive her. There was a delicious smell of baking coming from the oven. 'What have you got cooking, Liz?'

'It's a pie. I haven't made it, I didn't have all the ingredients. We've to do some shopping, lass. But Molly made us one and brought it over ready for the oven. By, she's a lovely lass, Tilly. We had a good chat today and I were able to pour me heart out to her. Somehow it helped. Her being nowt to do with me life before made it easier. She showed sympathy and even cried, but she didn't have the pain in her that you've got over me young 'uns. You loved them almost as much as me, and I knaw it hurts you to talk about them.'

'It does, Liz. And I knaw what you mean. It ain't just the hurt of your young 'uns, but of me own an' all. I daren't talk to you, Liz, about the pain I'm in as you loved me little Babs and Beth . . . Oh, Liz . . . Liz . . .'

They clung together, tears running down their cheeks and yet too drained of emotion to get any real release.

'You talk to Molly, Tilly. It's good to let it out, but we can't help each other much when it comes to our young 'uns. We can't.'

'Eeh, Liz, look at us. I'm sorry, lass. I'm just tired. We'll get through, we will.' Tilly took a deep breath, and then a big gulp of the hot tea and felt in control once more. 'By, I'm looking forward to that soak, lass, and here you are wasting time. I'll have supped me tea afore you knaw it.'

'Ha! Cheeky bugger! Right, I'll get on to it, and I have a big towel ready for you. Eeh, lass, it's of the quality you'd expect a lady to have. And I've dug out your clean nightie an' all. I won't be long.'

Liz didn't only get the bath ready, but scrubbed Tilly's back too, which soothed her and sealed the companionship she knew they would have for each other. They had been close at the asylum, and for years before they fell out, but this was different, as they were on their own now and reliant on each other. Taking Liz's hand, Tilly looked up at her. 'By, Liz, I love you like a sister. You're the best thing in me life.'

Liz smiled, her lovely kind smile, and though careworn, it lit her face. 'I reckon you were right that time when you said that God made sure we got back together, though he could have chosen a better way.'

'Aye, but to have each other is a blessing. Ta for being you, Liz.'

'Eeh, you daft apeth! Get away with you. And hurry up out of that water afore it gets cold, I'm going to get a quick dip in it meself.'

Once they were in their nightdresses, sitting next to the fire eating their pie to the soothing sound of the clock ticking, Tilly thought that despite everything they had a lot to be thankful for, and she would always be thankful for having Liz. *I'll allus take care of her and, somehow, we'll find happiness. I'm sure of it.*

TWENTY-FOUR

Over the next few days Tilly and Liz worked so hard making baskets that their fingers were red raw and scratched. Liz's job was to bore the holes into the bases that Tilly had fetched from the woodyard and then thread the thicker vines through, before plaiting them securely, leaving the long strands ready for Tilly to work her magic and fashion the basket.

Tilly had enjoyed seeing the woodman again. A jolly-faced man with rosy-red cheeks, he was small in stature, and almost as round as he was tall. His breeches were tied around his waist with a length of string, and at his neck he wore a kerchief which he tucked into his khaki-coloured shirt.

The smell of the woodyard always lifted Tilly; she'd drawn in a deep breath and enjoyed the scent of freshly cut wood and had wanted to run her fingers through the sawdust and curled wood shavings.

Henry, the woodman, had been surprised to see her but pleased to hear that she was all right and back doing what she should. He'd always been good to her, sometimes giving her a couple of bases that he'd said he'd made out of a piece of board he was going to throw away.

Always one for chatting on about this and that, he'd told her the news about her old neighbours. She'd been upset to learn that Martha was ailing and determined to go along to see her to make her peace and to help her if she could. The woodman had news of the vicar and Agatha too, telling Tilly that they had married. 'I tell you, folk around here reckon as sommat were going on afore she lost her husband and that's why he ... Eeh, I didn't mean ... Anyroad, you'll find them around here more forgiving of you as Agatha told the vicar's housekeeper that Joe used the fact that you had nowt to, well, you knaw ... By, I'm sorry I started this line of conversation. I'm digging meself a hole to bury meself in.'

Tilly had laughed. 'Naw, it's all right. I were duped by him and acted in the wrong way. I – I, well, I did it all for me young 'uns.'

When Henry had asked after Babs and Beth, there had been an awkward moment, as she'd not been able to explain without shedding tears. Her pain still held a rawness, and that was even more cutting as she walked the streets she'd walked with them.

'By, lass, I've heard of such things but never come across it afore. It don't seem fair that such a lass as yourself should have so much put on your shoulders.'

He'd wiped a tear from his own eye and then coughed and turned away, pretending to be busy shifting things around. By the time they had both composed themselves Henry had added to the pile that he intended to cut into more bases for her to collect. 'They'll be ready for when you next call, and I don't want owt for them. If I can find some more offcuts, I will an' all. I'll help you all I can, lass.'

Tilly had thanked him and told him that she would send a couple of lads she knew to pick them up.

As she'd left, she'd impulsively kissed Henry on the cheek and had once more seen tears in his eyes as he'd smiled a watery smile and patted her shoulder, unable to voice his goodbye.

'Eeh, lass, can't we ease up?' Liz cut into Tilly's thoughts. 'We've five made now. That'll bring in a bit, won't it?'

'Aye, it will. And you've a few bases made ready for me to tackle. You go and soak your hands and put some of that balm we got from Mr Lloyd on them. It works miracles.'

'What about you, lass?'

'I'm used to it. After a couple of days, me hands will harden up again. By, you'd think after all the weaving we did of them chairs that our hands would be toughened up, but the work wasn't as intense as this, as most of the frameworks were in place, and we had that good cane to work with.'

'If you're sure it's all right, I'll do that, and I'll put the kettle on an' all.'

They were working on the kitchen table, with the back door, which led to their small yard, stood open. It was the first of April and Easter Sunday was just three days away. 'Liz, it's a nice day, why don't you take a walk to the beach and see if you can secure us a pitch after we've had a cuppa? Seek out a chap called Dan. He has a bric-a-brac stall near to North Pier. He said I could pitch up next to him when I asked afore. He were a nice bloke. Not that I knaw much about him, but he were willing to help me back then.'

'Aye, I'll enjoy that. And I'll bring us a bag of mussels from Robert's Bar. Be a treat for all our hard work.'

With Liz out of the way, Tilly made a renewed effort and soon had another basket made – a small one that could be used as a fruit basket, or to stand a pot of flowers in. Thinking this gave her an idea. She would buy some fruit, and a pot plant, and make a display of a couple of them, and she could buy a few veg and clean them up and display them in one of the oval ones. The idea took hold and she began to imagine a row of baskets showing their purpose and looking colourful. Something else occurred for the future too. *Maybe I can build on that theme, and line some of the baskets with a nice gingham material, and pad them, so that folk can see the different uses – nannies could keep all the bits and bobs they needed for baby's bath in one and, like Florrie did, I could show one holding dusters and polish and a feather duster.*

Her thoughts went to the chairs she'd mended, and she began to think of making nursing chairs, and even rocking chairs. The woodman would help. He was able to cut wood into all kinds of shapes, and now that she was experienced in binding the joints of the chairs to make the frame strong, it all seemed a possibility.

An excitement built in Tilly as she began to dream big dreams of one day having a shop in Blackpool and her hand-made cane furniture being famous countrywide.

From this her mind drifted to Florrie, prompted by the thought of the basket Florrie had bought. *Once Easter is done, I'll visit both Martha to see if she'll accept me back as a friend, and Cook to find out about Florrie. It'll be good to catch up with the folk who treated me right. Maybe it will help me, and Liz an' all. We need more good folk in our lives. And Cook and Florrie were good folk; non-judgemental they were, especially Florrie. Eeh, I did like Florrie.*

As her thoughts turned to Molly and the friendship they had found with her, it was as if Tilly had conjured her up as the back gate opened and Molly appeared. 'How's it going, lass? By, I don't knaw how you do it, but I'd love to learn. Is it sommat as you can teach, Tilly?'

'Aye, though you do need to have a little talent to master some of the art of it. But, like owt, you never knaw till you try. Here, I've a shape here that won't make a decent basket; it were one of the offcuts the woodman threw in for free. You see that tool there? Aye, that one. That's called a bodkin. All baskets start with a base that has holes punched evenly around it. You make them with a bodkin. Try it.'

After a few moments of struggling with this, Molly gave up. 'Eeh, owt as difficult as that ain't for me. Is there a simpler process that I can help you with?'

'Ha, basket making ain't for anyone who finds it difficult to make holes with a bodkin! How about you test them willow out there that are soaking in the bath? Get hold of each piece and if it bends easily, then it's ready for me to use. Just get ten strands out for me, as I want the others to darken up and they have to soak longer for that to happen.'

'Oh, is that how you get the different colours?'

'Aye, they start to turn brown as you soak them, and the longer you leave them, the browner they become so you can achieve different shades. And you can steam them an' all to get a lovely black willow.'

When Molly had brought in the willow strands, Tilly set her to getting the thorns off the blackberry vines she had stored from her visit to the fields. 'The easy way is to run them through canvas that you hold in your hand around the branch and pull through, but I've not got any at the mo. I'll build on me equipment as I go, but first, I need to afford a shed to keep me tools and stuff, and to have room for me stock. Oh, and a cart or an old pram to transport me goods to the beach – that's a priority as me stock grows. Though I were going to ask your lads to help me and Liz get down there in the first instance.'

'They'd be glad to. They'll be off school all Easter, so that and collecting you some more hedgerow pickings'll keep them busy. How about I keep one of these vines and take it to them? It'll give them an idea of what you need.'

'Eeh, that'll be grand to have their help with finding me material, but best to wait till I can take them out after Easter. I need to show them a safe way of cutting, and exactly where to look and how to choose the thickness and quality needed. I saw some willows growing last time and some of them could be ready, but they're not easy to harvest.'

'I never knew as there were so much to it all. Just look at this. It's grand.' Molly had picked up an oval basket fashioned in light vine and with a pattern of dark leaves around it. 'My, it's perfection.'

As Molly began the task of clipping the thorns from the vines, Tilly told of her idea to line some of the baskets and then was surprised to hear that Molly was a seamstress and could make the linings for her. 'I worked alongside me ma and she taught me all the skills needed. I have her old sewing tin – eeh, lass, I just thought how much nicer to have all her sewing kit in a basket. I saw one once in the big house where she worked. It had a lid on it and was lined in silk. There were pockets in the silk for cottons and a flap made of felt that all the different-sized needles stuck into. And a little basket that fitted inside to hold pins. It was fashioned around a wooden interior. Then there were elastic hoops along one side that held scissors and crochet hooks of all sizes. It was lovely.'

'Eeh, Molly, I've never seen or heard of owt like that. If I could make the same, they would sell well, I knaw they would. The woodman would knaw of a carpenter who could make the little boxes for me and I could easily make the basket for them to fit in. They could be glued into place and then a little lid made for them. Was the lid to the basket loose fitting?'

'Naw, it were fastened by two leather straps that were attached to the basket and hung over the side. There was a hole in each then a toggle on the side of the basket that fit through the hole to fasten it. And it was padded on the inside and lined with the same silk.'

'By, the fastening sounds complicated, and too much to find all the craftsmen that would need to be involved. We'd have to come up with a different fastening. I'll give it some thought.'

'Oh, I don't knaw. Me man works in a saddlery, he's working with leather all the time. He makes things out of the offcuts that he's allowed to bring home. He made a lovely pouch for his tobacco, and bookmarks for the lads. Smart, they were, as he made one end appear as if it had tassels and he carved a different picture on each. He's very clever. I'll draw the fastenings and show them to him and see what he thinks.'

The excitement Tilly had felt earlier as new ideas had come to her really took hold now. She couldn't wait to get a little box made and to try out all the ideas Molly had given her. If she could pull them off, she knew she would make a fortune. This thought spurred her on and, ignoring her sore hands, she worked away at finishing another small basket.

As they worked, they chattered on. Mostly about how this or that could be made out of woven wicker and cane. Molly was a fountain of knowledge of the items that a rich family used, and also told her about a high-backed chair that the old lady of the house sat in in the summer house and the smaller ones that the family used. Molly had helped her mother to clean them and remembered the structure of them. She drew this for Tilly, who'd never seen such items of furniture. They looked complicated and Tilly knew it would take a long time for her to make each one, but she had a longing to have a go at doing so.

Now her dreams grew and grew as she saw herself not only with a shop, but with a shop with a workshop behind that held all the tools she would need.

'Tilly, lass, the more we talk, the more I see you making this humble beginning into a big concern. But you knaw, for that you're going to need other skills.'

Tilly couldn't think what Molly was referring to.

'I don't want you to be embarrassed by what I'm going to say, Tilly, but I reckon as you need to learn to read and write. And I'd like to teach you an' all. I knaw I have a talent for teaching as I've helped a few. I were taught alongside the Clefton children in their nursery. They had a governess. She were lovely, and believed all kids, no matter what walk of life they came from, should be taught at least the basic skills of reading and writing. By, it opens up so much to you, Tilly.'

302

'Oh, Molly, would you? Would you really teach me and Liz to read and write? I can't tell you how much we've longed to do so. I were going to get me tw – twins to teach me ... when they grew up.'

'By, Tilly, how do you cope, lass? Me heart bleeds for you.'

'I don't, but I have to, if that makes sense. Aye, and I have to hang on to the dream that one day they will come looking for me and that is why I'll never leave Blackpool. I see meself with me stall on the beach and one day, them walking along and spotting me. We'll run into each other's arms and I'll never let them out of me sight ever again.'

'Oh, Tilly, Tilly, lass. Here, take me hanky, it's clean. Dry your tears. I should never have led you to thinking of them.'

'I never stop, Molly. Allus they are there, but you knaw, as terrible as me situation is, it don't match that of Liz's. Poor Liz has naw hope. She can never imagine a day when her young 'uns'll come running into her arms.'

At this they both cried. Somehow, in doing so, it bound them together as firm friends and Tilly felt glad as it was a friendship that she could turn to that didn't hold any reminders of the past, and one she could gain strength from. It wasn't like that with Liz. She was constantly having to give her strength to Liz. Not that she would have it any other way as she loved Liz and would always be there for her.

Molly sealed Tilly's thoughts on their friendship by standing and putting out her arms. 'Can I give you a hug, Tilly, lass? As I need one meself an' all after that.'

Tilly put the basket down that she had been clinging on to and stood up. Going to Molly, she found comfort in her arms and knew some of her hurt to lessen.

'Right, can I put the kettle on now? Eeh, what a girl has to go through in this house to get a cuppa is matched by none!'

'Ha, cheeky bugger. Aye, let's have a cuppa. Maybe Liz will be back by the time the kettle boils, so we need to be cheered up by then an' all.'

The whistle shrieked, announcing that the water was boiling, just as Liz came back in. Her cheeks were rosy red, and she had an air about her that spoke of more excitement than securing the pitch for them that she told them she'd been able to achieve.

'By, the beach is already heaving, Tilly. And I found Dan and he were that glad to hear of you again. He wondered what had happened, of course, but I just told him that it was for you to tell him if you wanted to and he was happy with that. Eeh, Tilly, he's a nice bloke. He's going to let you pitch in part of his tent as there's naw room anywhere. Dan tells me that more and more hawkers are coming to Blackpool, and instead of riding their bikes around the streets to sell their wares, they are setting up stalls on the beach. It's that busy, I—'

'Eeh, lass, take a breath. You can tell us all about it over a cuppa. By, I've not seen you as lively for a long time.' Tilly didn't voice what she thought – that Dan had made more than an impression on Liz – as that might upset her, but something told her there was a truth in that and it warmed her heart with hope for Liz.

Blackpool buzzed over Easter, and all the stalls on the beach did a roaring trade. Tilly had sold out by the Saturday night and had even taken a few orders. Happy with how it had all gone, but wishing she'd had more stock, she determined to work even harder. 'We were a bit ambitious, you knaw, Liz. It were daft to set up with so little to sell, but by, it's given me a taste of what we can achieve.'

They were helping Dan to pack down his stall; his stock was amazing, as he had at least three or four of each item, with one on display and others stacked underneath the long bench he used as a counter. 'You helped my trade an' all, Tilly. Your baskets attracted the ladies and a lot of them looked through what I had to offer and made purchases. You're welcome here for as long as you want.'

'Ta, Dan, you're a good 'un. But I think I need to take a few weeks to get a good lot of baskets made. I can be ready for the early summer trade then. I'll make them orders first, though, and if you don't mind, Liz, you could bring them down on Monday and Tuesday as we arranged with the customers.'

'Naw, I'd be fine with that.' Liz looked at Dan as she said this, and he smiled at her, his face lighting up and his eyes twinkling.

'If you've the time, Liz, I could do with your help an' all. I'll be bringing more stock down, and it allus takes a bit of sorting.'

'I'd love that, Dan.'

Tilly smiled to herself as she saw colour flush Liz's cheeks. Meeting Dan had lifted Liz and made her interested in life again. It wasn't that she was ready to fall in love, Tilly knew that, but it was as if Liz had found a kindred spirit in Dan. Their banter was light-hearted and funny, and they made each other laugh a lot, when Tilly had hardly seen the joke.

They'd learnt a lot about Dan. He'd never been married. He got near to it once, but a tragedy had taken his fiancée.

She'd been run over by a horse and trap as she'd turned to wave to Dan. It was clear to see that his heart had been broken, and that the image of seeing his fiancée die in that way still haunted him. Liz had listened to him intently and had opened up a little about what had happened to her family, not telling him where she was at the time, but papering over that by saying she had been needed elsewhere. Tilly imagined that Dan accepted this as he had no knowledge of what life in the poorhouse was like.

The telling of each other's stories seemed to cement the friendship between Liz and Dan, and Tilly was glad of this and hoped in time that it may lead to happiness for them both. They were obviously attracted to each other, and more than they realised.

'Look, if you two don't mind, I'll leave you to it. It's only just on five, and I thought I would walk along and see an old friend. You remember Martha, Liz? She lived round the corner from your old street. Well ...' Tilly told Liz how she and Martha had become friends, leaving out that that friendship had ended and why, and the encounter she'd had on the beach.

'You never said owt afore, Tilly. Aye, I knaw Martha. Not that she had much time for me. But give her my regards anyroad.'

Dan showed his curiosity as to why anyone wouldn't have had much time for Liz. Tilly turned away, hearing Liz begin to tell Dan about her life before she left Blackpool as she did so. Never had she known Liz to talk so openly to anyone, but as she looked back and saw how engrossed they were in each other, she smiled.

★　　★　　★

Nerves and many other feelings assailed Tilly as she walked along Liz's old street. Many folk were outside enjoying the last of the warm evening as the weather was particularly mild for the time of year.

None seemed to recognise her, or at least, didn't take much notice of her, until she rounded the corner and came across Martha's neighbour sitting on her step. 'By, I ain't seen you in this good while, lass. Where've you been, and what's brought you round here again?'

The tone wasn't unfriendly, and Tilly felt glad of this. 'Hello, Mrs Ragton. How're you doing?'

'Well, me twinges are getting worse, but then, I've old bones. But apart from that, much the same as allus. Are you looking to call on Martha?'

'Aye. I thought I would.'

'Well, she's ailing, poor lass. But whether she'll be glad to see you, I don't knaw. She hadn't a good word for you after that affair with Joe. Mind, there's a different light on that now, and I'm sorry as you were hounded out how you were, lass.'

Although expected, this reference to her affair with Joe burnt Tilly's cheeks red, but she held her head high and managed a friendly reply. 'Ta, Mrs Ragton. And I hope as you feel better when the warmer weather comes.' She could have said that sitting on a cold step wouldn't help but it wasn't for her to give advice to an older woman.

Most of them, when left alone as Mrs Ragton now was, liked to be outside, in the hope of a few words with a passer-by. She understood that lonely feeling as she'd felt it many times herself.

Martha called out when Tilly knocked, so she opened the door and went inside. The familiar smell of lavender polish hit her and sent her reeling back to the time when she visited Martha regularly and she remembered the love they shared and how good Martha was to her. Her eyes filled with tears as she imagined she heard Babs and Beth calling, 'Ma, Ma, you're home.' And then bombarding her with all the things they had been doing with Martha. How different things would have been now, if Joe hadn't been the sexual predator he was, and she hadn't felt forced to take what he offered. But she couldn't change the past.

'Who is it? Come on through, I'm in me parlour.'

Not wanting to call out, Tilly went through the hallway and opened the door opposite. 'It's Tilly, Martha.' Tilly's heart thumped as she said this, and her only thought was, *Please don't let Martha reject me again.*

'Tilly! Oh, Tilly, I've dreamt of this day, but never thought that it would come. Come over here, lass, and give me a hug.'

Tilly's joy soared. She hurried over to Martha and flung her arms around her too-thin body. 'Oh, Martha, it's good to see you.'

Martha sat in her rocking chair, wrapped in a shawl, warmed by a roaring fire. 'Eeh, me lass, where've you been? I asked and asked after you. I needed to say I were sorry for how I were with you and that I shouldn't have turned you away. Then I condemned you when we met on the beach. I'm so sorry, lass. But ... well, I felt ... Oh well, none of that matters. I knaw now the truth of all that happened, and I'm sorry. I'm so sorry, me Tilly. Can you forgive me?'

'I have done already, Martha, and I understand. Don't think any more about it. We're all right now, and that's the main thing.'

'Where's me little lasses? Are they all right? Did you get them back?'

Tilly swallowed hard, then sank down onto the rug and knelt at Martha's feet. 'Naw. But I will one day. I will, Martha.'

'Eeh, lass, lass. And what of that one you were with?'

'I loved him, Martha. He was a gentle person.'

'Was?'

After Tilly told Martha how Jeremiah had died, Martha had tears streaming down her face. Tilly put her head in Martha's lap and let her own tears fall, till it felt that her whole body was crying.

'Naw, naw.' As Martha said this over and over, she stroked Tilly's hair. 'I'm to blame, I should never have turned you away.'

'Naw, Martha. There's naw one to blame but me. I made some bad mistakes. I were lost when me Arthur were took. I – I tried, but well, I took the easy way that was offered to me. The wrong way, and that's what led to it all happening.'

'You were used. I knaw that now. Even by Agatha. Oh yes, she has a part to play. Acting as if she was a good wife, and a good Christian, while all the time she knew what her husband were up to. But it suited her. She had her own agenda. Well, she got her way, her and that vicar, but she has to meet her maker one of these days, and they'll be naw hiding her cunning then.'

'Naw, Martha. Be glad for her that she has found happiness. Joe weren't what he seemed, and he treated her cruelly. She didn't set out to fall in love with the vicar. She tried to be a good wife.'

'Well, we'll leave it at that. I can be judgemental, as you knaw. It is the fault that I have to place in front of me maker when I meet him. And, Tilly, I don't think that will be long now. I have a growth in me stomach. It keeps growing and growing.'

'Oh, Martha, naw.' Tilly didn't ask if there was any hope; the nature of what Martha described told her there was none. As did what she saw when she looked properly into Martha's face for the first time. The signs were all there: the yellowing, sunken face, the skeletal appearance and the eyes, glassy and set deep into dark pools of skin. Patting Martha's hand gently, she told her, 'I will look after you, Martha. I'm here now. Let me get you a pot of tea.'

'Tilly, the Lord must have sent you, as they were about to move me to hospital, and I don't want to die there. They say there's only days, maybe weeks left for me now.'

Martha's bony hand took hold of Tilly's. 'I need to tell you sommat, Tilly. I've left me house and everything in it to you.'

Tilly was shocked to hear this. 'Naw, Martha. You shouldn't have. Why?'

''Cause I did wrong by you, Tilly. I should have taken you and the little ones in. I judged you and found you a sinner not worthy of help and that were wrong of me. Me solicitor has me will and instructions to find you, naw matter what it took, when sommat happened to me.'

'Awe, Martha, I don't knaw what to say. Naw one has ever done owt like that for me. Not ever. Ta, Martha. Ta.'

With this, Tilly, not able to take in the enormity of how her life would change, stood up and took the frail Martha in her arms, and rested her head on Martha's. 'I wish I could make you better, Martha. Life's so unfair.'

'Do what you like with the house, Tilly. You don't have to live in it, or keep it as it is. Me wish would be that you sell it and use the money to help you find your young 'uns.'

Tilly didn't tell her that it wasn't possible to find Babs and Beth, that there wasn't a place where she could look, or a soul she could enquire of, but just thanked Martha again and made the right words come out to the effect that Martha had opened up a way that would lead to her being able to try to be reunited with her children. *If only . . . if only . . .*

TWENTY-FIVE

Six months had gone by since Martha had passed away. The summer had been a busy one, and very profitable for Tilly and Liz. Now, with the autumn leaves crunching under her feet, Tilly walked towards the solicitor's office in King Street.

Today she was to hear the extent of Martha's legacy as the house and all the effects had now been sold. Tilly had kept the beautiful china fruit bowl that had stood on Martha's round, highly polished dining table. Its intricate design made it look as if it was edged with lace, and the pattern of various fruits that were beautifully painted around this edging made it a thing of delicate beauty.

Tilly had always loved it, and knew that Martha had too, and so it was a fitting reminder of her. She'd also retained the china dog that had stood on the mantelpiece. It was a model of a greyhound, and its sleek lines gave it an elegance. Martha had once said that her husband loved to go to the greyhound racing, and that he had bought it for her.

The fruit bowl had been passed down to Martha through two generations of her family. Tilly hoped to one day be able to give these ornaments to Babs and Beth. Babs, the animal lover, would get the dog, and Beth, who had seen the beauty in almost anything, would love the fruit bowl. She thought they would remind them of a small part of their childhood.

To this end, Tilly had wrapped the ornaments and written the girls' names on each – the first thing Molly had taught her was how to write her own and her girls' names. One day when she had learnt more of her letters, she would write on each 'to remember Martha by'. Though she wondered if either of her children would remember Martha as they had been so young when they had known her and loved her.

'Well now, Matilda.' Mr Fellows had called her by her proper name since they had first met, just after Martha's death. A fatherly figure of a man in his late fifties – Tilly knew this as he often said, 'When I retire on my sixtieth birthday, and that's not long now, just one year to go, I will work as your accountant. I love working with figures, and I can make sure your business goes in the right direction' – he leant forward now as he spoke. His full head of unruly hair flopped forward, making him look as though he had a fringe, and his friendly, twinkling blue eyes looked at her. A smile creased his face as he said, 'Its good news.'

These words increased the excitement Tilly was feeling. She had given up everything and had nursed Martha for two whole weeks until Martha had passed away, spending night and day by her side. During that time, they had talked when Martha had felt up to it, and together they had planned what Tilly should do with the proceeds of Martha's house. Doing so had made Martha happy and taken her mind off her pain as she'd made suggestions. Yes, finding Babs and Beth had been a big part of the plans they had spoken of, but so had the setting up of a shop and workshop for Tilly to run her business from, and this had pleased Martha so much.

'The house fetched the princely sum of seventy-five pounds, and—'

Tilly gasped. She couldn't imagine such a sum of money.

'Yes, I thought that would please you. The landlord of most of the houses around there bought it. He begrudged paying the price, but I wasn't going to let him get it for cheaper. And the furniture and effects realised fifteen pounds, which greatly surprised me, but Martha had one or two treasures among her possessions that did well at auction. And so, with the deduction of my fees, there is eighty pounds to be paid into the bank account we opened for you, and here I have two pounds and ten shillings, for you to treat yourself with.' He pushed the three notes towards her. In a daze, Tilly took them.

'Now, I have this for you to sign. I will read it out to you.'

'There's naw need, Mr Fellows, ta. I can read it meself.'

His eyebrows shot up. 'Oh, since when? Well, well, Tilly, this is good news.'

'Aye, it is. A new world has opened up to me. Me friend Molly has been on with teaching me, and though I may need help if there are any big words, I reckon I can manage to read most of it.'

'Well, I never. You never cease to surprise me. Good for you, and good for your friend. It was something I was going to suggest to you, as not being able to read would greatly hinder you in business, no matter how talented you are.'

Tilly took the sheaf of papers and leant back in the wooden chair. Slowly, she began to read, but not only that, she found that she understood what she was reading too, something that

314

had sometimes eluded her, leaving her just reading out words for the sake of it. *Eeh, I've mastered this now. To knaw the words and to follow what they are talking of means I'm reading good and proper.*

A pride entered her which wasn't marred by her having to ask Mr Fellows to read the odd word and explain its meaning to her.

Excited and grateful beyond words, Tilly almost ran home to Liz. The two young women did a jig around their small sitting room, laughing and clapping their hands together like children, until Tilly slumped down onto the sofa and burst into tears.

Her feelings were a mixture of the joy and relief she felt and sadness at how for a moment she'd thought her world was all better. But then it had hit her that it wasn't, and she wondered if it ever would be.

Two days later, still mulling over how best to go forward, Tilly pulled her shawl tighter around her against the bitter wind coming off the Irish Sea and felt glad she was wearing her sturdy black leather boots – a present she'd bought herself from the extra money Mr Fellows had given her – and her long, thick bloomers under her grey woollen skirt as she walked at a good pace towards St Anne's. With how busy she'd been, she hadn't carried out her promise to herself to visit Cook again.

With her head down, and tendrils of her hair escaping her bonnet, she let memories of Cook's and Florrie's kindness to her drift into her head, and she hoped and prayed that both were all right.

Cook greeted her with open arms. 'Eeh, lass, it's good to see you. Where have you been?'

Over a hot mug of cocoa, Tilly told the story she was weary of telling, but she knew she owed Cook an explanation.

'Eeh, lass, lass. Well, I'm glad as everything has turned out well for you – well, not everything, but some things have. And I've a surprise for thee. I had a letter from Florrie and she mentioned you, sending her love and good wishes.'

'So, she's not back yet, then? Eeh, I'm sad to miss her, but then, it's good that her ma is lasting this long.'

'But she hasn't. She died a good while back, Tilly.'

'Oh? So why ain't Florrie back here?'

'There's naw job for her. The new maid has her feet under the table good and proper. She does extras like dressing the mistress's hair, and looking after her clothes. She's seen as an asset and has been given the job on a permanent basis. We have a daily who comes in to do a lot of what Florrie did and as everything is running smoothly, Florrie was turned down when she came back looking to get set on again.'

'So, where is she, Cook? Has she found another position?'

'Naw. Poor lass. When her ma died, she lost the cottage as it was a grace and favour given to her ma on the death of Florrie's da. He worked down the mine and was killed down there, but the tenancy was only extended to his widow, not any offspring, so Florrie had to get out.'

Tilly held her breath, dreading what Cook would say next.

On a sob, and dabbing her eyes with her large hanky, Cook blurted out, 'She ended up in the workhouse, our lovely Florrie, and her letter says she is failing in health an' all.'

'Naw! Eeh, naw. Where? I have to go to her and pay her way out. I can, Cook. Me fortunes have changed. And though me and Liz, me friend as I live with, haven't much room, I can get another bed in my bedroom. Have you got Florrie's address, Cook?'

'Aye. By, lass, that's best news that I've heard in a long time. Let me see now, where did I put it?'

Tilly waited while Cook opened, one by one, the four drawers that were under the huge table top. Each held items Cook must have used a thousand times – whisks, wooden spoons, cutlery, and yet, Cook seemed confused as to which one she kept her notebooks, cookbooks and a few pencils in. When she finally opened it, she gave a triumphant cry and held Florrie's letter aloft. But then her face fell as she looked at it. 'Eeh, she don't say which workhouse, just that she is in one and helping in the kitchens. She says as it ain't too bad but that she never gives up hope that she will get out one day.'

'Well, there can't be many in Blackburn. I'll find her, Cook, I promise. She'll be standing on this doorstep with me any day soon ready to give you a hug.'

'God willing, Tilly. God willing. It don't bear thinking on what we can come to in naw time at all if fate plays us a bad hand. Look at you, you never asked for any of this to happen to you.'

'Well, let's not go down that road, Cook, or you'll have me blabbing, which I can do at a drop of me hat. I have to stay strong, and help those who allus helped me, or who made a difference in me life. I'll soon find Florrie, I'm sure of it. And if ever you need me, I'll be there for you, Cook. Remember that.'

Tilly's heart was heavy as she walked home. *Poor Florrie, how she's coping I dread to think.*

It was as she reached the top end of South Shore, a barren piece of sandy ground with a recently constructed wooden slide, and dotted with the wagons of the few gypsies who had camped there, that a voice called out to her. 'Tilly, is that yourself? My, you're looking grand. Did Jeremiah ever be after finding you?'

Tilly stood stock still as she faced Lucy.

'It is surprised you look at seeing me. Well, I was for marrying Jonas Gaskin and his clan are for working for Alderman Bean who is setting up a playground on this land.'

Tilly nodded, still unable to speak. She remembered Lilly Lee wanting to connect her family with the Gaskin clan.

'So, it is well that you are?'

'Naw, and I never will be so without me young 'uns. It was a cruel thing your clan did to me and me girls. If you have an ounce of decency in you, Lucy, you'd tell me where I can look for them.'

'I'm for guessing that Jeremiah didn't find you then? If he had, you would have been told that the twins were taken back to Romania where Jasmine is from.'

A moan came from Tilly. To have this confirmed seemed to close down the last shred of hope she had of seeing her girls again. How could they make their way from there, wherever it was?

'Look, it is sorry that I am. We didn't all agree with Lilly Lee allowing such a thing, but you had no way of taking care of the young ones, and what you did by lying with Phileas had to be punished, so it did.'

Tilly hadn't the strength to protest her innocence.

As if her hurt was nothing, Lucy changed the subject. 'So, it is a mystery to me where Jeremiah is. I've no contact with Lilly Lee either, as she has retired back in God's country of Ireland and will never venture out of there again.'

Wanting to hurt Lucy, Tilly told her without ceremony what had happened to Jeremiah.

Lucy let out a gasp of pain. 'No! Oh, for the love of the Lord, no.'

Ignoring the tears streaming down Lucy's face, Tilly turned and walked away. Her spirits were crushed. Her soul was on fire with pain, but somehow, she had to find it in herself to face the world. To rekindle the hope that she'd held in her heart, and to make a life fit for her girls when they came home – for no matter how futile, she had to keep hoping.

'Tilly!' Lucy's voice held a plea. 'It is that you're right about the cruelty of what me clan did. And if Lilly Lee knows of Jeremiah's passing, then she surely has been punished. I'm not for being the same as them, though I had to be acting their way when with them. I'll tell you the truth of what happened.'

Tilly felt a jolt of anticipation shoot through her. Her hope rekindled.

'Jasmine didn't cross the water. Her husband was for thinking that the pickings in England were better than they were in Ireland. But neither would he agree to go to Romania. That is the lie we were all told to tell you if—'

'You mean, Jeremiah lied to me too?'

'No, Lilly Lee knew of his intention to find you, and so she told him the Romanian story as if it was a truth, but she made us swear to keep her secret forever. I'm breaking it now

Jeremiah is no longer on this earth as he cannot now find out he was lied to and excluded from a clan secret.'

'But where did they go to, Lucy? Please tell me.'

'They went down the south to Somerset. It was apple picking season they were aiming for, and then they had a mind to stay in that area. The south of England, that is. They would travel from county to county as the work took them. Jasmine's husband was a man of the land, so he was.'

Tilly could have jumped for joy as hope seared in her once more. 'Ta, Lucy. You've eased me pain some and given me hope where I had none. One day me girls will come looking for me. Being in the same country, it will be so much easier for them to. I knaw as they'll never forget me. And they'll never forget Blackpool. When you're a Sandgronian the place is embedded in your heart.'

'And what will be a Sandgronian then?'

'Someone born in Blackpool. A true Blackpudlian. And that's what me girls are, and me and their da afore them, and aye, their grandparents an' all. Babs and Beth will come back, I knaw they will.'

'Well, it is that I hope so. And if you are passing by anytime, call in to see me. I'm for developing the powers of seeing into the future, and Rina Petrigolla is for teaching me how to let the spirits guide me. She says I am a natural but am resistant. Well, I can feel things that are going to happen, so me training is coming along. Maybe it is that one day I can predict when your girls will come.'

Tilly said she might do that, but in truth knew she wouldn't. She didn't want to associate with the gypsies ever again. For though she knew many were good people at heart, there were those who would harm her, and she didn't yet trust that Lucy wasn't one of these.

'Is that you, Tilly?' Liz's voice met her as she opened the gate.

'It is. Who were you expecting, Liz?'

'Naw, not expecting, but I wondered if it was Molly.'

Tilly detected a note of excitement in Liz's voice. Using the handle and lifting one foot after the other, she eased her boots off. New boots always pinched, and these ones had done a better job than most at giving her toes a good nipping.

'Hurry up, Tilly.'

'I'm coming. What's the matter with you? I'm not late for owt, am I? Tommy! Oh, Tommy, it's good to see you, when ...? How ...? I mean, what are you doing here?'

'The when is obvious. The how is by train, and I'm here to see the two loves of me life, so I am.'

Liz giggled in a silly girlish way. Tilly was too surprised to react; she just stared at Tommy, remembering the feelings he'd evoked in her as they now tickled the nerves in her stomach.

'How are you, me Tilly? I ...'

'Look. You two go on into the front room. I'll put the kettle on. You can catch up with all Tommy's news, Tilly.'

Once she'd discarded her shawl, Tilly led the way into the front room. A fire crackled in the grate, giving a welcome glow in the dim light. 'I – I'll just light the mantels. Make yourself comfy, Tommy.' Feeling nervous, Tilly turned away and lifted the box of matches from the mantelpiece and went to strike one.

'Don't, Tilly, I like this light. Come here so I can be giving you a hug.'

'Oh, Tommy, I – I'm still not ready. I—'

'I'm ready for the both of us, so I am. I can make you love me, Tilly. I'm just needing a chance to show me feelings for you.'

Tilly turned and looked at Tommy. In the half-light, he looked beautiful. His lovely Irish eyes twinkled, and his black hair shone as it caught the flickering light. His arms opened. Tilly couldn't stop herself from going into them.

As he held her close, she could feel his love for her. But she knew she couldn't give in; she had so much tangling her insides, and she'd vowed to never again let a man take her heart until she was ready. She needed to prove to herself that it was love on her part, and not the seeking of comfort, or of the pleasure a man could give her.

Tommy's lips planted kisses in her hair. 'You smell lovely, Tilly, you're for being like a fresh field.' His voice was low as his lips travelled to her neck.

'No! Tommy, please. I can't.'

Tommy jumped back, a look of disappointment on his face. 'Why? Why, Tilly? I know that it is that you have feelings for me.'

'I do, Tommy. Very strong feelings. But ... I ... well, I can't trust me feelings. I've had them before. I've given me all to others since me Arthur passed on, and all it's done is given me heartache. I'm happy on me own. Just me and Liz, and I've me business to think of. I have to build me business, Tommy.'

Tommy sat down, his head lowered. Tilly waited, unsure what to do. Her heart wanted her to go to Tommy, but she wasn't letting her heart decide, not this time. And in her head, she knew the path she should take.

'I'm for going back to Ireland. Me brother is dead and I'm the owner of the farm now. I wanted it to be that you came with me, me Tilly. I wanted you to marry me and to give me sons that we can rear to become good Irish citizens and farmers of the land.'

'Tommy . . . Well, that's sommat as I cannot do. After me twins were born, I were damaged in a way that meant I'll never have children again. Go to Ireland, Tommy, and forget me, I'm not the lass for you.'

'What? Is this the truth? Are you telling me that you . . . ? Oh, Tilly. It isn't for being important, I still want you. Holy Mother, is this the reason for you rejecting me?'

'Naw. It ain't, Tommy. I . . . well . . . I just need more time.'

'Well, I know it isn't because you don't love me. I know that you love me as I'm for loving you. But I'm not for understanding how it is that you can reject me. You're breaking me heart, Tilly.'

'I'm sorry, Tommy. I am. Write to me, eh? Let me knaw all that you're doing, and I'll write to you, and we'll see. Only, I ain't promising that I'll come to Ireland. I need to be here in Blackpool for when me girls come looking for me.'

A knock on the door proved to be a blessed relief for Tilly. 'Bring the tea in, lass. We're ready for a cuppa.'

Liz came into the room, bottom first. When she swivelled round, tray held aloft, she looked expectantly at Tilly.

'Tommy's going to live in Ireland, Liz. Ain't that sommat, eh?'

'And you?'

'Naw. I'm not going.'

323

Liz looked relieved, but then covered it up. 'Don't miss your chance at happiness, Tilly. I – I, well, I've sommat to tell you as might change your mind.'

'Oh?'

Tilly saw Tommy look up eagerly and felt sorry he had his hopes raised, as she knew for certain she wasn't going with him. Not yet she wasn't.

'Aye, well, me and Dan. Well … Dan's asked me to marry him and I've said yes!'

'What? Eeh, Liz, lass, I'm so happy for you. Come here and give me a hug.'

Almost dropping the tray on the table, Liz ran into Tilly's arms. 'So, you see, you've not got me to consider anymore. I'm going to be fine, Tilly. Just fine.'

'Well, you kept that quiet, though I've seen the looks going between you both, and you've allus got an errand to run and often don't come back for a while. I guessed sommat was going on.'

'I – I didn't mean to be deceitful, Tilly. I just didn't knaw how to tell you. I felt as though I were letting you down.'

'Naw, I couldn't be happier for you, Liz. Truly. You've made me day.'

The two clung to each other. Tommy's coughing broke them apart. 'And so, is it that I can hope, Tilly? Was it that you had the fear in you that Liz would be left alone?'

'Naw, Tommy. Liz isn't me only concern.' She told them both about Florrie. 'And besides that, I have me plans. I'm looking to do another season on the beach, and then to buy meself a shop. It's what I want, Tommy.' Not giving him time to speak, Tilly went on to tell them, 'And, I'll call it Tilly's

324

Basket Wares, so if ever me girls return, they'll find it easy to find me, as I'm going to make sure as everyone knaws of me shop. I'm going to make it the biggest shop in Blackpool.'

Tommy sighed. His face showed his sorrow, but he didn't argue any further. What he did say, though, made Tilly have a sinking feeling that nearly changed her mind. 'Well, if it's a no you're standing by, then I'm to accept that. And I am for thinking that you'll never change your mind, Tilly. So, I'm to be honest with you. There is a lovely colleen that I've known all me days. Bernadette Farren. She and I were for being girl-friend and boyfriend and it is that she has always written to me. I have a fondness for her, which I hope will grow to the depths of me feelings for you, Tilly. As with no hope coming from you, I'm for thinking that I cannot be a bachelor, but must plan on becoming a married man. So, I'll be saying me goodbyes, Tilly, and be wishing you and Liz all the luck in the world.'

Tilly wanted with all her heart to go after Tommy as he walked through the door, but she clung on to Liz to stop herself. *Oh, Tommy, Tommy. I do love you. I know in me heart that I do, but I have to think of me girls, and I have to be where they will be able to find me.*

TWENTY-SIX

Christmas was the jolliest that Tilly had known since before her Babs and Beth had been taken from her.

Dan made it so.

Tilly was surprised how much she enjoyed the fun Dan brought to their home as her mind was constantly on Florrie and trying to find her. Her trip to Blackburn had been fruitless.

There was only one workhouse in the town and Florrie wasn't known there. And yet, Tilly had always thought that when folk were sent to the workhouse under the Poor Law, it was to the local one in their area.

But she did have one hope. After the Christmas festivities were over, Mr Fellows was going to make enquiries for her. He felt confident that there would be a register of where everyone was sent. He just needed to find out if it was the court that decided or the local authority.

Tilly held on to that and let herself enjoy the lovely Christmas dinner of boiled ham and potatoes, finished off with a plum pudding.

'Eeh, that was a grand dinner.' Liz patted her overstuffed stomach and grinned. Tilly grinned back at her and nodded.

They were sitting together on the sofa, the fire was blazing up the chimney, and Dan sat in the armchair next to it, his feet on the fender, his head back, making little snoring sounds as he took forty winks. 'And Molly and her lot are coming around soon. I've made some fruit pies for them, Tilly. And we've a drop of good whisky to wash it down with. Dan is going to give us a tune on that piano he persuaded you to buy.'

'Well, that's a good thing. I've been wondering why I let him talk me into getting it. I knaw it were a bargain, but I can't play it, and neither can you. When you get married it can be me wedding gift to you, Liz, then Dan can play it all he likes.'

'Ha, I think that might have been his plan all along. He says his family allus had a piano when he were a lad. And when he saw this one and it was going for a snip, he thought of asking you to buy it as he has nawhere to put it in his place.'

'Aye, there were method behind the madness, I reckon. So, when are you two going to find somewhere of your own, then?'

'Once Christmas is out of the way. Though Dan is on with a plan he has already. You see, his elderly aunt lives in a house on St Anne's Road, and it's far too big for her. She says she is leaving it to Dan when she dies. Anyroad, he's talked to her about making her a home in two of the rooms and us having the rest of the house and taking care of her. I've met her, and she's a lovely old lady. She's taken with the idea, but Dan wants to be sure that she's happy, so he's going to show her how it will work out for her. Eeh, Tilly, I never thought as I'd live in such a big house.'

'You mean them double-fronted ones? By, Liz, that'll be grand, it'll be easy to make a space you can all enjoy without being under each other's feet.'

'Aye, we can, as his aunt only uses one front room, which she has her bed in an' all, and the kitchen that leads off that room. Dan says he can make a separate kitchen for us, so it'll seem as though we live on our own and his aunt will still have her independence.'

'Well, I'm pleased for you, Liz, and I've never seen you so happy. You deserve it, love. You do.'

'It don't mean that I've forgotten, Tilly. I'll never forget me young 'uns and what happened, and I'll try to remember the best of Eddie an' all, but I feel as though I've been given another chance.'

'Aye, you have, and you must take it, Liz. All your family would want that for you.'

'Dan's going to have a stone put up for them all, Tilly. He says as it'll be his wedding gift to me. He's buying a plot in Layton Cemetery and placing a headstone there, just as if they are all lying there, and I can put flowers there for them, like you see folk doing.'

Tilly couldn't say anything to this; she just took Liz's hand and squeezed it.

They fell silent.

The silence led to them napping, and not waking up for over an hour. Dan woke them. 'I've made a pot of tea, lasses. Wake up, you're like two sleeping beauties. You were snoring loud enough for two anyroad.'

'Ha, we couldn't have matched you, you were like a pig, grunting and snorting.'

Tilly smiled a sleepy smile at this light-hearted banter between Liz and Dan.

'Drink your tea and then I'll play us a tune, how would that be?'

Before they could answer the door opened and Molly shouted, 'We're here! Merry Christmas, everyone.'

Feeling wide awake now, Tilly jumped up. 'Come on in. Merry Christmas. Eeh, look at you, Gerry and Brian, don't you look smart?' The two lads had newly knitted dark green jumpers on, with matching knee-length socks that reached the bottom of their breeches. 'You look almost grown into young men. And handsome ones at that.'

Both lads blushed. Gerry, the youngest, handed Tilly a pie. 'Ma made it. It's got jellied crab apples and a drop of port in it.'

'Eeh, ta, lad, that'll go nicely with the brew that Dan has on the go.'

'And there's this an' all.' Brian handed over a bottle. 'It's Ma's homemade elderberry wine. Da says it'll knock anyone's socks off.'

They all laughed at this. Will, Molly's husband, playfully clipped Brian's ear.

A quiet man, Tilly and Liz hadn't had much to do with Will and had only passed the odd greeting with him, and yet Tilly felt that she knew him as Molly was always singing his praises. When he spoke, his voice surprised her as it had a lighter tone than she expected for such a big man. Tall, that is, and well built. 'Eeh, these lads of mine'll get me hanged one of these days.'

His face creased into a lovely smile, giving his square face a more rounded appearance and lighting up his brown eyes. In a gesture that showed his shyness, Will swept his fingers through his rust-coloured hair, lowering his head as he did so.

'Well then, I think we'll let that tea stew in its pot and all have a drop of elderberry wine instead, what do you say, Liz?'

'Aye, Tilly, I reckon as that's a good idea. I'll get some tumblers. Sit down, everyone. Brian and Gerry, you'll have to perch on the rug, lads.'

Within a few minutes everyone had relaxed, and Dan had begun to play, a honky-tonk sound that almost resembled some of the popular tunes of the day.

Prompted by the wine, which was watered down for the boys, soon they were all in full voice.

Tilly lost herself in the joviality of it all and didn't hear the knock on the front door. Gerry did, and he jumped up. 'I'll answer it.'

Tilly's heart lifted higher than it was already as Tommy entered. His presence heightened the love abounding in the room. 'Eeh, Tommy, I thought you were in Ireland?'

'And so I was, Tilly, but I caught a ferry over and have had to walk a good way as there's so few trains running.'

'You look frozen. Come in and sit by the fire.' This wasn't what she wanted to say; she wanted to shout her joy at seeing him.

'That's a lovely smile to greet me, so it is. I was unsure of me welcome.'

'Everyone's welcome around here, lad. Especially when we knaw who you are.'

Tilly laughed at Molly but was glad of the distraction of introducing Tommy. Fussing over him more than she intended, Tilly helped Tommy with his coat and scarf, and ushered him to take her seat on the sofa. 'Your nose is red with the cold.' As she said this, she noticed his bag. 'Where are you staying, Tommy, and how long for?'

'Sure, I only have a couple of nights. The next ferry from Liverpool is on Monday. I was lucky to find me brother had a right-hand man who lived in one of me barns and will take care of everything for me till I get back.'

'In a barn, eeh, I bet he's cold at night?' Gerry received one of his dad's gentle cuffs for speaking out of turn.

'No, it's cosy that he is. He has a big stove in the corner, and a sofa and his bed. And he's grateful for it. Some in Ireland are starving and, well, it's down to the British that they are.'

Tilly was surprised at this and embarrassed that Tommy had said it so boldly. Will saved the day. 'Aye, well, there's some injustices afoot by the upper classes of our country, but you won't find us in favour of it, even though the papers try to make you all out as the villains. As I see it, you are hard-working farmers and should have claim to your land.'

'It is that I know the thinking of the working man here, but it isn't you we have to fight for our rights. Not that I am in the same boat as many of me countrymen as me family have owned the land I farm for generations. It is the tenanted farmers who are most at risk as their rents go higher and higher. But, it isn't for us to be putting all this right on such a day. I'm not for spoiling the fun I could hear you were having. I just came to be with you, Tilly.'

Tilly blushed even more at this, but it wasn't all because of her embarrassment at Tommy's declaration, because the blush was also one of deep pleasure at Tommy's words.

'Tommy's right, no more politics – not that I understand them, but I knaw what you men are like when you get going. It's nice to see you, Tommy, and you'll be welcome to the sofa for a couple of nights, won't he, Tilly?'

This last, Liz said with meaning, and Tilly felt trapped into nodding. 'Of course. Now, Tommy, is it a hot drink, or a mug of wine you want?'

'Neither. I've brought a drop of good Irish whiskey with me, and it's sure I am that the menfolk will join me in partaking of it and leave you women to your wine.'

Both men nodded.

'I'll get the extra tumblers, Tilly, while you do the introductions.'

Tilly nodded at Liz and was glad to be doing something to take her mind off her wobbly tummy and to lighten the atmosphere.

With everyone knowing everyone, Dan decided he should resume his playing. As he did, Tommy pulled Tilly down to sit on his knee. 'I can't be having you standing, me wee Tilly.' His whiskey-tainted breath fanned her face. 'I think you've been at that bottle of yours already, Tommy.'

'Just a wee sip to keep out the cold, would you begrudge a man that?'

'Naw, but it is making you bold. Now behave yourself in front of the lads.'

Tommy laughed. 'To be sure, don't they know as you're me girl, then?'

Tilly didn't know how to handle Tommy in this mood, so she just laughed at him, which eased the tension. The singing resumed and once more the atmosphere was a jolly one.

'I have a song for you, so I do. Is it that you know "The Wild Colonial Boy", Dan?'

'I do.'

As the tune of the popular Irish song rang out, Tommy's voice, so beautiful with his soft lilt, filled the room. All sat in silence, even though most knew some of the words. When he'd finished, everyone cheered and asked for another song.

'To be sure, with a name like Danny, it is a wonder you're not of the Irish, Dan.'

'My grandfather, Daniel Feeley, came over from Ireland. He was a trader in all manner of things, and my grandmother, Verity, was talented in pottery making and embroidery – she used to make many of the things he sold. We still sell much the same on me stall now.'

'Ah, many a good man came from Ireland to make his way here on the mainland. Well, I'm something of a poet, and if you play that same tune again, I'll be singing a ditty to it that speaks of your grandfather.'

This fascinated Tilly. This was a side to Tommy she didn't know.

Dan played a few bars, whilst Tommy looked thoughtful, then putting his finger in the air as if something had occurred to him, Tommy began to sing.

'There was a wild tinker-man who sailed the Irish Sea
It was to sell his wares and to impress his Verity
But though they flourished and no matter what they saw
They were never to forget the beautiful Irish Shore.'

Everyone clapped and laughed as they knew the words were just put together because they rhymed.

Returning to the sofa, Tommy bent down and lifted Tilly up in the air. 'Play something as we can dance to, Dan. An Irish jig.'

Before they had a chance to think about this they were all up dancing around in a way that didn't resemble an Irish jig at all, but more a Scottish reel as they linked arms and twisted each other, then skipped under an arch made by Tilly and Tommy.

Tilly brimmed over with the joy of it all. Her head was in the clouds with the amount she had drunk. It was as if her body was receiving the nectar it had craved but been denied, as with the wine all gone, she turned to swigging the whiskey.

'Tilly, take it easy. You're going to have a sore head in the morning.'

Molly's face appeared to be swaying from side to side. 'Eeh, Molly, I'm jush having a good time.'

'I knaw as you are – we all are but remember what happened to you when you last drank in this way.'

'Ha! You're being a fudsy dudsy, Molly. Enjoy yourshelf.'

'Will, I think we'll get the boys home now. We'll say good-night, Tilly, and thank you for a wonderful Christmas afternoon.'

'Naw. Naw, you can't go. The party's jush beginning.'

'You go, Molly, lass. I'll take care of Tilly. Ta for coming. We've had the best Christmas for a long time. Don't worry. Tilly'll be all right. Christmas is a hard time for us to get through. But you've made it easier for us, lass.'

Molly hugged Liz and then turned to Tilly. 'Give us a hug, lass.'

Tilly went to hug Molly but tripped and fell forward. They both landed on the sofa. Tilly laughed out loud, but Molly cried out in pain. Hearing the sound sobered Tilly a little. Jumping off Molly, she couldn't apologise enough. 'Eeh, lass, what's to do?'

'I'm all right. I hit my back on the wooden frame. I'm just bruised.'

Tilly felt mortified. And the realisation that her drinking too much had caused this hit her, making her feel the shame of her behaviour. And yet the thing she wanted most in the world was another drink. The urge was so strong in her that she lurched for the bottle on the dresser. She never made it. The floor came up to meet her and her world went black.

Sometime during the night, Tilly had the sensation of being in someone's arms, but she couldn't sort out whose. She knew she was in her own bed. The pillows were hers and the smell of the bed linen was familiar. Her head hurt, and her throat felt as if it had been rubbed with sandpaper.

Trying to sit up was like fighting against a heavy load as her body felt weighted down. Gradually she worked out that it was someone's arm flopped across her. The someone stirred. 'Is it that you're awake, Tilly?'

'Tommy! What are you doing in me bed?'

'I wasn't for letting you sleep alone in case you vomited and choked. You were stinking drunk, Tilly.'

'You didn't . . . ?'

'No. Be Jesus, I wanted to, still do, but I'd not be taking advantage of you. Just keeping you safe. I wasn't meaning to fall asleep.'

'I need a drink of water, Tommy.'

Tommy eased himself up. As he did Tilly felt his bare leg rub against hers. A tremble zinged through her. Feelings that had lain dormant tingled into life, making her draw in her breath and clench her thighs together.

Tommy knew. He turned towards her, his hand tracing a path along her leg. 'Tilly, me wee Tilly.'

She couldn't speak. Her throat had dried even more so that swallowing was difficult. The first awakening of her was pulsating through her. She tried to fight it, but knew it was beating her. The longing in her to feel Tommy inside her made her gasp.

Tommy's arm came around her and gently lowered her body. 'Tilly, oh, Tilly.'

Her need for water forgotten, she went willingly into his arms. His words of love encouraged her. She didn't stop the progress of his hand as he sought, found and stroked the most intimate part of her, giving her sensations she drank in, and moaned at the pleasure of.

Clinging on to Tommy's strong, warm body, she allowed her own hands to explore. A shudder vibrated through her as she felt his need for her. The first tentative touch and gentle caress of him had Tommy asking, begging, to be allowed to take her.

Her arms enclosed him and pulled him towards her. Her eagerness to accept him didn't disappoint her as an explosion of feelings cascaded through her the moment he entered her. 'Ooh, Tommy, Tommy.' Her legs curled around him, clench-ing him so that he thrust deeply into her.

'I love you, Tilly. I love you.'

Though ashamed of what she must taste like, she accepted his kisses. His deep probing with his tongue, his sucking in of her lips, while her body drank of the pleasure that he gave her.

When the sensations built inside her she hollered out her love – the love she could finally acknowledge and give with a willing heart.

Tommy's deep moan joined her cries as he gave of himself to her.

Clinging to each other as if they never wanted to let go, they cried out the joy they had experienced in sobs that shook their bodies. Only these weren't tears of pain, but of blissful happiness.

When at last Tommy released himself from her, he did so while planting kisses all over her face. When he reached her lips, his kiss was a gentle pressing of his to hers. A loving kiss that held no demands. His hands caressed her face. His naked body slid off her, but as it did he rolled her towards him. 'My Tilly. My beautiful Tilly. I love you beyond words.'

'Eeh, Tommy. I don't deserve your love. I'm more deserving of the way you treated me when we first met.'

'No. Don't be saying that. Don't ever be referring to it. For sure it is that I am mortified when I think of it. I was misled. But still, I shouldn't have behaved in that way. I feel that I defiled you, my Tilly, and that it has been between us ever since.'

'Naw, I forgave you a long time ago, Tommy. It's . . . well . . . it's just that I . . . well, I don't come to you pure as I should do.'

'I think it is that you have been sinned against – used for what it is that you can give a man. Don't be hard on yourself, Tilly. You have been through a lot, so you have. You had to survive, and sometimes giving of herself is the only way a woman can do that. I love the Tilly that is right here, now. The Tilly that makes me blood coarse through me veins. What it is that you have been through has shaped you into this person, so I won't be condemning you, only grateful that you are in me arms at last.'

Tilly snuggled into him. The feeling he'd given her with his words was that of being completely forgiven. Her sins wiped off the slate. Maybe now she could build a future that wasn't dogged by the past. But what of Tommy? Could she go with him to Ireland? A voice she tried to ignore told her that she couldn't. She had too much tugging at her and keeping her anchored to Blackpool. It wasn't just the task she had ahead of her to find Florrie, or the burning need to be where her girls could find her, but something that Blackpool did to those born Sandgronian. Blackpool was in her soul.

TWENTY-SEVEN

Boxing Day brought sunshine, as often happened on the west coast of England, surrounded and shielded as it was by three ranges of mountains – those in the Lake District, the Black Mountains of Wales and the Pennines to the east. Mountains that batted away many a bout of bad weather, though the strong winds off the Irish Sea weren't deterred by any of these. Today, though, they were just a flutter, a light breeze.

Opening her eyes and feeling her body snuggled into Tommy's, Tilly felt a conflict light up inside of her. She wanted to have this feeling every morning of her life, but knew she was going to deny herself it.

Getting out of bed without disturbing him, she knew she must go along to Liz's room. She wanted to apologise for her behaviour, and as soon as she got her body and soul together, she would go to see Molly too.

Her feet froze on the cold lino, and her body shivered. Despite the sun beaming through the open curtains, she felt chilled to the core. Grabbing her housecoat, she wrapped it around her and tiptoed out of the room.

A smile curled her lips as she saw more than one body in Liz's bed. It seemed they'd both had a good night. Her heart swelled as she gazed on Liz and Dan curled around each other almost as if they were one. For Liz to find happiness and be able to give the love she did was a miracle. And one Tilly was glad of, though she wasn't looking forward to Liz moving out.

The door creaked as she stepped out of the room and tried to close it again. Tilly stood still. She felt ashamed, as if she had been caught in the act of being a Peeping Tom.

'It's a wonder you can get out of bed this morning, Tilly.'

Liz's sleepy voice sent the blood rushing to Tilly's cheeks as she wasn't sure what she was referring to – the frantic love-making of her and Tommy, or the drunken state she'd got into the night before. Both were a sauce of embarrassment to her.

'Put the kettle on and I'll forgive you, lass.'

A sleep-filled groan came from Dan. Liz appeared at the door grinning. 'Don't worry, he won't wake for a while, I've worn him out with me demands.'

They both giggled as Liz tucked her arm under Tilly's.

'I'd say we had a good Christmas, wouldn't you, Tilly, lass?'

'Aye, I would. But—'

'Don't be apologising. You slipped up, that's all, but look what it did for you, lass. Oh, aye, I heard you. By, I think you've met your match in Tommy. He'll tame you good and proper.'

Tilly laughed again, and Liz joined her. It felt good.

Unhooking arms, they made their way downstairs. The embers were glowing in the grate, giving the living room a warm feel. Liz crossed the room and poked the log that was smouldering; it broke up, spitting sparks as it did, and then jumped into life, sending flames shooting up the chimney. She swung the grate plate with the ever-full kettle on it over the flames. Reaching up, she lifted the tea caddy off the mantle shelf. 'Get the mugs, Tilly. I ain't waiting on you.'

Again, they giggled. Tilly thought they were like two naughty girls who'd got away with a prank. And that's how she felt, as after all, they had both misbehaved according to convention.

By the time the kettle let out a shrill whistle, the tea leaves were in the pot, and mugs, milk and sugar were laid out at the ready. 'By, I need a cuppa. I'm that thirsty . . . Liz, I . . . Look, I knaw you say I shouldn't apologise, but I am sorry, I shouldn't have drunk so much.'

'Naw. But it seems to me that once you have one, you're lost, Tilly. I reckon you should never have that one. Never forget where it led you to last time. And it could again, as it messes your head up.'

'I knaw. I just thought, well, after all this time, that I could enjoy a couple and leave it at that.'

'You can't. I don't knaw why, but there's too much for you in the bottle. A chance to forget – not care, even. And that ain't easy to resist once you've had a taste of it. And your first sip promises you that release from your pain. There's naw stopping after that. You've got to make a pact with yourself never to have that first sip. It ain't the answer, Tilly, it ain't.'

Tilly hung her head. Even now she could smell the whiskey bottle standing open on the dresser. Liz must have seen her eyes looking longingly at it as she jumped up, grabbed the bottle and went with it to the kitchen. Tilly heard the glugging sound of it as Liz poured it down the sink. She wanted to cry out against her doing so but stopped herself. *I have to fight this demon in me that's woken up once more. I have to.*

By the time the men came downstairs, Tilly and Liz had some tatties frying off in the pan with the leftover cabbage and onion. Tilly stirred the mixture while Liz beat an egg that would bind it all together and give it a fluffy texture. Tilly loved the Boxing Day breakfast fry-up of leftovers.

Tommy caught her by the waist and kissed her neck. Tingles travelled down her spine, but a sadness settled in her as she knew she had to dash Tommy's hopes.

But then he made her giggle as he did a little jig. 'For sure that Dan sneaked past me. You shouldn't have tempted me to tarry. I was ahead of him in the race to the lav, so I was.'

'Ha, you should have used the piddle pot before you came down. Go on with you, there's two out there. Mind, we share with the neighbour, so you might have company sitting next to you.'

Tommy looked aghast at this. It was a look that brought home to Tilly how much she hated visiting the lav out the back. She and Liz only did so when it was really necessary, but mostly they used the piddle pots, keeping them emptied and cleaning them regularly under the tap in the yard.

When they sat down to eat, both men had shiny faces as they'd swilled themselves under the tap, and the cold water had given them rosy cheeks. 'Innocence itself, look at them, Tilly. Butter wouldn't melt to see them all scrubbed up like this. You'd never think they were raging animals between the sheets.'

They all laughed at this, though Tilly felt a tinge of colour redden her cheeks and she wished Liz hadn't been so coarse in her remark as it seemed to mock the beautiful thing that had passed between her and Tommy.

Tommy looked up at her, his lovely Irish eyes full of love. Tilly couldn't hold his gaze.

Undeterred by the silence she'd caused, Liz deepened the embarrassment. 'Well, so, you two lovebirds will be thinking of wedding, no doubt?'

Tommy nodded. 'Aye, I'll be making Tilly me bride as soon as I can.'

'You haven't asked me yet, Tommy. How do you knaw what me answer will be?'

'I'll be asking you now, then, me lovely Tilly.' Getting out of the chair, Tommy came around the table to her and knelt on one knee. 'Is it that you can do me the honour of being me bride, Tilly?'

Tilly was mortified. Standing, she pushed by the kneeling Tommy and fled through the door, through the living room and up the stairs. When she reached her bed, she flung herself on it and sobbed.

Her heart told her how much love it held for Tommy – it was bursting with it – but her head told her that she must not, could not, go with him.

The creaking of the door alerted her to Tommy's presence. 'Tilly? Tilly, me wee darling. Please, Tilly. I – I can't live without you. I love you with all that I am, me Tilly. Life without you is for being an unbearable thought. Please marry me, Tilly.'

When she lifted her head, she saw that Tommy was kneeling by the bed. His hand came out and stroked her hair. 'Whatever troubles you have, I am for being able to sort them for you, Tilly.' But then it was as if realisation dawned on him and he lowered his head. 'I can never be for finding your girls, Tilly. If I could, sure enough I would be out there combing every street of every town, but there is no starting point. And if that's what it takes to have you as me bride, then I have failed, so I have. But I beg of you, Tilly. Don't spoil the rest of your life and mine by making the hope that's in you the only peg on which to hang your life.'

'I have to.' Twisting and sitting up, she looked deeply into Tommy's eyes. 'If you love me, Tommy, you will have to be the one to make sacrifices. I will never leave Blackpool while me girls are out there and may one day come looking for me.'

'Tilly, Tilly, I cannot leave me farm. If I do, it'll be taken over, if not by the thieving British landlords, then by those who would squat on it, and work it, and then claim it as their own.'

'But if you have the deeds to it, naw one can do that, and you say that fella who lives in the barn can run it for you. You could go over every few weeks and see that everything is running all right.'

Tommy shook his head. 'You don't know the way of it, Tilly. I have to be there. There are rebels who would take any land they see vacant and use it for their cause. There are the British who often sack the land, applying to the Crown to add it to their holdings, and there are the homeless and hungry who would take possession. I cannot let it happen.'

'Then we can never marry, Tommy.' The tears cascaded down her face as Tilly faced the reality of their situation and the years of loneliness without Tommy stretched before her.

Tommy stared at her. The desolation he felt was written all over his face and it seared her heart. The tear that trickled from his eye and traced a path down his cheek nearly undid her, but she remained silent, looking back at him.

His cry as he lunged for her was more of a moan of deep pain. Rising from the floor, he sank down on the bed and took her in his arms. 'Tilly, me little Tilly. I beg of you ...'

His arms held her close; she encircled him in hers. Their bodies moulded into each other, giving Tilly the sure knowledge that this was where she belonged and that not being so would break her heart.

Tommy's kisses covered her face, his hands sought to caress her. Undoing the buttons at the back of her blouse, he touched her bare skin. Tilly was lost. Her body could never deny this man – her man – even if her mind wouldn't let her go with him.

Feeling the pleasure of him pulling her blouse off and snuggling into her cleavage, she begged of him, 'Couldn't you visit me often? Please, Tommy, I don't want to live without you.'

Pulling away from her, Tommy once more gazed into her eyes. His fingers pulled at the lace in her corset as he said, 'If that is the only way, then so it must be.' His lips descended on hers, just as he'd freed her breasts from their stays. When his hands curled around the softness of her Tilly cried out, both from the agonizing pleasure she felt and the injustice of everything that had befallen her. But then she surrendered to the pleasure and gave her all to Tommy.

Waving Tommy off on the train the next day, Tilly couldn't cry. She was drained of tears. Drained of refusing Tommy's begging. Drained of energy.

As the train disappeared, leaving her in a mist of smoke and steam, she bowed her head. Once the air had cleared, she looked around the deserted station and felt a loneliness enter her like none she'd ever experienced. It consumed her and made her feel only half a person. A big part of the other half of her had been taken away on the train; another part had been missing a long time.

It was a week later, with Liz in a flurry organising her wedding, and Molly doing a final fitting of the frock she was making for Liz, that Tilly received news that Mr Fellows wanted to see her. The messenger boy had no other information for her, just that she should come to see Mr Fellows at her earliest convenience.

'Let's hope he has news of your mate and its good news, Tilly.'

'Aye, I hope so, Liz. Florrie's on me mind all the time.'

'It'll be like shifting one out and another in.' Molly laughed as she said this in a voice squeezed out between the pins she held between her teeth.

'You'll swallow one of those in a minute, lass. And Tilly ain't shoving me out, I'm going willingly. I hope you do move Florrie in, Tilly, as I feel bad about leaving you on your own.'

'Naw, don't.'

'I were only joking, Tilly. Sorry. I didn't mean owt, Liz.'

Tilly went to Molly, who'd stood up in her anguish and put her arms out. 'We knaw you didn't. Come here, we're overdue a hug after me behaviour at Christmas.'

'You can't keep apologising, Tilly.' Molly's arms hugged Tilly. 'It were a slip, that's all. Aye, and a lesson to learn.'

Tilly came out of Molly's arms and she looked Molly in the eyes. 'I've learnt it, I promise.'

'And having Florrie with you will help. Stop you from getting too down, though how you cope without the man you love on top of everything else and not hitting the bottle I don't knaw.'

'I don't, Liz, I just exist from day to day, longing for a letter to come from Tommy, and longing even more to have him walk through the door, but then that vies with me longing for me girls to do that an' all, and keeps me here in the hope.'

'It's hope as keeps us all going.' Liz put her arm around Tilly as she said this. 'And I for one think you are amazing, Tilly. You care about everyone, and not only care, but you do sommat about their situations. Look how you fought for me. You brought me out of the darkest pit I've ever been in. And one that threatens to engulf me every day, if it weren't for you and, well, Dan an' all.'

'Dan will take care of you, Liz. He's a very caring and understanding man.'

'Aye. You knaw, he desperately wants kids, but I ain't ready yet, so he makes sure he won't make me pregnant.'

'Do you reckon as you'll ever be ready, Liz?'

'Aye, I does. Sometimes I feel the urge so strong, I almost beg Dan to let things take their course, but I want to be sure. I want to reach a time when I don't want kids to replace them I lost, but for themselves, if you can understand that.'

Tilly found it hard to understand how Liz bore anything that she was forced to, let alone how she could bring logic to her situation. 'You knaw, Liz, I love you like you're me sister that I never had, and whatever you decide, I'll be here for you, lass.'

'Eeh, the day you two came to this street were a good day. I've never had any friends like you. Now, let me get on before I start blabbing.' With this, Molly knelt down again and began to stick pins in the hem of Liz's frock as if her life depended on it.

The news Mr Fellows had for Tilly was partly good. He'd located Florrie in a workhouse in Manchester. 'But, I'm sorry to tell you, Matilda, your friend isn't well and is in the infirmary. She has pneumonia.'

'Oh, dear God, naw.' Fear for Florrie clenched Tilly's heart. 'When can I go to her?'

'I have made approaches and told the governor that we will be applying to the court to have Miss Florence Stanley released to your guardianship. I have been able to prove to them that you are financially able to support her and that you will care for her, but that will take time. In the meantime, the governor has consented to you visiting once a week until she is free. He has said that this must be on a Sunday afternoon so as not to cause any disruption – though what disruption he thinks you will cause, I am not sure.'

'That's wonderful, ta, Mr Fellows. I'll see how the trains run on Sunday, but if that's not an option, I'll hire a cab to take me.'

'I have looked the trains up, and there is one in the morning that leaves Central Station at nine thirty a.m. and will take you to Preston, and then a connection that will take you to Manchester. You will need a cab to the workhouse as it is out of the city centre. Then, there is a train that comes back to Preston at four thirty, and a connecting one to bring you back to Blackpool. We are very lucky to have one of the busiest trainlines in the country, and the people to use it, as it seems the whole country flocks here, summer and winter.'

'Aye, we are, and to have the folk coming an' all. They're good for business.'

'Ahh, talking of business, how are your plans coming along?'

'Well, I have had a good batch of cane delivered, and the best quality an' all. And I'm about to begin working with it to stockpile for the season. As I said, I'm going to pitch with Dan – the man I pitched with last year. I'm hoping to get another good season under me belt and then see about premises next year.'

'I see, and you paid your benefactor back, I take it?'

'Aye, I paid Tommy off the money he leant me.' Tilly didn't let in the pain that threatened her at the mention of Tommy.

'Good. Well, I have news about the pitches that you are thinking of taking. I'm sorry to say, but the council are talking of banning all traders from the beach from the beginning of this 1897 season.'

'Awe, naw, why? We're a big part of Blackpool life! The holidaymakers love us, and the experience of mooching through what we have to sell and finding a bargain to take home. It'll be a tragedy to lose it. And besides, what will all the traders do?'

'It seems that the council are in talks with the owners of the houses along the promenade, and quite a few are willing to let out their front gardens, especially those who only come here every now and again – they see it as an income towards the upkeep of their second home. Those who are running their houses as guest houses are not so keen, though, so there are limited places available this year. Some traders may get a licence to trade from barrows on the pavement, but that wouldn't be big enough for you. How about I make enquiries for you? How much space do you need?'

'Between us, me and Dan'll need at least three parts of one of them gardens. And we'll need to be able to pitch our canvas an' all, to protect our goods if it rains.'

'Yes, of course, but I think there will be rules as to the type of structure you can have. Neither the owners nor the council want to see Blackpool's front looking a mishmash of the type of stalls that have been used on the beach – the sort of thing that is made of a piece of canvas slung over two poles. They are talking of properly constructed stalls all gayly coloured, and looking neat and tidy.'

'Oh dear, we haven't owt like that.'

'Well, I'll look into that too. Leave it with me. Come and see me next week. Bring the gentleman you are setting up with, and I'll have a plan for you. I'm sure the council have someone in mind to construct the stalls. And Matilda, we must look on this as the way the future for Blackpool should go. With everything looking nice and tidy, we'll attract more visitors and the mile that is being allocated for you stallholders could turn out to make your fortune – a Golden Mile, so to speak.'

Tilly liked the sound of that. 'You should suggest that that's what it's called: "The Golden Mile". It conjures up a picture that's exciting.'

Mr Fellows laughed. 'It does. And it'll be what you traders and the stalls that provide fun, like the hoopla and the other chance games, make of it. You are the future of Blackpool and the council recognises that.'

'Aye, by chucking us off the beach! But, I can see as it will work.'

Although what she had heard posed problems that had to be solved in just a few weeks before Easter was upon them, Tilly's thoughts were more centred on the knowledge of where Florrie was, and her worry of hearing how ailing she was. *Eeh, God, you've not been one for answering many of me prayers, but if you could see your way to saving Florrie and helping me to get her back here, then I'd be very grateful.*

TWENTY-EIGHT

As Tilly walked up the sweeping path to Crumpsall Workhouse she was surprised to see a beautiful ornate archway in front of her. Through this she could see a round garden bed with the paths to the main door skirting it. The garden was full of daffodils swaying in the breeze.

Although cold, the sky was lit by a strong winter sun whose warmth had almost dispelled the frost, leaving patches here and there of glittering white. Tilly couldn't believe she was in a place that held the misery of the poor.

There was a man bending over a brush with which he was fighting a losing battle against the debris that had fallen from the trees; no sooner did he sweep it into a pile than the wind scattered it again. He straightened when he saw Tilly approaching. 'Good morning to you, lady.'

Tilly smiled at him and was rewarded with a lovely grin that was marred by his yellow-stained teeth. 'I'm looking for the infirmary.'

'Just go and pull the bell on that door, they'll guide you.' He gave a little cough. 'I'm begging your pardon, miss, but have you any baccy on you?'

'Naw. I don't smoke. Sorry. I can give you a penny to buy some, though.'

The man, who she'd thought of as old, came over to her and she could see he was no more than around forty years of age. His suit was dirty, his shirt was collarless, and he wore a grubby neckerchief around his neck. 'Ta, that's sommat as I'd be very grateful of.'

Tilly gave him the penny. Her heart felt sore at the sight of the open raw spots on the man's face and the look of hope-lessness in his eyes. 'I hope as things get better for you soon. I'm visiting a friend who I lost touch with. I were shocked to find she were in here. I'm taking her out as soon as she's well.'

'It ain't Florrie, is it?'

'Aye! Does you knaw her? How is she?'

'Florrie's me girl, we're going out. We met when she was well and took walks in the garden with other lasses – that's when they were allowed. We got talking and, well, we fell for each other. We did our best to be together, but could only sneak a short time here and there, as they don't like the men and women mixing. But we find our ways. It breaks me heart that she's so poorly and I can't go to see her. Will you tell her that Reggie sends his love?'

'Aye, I will, Reggie.' Tilly liked Reggie, though she struggled to work out what Florrie would see in him; he smelt strongly of body odour and when he'd lifted his cap, she'd noticed that his hair was thick with grease and dirt. His hands were encrusted with grime and his fingernails were black. Florrie was such a clean woman and took care of her appearance.

But when Tilly entered the ward where Florrie was, she was shocked to see her friend. The young woman she'd remembered bore no resemblance to the gaunt one lying in the bed under a tent that had steam pumping into it from a large kettle that stood on a gas ring. Looking through the opening to the tent, Tilly's anguish showed in her voice. 'Florrie – oh, Florrie, love, can you hear me, lass?'

Florrie turned her head. Her eyes didn't seem to focus. Her laboured breathing became more so, but then a flicker of light in her eyes showed Tilly that Florrie had recognised her and Tilly was relieved to see a small smile appear on her face.

'Eeh, Florrie, Florrie, I'm so happy to have found you. You have to get well, lass, as I'm taking you home.'

Florrie's brows furrowed. Her cracked lips moved but no sound came from her.

'Aye, home, lass. Home to mine, where I'm going to take care of you. I have a house now. It ain't very big, but it's grand, Florrie.'

Florrie's mouth dropped open, but it was a good shock to her as some colour began to tinge her cheeks.

'And I met your Reggie an' all. He said to give you his love.'

The smile Florrie gave at this confirmed to Tilly that she did feel for Reggie how he had indicated. 'Look, Florrie. We'll get you out first, then we'll try to get Reggie out. We only have to prove that he has somewhere to go and a job, and I can give him both.'

Florrie's pale face lit up at this. Tilly knew in that moment that giving Florrie hope for her future had made a difference to her. She knew that feeling herself, only too well.

Florrie's mouth moved again. 'Don't try to talk. Your mouth looks so dry, Florrie. But it can happen and will. I promise you. You just have to get better. Fight, Florrie. Fight with all you're worth to get better.'

Florrie nodded.

'Cook's worried about you. You didn't give your address when you wrote. You've taken some finding. Me solicitor found you in the end . . . Oh, aye, you may look surprised, but I've come a long way since I last saw you. Not all of it's been good. Some has broke me heart, but some of what's happened to me has been good, and now I'm well set up. Hold on a mo, lass, I'll be right back.'

Tilly went towards the sister sitting at a desk near to the door. 'Can I have a word, please, Sister?'

The sister looked up. Her gaze took in all of Tilly until she felt dirty under the scrutiny, but then she remembered the standing she now had and lifted her head. 'I'm to become the guardian of Florrie, me solicitor is in the process of drawing up the papers, and—'

'Guardian? You?'

'Aye, me, and afore you judge me, I'm set up well, and have me own business in Blackpool, so I'm well placed to take care of Florrie. But all I want to ask you is if she can have sommat to drink, some water, or sommat to wet her lips. She's parched.'

'Oh? Well, yes, I suppose so. I'll be there in a moment.'

'Ta.'

Tilly turned back to go towards Florrie and was pleased to find how much brighter she looked. 'Eeh, Florrie, you're getting better already, lass.'

This time Florrie managed an even bigger smile and nodded her head.

When the sister came over, she showed her surprise at the transformation as she joined Tilly at the opening of the tent. 'Well, well, it seems a visit from your soon-to-be guardian has caused a miracle. I'd given up on you, Florrie.'

Turning to Tilly, she said, 'I'll get her a drink now. When you asked, I really didn't think it would do any good, I thought it was just a matter of time.'

This shocked Tilly, as without water, Florrie surely would have faded away in a very short time. She raised her eyes heavenward and said a silent prayer of thanks to God for getting her to Florrie's side before that happened.

Once Florrie had taken a few sips of water she was able to speak. 'Ta, Ti – Tilly. It's . . . good to . . . see you.'

Before Tilly could answer the sister spoke. 'Now then, don't overdo things, Florrie. You're on the road to recovery by the looks of you, but you've a way to go, so take it very easy for a start.'

'Yes, Florrie, love. Do as the sister says. I'll go now, but I'll be back next Sunday. Me solicitor has arranged that I can come every Sunday till you come home. Just get better, lass. Promise me.'

Florrie managed a smile and a nod of her head. But her weakness worried Tilly. Yes, she'd seen an improvement and the sister had confirmed that, but Florrie was just skin and bones and had a long way to go. From what she'd seen of this place it was none too clean. What if Florrie caught another infection while she was so vulnerable?

By the time she'd woken up the next morning, Tilly had a plan and now she stood once more in Mr Fellows' office.

'Please, Mister Fellows, there must be sommat you can do? Florrie is in grave danger if she stays in that place too long.'

'But it will take almost all you have to pay for your friend to be brought back here and placed in the hospital for treatment. What about your business? Matilda, don't give up on your dream, your way of making something of yourself, for this friend. I'm sure she would never ask that of you.'

'She don't have to ask. I don't care about owt but keeping her safe. I want to do this. Please arrange it for me, Mr Fellows, please.'

'Very well.' Mr Fellows shook his head. 'If I live to be a hundred, I will never understand how you poor folk form such alliances with each other that you'd give your life for each other, but you know, I wish I did. You have something the rich of this world will never have, and I envy you for it. You're an angel, Tilly, an angel in the sense of the good you do.' As if he'd embarrassed himself by this statement, Mr Fellows coughed and became business-like once more. 'I will make the arrangements. As it is only a formality that you will take guardianship of your friend, I can get that through court tomorrow.'

'And what about Reggie?'

'Oh, Tilly, Tilly, isn't it enough that you have secured your friend? You don't know this Reggie.'

'I knaw as me friend loves him and that's enough for me. She deserves a shot at happiness.'

'I thought you said your friend had barely been able to speak to you? Look, I want to strongly advise you not to do anything about this Reggie chap until you can speak to your friend and make sure this is her wish. He may have been trying to con you. Please be guided by me in this at least, Matilda.'

'Aye, it makes sense what you say. And he's a strong man so won't come to any harm by having to wait. But in the meantime, just in case, I'll ask around to see if I can get him work.'

'Do you know what he does? What skills he has?'

'Well, naw. But he were gardening, so he must have that one.'

'Umm, well, as it happens, I do know someone who is looking for a gardener. But before you start to smile in that way, it isn't cut and dried. I would have to know a lot about this Reggie, and it would all have to be good for me to even mention him as a possible candidate for the job.'

'You knaw, not many can help landing up in the poorhouse, Mr Fellows. I nearly did meself. And Florrie, well, if you'd have known her, she were a maid, and well thought of, an honest young woman, but as I told you, she hit hard times.'

'Yes, I understand that and think these things tragic, but I still have to check out that Reggie is of the same type. He could have been put there through his own doing – gambling, or drinking, or just idleness and getting into debt. I have to be careful.'

Tilly understood this and didn't think badly of Mr Fellows for it. He wasn't a man who judged anyone without knowing the facts. She just hoped Reggie wasn't found wanting as she was desperate for Florrie to find happiness.

The following week, Tilly felt some of the joy she'd felt on Christmas Day enter her. Florrie was safely in the hospital on

Whitegate Drive and making wonderful progress, and excitement was mounting for Liz's wedding on Saturday, which would give them all plenty of time afterwards to prepare for the season opening at Easter, which didn't fall until mid-April this year.

Tilly, despite everything that had been going on, was well ahead with her basket making, though struggling for space to put everything. This had been eased a little with Dan building a stepladder to her loft and taking some of her baskets home with him to put in his lock-up with his own stock. But both she and Dan were anxiously awaiting news from Mr Fellows about their pitch and the cost of a new stand. They'd heard rumours of the rents being very high and of traders vying for so few places available.

Tilly was particularly worried as her newfound fortune was dwindling at an alarming rate, as hospital fees came out of it. She was hoping and praying that when she visited Florrie later that day, she would find her well enough to bring home.

'Tilly, you're not paying attention.'

'Sorry, Liz, love, but we have gone over everything a million times. And you knaw as everything's in place.'

'But you haven't iced the cake!'

'Naw, and I'm not doing so. I told you, Molly has a friend who's really good at it, and she's taking it to her this afternoon.'

'Awe, I'm sorry, Tilly, I knaw as you've a lot on your plate, but I want everything to be so nice. I'm not sure of Dan's family yet.'

'They'll all love you. How many did you say will be coming?'

'Eleven of them. His ma, his two brothers and their wives, and they have four young 'uns between them, and his aunt, who is the only one I feel comfortable with at the moment. She's grand and is right pleased with the rooms she has and how Dan has set them out for her.'

'And, then there's me, and Molly and her lot. It'll be lovely, I promise.'

'Oh, Tilly ... I ... It's a bit of an ordeal to tell the truth. I just wish Dan had whisked me off to the registry office and married me and then told them all. And not only that, but ... well, I'm feeling guilty. I feel as though I'm shoving all me family out and making a new life that they can't make ... I ...'

'Come here, lass.' A sobbing Liz came into Tilly's arms. Tilly held Liz's shuddering body to her. 'It's nerves, Liz. It's all play-ing on your mind. It were bound to whenever you made a decision about how to spend the rest of your life. But, love, you can't alter owt. And sitting around going mad as you were in that institution ain't going to make owt better. Your young 'uns'll be glad to see you happy. They loved you so much, they'd have done owt for you. They'll be dancing for joy on them clouds on Saturday.'

Liz calmed. 'Their stone is ready. And I'm going to put some flowers on it soon.'

'Aye, that's a grand idea, and I'll put some on Martha's. By, I'm looking forward to being matron of honour. And it is an honour, Liz. And one I'm looking forward to. But, lass, you'll allus have these moments, just remember not to bottle them up, but to share them with Dan, or me. We'll allus be here for you.'

★   ★   ★

360

At the hospital, Tilly was overjoyed to find Florrie out of bed. She ran to her and took her too-thin body in her arms. 'Eeh, lass, by, you'll soon be coming home now.'

'Ta, Tilly. I'd be dead by now if it wasn't for you.'

'Well, you're not, lass, and I want you home as soon as possible. I'll go and speak to the sister.'

The ward sister was a different one to the one on duty the first time that Tilly visited. This one was a kindly lady in her late forties who Florrie loved and who was always nice to Tilly. She had a round face and body. 'Ahh, Tilly. I bet you're thrilled to find Florrie so well? And we are very happy with her progress. There's no infection showing now, we just need to build her up.'

'I can do that, Sister. Can you arrange for her to come home to me? I'll get her to eat and take her for little gentle walks, and make sure she rests up an' all.'

'I don't see a problem with that, my dear. I'll speak to the doctor. I am sure we will have good news for you tomorrow.'

'Oh, ta. Ta ever so much. That's a grand relief to me.'

The sister smiled knowingly. 'You've done well by her, Tilly. I wish I had a friend like you.'

Tilly blushed, but before she could speak, a voice she knew well called out her name. 'Cook! Eeh, I'm glad to see you. Florrie'll be over the moon. Excuse us, Sister ... Oh, it is all right for us both to see Florrie at the same time, ain't it?'

'It is. Go on with you, or visiting time will be over.'

Florrie was so happy to see Cook. It brought tears to Tilly's eyes to see them hugging and shedding tears of joy at being together, and she knew in that moment it was worth all the money it had cost her just to see this.

Once they were all calm, Tilly broached the subject of Reggie, explaining what she had in mind. 'I need to knaw how much you knaw about him and if you want him to come out and to be with you, Florrie.'

Cook looked puzzled. 'And who is this Reggie you're talking of, eh?'

'Oh, you'll love him, Cook. We ... Well, we fell in love on first sight. He came in to the workhouse a few months after me. It's been so difficult for him. He worked for an old farmer who was on his last legs. Reggie ran the farm and did all the work that was needed with no help. He sometimes worked sixteen or seventeen hours a day and lived in a draughty old barn. The farmer paid him a pittance, but kept him well fed. Then one day he found the farmer dead in his chair. He had no relatives and hadn't left a will, so his land reverted to the Crown. Reggie couldn't find another position and had no money. He lived on the streets for a while but got picked up for begging. The court sent him to the workhouse.'

'Eeh, Florrie, don't you worry, lass. Me solicitor will check Reggie's story and if it's true ... I – I mean, I believe it, but you knaw what these solicitor folk are like, well then, we'll soon have Reggie out, and hopefully he'll be given this job as me solicitor knaws of. And you knaw what? I found out that there's a cottage that goes along with the job an' all. Though the bloke who gets the job has to be married afore he can have the cottage, so you've got some serious courting to do, lass.'

Both Florrie and Cook laughed at this and the sound gladdened Tilly's heart. Everything seemed to be coming together in life ... except ...

'That were a big sigh, lass. And I reckon I knaws what prompted it.'

'I haven't told Florrie yet, but I reckon as you're strong enough now, Florrie, lass.'

'What? What is it? Is it sommat really bad?'

'It is, but you mustn't upset yourself. I'm coping, and I have a hope alive in me that I keep leaning on, so I get by. Having you back will help an' all, Florrie.'

'What is it? Oh, Tilly, tell me.'

After her telling of how Babs and Beth had been taken, Tilly couldn't stop her tears flowing. Florrie and Cook cried with her.

'Now then, what's all this, ladies? Come along, Florrie, it won't do you any good getting upset, and I'll have to ask your visitors to leave if they are the cause.'

'It's all right, Sister. I'm fine. I just heard some bad news, but I can cope. I – I, well, just do all you can to get me home. Me and Tilly need each other, and we should be together.'

'If you're sure. But I don't think you should talk about whatever it was that upset you all and instead revert to the laughter I heard a few moments ago. Laughter is a healer, crying weakens you.'

The sister was right, Tilly knew that. She wiped her tears. 'I'm fine now. It's good to share your sorrow with those you love, and I do love you both. You've been good friends to me. I can't wait to get you home, Florrie. I'll arrange it for Monday. Liz, as I told you of, will be married then and her room will be free. Then if we get Reggie home, he can have the sofa. But I'll be looking to get the pair of you wedded off and out from under me feet just as soon as I can.'

The joy on Florrie's face at this lightened the mood and made Cook clap her hands together. 'You're an angel, Tilly, a proper miracle worker.'

Tilly smiled; she'd been called that before but was sure that angels didn't behave how she sometimes did. And then, she thought: *If only I were one. I'd miracle me lasses here this minute.*

TWENTY-NINE

On the morning of the wedding, Tilly woke early. For a moment she stayed under the covers, steeling herself to make the trip to her dresser over the cold lino to wash her face, but suddenly she was compelled to throw the covers back, jump out of bed and grab her piddle pot. Just in time she caught the vomit that projected from her.

Stinging, nasty-tasting bile had her retching and retching, even after there was no more of it to bring up. Tentatively taking a sip of the water she always had on her side table, Tilly hoped she wasn't coming down with something. Not today of all days. But with the bout passed she didn't feel ill anymore.

Thinking she must have eaten something that didn't agree with her, she donned her housecoat and hurried downstairs with the offending pot. Warmth met her as the embers were still burning in the grate. Mentally going through what she had to do, she scurried into the yard. Darkness cloyed at her as she trod the well-known route to the back lav. The pot seen to and swilled out, she left it propped against the wall and set about lifting the tin bath tub down from its hook and dragging it in front of the fire.

Shivering from the cold, she ignored the strange feeling that she was going to faint and set about stoking the fire and putting the grate plate holding the kettle over the heat. This done, she hugged herself for a moment and gazed into the flames. A memory of the last time she was sick in the morning came to her, and though it provoked a longing for her girls, there was another thought that shifted that feeling from her and filled her with an incredible one. *Naw, I can't be. Naw, the doctor said I were too damaged to have another babby.* But then she realised that she hadn't seen her bleeding since before she and Tommy ... *Oh, God. I've been so busy, I hadn't given thought to it.* Not that she ever did as it was just a monthly occurrence that meant nothing anymore. *Could it be? And if it is, how will I cope?* A painful thought hit her then: *Oh God, what will me Babs and Beth think? Will they think as I'd forgotten them and went on to have other young 'uns to replace them?*

Fear vied with a feeling of wonderment that it could be possible she was having Tommy's child. But then another feeling hit her. A longing to be with Tommy, to have him protect her and tell her everything was going to be all right.

Not allowing herself to dwell, Tilly put all her energy into stoking the boiler in the kitchen and lighting the stove, then tugging the heavy pan of water over the heat. Both she and Liz wanted to bath and wash their hair this morning, so it was important she got hers done early and then prepared Liz's bath for her.

The kettle whistled impatiently, prompting her to fill the teapot they had left all set out on the table. Her hands shook as she did, and a confusion of feelings assailed her: they ranged from joy to sadness. Excitement to fear. But overriding these was disbelief. *Naw, I'm being daft. I can't have any more babbies and that's that.*

As she took two cups of tea up the stairs, she determined to put the idea out of her head and concentrate on making this a magical day for Liz. 'Come on, sleepy head, it's your wedding day!'

Liz gave a muffled moan.

Placing the cups down on the dresser, Tilly lit the gas mantle and then went to the fireplace and lit the paper and kindling that lay ready in the grate. She hadn't bothered to light the fire in her own room, knowing they were planning on dressing together in Liz's. As light flooded the room, she looked at the beautiful frocks hanging on the cupboard door. Liz's a pale blue, hers a darker, almost navy blue. Lying on the chair in front of them were the thick bloomers and the pretty corsets they were to wear underneath – the bloomers were made in winceyette and, it was hoped, would keep bodies and legs warm, while the frocks had matching long jackets lined with fleece. Tilly marvelled at the work Molly had put into the outfits, and the skill and talent she had shown. Both frocks had a fitting bodice that had a ruffle panel from the bustline to the waist. The skirt hung in folds down to the ankle, which would show the white silk stockings they were to wear and the white pumps – both of these items had cost a fortune and they'd had to be specially ordered in by the shop.

'Come on, Liz, love, sit up and drink your tea. We've a lot to do.'

As Liz looked up at her, Tilly smiled. 'Happy wedding day, lass. Aye, and I wish you a happy life with Dan an' all. Though I knaw as there's no doubting that.'

Liz didn't speak. Tilly could see that many emotions were assailing her. Keeping things cheerful, she chatted on about how excited she felt and joked that she couldn't wait to get rid of Liz, so that she could get the room ready and move another friend in.

'Eeh, you're a bad bugger, Tilly. Ha, I doubt you'll let me bed get cold.'

'Aw, Liz. It's like sommat's coming to an end.'

'Well, it is, but sommat's just beginning an' all. A new life for the both of us. Me with me lovely Dan, and you with your friend Florrie. I can't wait to meet her, you knaw, Tilly.'

'She's lovely. She didn't deserve what happened to her. Anyroad, shift up, let me in with you, there's still a chill in this room.'

With this, Tilly slipped into the bed next to Liz.

'By, your feet are cold, Tilly, don't touch me legs with them.'

'I wonder what you'll do if Dan has cold feet.'

'He hasn't . . . I mean . . . well, I've sampled them.'

They both burst out laughing at this. 'Eeh, Liz, that sounds like you've taken a bite out of them, you dirty mare.'

'I could have done an' all. I could eat him, he's so beautiful.'

Tilly wondered at this. Dan wasn't unattractive, but beautiful? No. Her Tommy was, though . . . *By, what am I thinking?*

'What's up, lass? You've gone quiet. And come to think of it, you look a bit peaky. Are you all right, Tilly?'

'Aye, I'm just tired.'

'Come on, what's troubling you? You can't fool me, you knaw. I've known you too long.'

'You have – a lifetime, Liz. And by, we've been through sommat together. But let's not think on that, or owt that might be troubling us. Today is a day of happiness. Your wedding day, Liz. Eeh, it's going to be grand.'

'It is, but we wouldn't be human if we didn't reflect on what went afore. And I want to an' all. I want to think of me young 'uns today. I want to remember them, not shut them out. Aye, I feel pain at their loss, but when they were alive, they didn't ever cause me pain. They were a grand bunch, and I want them in me heart today.'

Tilly marvelled at this, and a small hope entered her that Liz was healing a little. Oh, she knew it was impossible for her to completely heal, but for her to talk like this, to say she wanted to remember the best of her children, well, that was a beginning.

She found Liz's hand and squeezed it.

'Pass me me tea, lass. It'll be cold.'

In this from Liz, Tilly felt that she was putting a lid on her sadness for today. She knew she must do the same.

'By, that's good. Ta, Tilly. It were thoughtful of you to get me a cuppa in bed. Now, tell me, what's ailing you?'

'Awe, much the same as you, Liz. But I'm going to do the same as you are and hold me young 'uns close today. I reckon that will be more comforting than trying not to think of them.'

'Aye, having them with us will help us to enjoy the day more. But are you sure that's what's making you look so peaky and troubled?'

'Eeh, Liz, you knaw me better than most. I knaw I'm going to have to tell you. But you'll be shocked. You see, I were sick this morning.'

'And?'

'Well, what does morning sickness tell you?'

'Naw! But I thought … Eeh, Tilly, have there been any other signs?'

'Aye, me bleeding ain't visited me since Tommy were here and, well, I hadn't given it any thought, but me breasts are tender and have been pushing against the restrictions of me clothes lately.'

'I – I don't knaw what to say, lass. Part of me wants to shout for joy, but I don't knaw how you feel.'

'Scared. Overjoyed. Sad. Worried. Oh, Liz, I feel every emotion going. Should I contact Tommy? Oh, I don't knaw. I've even had the fleeting thought of visiting old Ginny.'

'Naw. You're not doing that, Tilly. She's been responsible for many a lass losing their life, and if she don't get the babby away, maiming the unborn child. It's wicked what she does with them knitting needles of hers.'

'I knaw. But what would you do if you were me?'

Liz was quiet for a moment, and Tilly had the feeling that she had something she wanted to say but couldn't.

'Let's get up and think on it, eh? Come on, we've a lot to do, like you say.'

'Liz?'

'What?'

'You're hiding sommat. I can tell.'

'Naw. Naw, I ain't. Now, come on. Today is my day. Don't go stealing me thunder.'

Tilly felt this like a blow.

'Eeh, I'm sorry, lass.' Liz's arms came around Tilly and she sank gratefully into the warmth and love of them. 'I just don't knaw what to say, that's all. But look. I'm allus here for you.

370

Me and Dan'll help you through this. You can ask owt of us, and we'll do it. Just don't press me to tell you owt as I shouldn't.'

Tilly accepted this, but her thoughts ran wild. What was it that Liz couldn't tell her?

'And, don't look like that, Tilly lass, it ain't owt bad.'

This intrigued her. And unnerved her a little. But she brushed this thought away as whatever the surprise was, it wouldn't be anything bad. Liz and Dan wouldn't do that to her.

They sat each end of the bath, giggling like schoolkids and chatting about this and that. 'Eeh, I'm glad I didn't have time to have me bath afore you as I planned, Liz. This time together is lovely.'

'Ha, with you taking all the room and splashing me it ain't.' Liz splashed water at Tilly as she said this, but then became serious. 'You knaw, Tilly, though me and Dan have coupled, he ain't ever seen me naked. I mean, well, me body shows the signs of bearing me young 'uns, and it worries me that he has his expectations high.'

'Don't be daft, you're beautiful, Liz. You're slim, firm, and aye, your breasts hang a little, but nowt so as you'd notice.'

'It's all right for you, you've allus been big-breasted, and small-waisted, and your titties don't sag, never have done. But mine, well, after feeding five of them ...'

'They're a medal to what you did for your young 'uns, Liz. Dan will love the sight of them.'

Liz was quiet for a moment, and Tilly regretted saying anything about her children as she knew that one moment you could face the loss, and the next it could overwhelm you. She prayed that she hadn't triggered this. But suddenly Liz

371

laughed again and chucked the sponge at Tilly. It hit her smack in the face, stinging her eyes with soap, but Liz's laughter was infectious, filling Tilly with relief and making her join in with the laughter even though she couldn't open her eyes.

'Eeh, Liz, give over, and let me swill me eyes.'

The laughter went on and lifted their mood as they climbed out and dried each other. 'You've a lovely skin, Liz. It's sort of milky and lovely and smooth. You've none of them marks like I have. Here, look.'

'Eeh, they've faded well. I remember bathing you just after you'd had the twins and you were really weak, and they were like jagged red scars. They're just silvery lines now, and you can hardly see them.'

Again, they laughed.

'Anyroad, enough about our bodies. We're two young women approaching thirty, what we expect, I don't knaw. Put your housecoat on and let's cook breakfast, then we'll do each other's hair and start to get ready, eh?'

Liz agreed, and as she turned away, Tilly traced her hands over her belly. *Are you in there, little one? Tommy's babby? Are you settling into me womb?* Suddenly she wanted it to be so and with the feeling came a longing to be in Tommy's arms.

The morning was a crisp, sunny one with a chilling wind that couldn't make its mark on the happiness everyone felt.

Liz looked beautiful and her smile held genuine happiness, which warmed Tilly's heart. The vows went well, with Dan stuttering a little over his words, and wiping a tear from his eye. Liz spoke out clearly and Tilly could feel that she meant every word. This was a chance at a new life that Liz was going to grasp with both hands and Tilly felt glad of that.

The congregation had been a blur to Tilly as she'd followed Liz up the aisle. She only remembered registering how many there were, but then, everyone loved a wedding and the townsfolk would gather to watch or take a place in the church to feel part of it.

It was as she straightened after helping Liz to turn in her dress to walk back down the aisle that she saw him. *Tommy!*

Her world collided with the stars. Her heart thumped a joyful rhythm. *Tommy! My Tommy!*

So this is what Liz couldn't tell me!

For a moment Tilly couldn't think why, but then, if she'd have known it wouldn't have been such a wonderful surprise and this is what Liz had wanted for her. *Oh, Tommy, Tommy.*

Liz turned and looked at her. She must have seen Tommy's expression and knew they had spotted each other. Liz nodded. 'Happy?'

'Aye, so happy. Ta, Liz. Best matron of honour present ever.'

To the sound of the bells ringing out, Tilly found herself in Tommy's arms being swung around. All her troubles left her. 'Eeh, Tommy, I'm so happy to see you.'

'Me Tilly, me lovely Tilly.' A flash of light told Tilly that their moment had been caught forever by the cameraman. She looked into Tommy's eyes, and her joy was complete.

After that, Tilly couldn't wait for the formal photographs to be done with so that she could be with Tommy.

In the church hall they found that they were sat together during the wedding breakfast. 'Eeh, Tommy, I'm that glad to see you.'

'I am for seeing that, me Tilly, and it is for gladdening me heart. Is it that you've had a change of heart? Has me absence made you know that we have to be together?'

'It has, Tommy. I love you. I love you more than I can say.' With these words that brought tears to Tommy's eyes, Tilly felt a sense of peace enter her. It encompassed all that had gone before and laid it to rest. Arthur had his place, tucked in her memory. A loving place that would always hold him. And Jeremiah too. Gentle Jeremiah. Resting now, as he was meant to be. And living in her thoughts, clothed in the deep fondness she'd had for him. And her twins too. They skipped and danced around her, telling her that they would find her one day but freeing her to give herself to Tommy and to bear his child.

'Tilly? Tilly, are you for being all right? What is it, Tilly?'

'Aye, why do you ask?'

'Well, it was that you seemed to be drifting away from me, as if on a dream.'

'I think I was. I was settling a lot of things that rage inside me and hold me back from seeking happiness. I'm ready, Tommy. I'm ready to come to you, but . . . well, it can't be yet. We must talk, me lovely Tommy.'

A flicker of disappointment showed in Tommy's eyes.

'It won't be a long wait, Tommy, I promise you, but well, there's things I have to see to.'

Tommy squeezed her hand.

It had been a wonderful day. Dan had played the piano that stood in the hall, and everyone had danced. Tilly had felt the excitement of being close to Tommy's body and had whispered to him that she wanted him to come home with her to spend the night with her. In answer he had held her closer and kissed her ears and her neck, but then remembered where they were and had pulled away from her. His eyes had twinkled as he'd breathed the words, 'Thank you, me little Tilly.'

His kisses had held a promise to her. She'd found it difficult to contain her feelings, and was filled with joy when finally Dan stood and told them, 'That's it, my lovely family and friends. Now, I have to take my beautiful bride home.'

Everyone had cheered. Liz had blushed.

'Throw your bouquet, Liz,' someone shouted. Liz looked bemused. Tilly turned and saw it was an elderly lady who had spoken. She'd been introduced as a friend of Dan's aunt.

'I was in America in the summer and attended a cousin's granddaughter's wedding. They have a lovely custom. All the unmarried ladies gather in a group and the bride throws her flowers. The lady who catches it is the next one to marry. It was such fun.'

Molly, who was stood next to Tilly, dug her in the ribs. 'Go on, Tilly. It looks to me like this should be your catch.' She nodded towards Tommy. Tilly laughed. 'I'm bound to catch it, all the other unmarrieds are little girls.'

'Naw, look, Dan's aunt and the lady who suggested it are joining in.'

Tilly lined up, determined not to catch the flowers and hoping one of the children did, but they came flying at her and if she hadn't have caught them, they would have taken her eyes out. Laughing, she felt herself blushing. Once the clapping had ceased, Tommy's voice filled the room. 'Ladies and gentlemen, it seems I have a duty to perform.'

All went quiet. Tilly held her breath. Then watched in amazement as Tommy went down on one knee in front of her. 'Tilly, or Matilda, as is your proper name, will you be doing me the honour of marrying me?'

The room remained silent. All eyes were on her. Tilly looked Tommy in the eye and, with no hesitation, answered, 'Aye, I will, Tommy, and ta for asking me.'

A cheer went up. Tommy stood and took Tilly in his arms. His kiss sealed how much she loved him as she melted into him. Her thoughts were that she must go forward with her life, and it was with Tommy that she wanted to do that. *Naw one knaws me future, or if I'll ever see me little lasses again, and that cuts me in two, but I have a chance of love now and a new future – a new beginning. One that the past is entwined into, with its sorrows and mistakes, but I will always hold on to the hope that one day a precious part of my past will join my future. I'll find a way of coping until that happens and a way of making sure that if me girls ever turn up, they will knaw where to find me.*

EPILOGUE

FINDING A KIND OF PEACE

'Is it the baby that changed your mind, then, Tilly?'

'Naw, me mind has allus been made up, but I couldn't see how I could be with you in Ireland and hold out hope of seeing me girls again. Realising yesterday morning that a miracle had happened was what spurred me on. I want to be with you, Tommy. To have you support me through the months ahead, and to be by me side when our child arrives.'

They were lying in bed together. Part of Tilly still held on to the feelings Tommy had given her during the night. She'd thought the time they'd made love that had resulted in her being pregnant had been the ultimate in lovemaking, but she'd been fuzzy-headed from drinking too much then. What she experienced in Tommy's arms this time was incomparable to that. Some of this was because now, she had no doubts. She returned his love and held him in esteem as the father of her unborn child. She'd wanted to give her all to him.

'Awe, Tilly, I will be, but weren't you for saying that nothing could happen yet?'

'I meant instantly. You see, I have things to sort out.' She told him about Florrie.

'Sure, are you going to be picking up waifs and strays all your life?'

'Naw. And Florrie ain't a waif and stray, I told you. Her and Cook were the saving of me at times. Anyroad, I don't think getting her settled is going to take much, I just need to get her Reggie freed from the workhouse.'

'And that has to be because he has a job?'

'Aye, mostly. Once that happens, he has to be released by the court as he was committed there by them.'

'And you're thinking him to be a decent man?'

'I am. If Florrie believes in him, then I do an' all.'

'Well, it is that I can offer him a job but being an Englishman in Ireland at this time is not a good thing to be.'

'Will I be safe, Tommy?'

'Aye. I'll make sure of that, but with a man, well, he'll want to go to the pub and that's where he'll get into trouble.'

Tilly could see that. Not that she understood the problems in Ireland or their hate of the English, but it was what it was.

'Eeh, I'd have loved a friend nearby an' all. I can't imagine what it'll be like, Tommy, or how I'll cope being among a lot of strangers – let alone them as won't like me for where I were born.'

Tommy was quiet for a moment. When he spoke, he said, 'It is that I'm asking a lot of you, Tilly, me darling. But I don't see a way we can be together unless you come to me farm or I give up what me father before me worked his fingers to the bone for.'

'Naw, I'd not ask that of you. I remember in the days when I went to church that there was sommat in the Bible about a wife laying her head wherever her husband lay his, and that's what I'll do.'

Tommy squeezed her to him. 'I'll make sure it is that you never regret doing so, me Tilly. But what of your basket making business?'

'That's one of the things I have to sort out. I'm thinking of going into partnership with Dan, rather than just sharing his pitch. Now, don't look like that. The way I'm thinking won't stop me coming to you.'

'But how is it you will run your half?'

'Through Liz. She and I are already partners, and Liz is getting to be good at making baskets. Last season she made all the simple ones. Before I come to you, I can teach her more skills, so she can make patterned ones an' all. And we were doing another line in them this year, which involved Molly lining some of them and adding pockets – sewing baskets and the like. So, I'll make Molly a partner, if she will take it on. You see, I was to pay half of the rent for the pitch this year ...' Tilly told Tommy about the new council rules and the extra cost they were going to have to bear. 'So, I can't just walk out on them all. Dan would never manage the rent on his own. But I can trust Liz and Molly to run the business in the proper way – they'll have Dan to guide them. And before I come to you, I can make sure they have a good stock to start them off. And, as I will visit at least twice a year, I can make some of the intricate ones in Ireland and bring them back with me.'

'It is for sounding a good idea, Tilly. I can help if more funding is needed.'

'Ta, Tommy. That's good to knaw. We don't knaw final figures yet, or even if we have a pitch. But, hopefully, funding it all won't be a problem.'

'Me little Tilly, you've so much to get sorted, I cannot see me fetching you over as me bride for many a month.'

'I knaw, but Tommy, I – I, well, would you marry me soon? I don't want to be an unmarried woman with her belly up. I want our child to have two parents.'

'Oh, Tilly, you've gladdened me heart. Yes. We'll be married soon. I just need to find out how. I mean, isn't it here, as it is in me own country, that we have to post the banns, and have to reside for three weeks in the parish?'

'Naw, I think it is fine as long as I am residing here. Girls meet boys from all over, but the boys cannot allus come to live in Blackpool.'

'Well, if that is so, and this being Sunday, why don't we up out of our bed and get to church?'

Tilly giggled. 'By, it's a long time since I went to church.'

'Well, you can start by going to confession, so you can.'

'Ha! You'd better do that an' all, having relations while out of wedlock. That's sinning, ain't it?'

'Aye, it's a powerful sin, and one I want to commit again, right now. Oh, Tilly, me Tilly.'

Tilly snuggled into Tommy. His caresses heightened the feelings and the memories of their unions during the night, till she almost begged him to take her.

They clung together afterwards. Their sweat mingled, their tears salted their mouths. Tears not of sorrow, but of utter and complete love.

It was difficult for Tilly to wave Tommy goodbye later that evening. She'd found it so the last time they'd parted, but now, aware of the depth of her true feelings for him, it broke her heart to be away from him. Even knowing he would return in three weeks to marry her didn't help to lift her.

Turning away as the train pulled out of sight, Tilly wanted to find a corner to curl up in and stay there till Tommy returned, but she had to get on with fulfilling her promises, to Florrie and to Dan and Liz.

Her first task when returning home was to sort out Liz's room. Dan had brought a small trunk for her to pack the rest of Liz's things into. There wasn't much as over the past week, Liz and Dan had shifted most of it to their new home, but there were some of the things Liz had needed for her wedding, and the nightie and housecoat she'd worn the day before. Tilly soon had them gathered up and pulled the trunk into her own room until it could be collected. With this done, cleaning the room and changing the bed linen took another hour.

By now, it was dark outside, and the house felt empty. A loneliness descended on Tilly. Making herself some cocoa, she snuggled up in front of the fire, trying not to think of bad things but to concentrate on all that was good in her life.

Plans began to form. She would go to her solicitor with Dan tomorrow and try to finalise the business side of things. And she'd make certain that he was looking into Reggie's case. All of that seemed an easy process. She trusted Liz and Molly, and once her capital was paid back and they could manage without hers and Tommy's support, she would withdraw from the business and leave it to them all.

Getting Reggie and Florrie settled might take a little longer, but she wouldn't leave for Ireland until they were.

But what of her girls? How could she make sure that they could find her if ever they returned to Blackpool to do so?

This question weighted her heart. Lucy came to mind. Lucy knew a lot more than she would admit to. Already, she'd said that it was untrue that the girls had gone to Romania and that they were in Somerset. *The times that Somerset has been a part of me life, and yet, I'm not sure where it is, and how far it is. I just knaw as it's a long way away and that it is where you get apples and good willow from. Maybe I could go there?* But as the thought came, Tilly knew the hopelessness of it. Yes, she now had the money to fund going, but she was with child and she had no idea where to start looking if she did go. Besides, Lucy had said that Jasmine and her husband intended going from county to county. It was hopeless.

And yet, her heart ached at the thought that she wouldn't be on the beachfront if ever Babs and Beth did come.

Her head spun with possibilities. But all of them confirmed to her that it would be years and years before the twins were old enough to even think about finding her. They were seven years old now. So, many years would pass before they could leave Jasmine and make up their own mind as to where they went. *Eeh, me lasses, when that day comes and I knaw as it will, you will only have to walk down the prom and you will see your Aunt Liz. She'll bring us together.*

382

Though she'd tried hard not to, Tilly couldn't fight the tears. She doubled over with the weight of her grief, for her girls, her Arthur and for Jeremiah. Her whole body wept. Her sobs turned to wails. Her fists clenched and beat against the back of the sofa till they were sore, such was her anguish. Till at last, exhausted, she lay back and calmed herself.

The light from the window woke her. Trying to think where she was, Tilly lifted her stiff, aching body and looked around the living room. For a moment she couldn't think why she was there, and still fully clothed. The clock struck ten times. *Naw, it can't be ten o'clock in the morning! I can't have lain here all that time.*

Rising, she went to the fire and poked the dying embers. They flickered a weak life. Stoking the fire with sticks and one log, she watched as the flames danced as if excited to be licking their way up the chimney.

Strangely, she felt very light. It was as if her soul had finally cleansed itself and given her an inner peace. And she knew she could cope once more.

She was startled when there was a knock on the door and Liz opened it.

'Are you ready, Tilly, lass? We have that appointment at your solicitor's, remember?'

Liz glowed. There was no other way to describe the happiness that shone from her. And yes, as had happened to herself, Liz had the look of someone at peace.

'I'll not be a minute. I'll just wash me face and change me frock.'

'I should think so, you look as though you slept in that one – you did, didn't you? Eeh, lass, what's to do?'

'There's a lot as it happens, but I'm all right, Liz. I'm better than I've been in years. I'll tell you all me plans as we go. Is Dan driving us?'

'Aye, he has the horse and trap outside. And he says he'll take you to the hospital to collect Florrie afterwards. Do you reckon as she'll be up to meeting us?'

'Oh, aye, Florrie's fine. A little weak, and wanting news of her man, but I hope to get that today. Wait there a mo, Liz.'

'Eeh, I'm a visitor now, am I? Confined to the living room.'

'Naw, you daft apeth. Ha, you can come up and dress me if you like.'

'I'll not do that, but I'll come up and sit while you get ready, and you can begin to tell me some of what you're planning.'

By the afternoon, Tilly was more settled in her mind than she had been in a long time. The peace that had descended on her this morning was still in her and she had a clear picture of everything she'd planned and knew it would all work out. And now, Liz and Dan had gone home, and she sat with Florrie.

'Eeh, Florrie, it's good to have you here, lass. And I've good news for you. Mr Fellows, me solicitor, has checked out Reggie's story – you knaw, I told you he'd have to, didn't I? Well, Reggie is what he says he is, which we knew all along. But having proof of it means that everything can go a step further and Reggie's freedom can be applied for.'

'Will he get it, Tilly?'

'Oh, aye, it's just a formality. Mr Fellows says he'll be out in a couple of days.'

'What? Oh, Tilly, Tilly . . .'

'Now then, naw tears, unless they are happy ones.'

'They are. Thank you, Tilly. Thank you from the bottom of me heart.'

Tilly smiled at Florrie. And in the smile she got back, she could see a glimmer of the old Florrie and this gladdened her heart. 'He can be released because of the job that Mr Fellows has secured for him. His friend, Lord Clefton, has agreed to take Reggie on as his gardener. He'll work with the present one for the time being, but he is retiring soon, and Reggie will take over the job. And, if it works out, then the cottage that goes with the job is his once you pair are wed. You do want to wed Reggie, don't you, Florrie?'

'Aye, I do. More than owt in all the world, I do.'

They were sitting on the sofa together and Florrie reached out her hand. Tilly took it in her own. 'I have a lot to tell you, Florrie. Are you up to hearing it?'

Florrie relaxed back. 'If you pour me another cup of that lovely tea you brewed, I am, Tilly.'

At the end of Tilly's telling Florrie all about Tommy, and her expected baby, they were in each other's arms. 'Eeh, Tilly, lass, you deserve all the happiness that's coming to you.'

'And you do an' all, Florrie. Everything's turning out all right for us all. Well, that is everything except having me little lasses back . . . But I've made me mind up that that will an' all. It may not be for years and years, but it will. I knaws it will.'

The peace that still lived in Tilly confirmed this to her and though she knew there would be many times down the years when she would suffer the pain of loss and separation, she also knew she was strong enough to do so.

She would have her Tommy by her side, and – she patted her tummy – have her little miracle to take care of.

One thing was for sure, he or she would know, as soon as they were able to understand, that they had two beautiful sisters, named Babs and Beth, and that when he, or she, grew up, they would meet them and love them.

'That was a big sigh, Tilly.'

'Aye, it held all me hopes and dreams that I'll never give up on.'

They were silent then. The fire flickered a comforting light around the room, leaving the corners dark and shadowy, and Tilly thought, *That's how me heart is, dark and shadowy in the corners, but full of light in the centre. I'm going to be all right. Me world will always be filled with half-light till I'm reunited with me girls, but there is a peacefulness in shadows and that will sustain me until the day we are together again.*

AUTHOR'S NOTE

The summer of 1897 saw the arrival of Blackpool's world-famous 'Golden Mile', with amusements galore. The town banned stalls from the beach, and traders moved into the gardens of houses on the promenade.

Along the South Shore, for many years the haunt of gypsies and fairground artists, the 'Pleasure Beach' was built. One of the very first rides, Sir Hiram Maxim's 'Captive Flying Machine', which began operating in 1904, remains today, though in a somewhat different form.

A Letter to My Readers

Dear Reader

I hope you enjoyed *Blackpool's Angel*. The book is the first of the Sandgronians Trilogy, set during the years of 1893–1920s, which follows the lives of Tilly and her twin daughters, Babs and Beth.

Most of the trilogy will play out in Blackpool at a time of great change as it develops into a seaside resort complete with a tower modelled on the Eiffel Tower, a fairground, and gradually becomes known for the benefits of bathing in its waters, which sees people flocking to its shores.

In the second of the trilogy, *Blackpool Sisters*, you will travel far and wide as we take up the emotional and heart-wrenching story of Babs and Beth in their quest to find and be reunited with their ma, through the fields of Somerset and the theatres of war in France and of course, where the heart of the story is – my beloved Blackpool.

And this is where the trilogy will conclude in the third book, *Blackpool Christmas*, as the family, torn and almost broken by all they have been through, struggle to overcome the differences their experiences have wrought on their lives.

Will Tilly ever realise her dream of uniting her family? Will the friendships she made, and those she helped along her life's path, sustain her? Now a successful businesswoman, will she pull off the Christmas she plans that holds her hopes of finally bringing peace and joy back into all of their lives?

All three books will be published by Sphere over the next twelve months. Look out for them in whatever format you enjoy – hardback, paperback or ebook.

If, while you wait for each publication, you would like to read more of my work, then you will find *Blackpool Lass* and *Blackpool's Daughter*, my first two standalone books by my pseudonym Maggie Mason, and my books under my real name, Mary Wood, in supermarkets, bookshops, online Amazon store, or any online book outlet.

Lastly, but as the saying goes – not least, an author is greatly helped and made very happy by receiving reviews. If you can take the time to review this or any of my books on Amazon and/or Goodreads and Facebook, I would be very grateful. And I would love to hear from you personally, too. You can reach and interact with me by email through my webpage and through Facebook and Twitter. I will always reply to you myself and hope that through our contact we become friends.

Much love to you all, Maggie (Mary Wood)

www.authormarywood.com
www.facebook.com/HistoricalNovels
Twitter account: @Authormary

ACKNOWLEDGEMENTS

My heartfelt thanks go to:

My editor, Viola Hayden, always there for me. And to all the hard-working team at Sphere, who believe in my work and strive to do all they can to make it shine and to find its place on the shelves of book retail outlets.

To my agent, Judith Murdoch, who had faith in me from the moment she read my first book and has been by my side for six years, guiding me through the complexes of the publishing world, fighting my corner, celebrating my successes, and supporting me through my down moments.

To my wonderful husband Roy, my children, their partners, my grandchildren and great grandchildren, and all my Olley and Wood family – I love you all – you are my world.

To my readers, especially those who interact with me and support me on my Facebook page and website – and to my friends. You all see me through my workload and make all my efforts so worthwhile. You are a joy.

Author's Research Notes

For information on the building of the tower I found the following article very helpful, sent in by Simon Entwistle and published on the BBC's history and local landmarks webpage:

http://www.bbc.co.uk/lancashire/content/articles/2008/04/17/history_blackpool_tower_feature.shtml

It makes fascinating reading.

Other sources of historical notes:

Blackpool's Seaside Heritage by Allan Brodie and Matthew Whitfield.

2/8/13